D0554276

The Eternal Zero

Naoki Hyakuta

VERTICAL.

The Eternal Zero

Naoki Hyakuta

Translated by Chris Brynne & Paul Rubin

VERTICAL.

EIEN NO ZERO

© Naoki Hyakuta 2006

First published in Japan in 2006 by Ohta Publishing Co., Tokyo.
Worldwide English translation rights arranged with Ohta Publishing Co.
through TUTTLE-MORI AGENCY, INC., Tokyo.

Published by Vertical, Inc., New York, 2015

ISBN 978-1-939130-82-2

Manufactured in the United States of America

First Edition

Vertical, Inc.
451 Park Avenue South, 7th Floor
New York, NY 10016

www.vertical-inc.com

Prologue

It was definitely right before the end of the war, but I don't remember the exact date. That damn Zero, though, is something I'll never forget. It was like the devil himself. I was a 5-inch artillery gunner on the USS *Ticonderoga*. My job was protecting the aircraft carrier from those crazy kamikazes that plunged right at us.

The 5-inch shells had so-called proximity fuzes. The proximity fuze emitted radio waves in a radius of 50 feet of the shell and was designed to detonate the instant interference from an approaching aircraft was sensed. It was an awesome weapon. I fired hundreds of those shells. And shot down most of the kamikazes before they got close to the carrier.

The first time I saw a kamikaze, I was seized by fear. I had deployed on the *Ticonderoga* in the beginning of 1945. I had heard rumors about the kamikazes, but when I first laid eyes on them, I thought, "They're gonna drag me down to hell with them." These suicide bombers were the height of madness. I wanted to think that it was a unique exception; however, their attacks came one after another. I thought they were not human. Far from not being afraid to die, they just threw themselves to death at us. Didn't they have families, friends, lovers—anyone that would mourn their deaths? I was different. I had wonderful parents back in the Arizona countryside and a fiancée.

Our Navy had magnificent artillery and the power of the proximity fuzes was astounding. Our ships could fire them all at once, the barrage darkening the sky. Rare was the kamikaze that could break through. Any that did were baptized with showers of bullets from 40-mm and 20-mm machine guns. And most of them exploded or fell into the ocean in flames.

Before long, my fear faded, replaced by anger. Anger incited by deeds committed by those who did not fear God. Or perhaps it was a desire for revenge for the fear that they had given me. We gunners focused the energy of our anger into our artillery and machine guns, and pounded away at them. Once my initial fear passed, it became a game. We shot down kamikazes like we were shooting at clay pigeons.

They usually approached from a shallow angle. By then, Japanese pilots were all rookies, and there were few that could come at us from steep dive angles. Our guns could move in almost any direction, but it was difficult to keep them in our sights if they dove at us from directly above the ship at close to 90 degrees. On the other hand, if they did come at us from such steep angles, it was extremely difficult for them to ram into the ship. A guy familiar with airplanes once told me that at high speeds an aircraft's rudder becomes ineffective. I saw many such diving kamikazes lose sight of their target and crash into the ocean.

However, shooting down kamikazes was also becoming increasingly painful. Heck, the target was not just a clay pigeon. It was a fellow human being.

Darn you, kamikazes. Please stop coming! I lost count of how many times I thought such words.

But if they came, I would shoot them. If I didn't, we would die. More than a few warships sank after being rammed into. Warships had thousands of personnel on board. If one sank, hundreds would perish. We couldn't allow hundreds of Americans to die because of one Japanese. Even if the ship hit by a kamikaze didn't sink, dozens of us could still die.

After the Battle of Okinawa in May, our defense against kamikaze attacks was nearly perfect. Radar picket ships positioned 100 miles ahead of the main flotilla picked up approaching kamikaze planes at a range of 200 miles, which allowed interceptors positioned far ahead of the warships to shoot down most of them.

By then, the kamikazes didn't have fighter escorts. They were like flocks of sheep with no dogs to guard them. Rendered sluggish with their heavy ordnance, the kamikaze planes were no match for our late-model fighters. That was why the majority of them never reached the flotilla.

That summer, we high-angle anti-aircraft gunners were open for business but had no customers. As August came, it was widely speculated that the war would soon be over.

That's when I caught a glimpse of that damn devil of a Zero.

Chapter 1
A Ghost

I was awakened by the *Star Wars* theme ringing on my cell phone. Glancing at the clock, it was past noon. It was my sister calling.

"What're you up to?"

"Just takin' a walk."

"You were sleeping, weren't you?"

"Am gonna hunt for a job this afternoon."

After a brief pause, she suddenly said, "You're lying! Are you going to goof off forever, not working? They call people like you a NEET, Kentaro."

"Do you even know what NEET stands for?" I replied.

She ignored the question. "If you're not doing anything, I can get you a good part-time job."

Oh, here we go again, I thought.

To be sure, even I thought myself rather pathetic—twenty-six and just hanging around without working. Waiting for another shot at the bar exam might sound good to some. But I hadn't even bothered to take it this year. I had for four consecutive years since my senior year of college and failed every time. The first time stung the worst. While I passed the essay section, considered the toughest, I completely screwed up the oral exam. That thoroughly disappointed my advisor.

Everyone thought I'd make it the next time, because those who passed the essay section were exempted from it the following year. However, I stumbled during the oral exam again. Being excused from the written portion, I'd taken it too easy. From there, I really bungled things. The next year I failed the essay exam, and the year after that I failed the short-answer test. I was in the worst possible mental state during that last exam, the girl I'd been dating since college having dumped me.

After that, I lost my self-confidence and motivation and spent my days goofing around aimlessly. I had been told that amongst my class I was the most likely to pass the bar exam first. Yet here I was, counted amongst the dropouts. Occasionally I worked part-time as a cram-school instructor. And when in the mood, I did some manual-labor jobs. But whatever I did, it was just to kill time.

I still felt confident that if I could get my engine going and studied in earnest, I could pass. But that essential motivation was missing, and more than a year had flown by as my law books gathered dust.

"So what is this part-time gig?"

"My assistant."

"Thanks, but no thanks."

My sister Keiko was four years older than me and worked as a freelance writer. Well, actually she was still just a fledgling reporter. After working four years at a publisher of trend magazines, she'd gone freelance. The bulk of her work was interviews for her former employer. Even so, she was renting an apartment in Tokyo, so apparently she was earning enough to get by. She always said that one day she'd be a top-flight nonfiction writer. And while that was probably just a dream, she was pretty ambitious.

"Well, to be honest, you wouldn't be assisting me with my regular work. I want to research our grandfather."

"Research what about Grandpa?"

"Not 'Grandpa'... I mean Grandma's first husband."

"Oh, I see."

Grandma lost her first husband in the war. They say he died during a *kamikaze* mission. Their married life was apparently very short, but my mother was born then. Grandma remarried after the war, and that husband was "Grandpa" for us.

I first learned all this six years ago when Grandma passed away. After the forty-ninth-day memorial service for her, Grandpa asked my sister and me to visit him, and then told us about our real grandfather. I was far more shocked that I had no blood ties to the man I had always thought of as my grandfather.

Grandpa had doted on my sister and me since we were young. And he got along great with our mother, even though she wasn't his biological daughter. After remarrying her second husband, my grandmother bore two sons (my uncles). And Mom and her step-brothers got along well.

Even after learning of the existence of my real grandfather, I didn't especially feel anything towards him. He had died thirty years before I was born, and since there wasn't a single photograph of him anywhere in the house it was impossible to even feel sorry for him. It's not a nice comparison, but it was as though a ghost had suddenly appeared.

Grandpa had apparently heard little from Grandma about her first husband. All he knew for certain was that her first husband had been a naval aviator who died as a kamikaze pilot. Mom had no recollection of him at all. She was three when he died, but he had been away at war well before then.

"Why are you researching that man?"

I purposely referred to him as "that man." I had Grandpa for a grandfather. I resisted the idea of calling my biological grandfather "Grandpa."

"The other day out of nowhere Mom said, 'I wonder what my late father was like. I don't know anything about him.'"

"Yeah," I said, getting up from bed.

"When I heard Mom say that, I found myself wanting to help her. I understand how she must feel. I mean, it's her *real* father. Of course Grandpa is important to her, and she thinks of him as her father. But it's like, those feelings aside, she's curious about what kind of person her actual father was."

"But why now?"

"Maybe 'cause she's getting old?"

"Doesn't Grandpa know anything else about him?"

"Apparently not. Seems Grandma didn't tell him very much about her first husband."

"Hmm."

I loved Grandpa. It was because he's a lawyer that I had decided to sit for the bar. A diligent man, he'd previously worked for Japan National Railway, but in his thirties he passed the bar and became a lawyer instead. Granted, he had the academic chops, having studied law at Waseda University. In practice, he ran around helping the needy. To use a worn-out phrase, he was a lawyer who lived in honorable poverty. Watching him inspired me to become a lawyer myself.

No matter how many times I failed the bar or how long I drifted aimlessly, he never got angry. When my mother and my sister discussed their concerns with him, he told them, "One day that boy will land squarely on his feet. So don't worry about him." They were disappointed by this.

"By the way, why do you need me to research our grandfather?" I asked her.

"Because I'm busy and can't let it take up all my time. And besides, it concerns you, too. But I don't expect you to do this as a favor. I will pay you."

I smiled wryly but thought, *Why not? It's not like I had anything better to do.* "But how can anyone do this research?"

"Have you decided to help out?"

"No, I just wondered if you had a clue to go on or something."

"Nothing at all. I don't even know if he had any relatives. But I have his name, so it should be possible to find out what sort of unit he was with."

"You really expect me to hunt down people who were in the same unit and ask them what kind of man he was?"

"You're a sharp one, Kentaro."

"Oh, give me a break. First of all, this was sixty years ago. Even if someone who knew him then is still alive, I can't imagine they'll remember much if anything about him. Besides, most of them are dead by now."

"We're discussing your biological grandfather, you know."

"Well, sure… But I don't especially care to learn about him."

"But I do!" my sister said in a forceful tone. "He was my real grandfather, and I'm keen to learn what kind of man he was. Heck, he's your roots, too."

I wasn't particularly moved by her speech, but I didn't feel like arguing with her.

"So, will you or won't you help?"

"Okay. I'll do it."

I wasn't totally incurious about our grandfather, but the real reason I accepted her request was nothing more than a desire to escape my boredom. Plus, there was the money.

The next day I met up with my sister in Shibuya, to talk about things over lunch. Of course, it was on her. We chose a chain restaurant that served Italian. Keiko had on very little makeup, as usual, and a worn-out pair of jeans.

"Actually, I might be working on a pretty big gig. I've been recruited by a newspaper company for its project on the sixtieth anniversary of the end of the war," she said with a hint of pride, naming the major newspaper.

"Wow, that's great. That's quite the leap up from a crummy little magazine."

"Don't call it crummy," she pouted.

I apologized.

"And if everything goes smoothly, they might publish my book."

"Oh, really! What kind of book?"

"A collection of war testimonials. I don't know yet if it'll really be published. I'll probably need a co-author. But anyways, that's on the table, too," she said, eyes sparkling.

I see. So that's what's up, I thought, finally comprehending. She was using the research on our grandfather as a dry-run. I was sure she genuinely wanted to learn more about him for her sake as well as Mom's. But more so, her objective was to hone her skills as a writer through our investigation. After all, she'd never even brought up our dead grandfather before now.

To be frank, I didn't think my sister was cut out for journalism. Sure, she was strong-willed, but she was too considerate. She was the type who couldn't ask tough or probing questions of her interviewees. Moreover, having a personality where your feelings showed right on your face had to be a disadvantage. She was likely already aware of these things even without me stating them. Perhaps she thought of the end-of-WWII anniversary project as a chance to peel off that skin and reinvent herself.

"So, is it true that he died as a kamikaze pilot?" I asked.

"Grandpa said as much," reminded Keiko, twirling pasta onto her fork. "We have amazing family," she added, sounding like she was discussing someone else's.

"Sure do," I chimed back, echoing her distant tone.

"But the kamikazes were terrorists."

"Terrorists?"

"Someone at the newspaper whom I met called them that. He said, 'From today's perspective, kamikaze pilots were on par with the people who flew planes into the World Trade Center.'"

"Hmm… I feel like it's wrong to label the kamikazes as terrorists."

"I don't really know, but some people see it that way. According to that journalist, although the era and context seem totally different, they are structurally similar. He said both were fanatic patriots and martyrs."

It was an audacious opinion, but I found myself unable to dismiss it out of hand.

"The person who told me this is quite brilliant. He used to be on the political beat for the newspaper. We were talking over lunch and I mentioned that my grandfather was a kamikaze pilot, so he lent me a book of last words by kamikazes. It brimmed with words like 'submitting' and 'fealty.' The most surprising thing was how the pilots were totally unafraid of death. Actually, some of the wills expressed joy over the prospect of dying a glorious death for the nation. When I read it I thought, 'So there was a time when Japan had a hell of a lot of fanatic nationalists, too.'"

"Huh. But my grandfather being a terrorist still doesn't ring any bell."

"Sixty years from now the grandkids of Islamic suicide bombers might say the same thing," Keiko argued, cheeks stuffed with pasta, before noisily chugging down some water. It was definitely not very feminine. My sister is fairly pretty, if you'd take her brother's word for it, but she sure didn't put much effort into personal grooming or matters of etiquette.

"Did our grandfather leave a will or any last words?"

"Apparently not."

"There's not a trace of his life at all?"

"That's why we need to investigate it."

"So what is it exactly that I'm supposed to do?"

"I want you to look up some of his war buddies. I'm super busy right now and just can't get around to it myself. That's why I've tasked you with that research. I'll pay you an advance, so please do it," she rattled off, retrieving an envelope from her handbag and handing it to me. "You're not exactly busy, right? You'll get somewhere with phone calls and faxes. If you can manage to find any of his comrades, I'll go to interview them in person."

I accepted the envelope, feeling slightly fed up already. "By the way, how old would he be if he were still alive?"

Keiko pulled out a notebook and flipped through the pages. "He was born in the eighth year of the Taisho Era, or 1919, so he'd be eighty-five."

"It might be tough to find any war buddies. In just a few years everyone who saw combat will have died out."

"Hmm," Keiko said. "We might be too late."

Even though I accepted the job, I didn't lift a finger for over a week.

It was only after countless pestering calls from my sister that I finally, reluctantly, got off my butt and got to work. Since I'd taken the advance money I couldn't get away with not working at all.

I learned of my grandfather's military service record after placing a call to the Ministry of Health, Labor and Welfare.

"Kyuzo Miyabe; born in Tokyo in 1919; enlisted in the Imperial Navy in 1934; killed in action off the southwestern islands in 1945."

That was my grandfather's entire life in a sentence. Of course, if one wanted, there were plenty of details that could be filled in. When he entered the Navy, he first became an ordnanceman, then underwent flight training and became a pilot; in 1937 fought in the Second Sino-Japanese War; in 1941 was assigned to an aircraft carrier squadron and participated in the attack on Pearl Harbor; fought numerous air battles in the southern Pacific; returned to the interior in 1945; and died as a *kamikaze* pilot just a few days before the war ended.

He gave the best years of his life, the eleven years from age fifteen to twenty-six, to the military, spending the last eight in continuous battle as a pilot. And at long last he was forced to die a kamikaze. The timing was most unfortunate. Had the war ended just a few days sooner, he would have survived.

"You were born in a terrible era, Kyuzo-san," I muttered without thinking.

Regarding his private life, he married my grandmother in 1941.

17

My mother was born in 1942. They were married for just four years, most of which my grandfather spent on the front. It's impossible to tell how long he was at home even when he returned to the interior. Perhaps Grandma never told Grandpa much about her first husband not because she was hiding anything in particular, but because there was nothing much to say.

Laying out his military background didn't reveal anything of my grandfather's humanity. In order to learn what kind of person he was, I'd need to get in touch with someone who remembered him. I was sure most of his comrades from the military had already passed away as well.

Guess we're a bit too late, I thought, echoing Keiko's words. But just as truly, now might be the last chance to learn anything.

The Ministry of Health, Labor and Welfare told me about the *Suikoukai* association of former Navy officers. I called the association, and they told me the names of various veterans' organizations. There were ones for comrades who had joined the marines division in the same year or who had served in the same squadrons or on the same aircraft carrier. However, as all the members were elderly, many of the organizations had disbanded in recent years. People who had experienced the war were exiting history's stage even as I worked.

I wondered how many members among the organizations had known my grandfather and how well they'd remember events that had taken place sixty years ago. If I were to be asked about any of my current friends sixty years in the future, what memories would I be able to call up?

But thinking such thoughts wouldn't get me started, so I sent letters at random to several veterans' organizations asking if there was anyone who knew about my grandfather.

Two weeks later, I received a response from one group saying that they had someone who'd served as a pilot with my grandfather in Rabaul. The reply was from an executive member, and not only was it ornately handwritten, there were *kanji* characters I didn't know. Unable to make out the whole letter, I brought it to my sister's attention.

She was busy, so it wasn't until late that night that we met up in a franchise restaurant. Even Keiko, who had majored in literature, had a hard time deciphering the ornate penmanship.

"Just a sixty-year difference between generations and their writing becomes illegible to us," I said innocently as I watched her stare down the letter.

"We only see the postwar simplified forms of these characters and never learned their traditional forms. Some bear no resemblance at all. Like this one," she said, pointing to a word. "Can you read this?"

I could not.

"I just happen to know it. It's Combined Fleet."

"So I guess this character means 'combined'? It's totally different. It has the 'ear' radical instead of the 'advance' radical, and the right half is completely different."

Keiko laughed. "Plus it's written in cursive which makes it that much harder to read."

I sighed. "I feel like I'm dealing with a different race of people."

"They're Japanese, like us. Does Grandpa seem like a foreigner to you? Ah, I mean our living grandfather."

"I don't think of Grandpa as a member of a different race. But eighty-something-year-olds who aren't family feel pretty darn foreign to me."

Keiko placed the letter on the table and sipped her ice coffee. "They might think the same thing of us."

Just the idea of dealing with such people made my heart sink a little.

Chapter 2
The Coward

Former Ensign Umeo Hasegawa's house was in the suburbs of Saitama Prefecture. His former surname was Ishioka, so perhaps he was adopted after the war to continue the Hasegawa family line.

We got off at a station an hour outside Tokyo. The hub area had an urban appearance, but after walking a short while the scenery completely changed into endless rice paddies. The sun was directly overhead. With not a cloud in sight, its light was intense even though it was still early in July, and insects were making themselves heard like you wouldn't believe. It got hot in the metropolis, but the piercing rays here held their own.

True summer.

"Hot, huh?" I said to my sister walking beside me.

"Oh, I'm enjoying myself."

What kind of an answer is that?

I was starting to feel irritated. Keiko had said that she would conduct the interview herself, but at the last minute she'd insisted that I join her. "Just at first, please," she'd practically begged, and without thinking carefully, I'd said yes. Walking down the sweltering countryside road, I was beginning to regret it big time.

"So, did you read up a bit about the war?"

"Like I have the time," Keiko replied. "Besides, I don't want to bring unncecessary preconceptions to the interview."

As self-serving as always, I thought, but held my tongue.

After walking thirty minutes from the station we were drenched in sweat. Even my sister stopped talking for the most part.

The address we were given brought us to a small farmhouse. The single-story building looked to be about fifty years old. It was surrounded by fields, and a light pickup truck sat in the vacant space in front of the entrance. The house was pretty shabby. From the title "ensign" I had imagined a fine estate, so I was mildly disappointed. I glanced at Keiko, who was gazing fixedly at the house, examining it.

I pressed the doorbell next to the glass door, but even after waiting a good while there was no response. The doorbell was apparently broken. I called out from across the door. Immediately a sturdy voice replied, "Come in."

In the vestibule stood a skinny old man. Seeing him made my heart skip a beat. There was no arm below the left sleeve of his blue open-neck short-sleeved shirt. This was Hasegawa.

He led us to a sitting room off of the foyer. The narrow, roughly 8x10-foot room felt somehow unnatural. There was a wooden table in the center, reproductions of paintings on the walls, and a cheap-looking chandelier hanging from the ceiling. The room was horribly hot. It was probably a prefabbed addition to the house. The moment I stepped inside, I burst into a full sweat. But I didn't ask for the AC to be turned on.

Hasegawa's white hair was all combed back and he had a mustache. He looked at us through narrow eyes like he was appraising us.

Keiko addressed the silent Hasegawa, reiterating the purpose of today's visit; namely, to learn about our grandfather, Kyuzo Miyabe. As she spoke, Hasegawa looked at both of us in turn. The heat of the room kept forcing the sweat to pour out of me.

"The letter was signed with a man's name," Hasegawa interrogated.

"That's because I put my brother in charge of communications," Keiko explained.

Hasegawa nodded in comprehension. Then he stared at both our faces again.

"So…" Keiko uttered, "you knew our grandfather?"

"That I did," Hasegawa replied without pause. "He was the biggest damn coward in the whole Naval Air Corps."

What? I thought.

"Kyuzo Miyabe held his own life dear above anything else."

Keiko's face turned crimson. I touched her knee under the table.

She pressed my hand to indicate that she was okay.

Keeping her voice as calm as possible, she asked, "What exactly does that mean, sir?"

"What exactly does that mean?" Hasegawa parroted. "Just that. He was a man who held his own life dear like it was everything. We pilots had given our lives to our country. Once I became a fighter pilot, I no longer considered my life my own. I absolutely would not die except in my boots. I had but one thought. *How*."

As Hasegawa spoke, he touched his left shoulder with his right hand. His empty left sleeve fluttered.

"I was prepared to die at any moment. No matter the battlefield, I never held my life dear. But Kyuzo Miyabe was not that sort of man. He was always running away from fights. His greatest desire wasn't to win but to save his own hide."

"I think it's a natural feeling to value one's own life."

Hasegawa glowered at my sister. "Such are woman's feelings."

"Just what do you mean by that?"

"Keiko," I muttered.

She pretended not to hear me. "I think men and women are the same. Isn't it normal to value one's life?"

"That, young lady, is the thinking in peacetime. We were fighting for the very existence of Japan. I didn't care if I died so long as my country remained. But Miyabe was different. He was always avoiding combat."

"I think that's wonderful."

"Wonderful?" Hasegawa raised his voice. "How can you fight a war if the troops avoid combat?"

"If everyone thought the same, there wouldn't be any wars to begin with."

Hasegawa's mouth dropped open. "What are they teaching you kids in school these days? Didn't you learn world history? Mankind's history is a history of war. Of course war is evil, the worst possible evil. Everyone knows that. But no one can get rid of war."

"Are you saying that war is a necessary evil?"

"It's pointless to debate whether or not war is a necessary evil with you. Go back to your workplace and discuss it with your superiors and colleagues to your heart's content. And if you find out a way to eradicate war, turn it into a book. Send it to the leaders of all the countries and the next day we'll have world peace. You could even go to war zones and tell them that if they all run away, the disputes will end."

Keiko bit her lip.

"Listen up. Battlefields are for fighting, not for running away. It makes no difference to us troops whether we were the aggressors or the defenders in that war. On the battlefield, we fire at the enemy before us. That's the duty of a soldier. It's the politicians' job to work for a ceasefire or a peace deal. Am I wrong?" Hasegawa touched his armless left shoulder again. "Miyabe was always running away from the fight."

Keiko could not respond.

"So you despised our grandfather, sir?" I asked.

Hasegawa turned to me. "The reason I call him a coward is because he was a pilot. If he had been drafted, then he could hold onto dear life all he wanted. But he volunteered. He wanted to join the military, and became an aviator. That's why I can't forgive him. Knowing that, do you still want my story?"

Since Keiko remained silent, I said, "Please tell us, sir."

Hasegawa blew his nose loudly. I asked if it was okay that I use a voice recorder. He replied that he didn't mind.

When I turned it on, Hasegawa said, "Fine, I'll tell you."

I joined the Navy in the spring of 1936. I was born the son of a farmer here in Saitama, the sixth of eight children. Our family were tenant farmers. It took everything we had just to survive. We were what you called peasants.

Now listen to me. If you don't know about the military and airmen back then, you'll never understand my hatred of him.

Since lower primary school, I was a good student. Not that it's anything to brag about but I was always top of the class. Still, my folks could barely afford to send me to higher primary school, so I never made it to middle school. Most village kids were in the same boat back then. Pretty much the only ones who went on to middle school were the sons of the village chief. My teacher kindly told my father, "It's a shame that such a bright kid can't continue his studies," but there was nothing to be done about it. My three elder brothers were very smart, too, but none of them went on to middle school, either.

After I graduated from higher primary school, my family sent me off to work as an apprentice to reduce the number of mouths that needed to be fed. My apprenticeship was with a *tofu* maker in Osaka. It was grueling work. Early mornings, late nights. Keeping my hands in the ice-cold water continuously made my fingers go numb. I was prone to getting frostbite to begin with, and it troubled me all winter long. My fingers would turn reddish brown, and the chapped skin bled, splitting open in new places before the old wounds could heal. Pain shot through my fingers every time I had to plunge them into the cold water.

I lost count of how many times I cried. The master was a relentless man. He told me I got frostbite because I was a spoiled brat. "I've done this job for decades and I've never gotten frostbite even once," he said.

He beat me all the time. Now I can look back and see it was a kind of sickness. He was brutal. He loved to beat people. He hit me daily, as if he'd hired me to be his punching bag. He would hit me for merely crying. And he immediately reneged on his promise to send me to middle-school night classes during my apprenticeship.

I had no choice but to endure, because I had nowhere to run. After two years, I was almost six feet tall and weighed 165 pounds.

It was as if my master didn't notice the change. One day, he was in a bad mood and took it out on me as usual, even though I had done nothing wrong. I got angry, and for the first time in my life, I hit my master. He flew into a rage, beating me with a club, yelling, "I'm gonna kill you!" But I caught hold of the club and hit him back with it. Suddenly he burst into tears and apologized. He went prostrate, begging repeatedly for my forgiveness. His wife rushed in and asked me to show mercy to him. A woman who'd never once tried to intervene when I'd been beaten countless times was in tears trying to put an end to it as soon as her husband was the one getting hit. The instant I saw this, I became violently furious. Had I been beaten so many times by people like them? I kicked her to the floor and flogged the master with the club. He screamed through his tears for my forgiveness until he finally passed out.

I fled the shop and headed towards the station. The only place I could return to was my country home. But the police caught me before the first train arrived. Since I was a minor I wasn't sent to prison, but the cops beat me until I fainted.

I had nowhere to go except the military. I applied to the Navy and was accepted.

I became a fireman on a cruiser. There too, I was beaten daily. There was no place as physically abusive as the Japanese military. They say the Army was terrible, but the Navy was even worse. This was supposedly due to the fact that Army soldiers had guns. Once they were in combat, bullets didn't always come from the front. There was talk of men settling grudges with a shot from behind on the battlefield. That's why Army beatings were said to be comparatively moderate. But most sailors didn't carry arms, which was why our superiors could beat us without any restraint. I'm not sure if that was the reason. I was always getting beaten, of that you can be sure.

Three years after entering the Navy, I heard they were recruiting aviators. I dreamed of becoming a pilot and studied for the entrance exam like mad, spending what little free time I had after finishing my duties on the ship.

I'd heard that it was extremely competitive, but I passed the test. I think that was pretty impressive, if I do say so myself.

Thus, I became a pilot in training according to Imperial Navy tradition. Come to think of it, Miyabe also did that program. He was several classes ahead of me.

Training at the Kasumigaura Naval Air Unit was intense, but it was a piece of cake compared to the daily work on the cruiser.

I felt happy to be alive for the first time since graduating higher primary school. I thought, "This really is the place for me." At the time, being a pilot required a willingness to sacrifice one's life. During wartime, pilots constantly flew deep into hostile territory to fight the enemy head-on. Even when they weren't, they always had death at their side. Aircraft back then weren't very reliable. Accidents weren't uncommon and more than a few pilots lost their lives during training. Yet I was never afraid. We weren't practicing how to fly safely under peaceful conditions. We were training to put our lives on the line.

I decided to stake everything on flying. I'm not exaggerating when I say I threw myself body and soul into training.

I think most of my fellow trainees felt exactly as I did. They all dove earnestly into flight training. It was a literal struggle, because not all trainees would become pilots. The instructors also gauged our natural aptitude, and those deemed unsuitable were delegated to be spotters or radiomen on bombers or attack aircraft. The ones who didn't become pilots wept.

Depending on the pilots' skills and aptitude, the instructors then separated them into separate pipelines for fighters, bombers, and attack aircraft. The cream of the crop were chosen to pilot the fighters. And I became a fighter pilot.

After graduating, I was assigned to Hankou in China. This was in the beginning of 1941. In China I flew the Type 96 carrier-based fighter. It wasn't as good as the Zero, but it was a very decent fighter. I shot down numerous Chinese planes with a Type 96 fighter.

Late that year, the Greater East Asian War began. When I heard about the attack on Pearl Harbor, I stamped my feet in frustration.

My dream had been to board the *Akagi*, an aircraft carrier with the 1st Air Fleet. I wanted to join that aircrew so I could fight the Americans. I was ready to die if I could be part of the *Akagi* crew.

But my dream didn't come true. I was promoted from a Type 96 to a Zero fighter but never received orders to transfer to an aircraft carrier, and instead spent day after day fighting the Chinese Air Force. By then, the Chinese single-mindedly avoided engaging with Zero fighters, so I was never able to down any of their planes with a Zero.

Early the following year I was transferred to the 3rd Air Corps and sent to Borneo. The Tainan Air Corps had destroyed an Allied military base in the Philippines the previous year, and the Japanese military vigorously advanced, capturing territories in Southeast Asia and the Dutch East Indies. It was like our forces were invincible wherever they went.

As part of the Imperial forces' invasion, we, too, advanced into

Borneo, Celebes, Sumatra, Java. In Java, there were dark-skinned natives all over the place. Like the characters in *Dankichi, the Adventurous Boy*, both men and women wore very little clothing. They looked at us in wonder, too.

I ended up on a military base called Kupang on the island of Timor, which served as a foothold for our attack on Darwin, Australia. There for the first time I took on American and British fighters. On the first mission I downed a P-40. I had been told that combat with Allied aircraft was nothing like fighting the Chinese Air Force, but they weren't really much trouble.

The Zero's greatness impressed me all over again. It was really a magnificent fighter. American and British aircraft just couldn't hold a candle to the Zero. When we tangled with them in a dogfight, we could easily get into shooting position behind them. We then blew them away with our 20-mm machine guns. I fought P-39s, P-40s, Hawker Hurricanes, and also the British Spitfires which had caused the German Luftwaffe so much agony over Europe. But none of them could equal the Zero.

The Zero was truly a heaven-sent warplane. The Zeros butchered many enemy planes on each mission. Our squadron must have downed over a hundred enemy aircraft while suffering fewer than a dozen casualties. I myself shot down five.

I always closed in tight on the enemy aircraft before firing. My squadron mates called it the Ishioka Ramming Tactic. Back then, my last name was Ishioka.

Most bullets failed to hit their targets. In training, we were taught to shoot at the target when it got within 100 meters. But in actual combat, out of fear most pilots started firing at a range greater than 200 meters. Of course, they missed. I would always get within 50 meters before firing. At such close range, the enemy plane fairly stuck out of the gun's sights, which is why I rarely missed when I pulled the trigger.

In any case, combat was the best training. At the time, we were quite competent. Carrier pilots were said to be brilliant, but they had nowhere near our actual combat experience. I'm sure they were highly skilled when they were assigned, but it was, after all, proficiency in carrier launches and landings and being adept at mock dogfights.

No matter how good a pilot is in a mock dogfight, it isn't the same as a real dogfight. There's a tremendous gap between those who've engaged in mortal combat day in and out and those who haven't. It's the difference between *kendo* fencing in a *dojo* training hall and dueling on a battlefield. Even if you're strong in a match with bamboo swords, that doesn't mean you can win with a naked blade. Someone who has repeatedly cut down people would be the stronger fighter. I was certain, and proud, that my skills were superior to those of the carrier pilots.

I was transferred to Rabaul in the fall of 1942. With the start of the Guadalcanal Campaign that began that summer, part of the 3rd Air Corps advanced on Rabaul under the command of the Tainan Air Wing.

Guadalcanal proved to be a harsh battleground. It was a long flight, a thousand kilometers from Rabaul, and we'd never launched such a long-range attack. Just to get there took three hours. And the enemy's aircraft were much tougher than the stuff at Port Darwin. On the first mission, two veteran pilots from the 3rd Air Corps who had been transferred to Rabaul along with me failed to make it back.

This is one helluva place, I thought.

We had combat sorties nearly every day, and lost many planes each time, a rare occurrence in Kupang. The Rabaul guys, though, didn't blink an eye. It was expected there. Most of the planes that did make it back were riddled with bullet holes. Rare was the aircraft that came back unscathed.

Yet Miyabe always came back from such an intense battlefield unscratched. He came back looking as if nothing had happened even from tough battles where nearly half of our guys had bit it, his airplane as clean as when he'd departed. Most of the planes in flights under his command came back unharmed, too.

You might want to say that he was very skilled. But that's not it.

I asked a veteran pilot stationed at Rabaul how Miyabe always came back unscratched. Was he really that good?

He laughed bitterly and said, "Yeah, at running away."

You must understand this: aerial combat is totally different from fighting on land. Once planes from both sides get jumbled together in a mêlée, you lose sight of who's friend or foe. In a way it's much more terrifying than ground combat. There are no trenches in the air. Everything is laid bare. Not only is the enemy on all sides, they're above and below as well. An enemy plane flies away, you give chase, and immediately another enemy fighter is on your tail. And behind him, there's one of our guys in pursuit. It is fundamentally different from a land battle where you are on one side and the enemy is on the other.

Then I saw it.

It was sometime in mid-September. We got into a mêlée with Allied fighters that had lain in wait for us in the skies above Guadalcanal. They were flying Grumman F4Fs—short, stout, sturdy planes. They weren't as nimble as Zeros but they could take quite a beating.

I was separated from my flight, and two F4Fs hounded me. They were very skilled. If I tailed one, the other one got right on my tail. If I shook it off and got behind it, the first one fell back on my tail. In formation air combat, it's standard to cover each other's blind spots, but we were never as thorough as these guys were. The big difference was probably due to the quality of their wireless communications. Our radios were very lame at the time, static making it nearly impossible to understand what anyone said. It was so bad that I had ripped out mine from the cockpit and sawn off the antenna. Getting rid of the useless thing reduced my flying weight, and I was glad to shed even the antenna's marginal air resistance.

But the performance of the Zero was such that it wasn't handicapped in a two-to-one fight. When one of the F4Fs tailed me again, I pretended to panic and flee, cutting right in front of the other F4F I'd been targeting. For a moment, I had two F4Fs pursuing me. I'd been waiting for that moment.

I pulled sharply on the control stick and went into a loop. Both F4Fs followed my lead and looped as well, which was their fatal mistake. No fighter could best the Zero when it came to looping as it had an extraordinarily short turning radius. They should have been well aware of that but must have forgotten, thrilled at the chance to get me. After completing one loop I was snuggled right behind one of the F4Fs. One volley from my cannon and it burst into flames. The other one fled away in a full-speed dive. Because of the loop I had just done, my plane had lost speed and I had to give up pursuing him.

It was then that I realized I was far from the site of the battle. When aircraft repeatedly bank, they lose a great deal of altitude. And during the fight with the two F4Fs, I had descended about 2,000 meters. There were still many planes engaged in combat in the skies above. I pulled up the nose of the plane, aiming to get back in the action. I glanced skyward and saw three Zeros leisurely flying along some distance from the battle. It was Miyabe's flight.

He apparently couldn't leave the battlefield soon enough, bringing the two other Zeros with him to stand idly by. Of course, I have no proof. Maybe he had temporarily moved away from the action as I had. But I doubt it. Call it a conviction on my part.

Why, you ask me? Because he was a big coward.

He was paranoid when it came to keeping watch during flights. Of course, there's nothing more important to a pilot than being vigilant. The best ones were all eagle-eyed, always keeping watch and spotting the enemy first. But he went completely overboard. Not a moment went by where he wasn't looking around restlessly. Everyone was appalled by this. There were many who said he was just a scared SOB. It was surprising to find such a pilot among the renowned Rabaul Air Corps.

Rabaul was called the Airmen's Graveyard. Yet he continued to survive there. Of course he survived. Do nothing but run away from the fight and you'll be spared.

His "precious life" antics made him the laughingstock of the squadron. Everyone was aware of his infamous declaration: "I want to get back home alive." I have no idea when and where he let the thought slip out, but given that it was the subject of so much talk, I assume he'd said it many times.

No member of the Imperial Navy ever said such things. Aviators, in particular, would sooner die than utter the words. We were not drafted into the military. We enlisted and then volunteered to become pilots of our own accord. And yet such a man had said, "I want to get back home alive"? If he had uttered the words in my presence, I'd have slugged him then and there. At the time he was a Flight Petty Officer 1st Class whereas I was just an FPO 3rd Class. I would face imprisonment for striking a superior officer, but even so.

I've said it before and I'll say it again—we were pilots. There is nothing a pilot is more intimate with than death. "Death" was always right by our side, ever since pilot training. Several of my classmates had bought the farm while practicing spins or nose-dive training. I've also heard that many test pilots got killed during the development of the Zero.

But in spite of that, and out on the front lines, he dared to say "I want to get back home alive"?

Your comrades are failing to return to base nearly every day. When you're all fighting nonetheless with everything you've got, one guy wants to save his own skin? The nerve!

Ah, but there's more. I've got another story concerning what a coward Miyabe was. It's about parachutes.

He never failed to carefully inspect his parachute. One day I sarcastically asked him, "Flight Petty Officer Miyabe, just where do you expect to land with a parachute?"

In response he laughed and replied, "A parachute is a very important thing to have. I always make sure my flight's planes are also fitted with parachutes."

You look puzzled. You want to tell me that parachutes ought to be indispensable items? If so, you're terribly mistaken.

We fought above the vast Pacific Ocean, usually in enemy territory. Even if we parachuted safely, we'd end up killed by the enemy anyway. And if we were returning from hostile territory and our aircraft failed, we'd be parachuting into the sea. We'd only drown or become shark food.

So at the time, none of us pilots had decent parachutes. Sorry to be indelicate, but we peed into them. Aviators spent hours inside their aircraft. When nature called, it wasn't like on the ground where we could just take a leak on the roadside. We did in fact have paper bags to relieve ourselves in, but it was incredibly bothersome to whip it out and insert it into a bag while piloting the plane. Besides, an enemy might attack while you were relieving yourself. If anything, it was extremely dangerous to be distracted in such a way. And after you were done, you had to dispose of it by opening the canopy a bit and tossing the contents outside. But in doing so, more often than not, the bag full of urine got buffeted by the wind and you ended up drenched in the stuff. I doubt there was a single fighter pilot who didn't get doused from doing that. So, what did we do? We urinated into the parachute. We placed it between our legs and let it gradually soak up our piss. Nearly all the pilots based at Rabaul must have done so, which is why most of the parachutes absolutely reeked. I didn't even want to imagine what their condition was like on the inside.

To be sure, plenty of pilots on the mainland used parachutes leading up to the end of the war because they could land on Japanese soil. And since they weren't invading, they weren't trapped in the cockpit for hours on end, dealing with annoyances like having to go.

But Miyabe always had a parachute equipped even in Rabaul. What's more, he would go so far as to regularly open up and inspect it just in case. It's too bad he never had to use the damn thing.

One day I saw Miyabe folding up his parachute and said, "Since you inspect it so carefully, sir, I guess there's no chance of it failing to open."

Apparently oblivious to my sarcasm, he replied without hesitation, "I sincerely hope I'll never have to use it."

I was dumbstruck.

Oh, talking of parachutes made me remember something else. He shot and killed an American who was parachuting. This happened at Guadalcanal. After downing a Grumman, he machine-gunned the pilot parachuting away from the craft. Talk of it spread like wildfire. I didn't see it happen myself but heard of it from one of my buddies there. There had been multiple witnesses.

When I heard what he'd done, I was disgusted. He was a disgrace to the whole Navy.

In a dogfight, once you down an enemy aircraft you've won. Of course an American pilot is an enemy, but is it really necessary to kill a man fleeing in a parachute from his wrecked airplane? Even in battle there is such a thing as showing mercy. What he did was equivalent to cutting down a man who'd lost his weapon on the battlefield and fallen, unable to fight. Once I'd heard what he did, I loathed him from the bottom of my heart. I'm sure there were more than a few other airmen who felt as I did.

I used my machine guns outside of dogfights, too. But it was to attack anti-aircraft emplacements or ships. I never once shot at an unarmed man. I believe only a coward would do such a thing.

Do you get it? That was the kind of man he was. He was always running from danger on battlefields but had no problem gunning down a defenseless human being. Or perhaps, it was because he was such a man that he was capable of doing such a thing.

Ever since I became a fighter pilot, I desired to fight bravely and die with valor in battle. In any case, I thought my life was forfeit, which was why I wanted to die heroically, like a man. I never ran away from dogfights. That's my medal. I was never actually decorated, but that alone is my pride.

I lost an arm in an air fight at Guadalcanal in October 1942.

That day I was providing cover for land-based medium bombers, the Mitsubishi G4Ms used by the Imperial Navy. They were slow, sitting ducks before enemy fire, which is why they always had a convoy of Zeros. Zeros were originally escort fighters.

The target for the bombers that day was a fleet of enemy transport ships. We had twelve bombers and twelve Zeros. Miyabe was part of the formation.

Enemy fighters were lying in wait for us in the skies above Guadalcanal. Their interception—*yougeki* rather than *geigeki* in Imperial Navy parlance—was particularly intense that day. There must have been over forty of them. We engaged the F4Fs while defending the bombers.

We did our damnedest to protect the bombers but the enemy avoided tangling with the Zeros and, instead, targeted the bombers. While we would pursue one enemy fighter, another one would swoop in and attack a bomber. One after another, the bombers burst into flames and plummeted. It was like being hunted by a pack of wolves.

Above all else, it was the duty of the escort fighters to protect the bombers. It was more important to keep the bombers from getting shot down than to shoot down enemy planes. If we went too far in chasing hostile planes and got separated, they'd take down our bombers. Each bomber had seven crewmembers and carried ordnance intended for a strike on the enemy's airfield. The bomber crews were risking their lives for that single attack. We escort pilots had been ordered to protect the bombers even if it meant offering up our lives. That was our mission.

Just as the bombers were about to turn course for the bombing, a gap momentarily opened in our formation. Two F4Fs swooped in. I didn't think I would make it in time, but on the spur of the moment I decided to slip in between a bomber and the enemy aircraft. It wasn't a conscious decision—my instincts as an escort fighter took over.

The next instant, I was fired on from above. My canopy was blown off. Something crashed into my head and for a second everything went black. But I immediately regained consciousness and looked behind me. The bomber was safe.

It was then that I noticed my left arm was killing me. I glanced down and saw that it was coated in blood from the shoulder down. I temporarily pulled away from the action to take stock of the damage. The wings and fuselage were riddled with bullets but thankfully the fuel tank and engine were still okay.

After the air raid, I flew back to Rabaul relying mostly on just one hand. Due to the pain and loss of blood I nearly passed out several times, but I willed myself to keep flying. Six bombers and three Zeros were lost that day. It had been a tough battle. Most of the Zeros that made it back were covered with bullet marks all over.

I learned this afterwards, but Miyabe's plane didn't have a single bullet hole in it. Even after such a ferocious battle, his plane was totally unscathed. He had been a part of the convoy. Where had he been while we were risking our lives fighting? Where was he flying around when my left arm was shot?

Ultimately I lost my arm. In the interior they might not have had to amputate it.

I was in Rabaul for just under two months. I'm not sure whether that was a lengthy or short stay. All told, my life as a pilot had lasted a year and a half.

Life after the war was a series of hardships. Society was cold to a fellow who'd offered up his life to his country and lost his left arm. Though I was discharged with the rank of ensign, such titles held no meaning in postwar society. Besides, I was only promoted after the war was over, as a so-called Potsdam Ensign. There were no jobs for a one-armed man. As a kid I had been thrown out of my hometown to lessen the burden on my family, but I ended coming back here after all.

And yet someone was kind enough to play the matchmaker, and I took a wife. Well, rather, I married into her family and took their name so perhaps "took a wife" isn't quite an accurate statement. If I hadn't lost my arm, perhaps a better life would have awaited me. No, if I hadn't lost my arm, I would likely have died in the skies. That would have been fine. I wasn't afraid of death in the slightest. Wouldn't it have been more splendid to die a manly, spectacular death than to eke out a miserable life covered in dirt in the countryside?

In my old age I've come to fully realize that I wanted to die a kamikaze. Had I not lacked a limb, I would have volunteered for sure.

Three years after I lost my arm, Miyabe died a kamikaze. I don't think he volunteered. There's no doubt they forced him into the Special Attack Force and that he begrudgingly followed orders. Thus a man who put his life on the line during every battle has survived into old age, while another man who held his life so dear ended up dead.

If that isn't an example of life's irony, I don't know what it is.

It was past six o'clock but the skies were still light.

My gait was heavy as we made our way back to the station. I'm sure it was the same for Keiko. Her expression was grim.

In her handbag was the voice recorder that contained Hasegawa's tale, but I was uncertain as to whether she would want to listen to it again.

It had been an unpleasant interview. No, it couldn't be called an interview. Hasegawa's monologue. The more he spoke the more he seemed to think back on his hatred of our grandfather, and he bluntly leveled that hatred at us, too. I was overwhelmed by his gaze, filled with so much malice and hostility.

"What a nasty old man," I said some time after we had left

his house. "He curses his fate. Maybe he thinks that his life was taken from him when he lost his arm. I bet he blames our grandfather for his missing arm, too."

Keiko was silent for a while. Then she sighed and said, "I feel sorry for him."

I was struck momentarily dumb.

"That was the first time I'd heard about the war from a vet. It wasn't easy. I feel like I understand how he feels. I'm sure he went through a lot after the war, too."

I didn't have a reply. If anything, I was ashamed for saying something so bitter after hearing what she said.

For a while we walked in silence back down the road we had traveled a few hours prior.

"But I didn't think the stories about our grandfather were fabrications," I blurted out.

Keiko let out a modest sigh. "Honestly speaking, I'm a little disappointed in him. They said he was a kamikaze so I thought he was brave. To learn he was actually a coward… Actually, I'm a pacifist, so I don't really want my grandfather to have been some war hero. But aside from that, I'm disappointed. Aren't you, Kentaro?"

I nodded silently. Hasegawa's phrasing, that our grandfather was a coward, weighed heavily on my mind. My grandfather was someone who flew around the skies fearing for his life. I realized that I was reacting to the word "coward" as if the old man had insulted me personally. That's because I was running away, too. So then, my grandfather's blood coursed through my veins.

Of course, my grandfather had been running from death, which was totally not true for me. Yet, it seemed certain that my grandfather had run from his duty as a pilot.

While I—well, what on earth was I running from?

"Ugh. This research is already too painful," my sister muttered to no one in particular. I felt the same way.

Chapter 3
Pearl Harbor

The week after meeting Hasegawa, I visited Grandpa to tell him that we were doing research on our biological grandfather.

Keiko said there was no need to go out of our way to tell him, but I hated the idea of sneaking around behind my beloved grandfather's back. I was also confident that he wasn't the sort to take issue.

But there was a concern. Ever since developing a heart problem the year before, he had been recuperating at home. He had essentially been retired from his long career as a lawyer for the past several years, leaving the running of his law firm to others. He had a regular housekeeper who looked after him and the house.

He used to often say, "Once you pass the bar, you'd better head straight to my firm." But recently he had given up saying such things, and I was a little saddened by that. Maybe he thought it was no big deal for me to take a three- or four-year detour since he himself had worked for the National Railway for a decade before passing the bar.

When I arrived, Grandpa was already entertaining someone.

Shuichi Fujiki had once been a part-timer at Grandpa's law office. An impoverished student planning to take the bar, even after graduating he'd studied for it while working at the firm. But several years ago, when his father fell ill, Fujiki was forced to abandon his dream of becoming a lawyer and to go back to his hometown to continue the family ironworks. He was paying Grandpa a visit after attending a college reunion the day before.

"Long time, no see, Fujiki-san."

"Same here."

Two years had passed since I'd last seen him. He made a point to visit Grandpa whenever he was in Tokyo.

"Ken-chan, you've grown into a fine young man. You were still in high school when I left the firm."

Fujiki had said the exact same thing when I saw him last. I was afraid that he was going to ask, "So how'd it go this year?" He'd always told me seriously that he'd "never seen a kid as smart as you. You should be able to pass the bar before you've even graduated." He was always very nice to me, and this time he didn't ask about my current circumstances. I appreciated his kindness.

"So how's your ironworks going, Fujiki-san?"

"Not well at all," he replied with a laugh. "We lose money just staying open. To be honest, I want to close up the factory but I can't do that to my employees."

He scratched at his head that was beginning to show signs of gray. He looked like a typical worn-out middle-aged man. It was a little hard seeing him like that since he'd always seemed eternally youthful. As I looked at this man who had failed to pass the bar year after year, I felt as though I was looking at an image of my own future.

"Are you married, Fujiki-san?"

"No, not yet. Working my tail off at the ironworks, I woke up to find I'd turned thirty-six," he laughed.

Fujiki soon bid us farewell and left. After he had gone, my grandfather said, "When he was with our firm I was on active duty and going strong." He looked briefly lost in nostalgia.

"Grandpa," I hazarded, making up my mind, "I'm doing research on Kyuzo Miyabe."

I thought I saw his features stiffen for a moment. *Damn*, I fretted. *Guess it doesn't sit well with him after all.*

"Matsuno's first husband, huh…"

I explained in a rush how my sister had asked me to help and that Mom wanted to know more about her real father.

"Kiyoko does?" Grandpa asked. Then he muttered, "I see."

"I actually understand how Mom feels," I said.

Grandpa stared into my eyes. There was something unnerving in his gaze.

When my grandmother had died, he had clung to her lifeless body and wailed. That was the first time I had ever seen him cry. He sobbed so hard that the hospital nurses were moved to tears. He loved Grandma from the bottom of his heart. Perhaps it was painful for him to recall that she had once been another man's wife. They say men prized pure women back in those days, but she'd even borne another man's child. Kyuzo Miyabe could hardly be a welcome figure for Grandpa.

"According to our research, Kyuzo Miyabe and Grandma lived together for a very short time. After they wed, he was almost always away with the military," I said, trying to be considerate of his feelings.

Grandpa merely nodded. "So how are you conducting this research?"

"I've sent letters to several veterans' groups asking them to find people who knew Miyabe. We've only been able to speak to one person so far, a man who was stationed in Rabaul with him for just a couple of months. He was a pilot like Kyuzo was."

"And what did he say?"

I hesitated but decided to tell him the truth. "That he was a coward, always fleeing from battle." Then I added, self-deprecatingly, "Maybe the reason I'm so spineless is because I've inherited grandfather Kyuzo's DNA…"

"Nonsense!" Grandpa rebuked me. "Kiyoko was a hard worker ever since she was a kid. She never whined or complained, no matter what. After her husband—your father—passed away, she managed an accounting firm and raised you kids single-handedly. Your sister Keiko, too, inherited that trait and is a tough cookie. The blood of a coward does not run in your veins."

"Sorry, that's not what I meant."

Seeing me wilt, Grandpa said gently, "Kentaro, you're a far finer man than you give yourself credit for. One day you'll realize that."

"You're always so kind to me, Grandpa. You say that even though, well…"

"We're not related by blood?"

"Uh, yeah…"

"I love you because you're kindhearted. Keiko is strong-willed but she, too, is a sweet girl," Grandpa said with a smile. "Speaking of kind-hearted people, Fujiki is one, too. He was always there for others even if he was going through hell. I'm sure that trait is the reason he's having such a hard time at the ironworks, too."

I nodded. It was true that Fujiki was a kind and sincere man.

"He's precisely the sort of man that should become a lawyer…" Grandpa said with a note of regret.

When Fujiki first came to my grandfather's firm, I was in elementary school and my sister was in junior high. He taught us about all sorts of things: interesting novels, history, tales of great artists. My sister and I loved to listen to him talk. He was the one who taught me that becoming a lawyer was a most wonderful career choice, and that Grandpa was the very model of a good lawyer. He may have influenced my decision to pursue a law career. In my very young eyes, he was like Superman. I adored him.

But unfortunately, he wasn't a very good student. Or rather, he wasn't very good at taking the bar. He loved novels and music more than legal tomes, which is why he didn't always pass even the short-answer portion of the test. Keiko always poked fun at him for it, but that was simply the flip side of her affection.

The week before Fujiki left for his hometown, he rented a car and took Keiko and me on a drive to Hakone. I was a high school senior and Keiko was in her last year of college. I had apparently asked to go on a trip to Hakone a long time before then, and while I had forgotten any such promise Fujiki faithfully kept his word.

On the drive, Keiko laughed, saying things like, "You worked so hard for ten years, all for naught…" and "You're gonna end up a middle-aged owner of a struggling ironworks in the sticks of Yamaguchi." Her jabs lacked the usual undertones of affection. But Fujiki simply gave a troubled smile in return, never losing his temper. I found myself getting offended on his behalf. I wanted Fujiki to be happy.

That night I had dinner with my mother for the first time in a while. Since she ran an accounting firm she always worked late, and we rarely got to eat together. She used to run the firm with Dad, but she had been in charge ever since he passed away from illness ten years ago.

"Had you really never been told anything about your real father, Mom?"

"Grandma didn't tell me a thing. Maybe she hadn't married him out of love. It wasn't uncommon for a couple to meet just once for an arranged match before getting married."

"Did you ever ask if she loved him?"

"I did, once, when I was a teenager."

"What did she say?"

Mom looked as though she was recalling the past. "She said, 'What do you want me to say?'"

"What did she mean by that?"

"I thought it meant that she didn't love him, but looking back on it now maybe I was wrong."

"I wonder if she did love him."

"I don't know. But I don't think she'd have said so even if she did. She was in love with Grandpa."

I nodded. I remembered Grandpa always being on Grandma's mind. Whenever something happened she'd run to him, saying, "Oh, Grandpa..." Grandpa cherished her, too. She was actually older than him but it didn't show. So I'd been genuinely surprised to hear that she'd had a husband before him.

"It'll be an eternally unsolved mystery whether my real father loved my mother, and whether she loved him. But I would like to know what kind of young man he was."

"Young man?"

"Yes, he was twenty-six when he died. The same age you are now, Kentaro."

I went over Kyuzo Miyabe's resume in my mind. I was struck anew by how young he was when he died.

"I wish Mother had told me what he was like," my mother said.

I risked asking a difficult question. "What if he didn't have a good reputation?"

"Is that so?"

"Oh, I just mean hypothetically. Suppose in the course of our research someone told us something you'd rather not hear."

"Hard to say," she said after briefly considering it. "In that case, maybe the kids were left with no stories because that was for the best."

My mood darkened at her words.

The next week, I headed to Matsuyama in Shikoku. We had found someone else who had known my grandfather.

At first, my sister was supposed to go on her own, but at the last minute she said, "I just got a gig that I simply can't turn down. Please go in my place." I wanted to refuse, but she implored me, saying, "Freelance writers are at the mercy of their clients," and I found myself unable to turn her down. I didn't think she was lying, but I couldn't quite rid myself of the notion that she didn't want to sit through another story like Hasegawa's.

That's why I ended up traveling all the way to Shikoku by myself. While I was disgusted by my trusting, good nature, since Keiko had given me double the usual per diem I decided to enjoy the trip as if I were on a mini-vacation. After finishing the interview at some appropriate point, I'd stop by the nearby Dougo hot springs or something like that.

Former Navy Lieutenant Junior Grade Kanji Ito lived in a large house in a residential area near the center of town. Ito was a small, elderly man with perfect posture and sprightliness to his movements. He was supposed to be turning eighty-five but looked to be in his seventies.

I was shown to a large sitting room. He handed me a business card that bore various titles. He seemed to be a bigwig in the local Chamber of Commerce. It also said that he was the chairman of some company.

"Do you run your business, sir?"

"No, I left my son in charge. Now I'm enjoying the retired life. Besides, it isn't much of a company."

The housekeeper served me some iced coffee.

"It's nearly August. August always makes me think of the war," Ito said with some feeling. "So you're Miyabe's grandson, eh? Hmm, to think he would have a grandson like you." He stared fixedly at me. "I certainly never thought Miyabe's grandson would pay me a visit sixty years after the war. But such is life."

I tensed up, remembering Hasegawa's tale. Flustered, I said rapidly, "To be honest, I don't know anything about my grandfather. My grandmother remarried after the war and died without talking to us about him. My mother, too, has no memories of her real father. I wanted to learn more about my own roots, so I thought I'd visit anyone who knew him personally and listen to their stories."

Ito listened silently to my explanation. He gave his head a small shake, as if attempting to call up old memories. Then he looked up at the ceiling, thinking of where to start.

I spoke first: "Sir, I heard that my grandfather was a cowardly pilot."

Ito gave me a puzzled look. "Cowardly? Miyabe?" he repeated the word as a question. Yet he didn't refute it. Then he looked up, seemingly a bit lost in thought. "Well, to be sure, I don't think that Miyabe was a particularly heroic pilot. But he definitely was an excellent one."

As I told you over the phone, I don't have many memories of Miyabe. Of course, I did converse with him. But it was over sixty years ago, and it's not easy to recall every little thing.

I fought alongside Miyabe for over half a year, from the attack on Pearl Harbor to the Battle of Midway. We were both crewmembers on the carrier *Akagi*.

Short for "aircraft carrier," a carrier is a warship loaded with planes. A small airstrip spans the length of the ship so planes can take off and land. The *Akagi* was the strongest warship of the Greater East Asian War.

After graduating from higher primary school, I enrolled in the Naval Preparatory Flight Training Program. I had grown up seeing the Iwakuni Naval Air Unit's planes near my childhood home and longed to become a pilot. I was a military brat of sorts. At the time the preparatory flight training program was very popular and the acceptance rate was about one out of a hundred. I jumped for joy when they took me. My program was distinct from the pilot-in-training course. The prep program's graduates entered the Navy as pilots, whereas the pilot-in-training course recruited sailors and turned them into pilots. Miyabe was a graduate of the latter.

After completing flight training I was ordered to the Yokosuka Naval Air Corps. I was with them for over two years before joining the crew of the *Akagi* in the spring of 1941. It was there that I flew the new state-of-the-art fighter. Yes, the Zero. We generally called it "the new-model fighter" or the *reisen* (Zero fighter).

Why was it called the *reisen*, you ask?

The nickname comes from the last digit of the Imperial Year 2600, when it formally entered service. Imperial Year 2600 was 1940. Nobody uses the Imperial calendar these days. Similarly, the Navy Type 99 carrier-based bomber was introduced the year before, in Imperial Year 2599. And two years prior, Imperial Year 2597, saw the introduction of the Type 97 carrier-based attacker. All three of these planes played major roles in the attack on Pearl Harbor. The Zero's official name was the Mitsubishi Type Zero Carrier-Based Fighter Plane.

The Zero was an incredible aircraft. Its combat performance was a full cut above the rest. Most impressive were its turning and looping abilities. It had a very small turning radius. That's why it was unbeatable in a dogfight. It was also very fast. In the early days of the war at least, I think it was probably the fastest aircraft in the world. In essence, it had both speed and maneuverability.

Typically, those two factors ran counter to each other. If too much emphasis was placed on combat performance, an aircraft's speed would drop. And if speed was the focus, then combat performance would suffer. But the Zero was a magical plane that somehow managed to excel in both areas. They say it was made possible thanks to the blood and sweat of two passionate young engineers, Jiro Horikoshi and Yoshitoshi Sone.

In addition to the standard 7.7-mm machine guns it was armed with powerful 20-mm cannons. The 7.7-mm guns could only put holes in airplanes, but the cannons were loaded with shells that exploded upon contact. You could blow apart an enemy plane with one shot. The cannons' slow muzzle velocity and low-capacity magazine were their weaknesses, though.

But the Zero's truly formidable weapon was its incredible cruising range. It could easily cover 3,000 kilometers. Most single-seat fighters at the time had a range of only a few hundred kilometers, so surely you can see how overwhelming a 3,000-kilometer range was in comparison.

This is a digression, but in the end, Germany was unable to defeat England. That's because the Germans had a weak navy. They made up for it by bombing England in the Battle of Britain. Nearly every day, German bombers crossed the Straits of Dover to assault England, but the Royal Air Force waged an all-out counterattack and eventually forced the Luftwaffe to abandon their air raids.

The Luftwaffe was defeated by the RAF because its bombers weren't sufficiently protected by fighter planes. Laden with heavy explosives, bombers lack both speed and agility, rendering them helpless against nimble fighters. That's why bombers need escorts, but the Luftwaffe's fighter planes weren't quite up to the task.

The Germans had an excellent fighter plane in the Messerschmitt, but it had a fatal flaw: a very short flight range, which meant it could only spend a few minutes fighting in British airspace. If a dogfight dragged out for too long, it was unable to get back across the Strait of Dover and plunged into the sea. Struggling to complete a round-trip crossing of a mere forty-kilometer strait…

In comparison, a Zero could have fought in the skies above London for over an hour and established total air supremacy. It's an absurd supposition, but if the Germans had had Zeros, England would have suffered terribly.

The Zero was designed to have such a long flight range because it was a requirement for a fighter that had to do battle above the vast Pacific Ocean. An emergency landing on water meant death, which is why the Zero had to be able to fly continuously for 3,000 kilometers. Battles over China's immense landmass was also part of the picture. An emergency landing there meant death just like on the ocean.

Warriors of old used to say that a fine horse can gallop a thousand miles out and back home again. The Zero was indeed a fine horse. It was an unparalleled fighter that combined the virtues of superior combat performance, speed, and an incredible flight range. And the most surprising aspect was that the Zeros were not land-based fighters but rather could take off from and land on narrow carrier decks.

Back then, Japan's industrial capability was considered much inferior to that of the West, yet out of nowhere it produced a fighter that set a new world standard. This is something that Japanese should really be proud of.

Experiencing war is certainly nothing to brag about. But even now, rushing about in the great skies in a Zero is one of my proudest achievements. I'll be eighty-five this year. In the span of such a long life, the time I spent piloting a Zero, not even two full years, is but a brief period. But those two years were so very fulfilling, and they've only taken on a greater significance in the twilight of my life.

Whoops. I got carried away a bit. There's no point in telling such things to a young person. Even I forgot about my experiences as a fighter pilot once the war was over. It was all I could do to put food on the table, and I devoted myself to providing for my family. I really worked my tail off.

Perhaps it's that in old age I can look back on my life and notice the brilliance of my youth. Probably when you've grown old, too, you'll look back on your life and see yourself as you stand now from a totally different perspective.

Sorry, I wandered off the subject.

Miyabe joined the crew of the *Akagi* in the summer of 1941 after serving in China. Several pilots who had fought in China were transferred to the aircraft carrier around the same time.

The first thing they practiced after joining the crew was landing on the carrier deck. Unlike runways on land, it's extremely difficult to touch down on a carrier as it pitches and rolls on the sea. It was daunting to many pilots who had never done it before.

Navy aircraft differed from Army planes in that they basically used a three-point landing. This was in order to catch the arresting cables strung across the deck with the plane's tail hook. If the hook failed to catch the wire cables, then there was no landing on the short deck.

But in order to execute a three-point landing, you needed to raise the aircraft's nose just before landing. The nose would then obstruct your view, forcing you to rely solely on intuition to find the unseen deck. Rush the landing and you crashed into the stern. If you feared that and got over-cautious, your hook missed the arresting gear and you collided with the brake plate installed near the bow. In the worst-case scenario, you fell off the front of the ship into the ocean. In fact, it wasn't rare to see planes screw up their landings and plunge into the drink. For this reason, destroyers called "dragonfly catchers" were on stand-by right behind the carrier during landing drills. Planes that ended up in the ocean were hauled up by cranes, making them look like captured dragonflies.

Incidentally, though it seldom happened, the arresting cables could snap, which was terrifying. The severed cable would turn into a whip that raced down the length of the carrier deck. I witnessed a crewmember's leg get sliced off in such an incident. I was unable to eat for the rest of that day. I would go on to witness countless harrowing scenes on the front, and developed a tougher stomach…

We went onto the deck to watch the carrier landing drills of the newly transferred pilots in order to observe their skills. As expected, their first landings were a mess. They were all seasoned pilots who had fought in China, and while most of them somehow managed to put their planes on the deck, there were some who fell into the ocean. We split our sides laughing at them.

But there was one among them who pulled off a top-notch landing. He approached at a shallow angle and gently set the plane down near the middle of the deck, caught the arresting cable closest to the bow, and came to a stop right before the brake plate. It was an ideal landing.

There were about ten arresting cables strung across the deck, starting aft and progressing forward. Catching the foremost cable and coming to a stop certainly made it easier for the deck crew to maneuver the aircraft out of the way, allowing other planes to come in for landings almost immediately. But it was a highly risky move, because if a pilot failed to catch the final cable, he would crash into the brake plate or fall off the bow. But that plane easily caught the foremost cable.

"Holy mackerel," we marveled. And that pilot was Miyabe.

"That's gotta be a damn fluke," someone said.

I called out to Miyabe after he completed his landing. As we were both Flight Petty Officers 1st Class, I didn't need to stand on ceremony, but it was also because I stood in awe of his display of skill. Miyabe was tall, probably close to six feet in height.

"That was really top-notch."

Miyabe gave a cheerful smile in reply, a very affable smile, and said, "That was my first carrier landing, but I managed thanks to following my senior aviators' instructions."

A pilot must have a really keen awareness of his aircraft to be able to pull off such a landing on the first try. At that point I had done over thirty carrier landings but still got nervous each time.

"I don't know anything about carriers, so please look after me," Miyabe said and bowed his head.

I was slightly taken aback because it was odd to hear anyone in the military talk that way. Of course, we were polite when we addressed our superiors. We had to be, or else they'd strike us. But Miyabe used the same form of speech with those of his own rank, and even those who ranked beneath him. Such people were rare specimens in the Imperial Navy.

His polite speech was probably the reason he was looked down on by much of the other aircrew. The Navy was a rough-and-tumble place, and I'll not mince words, aviators especially were a bunch of punks. The fact that we led such a precarious existence likely contributed a great deal to this. Most young men developed an attitude in that milieu, but Miyabe was different.

I somehow took to Miyabe the moment I met him. I was a hotheaded roughneck given to fighting with my squadron mates. Perhaps it was a case of opposites attracting.

Some of the lower-ranking crewmembers treated Miyabe with disdain, too, but he never let it bother him, always answering them politely, which only served to fuel their scorn. But nobody ever made fun of him to his face because they knew his skills as a pilot were first rate.

After his first landing, some sarcastic crew had said, "That's gotta be a damn fluke," but that was incorrect. Miyabe continued to land right near the bow of the ship. In time, a Miyabe landing became a must-see event for many of the crew. It's possible that he was the most adept pilot at carrier landings in the entire Imperial Navy.

Of course, landing skills didn't equal combat skills, but Miyabe was just as impressive in mock dogfights. Apparently, he'd downed over a dozen enemy planes over the Chinese mainland. Back then, anyone with five or more kills was considered a *mosa*, a stalwart. Overseas they're called "ace" pilots, yes?

In Miyabe's case, the disparity between his flying accomplishments and his everyday demeanor invited much malicious talk behind his back.

For you to better understand our battles, I should probably explain the difference between attack bombers and dive bombers. You might not be familiar with the terms, but on both the Japanese and American sides, no other aircraft fought costlier or tougher battles than those bombers. And their crews had the highest fatality rate.

Attack bombers were three-seat carrier-based planes generally used in torpedo attacks. Torpedoes weren't only used by submarines. These were the most dreaded type of attack for a warship because they could tear open the hull, causing water to gush in and sink her. The so-called unsinkable battleships *Yamato* and *Musashi* both suffered that fate.

Dive bombers were two-seat carrier-based planes chiefly used in dive bombings. Those, too, were fearsome. Diving from a height of 2,000 meters, the planes dropped bombs that crashed through the deck and exploded inside the ship. A warship was filled with explosives, fuel, and such. If any of it caught fire, the result was catastrophic. If the ship's propulsion system was hit and exploded, the damage was fatal.

Warships were fitted with anti-aircraft cannons and machine guns to repel aerial attacks, but this was quite a challenge. Using cannons and machine guns to shoot down an aircraft flying at over 150 meters per second was a tall order.

That is why fighters were the most effective defense against attack or dive bombers. The fighters would shoot down the bombers before they had a chance to attack the ship. As I said before, bomber planes were loaded with heavy bombs and torpedoes, so they were practically defenseless in the face of light, nimble fighters. Thus they flew with fighter escorts. Carrier-based fighters had two missions: protecting the fleet from hostile bombers and escorting friendly bombers to their targets.

Miyabe and I were fighter pilots.

We began an extremely intense training regimen from the moment we boarded the *Akagi*. For months we were worked nearly to death with literally no rest. Yes, the infamous *MMTWThFF*. During that time, the number of flight hours completed by pilots with the First and Second Carrier Divisions easily exceeded 1,000 hours each. We were all super-veterans, the mightiest outfit in the world, if I do say so myself, the world's best pilots flying the world's best aircraft.

It was the middle of November when the carrier group completed intensive training, gathered in Saeki Bay, and set course to the north. The aircrew was furnished with winter clothes, but they didn't tell us anything about our destination. We sensed that something special was in the works but had no idea as to the specifics. We were in the thick of the Sino-Japanese War at the time, and the Chinese alone were giving us plenty of trouble. We knew, however, that America and Britain were putting terrific pressure on Japan. Our allies the Germans were already fighting the British, so there was a sense that we, too, would end up fighting the Allied forces. Plus, the Navy had for a long time run drills where the hypothetical enemy was the United States.

We reached Hitokappu Bay on Iturup Island. The Sea of Okhotsk was frigid in November. A large number of military vessels of the Navy's Combined Fleet assembled in the freezing mist. It was quite a spectacle.

Then, on November 26th, once the entire aircrew from all the carriers was gathered together, the flight commander announced, "Simultaneously with a declaration of war, we will attack the American fleet at Pearl Harbor."

I was astonished but at the same time thought, "So the time has come at last." My whole body brimmed with tension like never before. I'm sure that all the other aircrew felt the same. No one even flinched at the thought of attacking Pearl Harbor. Everyone looked forward to making the hated Americans froth at their mouths.

After that, they announced our individual assignments for the mission. My name wasn't on the list of members of the attack force. Everything before my eyes went black. I was being delegated to combat air patrol. I would be milling in the skies above the fleet and protecting my mothership from hostile aircraft.

I tearfully begged the commander to let me join the attack force. Even though I knew that it wouldn't change a thing, I just couldn't accept it without complaint. Other aircrew excluded from the attack force or assigned to the reserve component were crying and pleading with the commander too. That night, several fights broke out among the pilots. I understood how they felt. We had all undergone excruciating training just for that day. If the operation was successful, even if it resulted in our deaths we'd have no regrets. There were some particularly intense displays of dejection among the attack and dive bomber pilots who found themselves in the reserve component.

That night, Miyabe called out to me on the afterdeck. There were two decks under the flight deck, fore and aft, reminders that the *Akagi* had originally been designed as a battle cruiser before it was rebuilt as an aircraft carrier.

"Ito-san, CAP is a very important mission." Miyabe had been chosen to participate in the first attack wave.

"Can't you understand my disappointment?" I shot back.

"CAP duty is more important than the attack force in my opinion. You're protecting the lives of everyone aboard the carrier."

"Then switch with me."

"I'd gladly trade places if I could."

"Then do it!"

But we both knew it wasn't possible. It would be unreasonable to allow aviators to rearrange mission assignments according to their own wishes.

I plopped down on the deck, tears of frustration welling up in my eyes. Miyabe sat down next to me.

I gazed out absentmindedly at the dark seas. There were no stars in the sky and it was a freezing night. But I didn't feel the cold.

Miyabe kept me company without uttering a word. After a while I started to calm down. I think having Miyabe sit quietly by my side probably helped.

Unexpectedly, Miyabe said with a sigh, "I told you I'm married, right?"

I nodded.

"I got married after coming back from Shanghai, before leaving for Omura. I had just one week to enjoy my newlywed life."

I hadn't known that. It came as a surprise.

"If I'd known I was going to participate in the attack on Pearl Harbor, I wouldn't have gotten married," Miyabe said, and then smiled.

That was the extent of that conversation, but for some reason I remember it very well. I still wonder why he decided to tell me that just then.

Hm? Did they marry for love? Oh, I didn't ask about that. In our day, such marriages were rare, though. You married the person that people around you said you should. Rushed marriages before heading to the front weren't uncommon. Parents and relatives probably wanted the young men to at least experience marriage before they faced possible death in battle. And of course there was probably also the desire to create an heir beforehand.

Back then, marriage wasn't thought of as some big deal. It was just something that everyone did. No one really considered the reasons for it. Young people these days seem to think differently—that you only get married when you find your ideal life partner. My granddaughter apparently feels that way, which is why she's still single even though she's in her mid-thirties. She says she'll happily spend the rest of her life alone if she doesn't find the right man. What a handful.

I don't know why Miyabe got married so hastily. Perhaps it was a marriage of love. Not getting married if he'd known he was going to attack Pearl Harbor can be taken either way.

Even though there were brawls and fights on the night of the mission assignments, the next day everyone, me included, faithfully carried out our duties without any hint of enmity. I just pulled myself together and resolved to fulfill my mission to protect the aircraft carrier.

At dawn on December 8th, I took off with the CAP team to patrol the skies above the carrier group. Soon afterwards the first attack wave departed. I saw off the formation with a salute from my cockpit.

During the operation, not a single enemy aircraft was spotted in the skies above the carriers, so I never engaged in combat.

As you are aware, the surprise attack on Pearl Harbor was a resounding success. In the first-ever, all-aircraft naval attack, the two waves sank five battleships and extensively damaged three more. Over 200 land-based aircraft were destroyed. It was an unprecedented exploit.

Right after the attack on Pearl Harbor ended in triumph, the pilots and crewmembers all celebrated wildly.

With one exception. Miyabe. "What's wrong? You don't seem to be enjoying yourself," I asked him.

"Twenty-nine planes didn't make it back today."

I was already aware of that. "It is unfortunate. But compared to the damage we inflicted, our losses are almost nothing."

Miyabe nodded silently. His face put a damper on my good mood.

"It's war. People are going to die," I pointed out.

"I saw an attack bomber destroy itself today," Miyabe said quietly. "After dropping its torpedo, it was hit by an anti-aircraft gun while passing over an enemy ship. Initially, the bomber ascended. I drew up to her. I could see a long white stream of fuel leaking from one of her wings, but luckily it hadn't caught fire. The bomber was flying toward the carrier, but suddenly turned around and headed back towards Pearl Harbor. I turned as well and pulled up alongside her. The pilot looked at me and pointed downward. Then he went into a dive and rammed the bomber into an enemy battleship."

His story made me shudder. In fact, I'd heard that many of the planes we had lost that day had similarly immolated themselves. We had been ordered to destroy our aircraft if it was damaged during battle in a manner that precluded a return trip. We'd been taught to avoid the shame of being taken captive, so it seemed inevitable.

"Before they dove, all three crewmembers looked at me and saluted, smiling."

"They were true soldiers."

Miyabe nodded. "I think it was mere minutes between their initial ascent and their turn back towards the harbor. They probably spent that time assessing the damage to the plane and gave up on making it back to the carrier. Either they saw that they'd run out of fuel or their engine was hit. In any case, in those brief moments they chose to blow themselves up."

Carrier-based attack bombers had three crewmembers: the pilot, the bombardier, and the radio operator. In the Imperial Navy, crewmembers of the same aircraft were called *pairs*, as in the foreign word. Flight teams had to become one in body and soul. They said that if the crew's breathing was not in sync, their torpedo attack would be imperfect. The bond shared by them was far stronger than your usual friendship. People sometimes speak of "sworn friends," and the crew on attack planes and bombers were literally that.

Most likely the pilot had decided to destroy the plane, communicating his resolve to the other two. They'd probably concurred straightaway.

"Their smiles were so vibrant. They didn't look like the expressions of men who were about to die," Miyabe added.

"Maybe that's because they were able to partake in a successful operation."

Miyabe mulled over my words a bit and then replied, "I suppose so."

"When I die, like them I want it to be after I've dealt a lot of damage to the other side."

Miyabe was silent for a while, but he sighed and said, "I don't want to die."

I was shocked by his statement. I had never expected to hear such words from anyone in the Imperial Navy. Of course, military men, too, feel that they don't want to die. Such is human nature. But a soldier cannot just leave it at that. Just as people in general must control all sorts of instincts and desires in order to exist in society, I believe it's important for military personnel to figure out how to relinquish that desire to survive. Isn't that right? If the troops prioritized survival, no war effort would be sustainable.

Our military had won an overwhelming victory. Yet, we had lost 29 planes and 55 lives. Looking back now, I understand something that I didn't back then. For the families of the pilots who died that day, the grief over the loss of their loved ones was far greater than the joy of victory. Whether it was a battle where thousands fought to the last man or just one soldier was killed in action, a bereaved family was robbed of an irreplaceable member. Thousands dying in action simply meant a greater number of tragedies; every one of those individual tragedies was the same.

But I didn't get it back then. And my reaction to Miyabe saying "I don't want to die" was intense contempt. Those were words that a sailor of the Imperial Navy, let alone a fighter pilot, should never utter. We should all have been prepared to die with our boots on the moment we became pilots.

"Why do you not want to die?"

Miyabe's reply was soft-spoken. "I have a wife. It's for her sake that I don't want to die. So I value my life more than anything else."

I was left momentarily speechless. And I was thoroughly disgusted. I felt like I'd caught a thief and asked him "Why did you steal it?" only to have him answer "Because I wanted it."

"Everyone values their lives. And everyone has a family. Although I'm not married, I have a father and a mother…" *but damn if I ever said I don't want to die*, I almost added, just barely holding my tongue.

"I'm a disgrace to the Imperial Navy, aren't I?" Miyabe gave a bitter smile.

"That, you are," I replied.

Miyabe went silent and hung his head.

Ito suddenly fell quiet.

He folded his arms, closed his eyes, and didn't speak. After several long moments had passed, he said in a voice barely louder than a whisper, "Miyabe was an odd man."

He continued, "Back then we pilots were living in a strange world, a place divorced from reason. We lived in a world where death was always right by your side, or rather where life and death always intermingled. You couldn't live in such a world if you feared death. Yet Miyabe feared it. He lived in the everyday world while fighting in a war. How could he manage to hold on to that feeling?"

Ito seemed to phrase it like a question for me, but it wasn't one that I could answer. Or perhaps he was asking himself.

"After the war and demobilization, I got married and started a family. It was only then that I was able to comprehend Miyabe's desire to keep on living for his wife's sake. But," Ito then said forcefully, "I cannot agree with Miyabe's words that he 'valued his life more than anything else.' Wars are not fought alone. Sometimes you have to fight on, even if it means sacrificing yourself."

"I couldn't say, sir."

"Here's another thing that happened. In February of 1942, during an air raid on Port Darwin, Miyabe returned from the mission early after his machine guns failed. Even if an escort fighter can't fire its guns, it can still chase off enemy aircraft. And just having a Zero by their side is heartening to the bomber crews. But Miyabe pulled out and left in a hurry."

"Oh…"

"It might sound like I am bragging, but had I been in his place I would have stayed, even if it meant getting shot down."

I simply nodded.

"Please don't misunderstand me. I'm not criticizing his principles. I just can't say they were praiseworthy. I feel bad saying this to his grandson, forgive me."

Ito bowed deeply. I could sense the old man's sincerity.

There was a knock at the door. A genteel old lady appeared.

"This is my wife."

She placed a plate of fruits on the table. "Please make yourself at home," she said and left.

"I married her after the war," Ito explained with a shy smile. "It was an arranged marriage, though." He glanced at a side table. On it sat a photo of the couple standing side-by-side on vacation somewhere.

"She seems very kindhearted."

"It's her only asset. Yes, she's been very devoted to me," he said quite earnestly.

"Where is that picture from?"

"Hawaii. We went there three years ago for our golden wedding anniversary."

I was a little surprised when he said Hawaii.

"It was my first time," he added, apparently sensing my reaction.

I looked back at the photo. Ito was standing at attention before a bright blue ocean, his wife's hand firmly clasped in his right hand.

"My granddaughter used to tell people, 'Grandpa went to Hawaii a long time ago.' But as I said, I actually never made it to the skies over Hawaii. It's been over sixty years, but I still regret it."

"Really?"

"On second thought, if I had flown over Hawaii back then, I might never have met my wife, let alone have a granddaughter," Ito said and laughed.

I recalled that 55 pilots had died in the attack on Pearl Harbor.

Ito seemed to remember it too, and lowered his gaze.

After a brief silence he said, "There was one very unfortunate thing about Pearl Harbor."

"What was that?"

"It ended up being a sneak attack made with no proper declaration of war."

"The declaration was delayed somewhere on the way, wasn't it?"

"That's right. We were told that we would be attacking at the same time the declaration was made. But that isn't how it panned out. They say the reason for the delay was that the Japanese embassy in Washington took too long decoding and delivering the declaration of war. But the delay was really due to the fact that the embassy staff were out drinking at a farewell party or something that went well into the night. They were late getting to work that day."

"Is that true?"

"We suffered the disgrace of being accused of foul play all because of some damn embassy staffers. Not just us, but Japanese as a whole were labeled a nation of cowards. We'd been told that the attack would take place with the declaration. Yet as it happened… Nothing could be more mortifying."

Ito's face contorted.

"At the time, yes, the U.S. was exerting extreme pressure on Japan, but they say the prevailing public opinion was anti-war. Back in those years, we were made to believe that America was a country with no history, whose disconnected, unpatriotic, and individualistic citizens enjoyed pleasure-seeking lives. We were told they didn't have our willingness to offer up our lives to our country and to the Emperor. Combined Fleet Commander-in-Chief Yamamoto wanted to smash the U.S. Navy's Pacific forces to pieces at the outset so the American people would completely lose spirit."

"And the exact opposite happened."

"Indeed. In response to our cowardly sneak attack, public opinion in America changed overnight to 'Remember Pearl Harbor' and giving us hell as many people rushed to enlist in the armed forces."

Ito continued. "Furthermore, even though the attack was called a tactical victory, that wasn't completely true, because we didn't send the third wave of attackers. While we succeeded in destroying much of their Pacific fleet and the aircraft there, we left the dry docks, oil reserves, and other important land-based facilities wholly intact. If we had destroyed everything, Hawaii would no longer have been viable as a military base, and total supremacy in the Pacific would have been ours. The squadron commanders offered to do a third attack, but were turned down. Vice Admiral Chuichi Nagumo, the fleet commander, chose to withdraw from the area. Looking back, I don't think Vice Admiral Nagumo had it in him to lead. The Imperial Navy missed more crucial chances after that throughout the Pacific, and it all stemmed from the indecisiveness and timidity of his leadership."

Ito sighed deeply. "I've really wandered off topic. No point in criticizing the Imperial Navy now, is there. Let's get back to Miyabe."

In the crew quarters on the journey back to Japan from Pearl Harbor, the squadron members who participated in the strike told the rest of us what it had been like. They raved about their magnificent attack. Those of us who'd been on CAP duty listened with one part excitement and two parts jealousy and envy.

Suddenly someone asked, "Hey, Miyabe, what were the American ships like?"

Miyabe replied, "The carriers weren't there." Everyone stared at him blankly, but he went on, unperturbed. "There were only battleships in Pearl Harbor."

That was common knowledge, as the pilots had already vented their frustrations over the lack of carriers. Everyone was confused as to why Miyabe was bringing up that point again.

He kept talking, unfazed by our reaction. "Eventually the Americans will attack us in the same way we attacked them today. That's why I wish we'd gotten their aircraft carriers."

"True, sooner or later we'll take on their carriers," someone said.

"Guess we saved the best for last, eh?" someone else joked, making everyone, including me, laugh. "Leave some for us," one of the CAP guys said. And another one of us, "Yeah, I want to be in the attack force next time, not in the CAP." Everyone who had been part of the patrol team that day agreed and laughed.

Miyabe was the only one not smiling. "That day will surely come," he said.

"Well, when it does we'll make mincemeat of any American aircraft carrier," someone retorted.

Miyabe finally cracked a smile at that. "I think we shall. Today was the first time I saw the attack bombers and dive bombers in action, and they were quite magnificent. Their airmanship is truly divine. I'm sure American carriers will be helpless in the face of such attacks. I don't know what kind of technology their bombers have, but they sure can't compete with our skills."

Since they weren't the hyperventilations of a blowhard but the detached observations of a calm fellow, Miyabe's words had a lot of impact. Everyone was well aware of his ability as a pilot, so his speech carried even more weight.

I found myself feeling profoundly disappointed that I hadn't been able to witness our attack force delivering its pinpoint strikes at Pearl Harbor.

"We can win, can't we?" I asked.

"If we take them head-on, we'll overwhelm them," Miyabe replied.

He was both correct and incorrect in that assumption.

Following Pearl Harbor, the Mobile Task Force under Vice Admiral Nagumo's command swept over the Pacific. "Mobile Task Force" refers to a carrier battle group. Aircraft carriers had greater speed and mobility than battleships, hence the term.

We freely ran riot from New Guinea in the south to the Indian Ocean in the west, our carrier-based aircraft sinking many enemy warships. "You'll see us run wild, for half a year," Commander-in-Chief Isoroku Yamamoto is said to have promised, and we were indeed invincible.

Of course, the Mobile Task Force came under several attacks from enemy aircraft, but the Zero squadrons protecting their motherships never let them lay a finger on our carriers. At the time there wasn't any fighter aircraft that could beat the Zero. If I do say so myself, Nagumo's fighter pilots were easily the most competent in the world. The bombers boasted near-superhuman skills as well. When we sank a British cruiser and small carrier in the Indian Ocean, our dive-bomber squadron had an accuracy rate of almost 90 percent. That was an astounding number for dive bombing.

The Nagumo Fleet controlled the Pacific. The country that had the most powerful aircraft carriers could claim naval supremacy. This smashed previously held military common sense.

For a long time, the world was caught in the "Dreadnought Era." According to the thinking, direct confrontations between battleships determined the outcome of naval warfare. Battleships were the most powerful weapons in history, and massive ones were thought to be necessary to claim mastery of the seas. The British Empire indeed came to dominate the world thanks to its fleet of powerful battleships. You can fathom the impression these weapons made just from how menaced the Shogunate felt by Perry's "Black Ships" anchored in Uraga. The history of the world was written by battleships.

Aircraft carriers first appeared after World War I. Back then, however, the aircraft were biplanes, and carriers only played an ancillary role. Some factions pointed out that attacks carried out by aircraft were effective, but it was believed that only small ships could be sunk that way, not larger ones like battleships.

Nevertheless, thanks to impressive developments in aeronautics, the power of aircraft carriers grew rapidly. The attack on Pearl Harbor at the outset of the war demonstrated this fact to the world. Aircraft alone were able to sink five battleships in one fell swoop. That was the moment when battleships, for hundreds of years the main actors in battles for naval supremacy, yielded the leading role to carriers.

There was another phenomenal battle that proved that airplanes, not battleships, ruled the seas. It took place two days after Pearl Harbor, off the coast of the Malayan peninsula. Our aircraft attacked and sank the pride of the British Royal Navy, Eastern Fleet, the state-of-the-art battleship HMS *Prince of Wales*, and the battlecruiser HMS *Repulse*. Thirty-six Type 96 land-based attack aircraft took off from Saigon and other bases, torpedoed both ships, and sent them to the bottom. It was about this naval battle that Churchill later said, "During all the war, I never received a more direct shock."

While the ships sunk at Pearl Harbor had been caught at anchor in a surprise attack, we sank the two British ships in open combat. In this respect, the outcome was far more shocking than Pearl Harbor.

That naval engagement proved that battleships with no escort fighters were easy prey for enemy aircraft.

Gone were the days of the Russo-Japanese War where fleets of ships faced each other in a decisive showdown. Now maritime battles pitted aircraft carriers against one another. Our Navy had six full-fledged carriers while the U.S. Pacific Fleet had five. We flexed our muscles in preparation for the carrier-on-carrier fight that we knew would come one day.

The chance came half a year after the start of the war. In May 1942, Japanese aircraft carriers supporting Army transport ships clashed head-on with U.S. carriers trying to prevent us from capturing Port Moresby, New Guinea. It was the world's first battle between two aircraft carriers. Incidentally, there haven't been any more carrier battles since Japan fought the U.S.

Unfortunately, my carrier, the *Akagi*, did not participate in that battle. The *Shokaku* and the *Zuikaku* of our Fifth Carrier Division fought the USS *Lexington* and the *Yorktown*. During this, the Battle of the Coral Sea, we sank the *Lexington* and severely damaged the *Yorktown*. On our side, the *Shokaku* was partially damaged while the *Zuikaku* was untouched. In the first-ever carrier vs. carrier battle, the Imperial Navy was victorious.

At the time, the aircrew of the First Carrier Division, assigned to the *Akagi* and the *Kaga*, was considered the most skilled. The next best was the Second Carrier Division, on the *Hiryu* and the *Soryu*. It was said that the Fifth Division on the *Shokaku* and the *Zuikaku* was slightly less capable. There was even a ditty about them that went, "If butterflies and dragonflies are birds, then so is the Fifth Division." When those of us in the First Division heard of the outcome of the Battle of the Coral Sea, we ruefully said, "Both American carriers would have gone down, had it been us."

The desire to take on a hostile carrier simmered in our veins. We got our chance a month later.

Yes, at the Battle of Midway.

It's a very famous battle. Four of our carriers were sunk at once: the *Akagi* and the *Kaga*, namely the First Carrier Division and the pride of our Navy, and the Second Division's *Hiryu* and *Soryu*.

After the war I read many books on the causes of our failure at Midway. Bottom line, it was all the fault of our military's arrogance.

The U.S. forces had known all about our operation, having successfully decrypted our Navy's code. Initially, though, their code-breaking team couldn't figure out the location of "AF," which we were targeting to capture. So the U.S. sent an unencrypted false message from the base at Midway that stated, "The water purification system has broken down and the base needs fresh water." Soon after on the same day, our military sent a message stating that AF appeared to be short on water. Thus, the U.S. figured out that "AF" stood for Midway.

The Americans were on alert, ready and waiting to ambush us. Actually, the Combined Fleet HQ had anticipated as much. Part of its plan for capturing Midway was to lure out and destroy the U.S. carrier fleet. Therefore, you could also say the U.S. Navy was suckered in.

Before the battle, the feeling that it would be an easy victory was prevalent among our entire Navy. HQ seems to have thought that the Americans might be too frightened of our might even to pit their carriers against us. I found this out in later years, but during the planning stages at HQ, when a certain commander asked Minoru Genda, senior staff officer for aviation, "What will happen if the enemy's aircraft carriers attack us at Midway?" he's said to have replied, "We'll beat 'em hands down," which indeed would have been typical. Slightly before that, on Hirashima Island in Yamaguchi, when HQ staffers were divided into friends and foes to do a map exercise of the Battle of Midway, nine bombs managed to strike the Japanese carriers. Chief of Staff Ugaki saw this and said, "I call one third of that—make it three," and continued the exercise, never revising the battle plan. There's no point in such a map exercise.

There were other instances of carelessness. We were supposed to deploy a submarine squad off the coast of Hawaii to detect the U.S. carrier fleet's departure, but by the time the subs got there the fleet had already left Hawaii. This, too, was probably due to the misguided assumption that the U.S. carriers wouldn't head out at all.

Over sixty years have passed, but I still clearly remember the events of that day—the Imperial Navy's, no, Japan's worst day. Of course, more terrible debacles would come. But everything started to go bad at Midway.

I took off in the morning as part of the escort for the bombers heading out to strike the base on Midway. The battle plan was two-fold: attack the base on Midway, and destroy the enemy Mobile Task Force if they showed up. Recon teams were being sent out constantly to search for the enemy.

In a carrier-on-carrier battle, the outcome is dependent upon good recon. Find the enemy task force speeding around the vast Pacific faster than they can find yours, and hit them. That was the essence of a carrier battle.

As I said earlier, the first such engagement was the Battle of the Coral Sea. Actually, something odd happened then. Both sides located each other and launched their bombers, but neither attack force was able to come into contact with the enemy fleet, and the first waves fizzled out. That's when the incident occurred.

Failing to find the enemy's task force, our Fifth Division's attack force returned to the carriers at night. Landing on one at night is very difficult. The first plane mistimed the landing and simply flew over the ship. It was then that the pilot realized the carrier was American! That pilot must have gotten quite the shock. The enemy carrier they'd tried so hard to find was right there where he thought his mothership would be.

That's how difficult battles involving high-speed mobile forces are. The carriers on both sides are moving at a rate of about 50 kilometers per hour. In two hours, they can end up putting 200 more kilometers between them. As a result, it was a given that when you returned, your carrier was in a very different location from when you sortied. That's how a pilot could find himself attempting a landing on an enemy carrier. I'm sure the American crew was just as astonished.

In the end, the attack force fled from the enemy carrier and made it back to their own carriers, but the whole episode sounds like a bad joke, doesn't it?

The next morning, both carrier groups sent out reconnaissance planes to locate each other again. A recon plane from the *Shokaku* discovered an enemy carrier and kept the American fleet in sight, communicating their position to our forces, until it was nearly out of fuel. Attack forces immediately took off from *Shokaku* and *Zuikaku*, and along the way they passed the recon plane. It had been heading back, but it turned around and guided the attackers to the enemy position. The plane had been on its way back because it was out of fuel. Guiding friendly aircraft to the enemy meant not making it back alive.

That reconnaissance plane was a Type 97 carrier-based attack bomber, and its leader was Flight Chief Petty Officer Kenzo Kanno, the spotter and bombardier. The other two crewmembers were FPO1 Tsuguo Goto, the pilot, and FPO1 Seijiro Kishida, the radio operator. Those three threw away their lives, praying that their comrades would triumph over the enemy.

Sorry. I'm easily moved to tears in my old age.

The attack forces did not let Flight CPO Kanno and his men's sacrifice go to waste. They swooped down on the enemy mobile task force, sinking the *Lexington* and damaging the *Yorktown*. Around the same time, *Shokaku* and *Zuikaku* came under enemy fire, but the CAP of Zeros, truly lethal, shot down almost all the enemy attack bombers and dive bombers. *Shokaku* took three hits but *Zuikaku* was unharmed. Amongst *Zuikaku*'s CAP at that time was Tetsuzo Iwamoto. He would become the Imperial Navy's top ace.

Yet it's said that the battle, though a tactical victory, ended in defeat strategically. That's because the Japanese military's original goal of seizing Port Moresby was thwarted. The Fifth Carrier Division's duty was to escort Army transports which were ferrying troops for a landing, but after the carrier battle, Fleet Commander Shigeyoshi Inoue ordered the retreat of the convoy. The enemy's task force had already evacuated far away, but in fear of it the operation was suspended. It was a decision that all but wasted the efforts of those who had bravely fought in the vanguard. Later on, the Army would carry out an extremely reckless operation to capture Port Moresby, giving its soldiers only enough provisions and fuel for a one-way journey via an overland route across the Owen Stanley Range. Tens of thousands of soldiers perished.

Setting aside the strategic view, though, in the Coral Sea carrier vs.

carrier battle, that is to say, aircrew vs. aircrew battle, we emerged victorious. The First and Second Carrier Divisions, more adept than the Fifth, participated in the next battle at Midway. It was only natural to assume that we would win there, too.

The Fifth Carrier Division was not part of the Battle of Midway. The *Shokaku* was damaged at Coral Sea and had lost a large number of aircraft and men. But I think that was odd. At the very least, *Zuikaku* was perfectly fine, and they probably could have replenished their aircraft somehow. Probably Combined Fleet HQ thought it was unnecessary to send in every aircraft carrier we had.

The U.S. military was completely different in that respect. The *Yorktown* actually required a month's worth of repairs, but they spent just three days patching her up and deployed her for the Battle of Midway. They say many repairmen were still aboard even as she sailed. Admiral Spruance was adamant that the *Yorktown* be sent to Midway even if it meant losing the ship. We had always thought that Americans were happy-go-lucky and spineless, but that wasn't the case. They sure had guts.

Let's get back to June 5th and the Battle of Midway.

I was resting in the stand-by area inside the carrier after returning from the first wave of attacks on Midway Island. Suddenly, the torpedoes on the formation awaiting sortie on the flight deck were changed out for land bombs. It seemed that the second wave of attacks on Midway was set to begin posthaste. Until then, in preparation for the American task force, the attack bombers had been loaded with torpedoes for use on ships, but after reconnaissance indicated there were no enemy forces in the area, we were apparently switching tactics and sending out a second wave of bombers to strike the land base. Looking back now, I can see that was our first bit of negligence.

I said that the torpedoes were changed out in favor of bombs. But that's not as simple as merely changing your shoes. The planes had to be lowered into the hangar on a lift; torpedoes removed, bombs loaded on, the planes were raised back up to the flight deck. This process had to be repeated for each aircraft, and there were dozens. Moreover, we're talking about ordnance, which had to be handled with care. It probably took about two hours to complete unloading the torpedoes and loading the bombs. During that time, a slew of hostile planes flew in from Midway, but the already airborne Zeros handily fought them off.

When the ordnance was finally replaced, a recon plane reported the discovery of what appeared to be an enemy task force. We thought, *American aircraft carriers, at last!* However, the planes on our decks were fitted with bombs meant for land-based targets. How utterly unfortunate.

Fleet Commander Nagumo ordered the land bombs to be unloaded and the torpedoes to be equipped again. This was the correct measure to take, since land bombs could damage a carrier but not sink her. The paramount objective of the operation at Midway was to lure out the U.S. mobile forces—namely, their carrier fleet—and to annihilate them all at once. If we sank all of their aircraft carriers, we would sail unopposed in the Pacific. Lightning strikes that sent a ship to oblivion with one blow—torpedo attacks—were an absolute necessity in order to accomplish that.

The entire carrier fleet simultaneously switched out bombs for torpedoes, a repeat of the job they had just finished. I watched the process impatiently. The enemy was a mere 200 nautical miles away, and I was anxious to take the battle to them as soon as possible. I felt miserable, thinking that if we hadn't just re-equipped, our attack forces could have taken off ages ago.

At some point, Miyabe appeared at my side. "Why the hell are we just loitering around? We must attack right away," he said, uncharacteristically ruffled.

"We can't sink a carrier with land bombs."

"We don't need to sink them. We just need to make the first move."

"But if we're gonna strike anyways, might as well sink 'em, right? If we only damage them and they run away at full speed, it'll all be for nothing."

"That's better than not striking at all."

"The goal of this operation is to annihilate their carrier fleet. There's no point if they escape."

"Then why were the torpedoes unloaded in the first place? If our primary targets are their carriers, then we should have kept the torpedoes loaded and waited for intel on their carriers."

I was at a loss for words. He was right. Our battle plan for Midway featured two fronts—a strategy that needed to be avoided like the plague.

"They might come after us while we're dithering," Miyabe muttered to himself. Like a fool, I hadn't even thought of such a scenario. I had just gone ahead and assumed that only our side had located the enemy.

Just then we fighter pilots received an order to increase the number of patrol planes in the air. The flight commander ordered Miyabe and several other pilots to provide air cover. Miyabe gave me a small wave, said "I'm off," and ran towards his Zero on the flight deck. That was the last time we would exchange words.

Even after Miyabe and the other pilots took off, the torpedo reloading process limped along. The enemy could spot us at any moment. I felt for the first time the frustration of knowing the enemy was right there but not being able to strike at them. I wasn't even a part of the attack contingent and I was positively itching, so the bomber guys must have been truly at the limits of their patience.

Suddenly a voice boomed out, "Enemy aircraft!" A formation of about a dozen planes was approaching at a low angle off the port side. They were still about 7,000 meters away. Our CAP guys were already on the move. The hostile aircraft were torpedo bombers. One strike from a torpedo could prove fatal.

I was seized by tension and fear. *Get it done, CAP,* I prayed.

The Zeros set on the cluster of torpedo bombers like a pack of hunting dogs. In the blink of an eye, the bombers burst into flames and fell from the sky. Every last bomber was shot down in mere minutes. It was a brilliant display. The crew on the carrier burst into spontaneous applause at such an amazing spectacle.

Then a voice called out, "Starboard!" I turned to see eight more torpedo bombers approaching from the other side. But there were three Zeros already in hot pursuit, and the bombers were shot down in rapid succession before they could come within range. The last two dumped their torpedoes and soared, attempting to flee, but these too were downed by the Zeros.

All the pilots of the attack force standing by on the carrier deck cheered the Zeros' bravura performance.

The torpedo bombers that attacked *Kaga* to our rear suffered the same fate. The CAP of Zeros swatted them down.

I was impressed anew by the Zero's prowess. Or rather, I was impressed by the incredible skill of the men piloting the planes. "Each a match for a thousand," as the expression goes.

The battle continued intermittently for nearly two hours. Over forty torpedo bombers attacked us, but nearly every one of them was downed by the Zeros. Not a single torpedo struck us.

The frantic reloading of the torpedoes continued inside the carrier the whole while. It was then that I heard a lookout scream. I'll never forget the sound of that cry for as long as I live.

I looked skyward to see four dive bombers descending upon us like demons. I stared up, engrossed by the demons, and thought despairingly, *Oh hell, we're done for.* I saw the bombers release their ordnance. It was a mere moment, yet it unfolded as though in slow motion. Four bombs fell leisurely, laughing. The shrill sounds they gave off as they glided through the air sounded like demonic laughter. They must have been laughing at our carelessness and arrogance.

The bombs exploded on the carrier deck with a thunderous roar. I was blown backwards into the bridge. Had it not been there I would have ended up in the sea.

Half-unconscious, I stared at the burning deck. Aircraft were catching fire one after the other. Aircrew leapt out of the crafts covered in flames. Planes whose propellers were already spinning went out of control, spontaneously lurching forward, some crashing, others falling into the ocean. The deck was in chaos. Further explosions came one after another from the hangar, the torpedoes and bombs triggering thanks to the fire. Each blast rocked the massive ship. I looked starboard to see the *Kaga* aflame as well. Another aircraft carrier far astern was also burning. Three of our carriers had been taken out in a flash.

I went down onto the afterdeck to escape the burning flight deck. A group of attack force crew was already there. Everyone's faces were drawn. There were many who were injured. A large number had lost limbs. The floor was stained with vast amounts of blood. It was hellish pandemonium.

Intermittent explosions echoed from the hangar. We ferried

buckets of water to put out the fire, but it was like pouring water on a hot stone. Eventually we ran out of water and there was nothing left to be done.

The flames on the ship blazed dozens of meters high and the smoke billowed hundreds of meters into the air. The entire ship was scorching hot. The metal ladders were hot enough to burn the soles of our boots. If you touched the handrail without thinking, you ended up with a serious burn. We found ourselves trapped on the afterdeck at a loss for what to do.

It was then that we caught sight of the headquarters staff abandoning the ship from the carrier's bow. Vice Admiral Nagumo and many of his officers were fleeing in launch boats. Seeing them left us crestfallen. Command had abandoned ship. The *Akagi* was done for.

After a while a destroyer's cutter drew close and came to our rescue. We boarded and left the *Akagi* behind. Once on board the cutter I turned back to gaze at the carrier. She was enveloped in a sea of flames so massive, it seemed like that was all the fire there could be in the world. The blaze was so intense that even at a distance of over a hundred meters I could still feel the heat waves.

But the *Akagi* did not sink. Because she had been bombed, not torpedoed, the ship had burst into flames but wasn't going down. But this merely prolonged her death throes, creating a hellish spectacle. Her steel went red and turned molten. Black smoke extended a full kilometer into the sky.

Two other streams of black smoke rose upward. A total of three carriers were destroyed.

I wept. The many other crewmembers aboard the cutter were crying, too.

Above us Zeros flew in vain, having lost their homes. Miyabe must have been among them.

That was the Battle of Midway as I experienced it. After the war, it gained infamy as the "five fateful minutes": had we just five more minutes, they said, our entire attack force would have been launched, re-equipped; even if the carriers had been dive bombed, they'd not have sunk since no bombs on deck would have gone up in secondary explosions; our attack forces would have dealt the enemy a knockout and turned their carriers into fish food. Luck was simply not with us, the argument went.

But that's a lie. When the Americans' dive bombers attacked, in actuality the reloading was still a long way off from being finished. I don't know how much more time it would have taken, but it certainly wasn't "five minutes."

There are no "ifs" or "buts" in history. The outcome of that battle was not due to bad luck. We could have launched our aircraft sooner if we'd wanted. We should have struck the enemy's carriers first, be it with land bombs. It was our arrogance that prevented us from doing so.

Also, the Americans' torpedo bombers had arrived without any fighter planes. Bombers attacking without escort is sheer suicide, and our Zeros took all of them out. But in effect, they served as a decoy. Our CAP was distracted by the torpedo bombers and neglected to keep an eye on the skies. The dive bombers that came later broke through that gap and devastated us.

Sure, you could call that bad luck, but I don't believe that's true. I learned this after the fact, but apparently, once the U.S. forces discovered our aircraft carriers, they sent out their attack planes as soon as each flight was ready even though the fighters couldn't be deployed in time, just in order to strike us straightaway.

When I imagine how the American torpedo bomber pilots must have felt, my chest swells with emotion. They surely understood what it meant to sortie without a fighter escort. They must have been well aware of the terror of confronting a Zero. There's no doubt that they were prepared for the possibility that they would not come back alive. Yet they bravely departed all the same. They swooped down on our carriers and were gunned down in rapid succession by the Zeros. Their risky attack drew our carriers' CAP into lower altitudes and prepared for the successful attack by the dive bombers.

I think the true champions of the Battle of Midway may very well have been the U.S. torpedo bombers. Just as our recon plane crew, knowing they'd run out of fuel, led their comrades to the location of the enemy on the Coral Sea, the American torpedo pilots sacrificed themselves for the sake of winning the war.

The Japanese weren't the only ones who could give their lives to the nation. We had our justification, which was to serve the Emperor. Surely the Americans didn't have the same sense of duty to their president. Then what were they fighting for? Purely for their country, I'd say.

In fact, we Japanese weren't risking our lives for the Emperor, either. For us, too, it was patriotism, the love of country.

In that battle, Japan lost four irreplaceable carriers. The U.S. lost only one, the *Yorktown*, which had received major damage in the Battle of the Coral Sea. Admiral Nimitz had ordered emergency measures and had the carrier, wounded as she was, participate in the battle at Midway. She dealt a severe blow to our carrier force and then sank. Yankee Spirit.

In comparison, the *Zuikaku*, which had emerged from Coral Sea unharmed, was merely resting back in Japan in the Seto Inland Sea— we had lost the Battle of Midway before it even began.

There's just one thing I want to praise our side for: the *Hiryu*, the only one of our four carriers to elude the enemy attack, putting up quite the fight. Led by the indomitable Rear Admiral Tamon Yamaguchi, commander of the Second Division, the *Hiryu* took on three American carriers all alone after our other three had been taken out. In the end, *Hiryu* and *Yorktown* died on each other's swords. Rear Admiral Yamaguchi went down with the *Hiryu*. As it happened, Yamaguchi was strongly opposed to Fleet Commander Nagumo's decision to unload the torpedoes and had advised an immediate launch of our attack forces. He'd also strongly recommended a third wave of attacks on Pearl Harbor.

Lieutenant Joichi Tomonaga, attack force commander of the *Hiryu*, boldly sortied on a Type 97 attack bomber whose tank had been pierced. He only had enough fuel for a one-way trip.

Had this been a sporting match, after the battle the crews of *Yorktown* and *Hiryu* might have praised each other for putting up a good fight, and perhaps friendship could have been forged between the two sides. But this was war. The two ships slaughtered each other, taking many lives along with them.

According to one theory, the loss of so many seasoned pilots in the Battle of Midway was the biggest blow to the Imperial Navy, but that's not quite true. Most of the aircrew aboard *Hiryu*, which fought to the end, did perish. But many of us on the three other carriers destroyed at the outset were rescued.

It was at the Battle of Guadalcanal, which began that fall, that we lost droves of seasoned pilots.

—What of Miyabe?

He probably continued to fight until he ran out of fuel and then ditched in the ocean. Or maybe he landed on the *Hiryu* and took part in the conflict with *Yorktown*. In any case, he, too, made it back to the interior alive. We never met again, though. The last I saw of him was when he took off from the *Akagi*. I heard that after Midway he was transferred to Rabaul along with a great number of aircrew.

My eyes were damaged in the bomb blast and my vision was reduced to 20:100, so I could no longer pilot a fighter. After I returned to Japan, I became an instructor for the Preparatory Flight Training Program. Had my eyes been fine, I probably would have been transferred from place to place, and I wouldn't still be here today. In fact, many of the carrier aircrew stationed at Rabaul ended up perishing in the Solomon Sea.

The Solomon Sea became an airmen's graveyard. From the latter half of 1942, a notice of transfer to Rabaul was considered a one-way ticket.

I heard that Miyabe survived for over a year in that hellish battlefield. Perhaps his cowardice is what allowed him to extend his lifespan. In the air, the brave are the first to fall. Miyabe was a different sort of man than Flight CPO Kanno, who gave up on ever returning in order to lead a friendly attack force to the enemy on the Coral Sea, or Lieutenant Tomonaga, who sortied at Midway knowing his mission would be one-way only. But Miyabe's cowardice isn't grounds for criticism.

I will say this. His skills as a pilot were first rate. I'm a little embarrassed to say this myself, but during the war, being assigned to the First Carrier Division was proof that you were a first-rate pilot. That he survived the living hell that was Guadalcanal was also thanks to his skills as a pilot.

The ice in the iced coffee set before me had long since melted. I had totally forgotten to even take a sip. Former Lt. JG Kanji Ito's tale had overwhelmed me. I knew next to nothing about the War in the Pacific, so everything he said came as a shock.

The battles may have taken place between aircraft carriers, but in the end it was humans fighting. The forces' specs weren't the only factor. Bravery, decisiveness, and cool judgment decided who won or lost, who lived or died.

Still, what a cruel world it was for the soldiers. The battles had happened a mere sixty years ago. My grandfather had fought in them.

According to Ito, my grandfather was not just a cowardly man but also a competent pilot. His words gave me a small amount of consolation.

"So Miyabe died in a kamikaze attack?" Ito suddenly asked.

"Yes, sir. In August 1945, off the southwestern islands."

"August, eh? Right before the war ended. So they forced pilots as experienced as Miyabe to kamikaze."

"Was it so rare for skilled pilots to become kamikazes?"

"Most were student reservists or young airmen. The Army and Navy put them through brief training to hurl them at the enemy." Ito looked pained. "I trained many student reservists myself. It took at least two years to turn someone into a full-fledged pilot, but those guys were given less than a year of flight training. The higher-ups probably thought that was sufficient for suicide attacks."

Tears shone in Ito's eyes again.

"That's terrible," I said.

"It was. But tactically speaking, it was a waste to kill off a seasoned pilot in a single kamikaze mission. The experts were instead tasked with escorting the kamikazes to the enemy fleet and also with defending the skies over the mainland. But it was obvious in the final days of the war that we would be defeated. The mood was 'all one hundred million fighting to the death' and 'all planes be kamikazes,' so I guess even a veteran pilot like Miyabe was ordered to mount a 'special attack' as well."

For the first time I was able to understand, if only a little, the chagrin my grandfather must have felt. Forced to fight continuously from the Sino-Japanese war, then used and thrown away as a kamikaze. That must have been infuriating for someone who'd wanted so badly to return home alive.

"Please tell me one more thing, if you can," I said. "Did my grandfather say that he loved my grandmother?"

Ito got a faraway look in his eyes. "He never said, 'I love her.' Our generation didn't use the word. Miyabe was the same. What he said was that for his wife's sake, he didn't want to die."

I nodded.

Ito concluded, "For our generation, that's the same thing as saying, 'I love her.'"

Chapter 4
Rabaul

"What a nice surprise!"

Those were my sister's first words on the phone. It was the day after I'd sent over the voice recorder containing Ito's story.

"I listened to the whole thing in one sitting."

She sounded somewhat excited. She was pleased to learn that our grandfather was a skilled pilot, but even more moved to hear that he had loved our grandmother. After briefly expressing her impressions, she asked if I was free that night and invited me to dinner with someone from the newspaper she was working with.

"I told him about our research, he's very interested and wants to do dinner with us."

Since I didn't have anything in particular planned for the evening, I agreed.

I arrived at the hotel in Akasaka where we were to meet up and found Keiko alone. The newspaper guy had gotten tied up with a last-minute assignment and was running a little late. We decided to go on ahead to the restaurant and eat while we waited.

"Grandma was loved by her first husband," Keiko said with feeling after we'd placed our orders.

"I wonder how she felt about him."

Keiko thought for a moment. "She really loved Grandpa. I'd never have imagined her loving someone else before him."

I nodded.

"But you can't ever know what's inside someone's heart. Maybe Grandma really did love Miyabe-san." That was what Keiko was calling him now, *Miyabe-san*.

"But they were married for just four years, most of which they spent apart, and then he died in battle. So maybe it wasn't so hard to forget about him."

Keiko neither agreed nor disagreed with me.

After a little while a tall man in a suit approached. It was Ryuji Takayama, the newspaper reporter. He apologized for his tardiness and hinted that he wouldn't be able to stay long due to his last-minute assignment.

Takayama had a gentle demeanor. I'd heard he was thirty-eight but he looked younger than that.

"So you're Kentaro? I've burdened your sister at work," Takayama said with an affable smile after placing his order with the waiter. Since Keiko had said he was an incredibly capable reporter, I had expected him to be a more self-confident and assertive type. Instead there was a soft, kindly presence about him.

He said that the newspaper was planning all sorts of features looking back at the postwar era as next year would mark the sixtieth since the end of WWII. That was why he had taken an interest when he'd heard that Keiko was researching her grandfather who had died as a kamikaze.

"I think the *kamikaze attack*"—Takayama appended the English word, making the whole phrase sound foreign—"is a theme we absolutely must include in the feature articles. The pilots were truly unfortunate." As if in silent prayer, he briefly bowed his head and placed his hands flatly together on the tabletop. "Yet, this isn't just an issue from the past. It's extremely depressing to think about, but as we saw with 9/11, the world today is full of terrorist suicide bombings just like the *kamikaze attack* of old. I wonder why." Takayama gave a faint sigh, then leaned forward slightly and said, "I think that in order to comprehend the phenomenon, it's necessary to reconsider Japan's *kamikaze attack* from a whole new point of view."

"Takayama-san, are you saying that the structure of terrorist suicide bombings and the Japanese kamikaze were the same?"

Takayama nodded. "Historically speaking, organized suicide attacks are extremely rare, and the *kamikaze attack* of old and the terrorist suicide bombings of Islamic fundamentalists today are the two representative instances. Yes, I think it's natural to assume there are common traits between them. In fact, there are newspapers

78

in America that refer to the contemporary terrorist incidents as a *kamikaze attack*."

Takayama spent more time looking at my sister than me during his reply.

It was obvious he was the person Keiko had in mind when she said she was just "parroting" her take on kamikazes. However, researching my grandfather, I'd come across more than a few experts on the Internet and elsewhere who held that "kamikaze" and "terrorist" were one and the same. It apparently wasn't all that rare a view. Some famous TV newscasters had voiced similar opinions. As I was sadly uninformed about the kamikazes, I found myself unable to agree or disagree on that issue.

Takayama continued, "Reading the kamikazes' diaries, you see that many of the pilots were willing to give up their lives out of a religious spirit of martyrdom. Some even wrote that the day of their sortie was a day of great joy. But that shouldn't merit surprise. Before the war, Japan was considered the land of the gods, ruled by the Emperor, himself a living god. Perhaps it was only natural that many youths felt joy at the prospect of martyring themselves for the sake of their country." Takayama cast his eyes downward. "To put it plainly, it's martyrdom, and it's this spirit that Islamic extremists who conduct suicide attacks as acts of terrorism share."

Takayama's argument was logically consistent, but I wasn't able to readily accept everything he said, probably because I wasn't willing to concede that my grandfather was a terrorist.

"You said your grandfather was a *kamikaze attack* pilot?" Takayama asked Keiko, to which she nodded. "Well, it gives me great pain to say this regarding your late grandfather…"

"I don't mind. Please, continue."

Takayama seemed hesitant but gave a slight nod at Keiko's words and said, "I think the *kamikaze attack* people who gave their lives for the Emperor and the state were fanatical nationalists."

My sister nodded again, but I found myself wanting to argue. "Our grandfather was someone who valued his life, though. He wanted to live for his family's sake."

"People always love their families. But before the war, all Japanese were taught that the Emperor was a living god, and many people accepted their indoctrination. This wasn't your grandfather's fault. The blame lies with the times."

"I can't be sure, but I doubt my grandfather placed the Emperor above his own family."

Takayama nodded and took a sip from his coffee. "You don't know very much about that era. Before the war, Japan was a country of fanatics. A large percentage of the populace was brainwashed by the military and believed that dying for the Emperor was not only sufferable but even a joyous deed. I believe it's the mission of us journalists not to allow this country to become like that again."

"But I never ever heard my grandmother, who survived the war, say, 'Banzai. Long live the Emperor.'"

"That's because the brainwashing came undone. I believe that an army of political theorists and journalists who came before me brought the populace to its senses after the war. I became a newspaperman because I wanted to follow in their footsteps. And I still aim to become a true journalist."

Takayama gave a bashful smile. He seemed very sincere. Keiko was staring at his profile with a trusting expression.

I pondered what he had said and concluded that on the whole, he was correct. But deep in my heart I felt something was off, even though I couldn't say what. After considering for a moment, I ventured, "I don't believe the mental make-up of Japanese and the Islamic extremists are the same."

"I didn't say all Japanese. I am speaking of the similarities between kamikazes and suicide bombers."

"Doesn't that amount to arguing that the kamikazes were special?"

Takayama inclined his head questioningly. "What do you mean?"

"Were the kamikaze pilots so special, so unique? I don't think they were. I think they were typical Japanese. Aside from the fact that they happened to be pilots, weren't they just ordinary people?"

Takayama lowered his gaze and fell into a brief silence. "This is a very basic thing, but those men who volunteered for the kamikaze forces were not conscripts. They weren't called up by the draft and forcibly sent to the battlefront. Had the *kamikaze attack* been carried out by conscripts, I think I, too, would view the matter in a different light. But at the time, aircrew were comprised entirely of volunteers.

The student reservists, the boy pilots, all of them. Which is why I'd go as far as to say that all kamikazes were people who wanted to join the military, who chose to fight."

I saw what he was getting at.

"Your grandfather joined the Navy at age fifteen, right? That means he enlisted, he wasn't drafted."

Before I could respond, Keiko interjected, "Takayama-san, you mean to say that the mental make-up of conscripts and volunteers were different to begin with, correct? That those who enlisted of their own free will already had what it took to be part of the kamikaze forces?"

"Exactly, Saeki-san. But I'm not saying they were completely different. I just think that the volunteers had a stronger than average desire to dedicate their lives to their country to begin with."

He had valid points. Maybe one couldn't discuss conscripts and volunteers in the same terms. Had something within my grandfather made him consent to becoming a kamikaze? Why had he joined the Navy in the first place? Hasegawa had joined the Navy to escape from reality, and Ito had joined out of an admiration for the air corps. Had my grandfather also been a militant youth who yearned to become a pilot?

"By the way, I have a request for you, Kentaro. Will you allow me to write an article about you gathering information about your grandfather?"

"You want to write about me?"

"I could write about your sister, but I think a young man is preferable. I'm not sure yet what the final product will look like, but a young man hailing from a generation that knows nothing of war tracing the itinerary of his grandfather, who died as a kamikaze, and visiting former comrades is an extremely fascinating project."

"I don't know about that," I tried to refuse.

"Why not do it, Kentaro?" Keiko butted in.

"Um, let me think it over."

"Of course. Please take your time."

After Takayama had left, I asked Keiko, "What the hell was that all about? A project about me? Was that the point of this meeting from the start?"

"No, Takayama-san came up with that today. He probably thought of it after I told him about our research." She didn't seem to be lying.

"He has a crush on you, doesn't he?"

Keiko didn't deny it. She had always been popular with men. She was turning thirty this year, but looked much younger and was fairly attractive.

"Is he single?"

"Yes, but divorced."

Keiko said she met Takayama at the beginning of the year through work. Thanks to his introduction, she got to do an article for the newspaper company's weekly magazine. Naturally, it was Takayama who had recruited her for the sixtieth anniversary project too.

"He likes you. That's why he's doing you so many favors."

"Don't put it that way."

"So what about you? Do you like him?"

"Hmm, I don't really know. I don't mind him. I think he's quite a guy."

"So he's the one who hit on you?"

"Pretty aggressively, yeah," she said and gave a forced laugh. "But I don't really mind men being that way. Besides, I'm getting to the age where I should settle down, and I've got no objections to him as a potential spouse."

"Sounds like a calculated marriage."

Keiko looked annoyed by my remark. "There aren't many men out there who are sympathetic to working women like me. For men, whom they marry might not have that much of an impact on their careers, but it's a considerably more weighty decision for a woman. You could even say it's the biggest job-related issue. Right? The type of man a woman marries determines what kind of work style and life-style she'll be pursuing. So don't call my being careful 'calculating'!"

"I'm sorry," I said.

"That's okay," she quickly assured me. "Sorry for flaring up. But women like me who don't jump right into it might be the permanent part-timers of the marriage world."

Though she smiled as she said this, her expression was a little lonely.

On the weekend after meeting Takayama, my sister and I visited former Imperial Navy Flight Chief Petty Officer Genjiro Izaki.

Izaki was in a university hospital in the city. We had been contacted by his daughter. From the outset I planned on going along with Keiko on the interview; Ito's story had really spurred my interest in researching my grandfather.

A woman in her fifties was waiting in the hospital lobby. "I'm Izaki's daughter, Suzuko Emura," she greeted us. "This is my son," she also introduced a young man standing beside her.

He lazily jerked his chin out. He looked to be around twenty. His hair was dyed, and he wore a Hawaiian print shirt. In his left hand was a gaudily painted motorbike helmet.

"My father is quite ill, so he can't talk for very long."

"Please, we don't want him to overexert himself," Keiko said.

"He once told me about Miyabe-san. That it was only thanks to Miyabe-san that he was still alive."

"Oh, really?"

"I ain't heard nothin' like that," the young man said brusquely.

His mother ignored him. "My father was very surprised to hear from the veterans' organization that Miyabe-san's grandchild had contacted them."

"He must've cried himself to sleep that night," the young man mocked.

"My father is in poor health and the doctors have cautioned him against discussing anything that could upset him. But he ignored them and insisted on meeting you."

"I'm sorry for all this trouble," Keiko said, bowing her head deeply.

"Also, he wanted his grandson to hear what he had to say as well, which is why I've brought my son along. I hope that's all right."

"Yes, of course."

"Whatta pain in the ass," the punk-haired youth muttered, but his mother seemed not to have heard him.

Izaki had a private room. Upon entering, we found a skinny old man sitting upright on the bed.

"Father, should you really be sitting up?" Suzuko said in a fluster.

"I'm fine," the old man responded in a sure voice. Bowing his head towards me and my sister, he said, "I am Genjiro Izaki. I apologize for my state of dress."

He was referring to being in his pajamas. He stared at Keiko and me.

"To think I'd be able to meet Miyabe-san's grandchildren after all these years…"

"I was born thirty years after his death," Keiko said.

"I hear Miyabe-san died a kamikaze."

"That's correct, sir."

Izaki looked up at the ceiling. "In the past week since you contacted me, I've been recalling all sorts of things about Miyabe-san. I lay in bed remembering those days of the war, sixty years long gone, buried for over half a century at the very bottom of my memories. I'd forgotten plenty of things." He turned to his grandson. "You listen to this, too, Seiichi."

"Got nothin' to do with me."

"It doesn't. But I still want you to hear it."

Seiichi signaled his acquiescence with a wave of his hand.

Izaki turned back to us and righted his posture anew. "I first met Miyabe-san in Rabaul," he began slowly.

I graduated from pilot training at Yatabe in Ibaraki Prefecture and was assigned to the Tainan Air Corps. That was in February 1942. I was twenty by the old reckoning, eighteen going by the Western style.

After graduating from higher primary school, I worked at a local silk mill. I joined the Navy when I was fifteen. The first year I was a gunner on the battleship *Kirishima*, but when I heard they were recruiting sailors to join the air corps, I went through pilot training and became part of the aircrew.

Why did I join the Navy?

Hmm, sometimes I wonder why. In those days, I'd have been drafted once I turned twenty anyways. I figured if I was going to join the military in any case, I preferred the Navy. The wages at the silk mill were meager, the work was grueling, and it had poor prospects.

Looking back now, I think it's strange that those were the reasons I joined the military when I could die by doing so. In those days it was pretty typical, but when I think back to it, I believe that poverty was behind my choice to join the Navy.

We had gone to war with the U.S. in December of the previous year. I'd heard of the attack on Pearl Harbor while part of the Yatabe Air Unit.

The following year, I was sent to Clark Air Base in the Philippines. It had once belonged to the Americans, but the Tainan Air Corps destroyed all of their planes in an air raid two days after the start of the war, and subsequently the Japanese military occupied the base. Apparently the thirty-four Zeros in the Tainan Air Corps knocked out almost all of the Americans' sixty fighters, while our side suffered just four lost aircraft.

By the time I went to the Philippines, the Americans had been eradicated so we had it pretty easy.

The Tainan Air Corps was filled with some of the bravest and most experienced aircrew, but I was still green. My rank was Flight Seaman 1st Class—basically a plain soldier. The Navy's ranks included seamen, non-commissioned officers, and officers.

As soon as I arrived at Clark Air Base an NCO said, "Let's dogfight." By that he meant a mock air battle. We were to practice going around and coming up close behind the opponent as in a real air battle.

"I haven't seen combat in a while, so I just want to spar with you," he said. It was obvious that his ulterior motive was to see if I was any good. The other senior crew were laughing.

"With your permission, sir," I said humbly, but in fact I was quite confident when it came to mock dogfights. Back at Yatabe I had been at the top of my class or near it. I wanted to impress on my seniors that I was pretty good.

The battle began with me in an advantageous position, as was a-greed beforehand. It was like he had given me a leg up. In aerial combat, the aircraft at a higher altitude has an overwhelming advantage.

I dove from that higher altitude. My opponent smoothly turned and broke away, but I still had the advantage. Making good use of my speed I went right after him. He attempted to evade by pulling up into a loop. I followed. But the next instant, I lost sight of him. I'd never experienced anything like that before. My opponent's plane was nowhere to be seen. Then I looked behind me to find him right on my tail!

He pulled up alongside me, opened his windshield, and indicated another round, just as I'd hoped for.

We began again with me at a higher altitude, but the match ended in the exact same manner. At some point while I was pursuing him, he snuck right up behind me. We went a third round. It ended the same way yet again.

When I got back to the base, the NCO long-timers laughed at me.

"With piss-poor skills like that, you'd never survive even if you had countless lives."

My opponent, Flight Petty Officer 3rd Class Hayashi, was a year older than I.

"I lose, sir," I said meekly. "You're really an excellent pilot, Petty Officer Hayashi."

"Me? I'm one of the shittier ones in the Tainan Air Corps. I can't hold a candle to the likes of CPO Miyazaki and PO1 Sakai."

"Really?"

"The only way is up, as they say," PO3 Hayashi said, slapping me on the shoulder.

I totally lost my self-confidence.

Piloting an airplane isn't as simple as driving a car, where turning the steering wheel turns the vehicle. With an airplane, you have to integrate use of the foot bar, too, to bank, and the rudder's effect is intricately intertwined with the plane's velocity. This is because aircraft move along a vertical axis as well as horizontally. Up until that point, I had been pretty confident in the cockpit, but the skills of these first-rate pilots far exceeded my expectations.

After that, my superiors drilled me via mock dogfights. They were totally different from the mock fights we did at Yatabe. I realized that actual combat was like these drills. You can bet that I desperately tried out all sorts of maneuvers. It was thanks to the precious training my superiors gave me back then that I was able to somehow survive the war.

While I say "superiors" they were all barely past twenty themselves. Flight Petty Officer 1st Class Saburo Sakai, the oldest NCO there, was only around twenty-five at the time. But to me, they seemed almost middle-aged.

Looking back now, we were all so very young.

Around then, Nagumo Mobile Task Force was taking southern island after island by storm, and the Navy built forward bases on each. To these, aviation units from the interior moved out in quick succession. Soon, the Tainan Air Corps received orders to advance to Rabaul, located on New Britain Island, past the equator, in the northeast part of New Guinea. The island had just recently come under Japan's control, in February of 1942, and the base was some 6,000 kilometers away from Japan proper. It became our farthest-flung base in the South Pacific.

We traveled to Rabaul in the spring of '42 on a troop transport ship. On the way, there was intel that a submarine was tailing us, so until we reached Rabaul we felt very helpless. The transport ship was the *Komaki-maru*. We had only a small submarine chaser as our escort, so if an enemy sub attacked us in earnest, we were as good as dead. The day after the transport ship docked at Rabaul, it was bombed by enemy planes and sank there in the harbor. The ship was later converted into Komaki Pier.

I realized this later, but had the *Komaki-maru* been sunk at sea, it would have dealt a major blow to the Tainan Air Corps and to the Imperial Navy as a whole. Losing so many highly skilled fighter pilots at once would have been an incalculable setback. At the time, the Combined Fleet had many warships merely idling in the Truk Lagoon, so they could have sent a couple of destroyers to protect us pilots. But perhaps the brass thought of pilots as easily replaceable commodities.

Rabaul was a beautiful place, with limpid blue waters and clear skies, palm trees along the shoreline, and a volcano in the distance. There was an old town near the airfield with houses where Westerners had lived. These houses were European in style, of course, and the look of the town was elegant and refined. But apart from that town, the rest of the island was unspoiled nature. The so-called airfield was actually just a broad field. When we arrived, our planes weren't there yet. Just a few seaplanes floated in the harbor. Rabaul had a good natural one that later became a berth for warships.

I felt like I had arrived at a paradise on the southern seas. I never dreamed back then that such a place would come to be known as the Airmen's Graveyard.

Afterwards, the converted aircraft carrier *Kasuga-maru* brought the Zeros to Rabaul. We boarded the carrier to receive the planes, and it was there that I did my first carrier takeoff. It was far easier than I had anticipated.

"Aircraft carriers don't seem so hard to deal with," I said to an NCO once we were back in Rabaul.

"Try saying that after doing a landing," he reprimanded me. At the time I thought he was just being self-important and patronizing, but later when I became carrier-based, I got an ample taste of just how terrifying the landings are.

Later, we were transferred from Rabaul to Lae further south on New Guinea. It was a forward base built to capture Port Moresby, also on New Guinea. Port Moresby was 400 nautical miles from Rabaul, a tough distance even for the long-range Zero, so another one was built in Lae. Four hundred nautical miles is about 700 kilometers.

Lae was even emptier than Rabaul. Before the war, Australians had settled in a small town there, but after an earlier air raid by our military, most of the town had burned down. There were several charred houses still standing, and we aircrew dragged simple bedding into the houses and slept there.

Port Moresby was on the same island and due directly south, over the Owen Stanley Range. For days on end, we escorted medium bombers across the neighboring sea to attack Port Moresby. These medium bombers were land-based twin-engine affairs, and the seven-man Mitsubishi G4M was the main type.

The air corps stationed at Port Moresby were mostly American and British. We battled their fighters nearly every day.

It was there that I experienced my first real dogfight.

It happened when I participated in an air raid on Port Moresby as Flight Three's third man. At the time, a flight of fighters consisted of three planes, a leader and two wingmen. Our mission was to establish air supremacy above the enemy's base.

Above Port Moresby, the flight leader suddenly entered a steep turn. Plane two followed almost instantly. In a panic, I tried to follow, but they were so fast that we quickly became separated. The entire formation began moving at high speed. I had absolutely no idea why. All I could do was try to catch up with the flight leader. The Zeros were fitted with radios that were totally useless. We relied on reading each other during battles, but that certainly had its limits. If we'd had functioning radios back then, those battles would have been so much easier.

Anyways, the leader and plane two were flying upwards, downwards. I frantically followed, completely ignorant of where I was going. A few minutes later, the other two entered a level flight path at long last, and I was finally able to catch up.

It wasn't until after we had landed at the base that I learned that we had engaged in combat.

Yes, of course. I was shocked. I hadn't seen a single enemy aircraft, after all. I asked my flight leader, and he said there'd been about a dozen enemy planes. What's more, he and plane two had gunned down one of them. They speak of having wool pulled over your eyes, and that's exactly what it felt like. All told, he said we'd shot down nearly ten enemy planes.

That made me terribly depressed. How do you take part in a dogfight if you can't even spot the enemy? But PO3 Hayashi, the pilot of plane two, consoled me, saying, "When I first started out, I never saw any enemy aircraft, either."

The funny thing is that I saw the enemy very clearly in my second air battle. I must have been nervous during my first. They used to say that if a rookie doesn't get shot down during his maiden battle, he's got a good chance of surviving a decent number of sorties. I suppose I know pretty well what they meant by that.

The second battle took place over Port Moresby as well. We engaged with hostile fighters that ambushed us, and this time I could see the formation of enemy planes. Before setting out, though, Flight Leader Ono had sternly cautioned me not to get separated, so I strove to keep close to him.

In a flash, we were caught up in a mêlée. Tracer bullets streamed through the air, and a plane fell from the sky. I couldn't tell which side's; all I could do was keep close to the flight leader. Tracer bullets burn as they fly, and one out of every four machine-gun rounds is a tracer. They give off a flare that shows the ballistic course so the aircrew can adjust their aims accordingly. The other side also used tracer bullets, and during a dogfight we could see their tracers flying towards us.

I saw the flight leader and plane two take down an enemy aircraft. The leader shot down yet another. Seeing such an admirable display made the fighting spirit surge within me. *I wanna take one out, too,* I thought. Perhaps I felt at ease, seeing that our side was winning handily so far.

I looked around and spotted an enemy aircraft about 1,500 meters below me and to the right. He hadn't noticed me. In pursuit, I pulled away from the flight leader. The enemy still didn't see me, and I thought, *I can do this…*

My body was rigid from tension and delight. Shortly I made a mistake. I fired before the enemy was in my gunsight. He noticed me immediately and rolled over.

Seeing that, I fretted. I gave chase, firing with reckless abandon. That made him panic for his part, and he turned, right into my stream of bullets. Machine-gun fire struck his fuselage, and his plane burst into flames and fell away.

I shivered at my first kill. I confirmed it, the enemy plane going into a tailspin and crashing into the ocean. I shouted in my heart: *I did it!*

I frantically looked around at the same time. I couldn't see a single airplane. I'd forgotten myself in the fight and strayed far from the combat zone. When I banked my plane to look behind me, there were two enemy fighters on my tail. My spine froze.

Flustered, I tried to flee by going into a dive. But then I noticed that a Zero with rising suns painted on the wings was tight at my side. It was Flight Leader Ono's. The planes that I thought were hostile were in fact friendlies. PO3 Hayashi was behind us.

When they had seen me break away to pursue the enemy, they had followed to provide backup. They had watched over me, wanting to let me have my first kill and to be there to help out if things got dicey. They told me as much after we got back to base.

My first kill became the formation's laughingstock, what with my letting loose from more than 500 meters away. There's no way to land a hit at that range. All it accomplished was to alert the enemy to my presence. Fortunately for me, he made a major mistake, too, by trying to turn and face me head-on. Given the difference in altitude, it amounted to suicide. Immediately realizing his mistake, he banked, the worst possible choice, and my machine-gun fire hit home. "Amateurs brawling," my seniors said, and they also got a laugh out of the fact that I had spent all my ammunition on one plane.

"If you need to spend all your bullets on one kill, no amount of ammo will ever be enough," laughed PO1 Ono.

PO1 Ono and PO3 Hayashi were very kind superiors. They were seasoned pilots who'd fought since the Sino-Japanese War, but later the same year, they both died at Guadalcanal.

It was Lae that tempered me as a pilot. I learned a great many things that I wasn't taught in flight school. For a fighter pilot, there's no better lesson than a dogfight. The difference from flight-school training is that if you don't learn, you die. At school, if you mess up on your exams, all you do is repeat the grade. Flunking a dogfight equals death.

That was why we were so driven. In a way, it was only natural that Rabaul produced so many aces. They were sifted through death's sieve and lived to tell the tale. The famous Saburo Sakai, Hiroyoshi Nishizawa, and Lieutenant Junichi Sasai honed their skills there and went on to become aces.

Lt. Sasai was a graduate of the Naval Academy. It was very rare for an officer from the academy to become a flying ace. In fact, most aces were self-made types who had worked their way up through the ranks, namely, NCOs from Preparatory Flight Training or the Pilot in Training Program. Officers who'd attended the Naval Academy couldn't hope to compete with NCOs when it came to piloting and dogfighting techniques. Yet, every unit larger than a flight was placed under the command of an officer, an academy graduate. NCOs had far more experience, better skills, and better judgment than the officers. But in the Imperial Navy, non-commissioned officers simply weren't to command formations.

I can't even begin to list battles that went awry thanks to poor judgment on the part of unit leaders. *If only CPO Gitaro Miyazaki or PO1 Sakai were in charge*, I thought again and again.

Rank is meaningless in the air. It's a world where only experience and skill matter, experience in particular being the most valuable weapon. The stalwarts of Rabaul gained valuable experience through an abundance of action, literally with their lives on the line. And even though the academy-bred officers lacked experience, they had plenty of pride, which prevented them from trying to learn anything from us seamen and NCOs.

However, Lieutenant Sasai was different. He went out of the way to mingle with PO1 Sakai and other NCOs and thought nothing of soliciting advice from his subordinates. PO1 Sakai, too, apparently felt that his friendship with Lt. Sasai transcended rank. Under PO1 Sakai's tutelage, Lt. Sasai's skills improved by leaps and bounds.

By the way, the Naval Air Corps' callousness towards NCOs and seamen was something else. Officers had private quarters and orderlies and were catered to in all sorts of ways, while the rest of us, NCOs on down, slept on the floor in common rooms. Plus, the officers' quarters were far away, so we rarely interacted. The meals were as different as night and day. Even though we were all part of the same team up in the sky, we lived in totally different environments.

As far as meals went, though, aircrew were lucky. The maintenance and ordnance crews were stuck with even poorer fare. Essentially, the military is a thoroughly stratified world. I would later join the aircrew of a carrier, and it had an elegant officers' mess called the Gunroom.

This is a vulgar topic, but there were military brothels at Rabaul, and those, too, were segregated for officers and the rest of us. Was the idea that an officer couldn't possibly be serviced by a lady who'd just seen an NCO or an enlisted man?

It took more than ten years even for the ace Saburo Sakai to be promoted to the rank of ensign. Meanwhile, Naval Academy graduates automatically became ensigns. It's just like the "career" and "non-career" tracks in today's ministries and bureaus. What's more, ensigns who came up through the ranks were referred to as "special duty officers" and considered a step below the ones with degrees from the academy. The Navy was like that.

My final rank was Flight Chief Petty Officer, but only after a postwar promotion. I was a Potsdam CPO.

Let's get back on subject.

At the outset of the Pacific War, the Zeros' might was overwhelming. It's no exaggeration to say that they almost never lost a fight. The enemy pilots were brave, taking the Zeros head-on, but that was akin to suicide. The Zero's combat capabilities were beyond compare, and an enemy aircraft engaging in a dogfight usually went down by the third loop. In a dogfight, two aircraft twist and turn to get on each other's tail.

Around that time, we found an astounding directive in the manual of a downed Allied plane. The circumstances where pilots were permitted to abort their mission and retreat were listed as "(1) encountering a thunderstorm, (2) encountering a Zero."

I met a good number of Allied pilots after the war, among which was Charlie Burns, an Australian pilot who fought at Port Moresby. Charlie was a jovial giant, standing 6' 3".

He told me, "The Zero fighters were truly terrifying. They were unbelievably quick, and we could never predict how they would move. They were like will-o'-wisps. We felt inferior every time we engaged with them. Then we got orders telling us to avoid combat with Zeros, period."

"I've heard about that order."

"We knew that the new Japanese fighters were codenamed Zero," he continued. "Talk about an uncanny name. 'Zero' means 'nothing there,' right? Not to mention, the fighters performed magic on us with their unbelievable moves. I couldn't help but think, 'So this is the mystery of the Orient.'"

"We were desperate ourselves," I told him. "We had been training like mad."

"We thought the pilots of the Zeros weren't human. We figured they were either devils or fighting machines."

"I'm quite human," I assured him. "Now I fight to get food on the table. I run a freight company. I drive a truck instead of a Zero."

He laughed heartily at that. "These days I ride horses at my ranch."

Charlie had been the son of an Australian rancher.

Afterwards he and I exchanged letters for a long while, but five years ago his family informed me that he had passed away from illness.

I keep repeating myself, but the Zero was truly invincible. The Allies didn't have a fighter that could fight on par with a Zero. Even the Spitfire, the pride of the RAF, was no match for the Zero. The renowned aircraft that had defended London from the Luftwaffe's Messerschmitts during the Battle of Britain dropped like flies before the Zero.

This was partly due to the fact that they had no idea how to engage the Zero. There was no fighter then that could tangle with a Zero and win. Unaware of this, the Allies sent their pilots to take us head-on, and those pilots met tragic ends.

Perhaps they just hadn't taken Japan seriously enough. An aircraft is the quintessence of a country's industrial technology. They probably thought that a third-rate country's yellow monkeys could never produce a superior fighter. To be sure, back then Japan wasn't even capable of manufacturing decent cars. And yet the third-rate nation created a miracle fighter in the Zero. It was a masterpiece that its young architects had devised through unstinting effort. The enemy came at us totally ignorant of what we had.

But the Zero was not indestructible. If struck by bullets, it burst into flames and got shot out of the sky. The Zero's shortcoming was a lack of armor. While it may have been unbeatable in a methodical duel, in a brawl it could easily be hit by stray bullets. If it pursued a hostile aircraft too far, it could get nailed by a different enemy.

Surprise attacks were the most terrifying. Snuck up on from a blind spot, even a Zero was helpless. CPO Gitaro Miyazaki, a masterful pilot on par with Saburo Sakai, was killed in such a surprise attack. That day, CPO Miyazaki had sortied in spite of illness, and a moment's inattention resulted in his plane getting shot down. His death in the line of duty was announced to the entire military, and he received his posthumous promotion by two ranks. That was how esteemed he'd been.

The most dangerous surprise attacks came after supporting an air raid, when we didn't exercise caution in regrouping for the return trip. The enemy, which had been unilaterally tormented by Zeros in dogfights, realized that they couldn't defeat us head-on and frequently resorted to surprise attacks and ambushes.

About a month after our initial strike on Port Moresby, the Allies started avoiding us if our numbers were about equal. They engaged if they had twice as many planes, but we were confident of holding our own even outnumbered two to one. During my tour at Lae, I became an adequate pilot. From April to August, Lae-based fighters' kills reached 300, while we lost a mere twenty aircraft.

As Charlie said, the Allied pilots called us Zero pilots *devils*—"devils gripping control sticks." I don't consider that an exaggeration. Lae's veteran pilots were truly that good, and Sakai-san and Nishizawa-san seemed like demons even to us.

There's a funny story about them.

Namely, Petty Officers Sakai, Nishizawa, and Ohta once did a loop in formation over the enemy's base. PO1 Ohta was PO1 Sakai's wingman, and as good an ace as the other two. By then, the three of them had probably downed over a hundred enemy planes among them. Sakai-san had planned on doing the loops for some time, and before taking off, he told the other two, "Let's do it today."

After the air raid and dogfights, the trio formed up above the enemy's airfield as though they could communicate. And they wheeled through the air. Three times. Those were marvelous loops. The three fighters moved as one, in perfect order. The rest of us, who hadn't been forewarned, watched dumbfounded.

They boldly swooped down even closer to the base, then climbed, executing yet another loop that was no less breathtaking. I thought, *So you can perform such a beautiful maneuver in formation if all three pilots are masters.*

Surprisingly, not a single anti-aircraft shell was fired by the enemy's airfield as the trio did this. They dropped quite low for the second round, and an anti-aircraft gun had a pretty decent chance of scoring a kill. I think it was out of chivalry and a sense of humor that the enemy didn't fire. Had it been us, an academy-trained officer would have turned red in the face and screamed, "Fire, fire! Shoot them down!"

"That was mature of them," PO1 Ohta admitted of the Allies' bigness.

A few days later, they sent bombers to hit our base at Lae. But I heard their planes also dropped copies of a letter that read: "Your formation loop the other day was spectacular. We're ready to welcome your next visit."

This happened between bouts of mortal combat, but it only ever did because the Rabaul aircrew were so skilled.

I think Rabaul Air Corps' Zero fighter force was truly the best in the world at that point in time.

Miyabe-san came to Lae in mid-July that year. Around then, aircrew arrived intermittently from the interior, and some had served on carriers.

It was never announced, but rumors quietly spread among aircrew that we had lost four carriers at Midway. We thought it was dreadful, but the news didn't carry a real sense of danger. We were practically invincible, and we were hardly scared of American and British fighter planes. We figured we'd never lose so long as we had the Zero.

I'd heard that the newly arrived aircrew included fighter pilots from the First Carrier Division, and that stirred up a spirit of rivalry in us. Sure, carrier pilots had to be excellent, but it wasn't like they saw aerial combat every day. We felt something akin to pride over the fact that we were risking our lives day in, day out. And to be honest, we thought that they wouldn't have screwed up so badly and lost their carriers if they were indeed so excellent.

Guided by medium bombers, Miyabe-san and the others flew Zeros from the mainland, arriving at Rabaul on a 6,000-kilometer course via Taiwan, the Philippines, and Truk Lagoon. After we were dismissed from the official welcome-aboard for them, one of the pilots called out to me.

"I'm looking forward to working with you," he said. It was Miyabe-san.

He was a tall man. I glanced at his insignia and saw that he was a Flight Petty Officer 1st Class, the highest subordinate rank.

Flustered, I raised my voice and replied, "The pleasure's all mine, sir."

Miyabe-san smiled. "So how do you fight here in Rabaul?"

"Yes," I said, unsure as to how to reply.

"How do the enemy fighter pilots fight?"

"They are rather not bad either, sir."

"Interesting. I look forward to hearing all about it."

I was greatly puzzled by his politeness. Rank was everything in the armed forces. There was an enormous gap between a Flight Petty Officer 1st Class and a Flight Seaman 1st Class.

I could only reply loudly, "Flight Seaman 1st Class Izaki, sir!"

"FS1 Izaki, is it? I'm FPO1 Kyuzo Miyabe. Think well of me, please," Miyabe-san said, slightly bowing his head.

I had no idea how to respond. My military career wasn't long by any means, but I had never before met a superior like him. I figured he was either extremely well-bred or a fool.

"Flight Petty Officer Miyabe, sir. If I may ask, were you on an aircraft carrier?"

He momentarily clammed up. I immediately realized that what had happened at Midway was a military secret and was about to quickly change the subject, but he spoke first.

"Yes, I was on the *Akagi*," he said, following it up straightaway with, "But that's no longer a possibility."

The rumors were true, then, I thought.

"Don't take the U.S. forces lightly. They are formidable opponents," he stated firmly.

I couldn't press him for details. We fell into a brief silence, after which I informed him about our standard method of aerial combat. I told him that the other side preferred fighting air battles in formation, just as we did, and that they sought opportunities for surprise attacks. I explained how they sometimes waited for the moment we were regrouping after an air raid. Miyabe-san listened intently to everything I said.

His attitude was wholly unexpected. More than a few veteran pilots who had fought in China were extremely proud of their records and didn't care to listen to anything aircrew like me had to say. There, most air battles were one-on-one dogfights, but here the enemy attacked in formation, using radios to coordinate among themselves. Many a veteran pilot downplayed this and chased an enemy too far, believing it would be no different from their engagements in China, only to be taken out by a third plane.

The next day we sortied to Port Moresby. We the tactical air control team consisted of three flights, or nine planes. Miyabe-san was PO1 Hashimoto's plane two, me the third man.

The skies over New Guinea were dotted with clouds that day. They were a huge bother to pilots since we couldn't see if the enemy was lurking on the other side. A cloud straight ahead was one thing, but any to the side or rear were unsettling. An enemy aircraft could appear all of a sudden and shoot us down. Of course we used clouds to our advantage as well, but more often than not cloud cover worked in favor of the intercepting side lying in ambush.

On our way I looked towards Miyabe-san a number of times. He seemed agitated, constantly scanning the area, occasionally repositioning his aircraft, keeping a sharp lookout. On more than one occasion, he rolled so he was flying upside-down, not neglecting to pay attention to the blind spots below. *He sure is cautious*, I thought. The pilots at Rabaul were as cautious as anyone, but I thought his vigilance was a bit too extreme.

About an hour in, all of the crew were visibly laughing at his bizarre movements. Here as we flew in neat formation was a single aircraft restlessly shifting about to check the surroundings, and it sure did stand out.

I thought he either had a terribly prudent mindset or was just a big coward.

The Owen Stanley Range came into view. The magnificent mountain range had 4,000-meter-class peaks and divided New Guinea in half lengthwise. Port Moresby lay to the south of this range, and our base at Lae was on the north.

Actually, I loved those mountains. They had a severe sort of beauty. It sounds strange, but flying over them gave me courage.

After crossing the Stanleys and just when Port Moresby was

about to come into view, enemy planes suddenly pounced through a break in the clouds in the sky ahead. It was a perfect sneak attack. We banked hard to the left, but my flight in the far rear of the formation was late in making the turn. The enemy's lead plane took aim at me and latched on. I was positioned such that my topside was exposed to him. *Oh boy, I'm a goner!* I thought.

Just then, the plane that was pursuing me suddenly burst into flames and blew apart. A piece of its fuselage hit my plane. The next instant, a Zero slipped past me incredibly fast. It was Miyabe-san's plane two. His Zero shot down another enemy plane, then made a sharp turn and got behind yet another one that was attempting to flee, pelting it with bullets until it, too, fell from the sky. This all took place in a matter of seconds.

What remarkable technique! And so fast!

It gave me goosebumps. I didn't even know when Miyabe-san managed to move into a position to attack the unfriendlies. He'd been flying alongside me.

Our formation of Zeros reassembled and took it to the enemy with great ferocity. As they had the initial advantage, they gave us one hell of a fight at first, but we quickly turned the tables. Even I got it together and downed one plane.

Once they saw that the tide had turned, the enemy pulled back. Instead of giving chase, though, we formed up again and proceeded to the skies above Port Moresby. Our side had not suffered any casualties during the surprise attack.

No aircraft lay in wait for us above Port Moresby, and we only encountered anti-aircraft fire. When we landed back at our base after the air raid, I went straight over to Miyabe-san to thank him. He merely laughed in reply.

"Did you see the enemy above the clouds back there, sir?"

"Yes, I caught sight of them through a break in them. I fired off a round of machine-gun fire to alert the formation leader. Then I ascended to fly out past the formation, but the enemy dove too quickly and I didn't make it in time. If I'd managed to notify all of you sooner, it wouldn't have been an ambush at all."

I let out a silent groan. The pilots in that day's formation of Zeros were all Rabaul stalwarts. But Miyabe-san had discovered the lurking enemy before any of us, and even beat them at their own game. I thought, *This man is a first-class pilot.*

But there was one thing that bugged me. In the chaos that followed, Miyabe-san wasn't the terror I'd witnessed at the beginning of the ambush. He behaved like a different person, almost. He assiduously backed up the flight leader but hardly shined. I don't know, he just wasn't aggressive. Instead of shooting down hostile aircraft, he seemed to be more focused on not getting shot himself.

Soon Miyabe-san became the talk of the unit. Specifically, the way he always scanned his surroundings during missions did. Once, when a group of aircrew were chatting, a conversation like this took place.

"I can understand being cautious, but that's going too far," a veteran pilot said.

"I mean, we're all plenty vigilant if we're somewhere we might run into the other side. But he's on guard the instant he takes off from Rabaul and keeps it up the whole time until he returns."

"He's gonna give himself a nervous breakdown at that rate."

"Maybe he's had some bad experiences that make him like that."

"Or he is a born coward."

Most of the group laughed at that, including myself. But there was someone who did not—Flight Petty Officer 1st Class Hiroyoshi Nishizawa.

"I personally think we should follow his example," FPO1 Nishizawa said, and everyone else fell silent.

FPO1 Nishizawa was a master dogfighter, the best or thereabouts even amongst the aircrew at Rabaul. The Americans would come to fear him, calling him the "Devil of Rabaul." He and FPO1 Sakai had exceptionally sharp eyes, always spotting the enemy before the other side saw them.

While you may think that aerial combat involves locking in a grapple like in judo, and that's true in part, it's far more effective to discover the enemy before they see you and to attack them from a higher position. Spotting the enemy even a second sooner gives you a serious advantage in the air, which is why good eyes are a major weapon. And by "good eyes," I don't just mean sharp vision. You need concentration, and a certain type of intuition as well. Singling out enemy aircraft as small as ants in skies that are wide open 360 degrees around you is easier said than done. Having 20/20 vision doesn't guarantee it.

Anyway, everyone fell silent at PO1 Nishizawa's words. But even so, more than a few still thought that Miyabe-san's extreme cautiousness stemmed from cowardice.

What about me? Well...

To be honest, I did too. Caution and cowardice are two sides of the same coin, but in Miyabe-san's case, I thought that cowardice won out; and that his performance during his first mission was a sort of fortuitous byproduct of his cowardice. I know it was pretty wrongheaded to think that about someone who'd saved my life.

In short order, Miyabe-san was made flight leader, and I became part of his flight. I made use of the opportunity to ask him to please stop using formal speech with me.

"You're the flight leader, sir. Please speak to me more sternly like the superior you are."

"Is it so awkward for you?"

"That's part of it, sir. And the crews of other flights might think it strange."

Flight Leader Miyabe thought about it for a moment, then laughed. "Okay, sure thing, Izaki."

Even after becoming flight leader, Miyabe-san still kept up his signature persistent watch-keeping. He incessantly checked his six o'clock. Every time he did so, his aircraft banked, so as his wingman it was a bother. He would also frequently flip over and fly inverted.

Nearly everything below an aircraft is a blind spot, but since most of the time the enemy approached from above, taking advantage of a higher altitude, we didn't really need to worry about what was underneath us all that much. Pilots often neglected the airspace beneath them, and in that sense it could be considered the most dangerous area. In fact, Sakai-san sometimes chose to sneak around behind and below an enemy aircraft he'd spotted in order to skewer its underbelly. The risk involved in attacking from below was being discovered by the enemy before you could take them by surprise, in which case they could strike from the dominant position above you. As I mentioned earlier, in a tangle between fighter planes, being at a higher altitude gave you an overwhelming advantage.

Even though I understood that you could never be too careful when it came to being on the lookout, I thought that Flight Leader Miyabe's cautiousness was a little too extreme.

His fighting style was the other reason I thought him a coward. It was something I learned once I was part of his flight, but he never stayed for very long in the area of combat. Once the fight turned into a mêlée, he promptly took refuge and went after enemy aircraft that similarly fled the combat zone.

Since I was young at the time, once a mêlée started I would become entranced, hoping to take out at least one enemy aircraft. But when the flight leader breaks away, his wingmen must follow. Many times I came very close to making a kill only to let the opportunity slip through my fingers. Those moments always left me feeling extremely disappointed.

Once, however, I tore away from my flight leader to pursue a hostile fighter.

I clung fast to the tail of a P-40 Warhawk that was attempting to withdraw after attacking one of our medium bombers. The Warhawk went into a dive to throw me off, but I went around, cut in close, and got on his tail. He tried his damnedest to escape, but I didn't let him. I drove him close to the surface of the ocean and fired on him with both my 7.7-mm machine guns and 20-mm cannons until his aircraft crashed into the waves. It happened then—a tracer bullet streaked past the side of my plane. I was being fired on from behind.

I turned around and looked back to find two P-40s hard on my tail, catching me in a pincer attack. I could've sworn they hadn't been there when I'd checked behind me a moment before.

There was still some distance between us, but the unfriendlies dove down, quickly closing the gap. I saw tracer bullets speed past both sides of my aircraft. I would be struck down whether I tried to flee left or right. I prepared for death.

In the next moment, the tracers that had enclosed me suddenly vanished. I looked back to see one of the planes spout fire and fall into a tailspin. The other one dove down and sped away. There was a Zero behind me. It was my flight leader. That was the second time Miyabe-san saved my life.

When we landed back in Rabaul, I addressed Flight Leader Miyabe. "Thank you very much for today, sir."

"Listen up, Izaki," he said with a very serious expression. "It is far more important to avoid getting shot down than it is to shoot down the enemy."

"Yes, sir."

"Or do you want to trade your life for that of a single American?"

"No, sir."

"Then how many enemy lives is your own life worth?"

I thought for a moment and then replied, "About ten might do, sir."

"Idiot." Flight Leader Miyabe finally cracked a smile. Then he said in an uncharacteristically blunt tone, "Is your life so cheap?"

I burst out laughing, in spite of myself.

"If you fail to kill an enemy but manage to survive, you'll have the chance to kill him later on. However," Miyabe-san continued, his eyes no longer smiling, "if you are shot down just once, Izaki, it's all over."

"Yes, sir."

Miyabe-san took on an authoritative tone at the end. "Therefore, Flight Seaman 1st Class, prioritize your own survival."

His words reverberated deep within my heart. Maybe I was able to take it especially seriously because his advice had come not long after I'd prepared to die. It was thanks to Miyabe-san's words that I managed to survive the innumerable air battles that followed.

That wasn't the only thing I learned from Flight Leader Miyabe.

He always left his quarters in the dead of night and disappeared for over an hour. When he returned, he was covered in sweat and a little out of breath. Ridiculously enough, I thought maybe he had a habit of going somewhere far from our quarters to, you know, pleasure himself.

All of us were healthy young men in our late teens and early twenties. Even though we spent our days in battle not knowing if we'd live to see tomorrow, we had sexual appetites. Or rather, it was precisely because we lived in such close proximity to death that we felt such powerful urges. Oh, I don't know. We had but one adolescence, and it's impossible to compare it to some other life.

This is embarrassing to say, but I did it too, many times, in my bunk or in the toilets. Sometimes I wandered off away from the barracks where no one was around and did it out in the open. There were military brothels at Rabaul and I made use of those as well, but there weren't any around Lae. If someone like me was beset with sexual desire, I imagine a married man like Miyabe-san felt even more restless. That is why I never inquired as to where he went on his midnight sojourns.

Then one evening, making my way back from fishing in a river some distance from the barracks, I heard groaning from a thicket. At first I was startled, but then, unable to contain my curiosity, I quietly crept closer toward the source of the voice.

In the shadows of the thicket was a man lifting something. It was him. Stripped to the waist, Flight Leader Miyabe was gripping the barrel of a broken aircraft machine gun in his right hand and lifting it up repeatedly. Since I'd snuck up, I was unable to announce myself and ended up peeping at what he was doing.

His body was flushed all over. In the end, he let out a cry that was close to a scream.

He rested briefly, then swung his legs over the branch of a nearby tree and hung upside-down. He stayed in that position for as long as he could endure it. His face turned beet red and the veins on his forehead bulged out so far they looked like they might burst open at any second. I wonder how long he held that pose for. I can't remember, but it seemed like an incredibly long time.

At long last I realized what he was up to—training for air battles. During turns and loops, the Gs increase and the control stick gets incredibly heavy. The G is the gravitational force exerted during flight. Fighter pilots must manipulate the heavy control stick with one hand during battle. In order to build up the muscles in our arms we did push-ups and pull-ups, but I had never seen anything like Miyabe-san's workout. And hanging upside-down had to be training for when the blood rushes to the head during sharp turns and loops in battle.

After Miyabe-san left, I went over and tried to lift up the gun barrel he'd held. I was absolutely stunned. I couldn't lift it at all. No matter how hard I tried, it wouldn't move, as if it was stuck fast to the ground.

I tried gripping the barrel with both hands. I finally managed to lift it up using every ounce of strength in my body. For him to lift and lower it with just one hand, he must have had incredibly powerful arms.

Monstrous strength underlay his elegant piloting skills.

The next day, I called out to Miyabe-san as he left the barracks. "Would you mind if I accompanied you, sir?"

He seemed a bit taken aback, but then smiled pleasantly. "Oh, saw me, did you?"

"My apologies, sir. I didn't mean to spy on you. I just happened to find you on my way back from fishing."

"It's fine. It's not like I was keeping it a secret or anything."

Miyabe-san went back to the same spot as the day before and went through the same drills. I couldn't very well stand there in silence as he sweated, so I dropped and did push-ups.

As we sat on the ground afterwards, I said, "You're amazing, sir. I tried to pick that up yesterday but couldn't lift it at all."

"Practice does it, whatever it is. You just need the perseverance to continue. You'll definitely get stronger the longer you train."

"Really?" I asked giddily, but realized he was only trying to console me. "You are an incredible man, Flight Leader Miyabe, sir."

"No, I'm not. Everyone does this."

"Is that true, sir?"

"Sure, Sakai-san, Nishizawa-san, all of them."

"I didn't know."

Miyabe-san laughed. "Nobody does it where everyone can see."

Once he mentioned it, I recalled that Sakai-san often did pull-ups on the crossbeams in the barracks. I felt like a total fool for assuming that was just a hobby of his. I had simply thought him a natural when it came to flying aircraft.

As a pilot in training back in the program, I was put through a grueling physical regimen every day, long-distance running and swimming, chin-ups, etc. But once I became a pilot, I no longer had such obligations. I was ashamed to have been so grateful for that. I realized that it had all been for my own benefit.

"But isn't it difficult to keep up with regularly?" I asked him, as if making excuses for myself.

"It's not easy. But it's nothing compared to the pain of death."

I felt like he was scolding me. "You train every day, sir?"

He nodded in silence.

"Even on days that you've sortied?"

He nodded again. I was impressed. The night after a mission, I was always so tired that I couldn't bear moving more than necessary. And yet he...

"Don't you ever think, 'I'm not going to bother doing it today'?"

Instead of answering me, he abruptly pulled a small bag of cloth out of his breast pocket. In it was a folded piece of paper. He unwrapped it to reveal a single photograph neatly coated in cellophane.

"A photo of my family."

"Please show it to me, sir?"

Flight Leader Miyabe passed it to me gently as if it were some kind of treasure. I took it gingerly, using both hands. In the photo was a young lady holding a newborn baby.

"Apparently, she had this taken at a photo studio in our neighborhood," Miyabe-san explained. He'd reverted to his polite way of speaking, partly because we were alone, but no doubt more because remembering his wife and child brought out his native sincerity.

The woman in the photograph was very lovely. I recall feeling envious.

"Her name's Kiyoko. As in 'pure child.'"

"*Kiyoko-san* is a lovely lady."

Flight Leader Miyabe laughed a bit bashfully. "No, my wife's name is Matsuno. Kiyoko is my daughter's name."

My face flushed in embarrassment. Flustered, I said, "She's an adorable baby."

"She was born in June, right after I returned from Midway. But I couldn't get any time off, so my hopes of seeing her were dashed. I haven't even met my own daughter yet."

It seemed that the rumors that Midway survivors had been quarantined were true.

"Whenever I think, 'This is too much, I'm quitting,' I look at this photograph. It gives me courage," Flight Leader Miyabe confessed with a shy smile. "Pretty pathetic that I lose my conviction if I don't look at this picture."

"Not at all, sir," I replied, but he was no longer listening. He stared intensely at the photograph, and carefully put it back into his breast pocket.

Then he said in a voice barely louder than a whisper, "I just can't die until I meet my daughter." His face, which usually was so gentle, looked incredibly scary then.

After that day, my view of the flight leader changed. I'd been taught the importance of survival in a way that a million-word lecture couldn't have. From that point on, I listened to everything he said. Before every sortie, he would repeat over and over until it became almost tedious to hear, "Absolutely stay in formation," and "No matter what happens, stick close to me."

The reason I am able to tell you this story today is because from then on I followed Miyabe-san's instructions to the letter.

An air mêlée is incredibly terrifying. You never know when someone might take you out from behind. It was a matter of luck. When I was young, I figured that if that happened, then that was when and how I was destined to die. But Miyabe-san was loath to stake his life on sheer luck.

Until then, I had dreamed of becoming a flying ace like Sakai-san, but after becoming part of Miyabe-san's flight, I considered coming out alive by far the most important thing.

However, we were soon embroiled in a battle where even survival was difficult. I'm referring to the Battle of Guadalcanal. Compared to Guadalcanal, our earlier attacks on Port Moresby were mere skirmishes.

For us pilots, Guadalcanal was the opening act of true hell.

Guadalcanal is a small island in the South Pacific, part of the Solomon Islands farther east from New Britain Island where Rabaul is located. It was a lone, undeveloped outcropping covered with jungles. Had the Pacific War not taken place, the name and its very existence would have gone forever unknown by the world at large.

At the time, the Japanese military was attempting to sever lines of communication between the U.S. and Australian forces. We hoped to build an airfield on Guadalcanal that would serve as an unsinkable aircraft carrier glaring out over the South Pacific. We advanced to Guadalcanal and began construction on the airfield in the summer of 1942. The plan was to move most of our aircraft from Rabaul to Guadalcanal once the airfield was completed.

An IJN construction unit spent a whole month clearing virgin jungle and building a runway, but as soon as they were done, U.S. forces mounted a ruthless attack on Guadalcanal and took our just-finished airfield. The Americans had held off until the runway was done. Most of the Japanese troops at Guadalcanal at the time were construction crew and didn't stand a chance. Our side was annihilated in no time.

I learned all this after the war had ended. At the time, I had never even heard of a place called Guadalcanal, let alone that our Navy was building a base there.

I suppose Imperial Headquarters never thought the U.S. would launch a full-scale attack on such a tiny island. They must have assumed that at most it would be a minor archipelagic conflict. But that obscure island would become the site of the hardest-fought battle in the Pacific theater.

August 7, 1942, was the fateful day.

As if in anticipation, we were transferred from Lae to Rabaul several days before. About half the pilots were back in Rabaul for R&R and aircraft maintenance. That morning, even those of us at Rabaul heard the news that Guadalcanal had been taken. Our planned air raid on Milne Bay was scrapped, and we were to attack the enemy's troop transport fleet headed for Guadalcanal instead.

"Where the heck is Guadalcanal?" I asked PO3 Saito, a member of my squadron.

"No idea. Nor did I know we had an airfield there."

None of the aircrew knew of the place. But soon information trickled in that a garrison on Tulagi, an island facing Guadalcanal, had died to the last man, and an incredibly heavy mood overtook our unit.

We gathered before HQ, where we were handed aerial maps. We found out that it was a whopping 560 nautical miles from Rabaul.

That's about 1,000 kilometers.

"Impossible," someone muttered. It was Flight Leader Miyabe. "We can't fight at such a distance," he objected in a sorrowful tone.

Someone yelled, "Who the hell just said it's impossible?!" A young officer boiling over with rage stalked towards us. "You bastard! What the hell did you say?" he barked, striking Miyabe-san across the face before he could reply. "Just this morning our comrades were killed in action on Tulagi. The entire seaplane contingent on Tulagi was wiped out as well. It's a military man's duty to avenge his brothers-in-arms!"

"I'm terribly sorry, sir," said Miyabe-san, but the officer punched him again, splitting his lip open.

"You're Miyabe, aren't you? I've heard the rumors about you, damn coward!" yelled the officer. "If I hear any more cowardly bullshit from you, you're gonna pay for it!" the officer shouted and walked away.

"Flight Leader, you can't voice such thoughts," I said, wiping at his bloodied lip with my scarf.

Miyabe-san's eyes were dark as he muttered, "This battle will be unlike anything that's come before."

"Do you know Guadalcanal?"

"No, I don't. But I do know how far 560 nautical miles is," he said softly. "It's not a distance that Zeros can do battle over."

The air supremacy team picked earlier that morning included Lt. Sasai, PO1 Sakai, PO1 Nishizawa, PO1 Ohta, all the Rabaul stalwarts. Miyabe-san was not among the names listed. Of course, neither was mine.

Flight Petty Officer 1st Class Saburo Sakai—I've mentioned him several times now, and from back then, he was so famous that there wasn't a single Navy pilot who didn't know his name. He was truly a genius ace who already had over fifty kills. His eyes were so sharp that they said he could pick out stars in the daytime skies, and his dogfighting skills were practically divine. Meanwhile, PO1 Nishizawa would later become the ace pilot most feared by the American forces. Lt. JG Sasai and FPO1 Ohta were remarkably expert pilots as well.

The Zero fighter pilots chosen for the attack on Guadalcanal that morning included Flight Chief Petty Officer Toraichi Takatsuka,

FPO2 Ichirobei Yamazaki, FPO2 Masaaki Endo—all amazing, master pilots, too.

Command must have known that making a strike at a distance of 560 nautical miles was at best a risky mission. Eighteen of our best men were chosen for it.

At 07:50, twenty-seven Type 1 land-based bombers took off from Vunakanau Airfield located on a plateau, and eighteen Zeros took off from the eastern airfield in the foothills. But one had to turn back due to engine trouble.

Thus seventeen Zeros fell into an orderly formation above Rabaul and flew due east into the deep blue sky. Even now I remember the sight of the greatest pilots in the IJN flying in formation that day. It was a truly beautiful formation. We waved and waved as we watched.

Later that day, nine Type 99 carrier-based bombers also departed. However, the 99's flight range was insufficient, so they all sortied knowing it would be a one-way trip. They were ordered to attack the enemy's troop transports, then to ditch in the ocean in a designated area and to wait for rescue from seaplanes. I remember feeling very uptight once I heard of such a suicidal mission.

"They'll be okay, won't they?" I asked Miyabe-san, who stood beside me as we saw off the Zero formation.

"With Sakai-san and Nishizawa-san, there shouldn't be anything to worry about," Miyabe-san replied. "Even so, 560 nautical miles is a punishing distance. At cruising speed, that'll take them over three hours. They'll have only a little over ten minutes to fight over Guadalcanal."

"Over three hours?"

"Considering how much fuel they'll need for the return trip, they can't risk fighting for much longer. The medium bombers have a better flight range than the Zeros, and a navigator calculates the route, which is reassuring. But the Zeros are single-seated. If any of them wanders off-course or takes unnecessary detours, there's a real chance the Zero won't make it back."

"But they've got the bombers with them, so they should be able to stay on course. Isn't that right?"

"Getting there, yes. But if they get separated from the formation during the air battle at Guadalcanal, they'll have to get back to Rabaul unaided. It's not exactly easy to navigate 560 nautical miles over open seas with nothing but a map and a compass."

Listening to Miyabe-san, I realized his explanation was that of a former aircraft carrier pilot. They were the words of a man who'd traveled over the ocean in search of the enemy's military vessels with no landmarks to guide his way, returned back to his home carrier after the attack, and done it all over again numerous times.

That morning, the whole base was filled with a heavy, oppressive atmosphere. The aircrew had at first been enthused over the chance to avenge our fallen comrades at Guadalcanal, but once they had calmed down they realized just what it meant to attempt a strike on the enemy on an island 560 nautical miles away.

According to the map, if you flew due east over a string of islands, you reached the target. Even separated from the formation, you could simply fly back along the same route. In case of heavy cloud cover, though, the islands wouldn't be visible, and you'd have to depend on your map and compass.

At around 15:00, we heard a familiar roar. We dashed out of the barracks and looked skyward to see friendly planes. The attack force had returned from Guadalcanal, seven hours after sortieing. They weren't in formation and landed as they pleased. Most of the medium bombers bore bullet holes, proving that it had been quite an arduous battle.

The biggest shock was the number of Zeros that made it back. There were only ten. Seven had been downed.

All the faces of the Zero pilots as they stepped out onto the tarmac spoke of bone-deep exhaustion. FPO1 Nishizawa looked downright gaunt, and it seemed to be all he could do just to get out of his aircraft. I learned afterwards that PO1 Nishizawa had been like a whirlwind, downing six Grummans that day.

All the pilots headed directly to the command post for the debriefing. I ran up to PO1 Nishizawa.

"Where's PO1 Sakai, sir?"

"I'm pretty sure he's all right, considering who it is we're talking about. No easy prey," he replied with a laugh and slapped me on the shoulder. But it seemed to take all the strength he had left to put a smile on his face.

It was fairly common to split up during combat and return in smaller groups, so I shouldn't have been particularly worried, but realizing that PO Sakai's plane was one of the seven that hadn't made it back intensified my anxiety.

Petty Officer Sakai was a flight leader. As I said before, a flight consists of three planes. PO Sakai was an extremely gifted flight leader. Up until that point, he had never once lost a plane under his command. "Saburo Sakai" always gets the limelight as a flying ace that shot down dozens of enemy aircraft, but I thought it was far more magnificent that he had never once lost a wingman. By the way, Nishizawa-san had a similarly excellent track record as flight leader. I heard that the only time he lost a man was in his final air battle.

In any case, it was highly unusual for Sakai-san to have become separated from his flight.

After a while, a report came in that five Zeros had crash-landed on Buka Island, to the east of Rabaul. They had run out of fuel and couldn't make it back to base. However, PO Sakai was not among those pilots either.

Another hour passed and still there was no sign of him. He would have run out of fuel by then.

Just after 16:00, a Zero suddenly appeared on the far side of the airfield. A commotion erupted on the base. The Zero tottered and staggered as it came in for a landing. I thought it was strange. PO Sakai would never be so wobbly during a landing.

The Zero slowly approached the runway. I saw the windshield was shattered, which meant bullets had gone through the cockpit. The Zero bounced on landing as though a novice pilot was at the controls. It taxied down the runway, eventually coming to a standstill.

Squadron CO Lieutenant Commander Nakanishi and Lieutenant Junior Grade Sasai clambered onto the wings, pried open the shattered windshield, and dragged FPO1 Sakai from the cockpit. All the crewmembers who had rushed forward to help gasped when they caught sight of him. Dried blood had given his face a dark cast, and his upper body, too, was covered in blood.

After getting out of the plane, Petty Officer Sakai said sharply, "I will go to make my report."

"You need medical attention first," Lt. JG Sasai yelled. He and

PO Nishizawa held up PO Sakai's body in their arms. I helped by propping him up from behind. His whole body reeked of blood.

"No, I will report first," PO Sakai declared. I thought he surely had to be some kind of a demon.

"Pilot senior, you're not fully aware of the extent of your own injuries," PO Nishizawa said, but PO Sakai kept on walking towards the command post on his own two feet. The moment he finished his report, he was carried to the infirmary.

Details of PO Sakai's report quickly spread through the ranks. On the way back after the raid on Guadalcanal, he had mistaken a formation of enemy carrier-based bombers for fighters and attacked them from behind.

He had made a terrible mistake despite being a pilot of his caliber. A fighter is completely defenseless from a rear attack, but bombers have a pair of swivel-mounted machine guns in the back. PO Sakai had charged into a formation of eight carrier-based bombers from the rear. Even though the swivel-mounted guns on bombers had a far lower accuracy compared to fighter planes' fixed guns, facing eight bombers' rear gunners was a different matter. A barrage of bullets fired from sixteen machine guns greeted him.

They blew away his canopy, a bullet grazed his skull, and shards of his windshield pierced both of his eyes, effectively blinding him. With his vision clouded over and his left arm paralyzed as a result of the impact to his head, he flew back to Rabaul using just his right hand, blood flowing profusely from his head wound.

"Only Petty Officer Sakai could have made it back under such conditions. He is incredible, just incredible," Flight Leader Miyabe said. I could only nod silently in agreement. "But the rest of us aren't up to it. Petty Officers Nishizawa and Sakai are true masters. Not everyone can pull off what they did. This battle is going to be really tough." The flight leader's voice had a grim tone as he predicted the hellish fighting to come.

That day, five medium bombers were lost, and there were six unreturned Zeros including those that had crash-landed on Buka Island. Most tragic was the fate of the nine carrier-based bombers that had undertaken a one-way mission. The bombers had received orders to ditch in a designated area of the ocean after attacking, but only four crewmen were rescued by seaplanes. Fourteen expert aircrew lost their lives that day.

The next day at 0800, I set out for Guadalcanal as Miyabe Flight's second plane. A total of fifteen Zeros—every single one at Rabaul that could be deployed—sortied that day. The formation of medium bombers, all of them armed with torpedoes, numbered twenty-three. Apparently, they had carried bombs the previous day. They'd initially planned to carry out a raid on Port Moresby when new orders to attack the troop transport convoy had suddenly come down, and they hadn't had time to switch to torpedoes.

We Zeros were escorting the bombers, and while we flew and flew, nothing but clouds and the sea greeted us. I realized in spades just how very far Guadalcanal was from our base.

The medium bombers were slow, and the Zeros had to fly in a zigzag pattern shaving the air to match their speed. As the Zeros had shorter flight ranges and needed to conserve as much fuel as possible, the zigzagging wasn't exactly enjoyable. As we could be on our own for the return trip, I periodically marked my location during the flight, relying on compass and ruler.

Before departing, Flight Leader Miyabe had insisted, "The battle isn't just aerial combat with the enemy. It lasts until you return to base." He'd also told me that more than a few planes lost track of their course over the seas and failed to return. Not making it back to base equaled death.

I glanced at the clock. It was nearly 11:00. We would be close to Guadalcanal at that point. I passed through a cloud and saw the island far in the distance ahead. I looked at Guadalcanal's waters and gulped. Innumerable warships lay at anchor in the island's bay.

I was horrified to discover that the Americans sent out so many ships to capture just one little island. How much could we accomplish by taking on such a huge force with just twenty-three medium bombers? I felt gloomy about the prospects but was committed to my mission. I roused my fighting spirit.

That day, I was guarding the medium bombers. Escorting consisted of two tasks: tactical air control and guarding the bombers. TAC was about establishing supremacy in hostile airspace, while the guard contingent stayed close to the bombers to protect them from enemy fighters.

I caught sight of hostiles ahead. The TAC which had sortied first was already engaged in combat with enemy interceptors. The TAC fought hard, trying to keep them away from the bombers, but slipping through, the enemy approached.

These fighters were Grumman Wildcats, and it was my first encounter with them. I would learn after the war that the U.S. fighters there belonged to the aircraft carriers *Saratoga, Enterprise,* and *Hornet.* The U.S. Navy had deployed every carrier it had on hand to take Guadalcanal.

The hostile fighters took advantage of their higher altitude and swooped down. Their tactic was the simple hit and run. They would plunge down, fire a volley of bullets, and then continue downward to escape.

Their fighters did not engage the Zeros. They dove in and focused their attacks solely on the bombers. Since our primary mission was to guard the bombers, we devoted ourselves to driving away the enemy rather than dogfighting. The guard contingent could not stray from the medium bombers. That would be playing right into the enemy's hands. The fighter guard's mission was to protect the bombers even if it meant giving up our lives.

The TAC team, too, had to conserve enough fuel for the return trip, so they could not chase the enemy very far. After diving down to flee, the Grummans pulled up into a climb to repeat the same style of attack. Once they were high in the air, the TAC team tried to close in on them, but the Grummans shied away and instead went after the medium bombers again. That day, we suffered a number of these recurring strikes.

The fighter guard strove desperately to protect the bombers, but in the face of such persistent interception, they began spewing flames and dropping one after another. It was humiliating.

Although the land-based Type 1 attack plane was the Imperial Navy's standard-bearing bomber craft, it had exceedingly poor defenses. The Americans gave it the unenviable nickname of "one-shot lighter" since it could catch fire from just one shot. Despite the fact that it was a slow-moving bomber, its fuel tanks were unprotected and there was practically no armor for the cockpit, which meant it was easily taken out by fighters. In fact, Admiral Isoroku Yamamoto, Commander-in-Chief of the Combined Fleet, was killed in 1943 when a Type 1 that had been transporting him got shot down.

Even so, the bomber formation managed to draw close to the troop transports. Just when we thought the enemy fighters had scattered, we faced a storm of anti-aircraft fire. The fighters soared to escape the onslaught, but the bombers had to continue their descent headlong into the barrage in order to launch their torpedoes. The tempest of AA fire from the enemy fleet made columns of water spout up around the bombers as they entered level flight. One plane after another caught fire and crashed into the waves, but the other brave crews pressed on through the blaze of gunfire. It was a bloodcurdling sight.

I watched as a torpedo delivered a death blow to the hull of a transport.

As the surviving bombers attempted to flee after the torpedo attack, enemy fighters pounced on them, and Zeros set upon them once more in turn. The enemy was tenacious, and our escorting fighters had a hard time of it.

The fruits of that day's battle according to our reports: two warships and nine transports sunk. A splendid achievement—only, the American tally made available after the war lists the loss of just one destroyer and one transport.

I departed at 0800 and finally returned at 1500, having spent seven hours in the cockpit. My first sortie to Guadalcanal had been unbelievably exhausting, and for a moment I felt faint when I landed at Rabaul. I'd never experienced such severe fatigue. I barely managed to crawl out of the aircraft, feeling like every bone in my body was about to rattle right out of my skin. I remember walking back to the barracks feeling like the ground was slowly rolling and pitching beneath my feet. I wanted to just collapse if I could.

That day, we lost eighteen medium bombers and two Zeros. Twenty-three bombers had taken off and only five had returned. In just two days, we had lost nine Type 99 bombers, twenty-three Type 1 bombers, and eight Zeros, which were almost all the attack planes and nearly half the Zeros at Rabaul. We had lost the lives of some

150 aviators. Since the medium bombers had a crew of seven each, the loss of one plane took the lives of seven men at once. Pilots, bombardiers, mechanics, radio operators—all of them first-rate in their fields, valuable aircrew who had spent years to get there. And we had lost 150 of them in just two days.

I thought back on Miyabe-san's warning that this battle was going to be incredibly tough.

And our losses that day would be hardly exceptional.

Chapter 5
Guadalcanal

"May I rest for a moment?" Izaki asked, reclining on his bed. His daughter Suzuko pressed the call button for the nurse.

"Are you all right, sir?" I asked.

Izaki, still lying down, raised his right hand in reply.

After a moment, a nurse entered the room. "I'm in a bit of pain," Izaki told her. She gave him an injection. He closed his eyes and turned onto his side.

"We probably should be going," my sister said to Suzuko Emura.

As soon as he heard her, Izaki practically shouted, "Wait a minute. I still have many things I need to tell you."

"Are you sure, Father?" Suzuko asked worriedly.

"I'm fine. The pain is already gone." Izaki sat up, but his face belied him.

"We'll come back again in a few days."

"That won't be necessary," Izaki said. "After living for eighty years, it's a given that one's body starts to fall apart."

The nurse sat down in a chair and told us that she could stay a bit since her shift was over.

"With a nurse on hand, we're all set," Izaki joked, but his smile looked forced, and his daughter looked at him anxiously. "I had such confidence in my physical strength when I was young. When I was at Rabaul, I was the same age as Seiichi is now."

Seiichi's expression stiffened momentarily.

"Izaki-san, it sounds like you had strong ties with our grandfather," Keiko said.

"As I mentioned before, it's entirely thanks to the fact that I was Flight Leader Miyabe's wingman that I survived. And precisely for that reason, I came to fear death. I only say this now, but when I first arrived at Rabaul I was totally unafraid of death. A kid of nineteen can't possibly understand how sacred life really is. This is a slightly odd analogy, but it's like someone with only a little money going out gambling and, assuming he'll lose anyway, happily betting everything he has. But then somehow he keeps on winning, and as the jackpot grows he becomes fearful and starts to not want to lose."

"I think I understand, sir."

"Beginning in the fall of 1942, veteran aircrew who'd survived Midway were transferred from the interior to Rabaul. But even for those seasoned aviators, Rabaul was a harsh place."

"It was the Airmen's Graveyard, right?" Keiko asked.

Izaki nodded. "But even so, Saeki-san, we were among the fortunate. The ones who really went through hell were…" Izaki paused and sighed quietly, "the Imperial Army soldiers who fought at Guadalcanal."

Do you know about the battle fought by the Imperial Army soldiers at Guadalcanal?

No? Ah, I see. Well, I guess young people these days wouldn't know anything about it.

This is getting off the topic of Flight Leader Miyabe, but I want you to hear about those soldiers that fought at Guadalcanal. In fact, I don't want any Japanese to forget about that tragedy. I definitely want Seiichi, here, to know about it, too.

And unless you know about the Army's battle at Guadalcanal, you won't be able to comprehend why the Rabaul Air Corps, to which Flight Leader Miyabe and I belonged, fought so hard grinding down our very lives.

It wasn't until after the war, though, that I became fully informed as to what had happened on the island. And when I finally learned the full story, I realized that Guadalcanal was a microcosm of the Pacific War. The foolishness of Imperial General Headquarters and the Japanese military came into full play in the battle for that island. No, it was Japan, as a country, that laid bare its worst weaknesses on that battleground.

That's exactly why I want all Japanese people to know about Guadalcanal!

This battle that spanned six months was the very turning point of the Pacific War.

When the U.S. forces attacked Guadalcanal on August 7th, the Imperial General HQ apparently assumed the conflict would be local. They seemed to have concluded that the U.S. merely wanted to score an easy hit on a weakly defended island. This, too, I only learned after the war was over.

As I just said, those of us in the Rabaul Air Corps immediately attacked their troop transports when the island first fell. But the following month, the Imperial General Headquarters sent Army soldiers to recapture the airfield on Guadalcanal. That was the beginning of the tragedy.

After sizing up the U.S. forces to number about two thousand without properly reconnoitering them, IGHQ sent an attack wave of just over 900 troops. It's a mystery as to where they got "2,000," but what's shocking is that they thought a force less than half as strong could recapture the island and airfield. Maybe they believed the Imperial Army was simply that powerful. However, it turned out that there were 13,000 U.S. Marines on the island.

After the war, I read in a book that the night before the assault, the Army's landing forces were in celebratory spirits as if they had already won the battle. The commander, Colonel Ichiki, was a cocksure man himself. Apparently, when he received his orders he asked his superior, "Can we attack Tulagi to the north of Guadalcanal as well?"

That battle was the first showdown between the Imperial Army and the U.S. Marines. It seemed that our soldiers went into battle thinking they would kill every last one of those spineless Yanks. Back then, it had been drilled into our heads that Americans were total cowards and sissies. That they put their families first and had cushy lives waiting for them back home. That they all hated war and valued their own lives above all else. They'd all surrender without hesitation if the fighting got too fierce. They lacked the fearless resolve of Imperial troops who would opt for a hero's death over the lot of a captive. So defeat wasn't possible. It was thanks to such a bias that they figured a force half the expected strength of the enemy would be perfectly sufficient. So I can't really blame the troops in Ichiki Expeditionary Force for laughing and thinking that an easy victory awaited them the next day.

But the results—it pains me even to say this, but Ichiki Expeditionary Force was totally annihilated when they mounted their first night raid. The Japanese military's assault charge was utterly ineffective in the face of the U.S.'s overwhelming firepower.

Back then, the Imperial Army's basic tactic was the bayonet charge. Troops threw caution to the wind, rushed the enemy's position, and stabbed the enemy with their bayonets to kill them. Meanwhile, the Americans used heavy artillery, as well as heavy and light machine guns. The U.S. forces rained shells on and inundated with machine-gun fire the charging Japanese troops.

There was no way our side could win. The Japanese ground forces at Guadalcanal were like the Takeda Cavalry challenging Nobunaga Oda's musket lines during the Battle of Nagashino centuries ago. Why on earth had our side chosen to carry out such a stupid operation? What was the IGHQ staff thinking? On what grounds did they conclude that such medieval battle tactics could defeat the Americans? I just can't fathom the idiocy of it all.

After the war, I saw a photograph taken in the immediate aftermath of that battle. It showed countless Japanese soldiers strewn along the sandy shore the morning after. The bodies had no blood on them; perhaps the waves had washed them clean. The photo clearly depicted their expressions. They'd all had fathers and mothers back in their hometowns, even wives and children waiting back home. I could barely see it after a while because my eyes welled with tears.

Of the approximately 800 troops who participated in the charge, it's said that 777 died, on that one night. Colonel Ichiki burned the battle flag and committed suicide. It is said that casualties on the American side could be counted on one hand.

Upon receiving news of Ichiki Expeditionary Force's fate, IGHQ said, "Well, in that case," and decided to send in a much larger attack force, of 5,000. That would surely do?

But the Americans outdid us. They'd repelled the Japanese forces, but predicting that we'd strike again with more troops, they increased their garrison to 18,000 troops.

The General Staff's plans were entirely haphazard. At first, they didn't bother finding out the size of the enemy's forces, made assumptions that worked in their favor, and thought they could win back the island with an expeditionary force of less than a thousand. When that failed, they simply concluded that five thousand should do the job. Sending in troops as they come instead of amassing them is a tactic that should be avoided at all costs, but the elite staff at IGHQ didn't even know the ABCs. Sun Tzu's *Art of War* famously states: "If you know the enemy and know yourself, you need not fear the result of a hundred battles." They were fighting without knowing the enemy, which was out of the question. Pity the soldiers who were used like pawns in such a haphazard operation.

The second wave of Japanese troops was thoroughly defeated too, and many fled into the jungle, where they were beset with starvation. Guadalcanal had been *Ga* Island for short, but the character for "starve" is used for that first syllable off and on because of this. IGHQ continued to commit separate waves of troops, and most of them, too, faced starvation, dying not from battle but from malnourishment.

The troops on *Ga* Island developed a metric for determining the lifespans of their comrades: "If he can stand, he has thirty days to live. If he can sit, he has three weeks. If he's bedridden, he has one week. If he wets himself while sleeping, he has three days. If he can no longer speak, he has two days. If he no longer blinks, he has one day left."

In total, we sent over 30,000 troops to attack Guadalcanal, out of which 20,000 lost their lives. Of that number, 5,000 perished in battle. The rest died of starvation. They say even the living were ridden with maggots. You can imagine just how deplorable the situation was.

By the way, there were other Japanese military operations that resulted in soldiers suffering starvation. Tens of thousands of officers and grunts died of starvation in New Guinea, Leyte, Luzon, and Imphal.

Why did they starve? Because the military hadn't prepared rations. In all these instances, they sent the troops into battle with only the amount of provisions stipulated in the operation plan. The thinking was that the troops would take the enemy position in so many days; they could seize the encampment's provisions and be resupplied via the captured base. Perhaps the brass thought soldiers without food would fight with blind fury, their only option to win. The Kawaguchi Expeditionary Force sent in after Ichiki's is said to have referred to the U.S. provisions that they were counting on acquiring as "Roosevelt's grant."

But war rarely goes simply according to plan. On the battlefields that I just mentioned, instead of wiping out the enemy our forces ended up getting pulverized, and those who survived fought starvation. Logistics is basic to war. It means supplying rations and ammunition and such. They say that generals of our Warring States period considered logistics to be of the utmost importance. Yet, the staff at IGHQ didn't even think of such essentials. Top graduates of the Army War College, they were all exceptionally bright, too. The Army War College's top graduates back then were on par with the cream of the cream of Tokyo University's elite Law Department.

That was how 30,000 officers and soldiers ended up isolated and abandoned on Guadalcanal. But we couldn't leave them to die. The IJN did send many ships to replenish their supplies of ammunition and food, but before the slow-moving transports could reach the island, planes launched from the airfield on Guadalcanal attacked and sank them. At long last, in a desperate measure, high-speed destroyers were deployed to deliver provisions. Rice and other staples were packed into metal drums which were then allowed to drift to shore at night via ropes. "Rat Transportation," the destroyers' captains self-deprecatingly nicknamed it. But even with this risky method, a single destroyer could only deliver several days' worth of provisions for the more than 20,000 troops. A number of these destroyers, too, were sunk in enemy ambushes. Plus, come morning, many of the supply drums would be strafed by American fighter planes and sink, riddled with machine-gun bullets.

Eventually, submarines unloaded the torpedoes that were more valuable to them than life itself in order to ferry in rice.

During this period the IJN fought many battles in the seas around the Solomon Islands. In some battles, the Combined Fleet managed to defeat the Americans, while in others the U.S. forces sank our vessels.

Actually, we had had a good chance to claim victory in the early stages of the naval battle at Guadalcanal.

I mentioned that the Americans launched a surprise attack on Guadalcanal on August 7th. The IJN's Eighth Fleet, located at Rabaul at that time, immediately headed out to attack the enemy's transport convoy. The night next, on August 8th, they happened upon an American fleet escorting the convoy off the coast of Savo Island. This would later be referred to as the First Battle of the Solomon Sea. Led by Gunichi Mikawa, the Eighth Fleet trounced the American cruisers by pulling off a surprise attack by night, a specialty of the IJN.

But Mikawa Fleet immediately withdrew. If they had taken the opportunity to press forward and attack the transport ships, they probably could have destroyed most of the convoy.

Even though Captain Hayakawa of the cruiser *Chokai* strongly suggested pushing forward to wipe out the transport convoy, Fleet Commander Mikawa chose to withdraw instead.

Reportedly, he feared U.S. aircraft carriers. He thought that even if they managed to destroy the convoy, if carrier-based planes attacked them come morning, a fleet that lacked a fighter escort would be in dire straits.

However, at that time the three U.S. aircraft carriers he was worried about were far away from Guadalcanal. That is because their fighter squadrons had sustained heavy damage from Rabaul's Zeros. Petty Officers Sakai and Nishizawa and others had fought bravely the day before, and that very morning Flight Leader Miyabe and I had participated in a desperate attack. The commander of the carrier air group, Admiral Fletcher, felt that Japanese carriers were approaching, and judging that he wouldn't be able to fend off an attack since he'd already lost many fighters, he retreated eastward. Those two days of do-or-die fighting on the part of the Zeros had driven away the enemy carriers.

But Mikawa Fleet let this chance at victory slip away. The enemy's transport ships hadn't yet offloaded their heavy artillery and such, so if only Mikawa Fleet had attacked, they could have sunk much of the convoy's weapons and ammunition. Had that happened, the engagements of the Ichiki and Kawaguchi expeditionary forces would likely have taken totally different courses. The foot soldiers on the front line were risking their lives in combat, yet the weakness of those in charge caused such an outcome. So very unfortunate...

Here's something else I learned after the war: when Fleet Commander Mikawa was appointed to lead the Eighth Fleet, General Staff Chief Nagano apparently told him, "Our country's manufacturing industry is quite small, so do your best to keep our ships from sinking." What a philosophy. Perfectly fine with treating soldiers and airmen like sacrificial pawns, they treasured the expensive warships with utmost devotion.

There's another ugly rumor that I heard. The Order of the Golden Kite, the highest honor that could be bestowed on a commander of a military fleet, was granted based on sinking enemy warships in battle more than anything else. Battleships were worth the greatest number of points, followed by cruisers, destroyers, and so on. But transport ships didn't count for any, no matter how many you sank. Moreover, losing any of your own ships meant a significant deduction. Is it much of a stretch to imagine that after sinking the cruisers and destroyers, Fleet Commander Mikawa withdrew without so much as a glance at the transport convoy for precisely this reason?

In any case, Mikawa Fleet's withdrawal was a terribly regrettable decision in the Battle of Guadalcanal.

Subsequently too, the Navy managed to deal some crushing blows to the American fleet. Our submarine, I-26, torpedoed the *Lexington*-class carrier *Saratoga*, rendering her incapable of combat. Another sub, I-19, sank the aircraft carrier *Wasp* in September.

During the Battle of the Santa Cruz Islands on October 26th, in the first carrier showdown since the Battle of Midway, our carrier-based pilots fought like fiends, sinking the U.S. aircraft carrier *Hornet* and badly damaging the *Enterprise*. The *Hornet* had carried out an air raid on Tokyo. Our pilots sortied knowing the mission was a long-range attack from which most would not return alive, and sank the *Hornet* at the cost of a very high number of casualties.

The Japanese military didn't know, but immediately after the Battle of the Santa Cruz Islands, the Americans were in a very precarious position, as they were left without a single operational aircraft carrier. That day was apparently Navy Day in the United States and was dubbed "the worst Navy Day in history." Supposedly, the Americans even considered withdrawing their garrison from Guadalcanal. In fact, after the war, many of their military historians noted that Japan could have recaptured Guadalcanal by mobilizing the Combined Fleet's entire might at that juncture. But the IJN missed the chance of a lifetime by choosing to attack incrementally, once again, with small forces. It was the Americans, in their sink-or-swim position, who threw their entire force into battle.

The world's largest battleship *Yamato* was anchored in Truk Lagoon just over 1,000 kilometers north of Rabaul but was kept safe, never once showing up at Guadalcanal. Admiral Yamamoto and HQ staffers dined on lavish lunches to musical accompaniment courtesy of a military band while they issued orders to the officers and sailors fighting on the front lines. Do you know what us rank-and-file sailors called the *Yamato*?

The Hotel Yamato.

Nevertheless, the men on the front lines fought with everything they had. At Lunga Point, destroyers conducting a "rat transportation" were ambushed by four American heavy cruisers. While we did lose one of the destroyers, they accomplished the incredible feat of sinking one enemy cruiser and badly damaging the remaining three. Normally, there's no contest between destroyers and heavy cruisers. It's like pitting a compact car against a tractor trailer. But with a valiant counterstrike Fleet Commander Raizo Tanaka defeated the heavy cruisers.

I'm getting off topic here, but Fleet Commander Tanaka, who pulled off such a victory, fell into disfavor after the battle for some ridiculous reason. This was a man who earned the highest praise from the American naval forces, who called him "the bravest, most dauntless admiral in the Imperial Japanese Navy." By the way, even though the submarine I-26 put the USS *Saratoga* out of commission for three months, because it was thanks to a single hit with a torpedo, none of the crew from the captain on down were honored for their efforts. Those men had persevered just to make that strike and only survived after suffering twelve hours of ferocious retaliation from the enemy's depth charges.

In general, the IJN was incredibly callous to those who risked their lives fighting on the front lines. It was an organization where commissioned officers from the Naval Academy rose up no matter how badly they screwed up, while self-made men were rewarded for their efforts only once in a blue moon.

We rank-and-file seamen and petty officers were treated from the start as nothing more than tools. For the joint staff, our lives didn't rate higher than ammo. Those Imperial HQ people and Command were hardly human beings!

Oh, sorry. I got a bit worked up there. Let's get back on topic.

So, while we managed to score some gains in combat, there were more than a few battles where we suffered major losses. During the night battle off Savo Island we lost a heavy cruiser to radar-guided fire from the American fleet, and in the Third Battle of the Solomon Seas two older battleships were likewise sunk. That time, too, the Combined Fleet was reluctant to deploy the *Yamato* and only sent out second-class battleships.

But worse still than individual naval battles were the dismal results of the transport operations. This was due to the fact that we did not control the airspace. Those 560 nautical miles proved too far a distance for aircraft to provide a screen for the Japanese supply ships. Later we built an air base at Buin on Bougainville Island, situated between Rabaul and Guadalcanal, and while that granted us some leeway, it was not close enough to regain mastery of the airspace over Guadalcanal.

That left support from aircraft carriers, but it was extremely dangerous for them to get anywhere near a powerful enemy air base situated on solid land. We had lost four carriers at Midway, which made the General Staff and the Combined Fleet Command too skittish to devise any remotely risky operation. They really should have, though.

It beats me why the Imperial Army and Navy chose to fight in a location where they couldn't even supply their troops.

Regardless, the battle had already begun. In order to recapture the airfield on Guadalcanal, we absolutely had to destroy the enemy's air power. And it was us, the pilots of the Rabaul Air Corps, who were tasked with the mission. It was from that point onward that Rabaul came to be known as the Airmen's Graveyard.

The Rabaul Air Corps was rapidly depleted after the start of the conflict at Guadalcanal. The sorties continued day after day, and we lost no small number of aircraft each time. The unit that had the highest number of casualties was the medium bomber squadron comprised of Type 1 land-based bombers. I mentioned before how the Americans had dubbed the Type 1s "one-shot lighters" because of their poor defenses, right? The Zeros also had extremely poor defenses, but their exceptional maneuverability and combat prowess made up for their lack of armor. But the Type 1 bombers were horribly slow and defenseless in the face of enemy fighters.

By the fall of 1942, nearly half of the medium bombers launched were failing to return. On some missions, we lost every single one.

The bomber crews seemed to have given up all hope of surviving. And who could blame them? On each mission, there was a higher than fifty percent chance they would be shot down, and the sorties continued on and on and on. All trace of vigor had vanished from their faces, and their bodies gave off an aura of utter exhaustion. Yet they were brave up to the bitter end. They never once complained as they carried out their assigned duties. Just as the kamikaze pilots that came later took off having fully accepted their fate, the bomber crews of Rabaul went into battle with death as the premise.

The Zero fighter squadron also saw losses of one or two planes on each mission. The personal belongings of the pilot left behind in the barracks were collected and sent to his family back in the interior. Some of the men had written wills. Others hadn't. I wrote one just in case, but more than a few felt that preparing for death might actually get them killed in action.

It wasn't immediately after a battle when the pain of losing a comrade was keenest. It was at night, in the mess hall. The fellow pilot that you had breakfast with wasn't there. They always cooked enough meals for everyone for dinner. Our seats weren't assigned, but out of habit we tended to sit in the same places each time. That happens in company meetings, too, doesn't it? People tend to always sit in the same places.

So at night, if there was an empty seat in the mess hall, it meant that the pilot who always sat there hadn't returned to base. It was unbearable if it was the guy next to you. He'd been wisecracking just the day before, or rather that morning at breakfast, but was now gone. When a pilot dies in battle, there is no corpse. After a particularly intense battle, several seats in the mess hall would become empty all at once. That's why we all stopped cracking jokes during dinner.

One day in September during breakfast, FPO2 Higashino, a senior of mine from the Yatabe Air Unit, said loudly, "Just once, I wanna eat a delicious rice cake stuffed with bean jam!"

Upon hearing that, I began to imagine a sweet rice cake and gulped audibly. I hadn't had a single sweet rice pastry since arriving at Rabaul.

"We're risking our lives fighting out here. You'd think they'd at least let us eat sweet rice cakes," PO Higashino joked, and everyone laughed.

That night, there were bean-jam rice cakes lined up on the mess hall tables. The kitchen staff had overheard PO Higashino and had gone all out making rice cakes for us. But PO Higashino, himself, wasn't there for dinner. No one dared to touch his rice cake.

Eventually such scenes became commonplace.

FPO1 Sakai, who had returned from the first battle at Guadalcanal despite severe injuries, ended up returning to the interior blind in one eye. Only three weeks into the fighting, "The Ace of Rabaul" Lieutenant JG Junichi Sasai, second only to FPO1 Sakai, failed to return to base. In September, we lost FPO1 Toraichi Takatsuka, a veteran pilot, and FPO3 Kazushi Uto, an expert dogfighter despite his youth. In October, FPO1 Toshio Ohta, who had performed the formation loops above Port Moresby with POs Sakai and Nishizawa, didn't make it back to base.

The situation was unbelievable. Maybe it would have been understandable if they were new recruits who had arrived just the day before, but week after week these expert pilots, the pride of the navy's aviation corps, were failing to return.

But when you think about it, this was only natural. For days on end we were ordered to make a round trip of over 2,000 kilometers to engage in combat in enemy territory. Once we took off, we were in the cockpit for about seven hours straight, and the whole time death was looking over our shoulders. The fatigue was immense.

We couldn't let our guards down on the way to Guadalcanal, either. The enemy could attack at any time. And upon reaching hostile airspace, we were confronted by their interceptors. Thanks to their superior radar they were able to detect our attack formations in advance and were always in an advantageous position to ambush us. At the time, we suffered a huge gap in radar detection technology.

Engaging in air battles from a disadvantageous position was no cakewalk even for Zeros. Moreover, the Zeros had the very important job of defending the medium bombers. We were unable to fight freely. Plus, our fuel tanks were filled to the brim for the return trip, weighing us down and ruling out nimble maneuvers.

After our bombers completed their run, we evaded the enemy aircraft in hot pursuit to make the long 1,000-kilometer journey home. Sometimes the enemy would be lurking along our return path, so even then we couldn't relax for a second. I'd never experienced such intense physical and mental fatigue. And if you got separated from your formation on the way back, you had to calculate your course with map and compass as you flew.

If your aircraft took a hit during combat, even if it didn't cause you to immediately crash, it often manifested as major damage soon enough. I keep repeating this, but Guadalcanal was 1,000 kilometers away from Rabaul. An airplane is a very delicate piece of machinery. The smallest bit of engine trouble could render it inoperable.

There was also the fuel issue. Like I said, Zeros carried just enough fuel for the round trip to Guadalcanal. If you burned up too much fighting above the island, you didn't have enough left to get back to base. If the fuel tank was shot and leaking, you weren't going to make it back. If you made a navigational error and lost track of your position, same thing. The slightest detour could prove fatal.

Pilots like Saburo Sakai who made it back alone and severely wounded were miracles. They were few and far between.

After a mission, your exhaustion didn't go away after a day or two. Yet before you had the chance to recuperate, you were ordered to sortie again. Three or four times a week wasn't rare. Many airmen, including myself, were going into battle close to our limits. I'm sure many ended up getting shot down thanks to mistakes brought on by sheer fatigue. When Lieutenant Sasai was shot down, he had sortied every day for the previous five days as formation leader. Had the pilots, including Lt. Sasai, been granted enough time to recover, we surely would have had far fewer casualties.

On the days I was not on a mission, I slept. It was Miyabe-san who taught me to do so.

"Izaki, listen carefully. When you have the time, rest. Eat as much as you can, then sleep. Get the maximum amount of rest like you're fighting for it."

I followed Flight Leader Miyabe's instructions to the letter. Whenever I had some free time, I simply slept. It's such a strange thing, but getting sleep is a kind of skill. Once you absolutely decide to, you can fall asleep no matter how noisy or bright the room is.

After the war I started a freight company, and I always told my employees until I was blue in the face to get a good night's sleep and not try to soldier through with willpower, guts, and all that. I'm not sure if that's the only reason for it, but our drivers have caused almost no major accident.

But some of the pilots badmouthed Flight Leader Miyabe behind his back. This was due to his tactics while on escort duty for the medium bombers.

On those missions, we were ordered to protect the bombers even if it meant giving up our own lives. Protect the bombers loaded with deadly ordnance until they reached the enemy's airfield, then ensure the success of their bombardment of the target. That was the duty of the escort fighters, and many highly skilled Zero pilots died protecting bombers.

Meanwhile, even though Flight Leader Miyabe fought off hostile aircraft that attacked the bombers, he would never place his plane in the line of fire to shield the bombers nor allow those of us under his command to do so. Some other pilots thought he was "a weasel" for this. As I was often part of his flight, they thought the same of me, too.

What did I think? That's a tough question to answer.

Zeros had just one seat, while the bombers had seven. If the loss of one life could save seven, then perhaps that's a sacrifice that should be made, tactically speaking. But if we were to lose a superior pilot like Miyabe-san, wouldn't we suffer more casualties eventually? Guess that doesn't really answer your question. And I don't know what Miyabe-san himself thought.

Well, I bet he probably just didn't want to die.

Beginning in the latter half of 1942, the Americans' battle tactics for engaging Zeros totally changed.

They had rarely come after Zeros before then, but from mid-'42 they plainly avoided dogfighting with a Zero. The American fighters stuck to hit-and-runs and two-on-one attacks, and these new tactics bewildered us.

I learned well after the war that the Americans had gotten hold of a relatively intact Zero in July of '42 and had studied it to come up with anti-Zero tactics.

Apparently, that Zero had crash-landed on Akutan Island during the Aleutian Islands Campaign. The pilot had died on impact, and the fuselage was discovered by a U.S. patrol plane.

Until then, the Zero had been a mystery fighter for the Allies. They'd been doing their utmost to capture a Zero fighter but only obtaining the wreckage of downed planes, so it was a godsend for them to discover a near-perfect one.

The Zero was brought back to the mainland where it was thoroughly researched. It was then that the U.S. was able to peel back the veil of secrecy that had cloaked the mystical fighter.

They say American aviation personnel were shaken by the test results. The "Japs" they'd derided as "yellow monkeys" had created a truly fearsome plane. Astonished, they were forced to acknowledge that at that stage, the U.S. did not have a fighter capable of taking on a Zero on equal terms. That answer appears to have been a scary one for them.

But at the same time, their research granted them insight into the Zero's vulnerabilities: the total lack of bulletproof armor, limited diving speed, reduced performance at high altitudes, etc. And so the U.S. military worked out battle tactics that mercilessly exploited the Zero's weaknesses.

The Americans issued "three absolute no-no's" regarding Zeros to all of their pilots: never dogfight a Zero; never perform the same maneuver as a Zero at speeds lower than 300 mph; and never pursue an ascending Zero at low speeds. Those who violated these rules would end up gunned down by a Zero, they were told.

Thus the Americans completely switched to using hit-and-run attacks on us, and their pilots were ordered to number two or more planes for each Zero.

It was thanks to the American forces' ample materiel that they could employ such a method. And we suffered attrition from these new battle tactics that relied on their ability to mass-produce fighters.

While the Americans pressed with ample materiel, they valued the lives of their pilots. I think it was that autumn when a captured American pilot was sent to Rabaul.

An American fighter had been shot down in a dogfight over Guadalcanal, and the pilot was picked up by one of our destroyers and held as a prisoner of war. What he said astounded us. After participating in battle for one week, American pilots were moved to the rear and allowed to fully recuperate before heading back to the front lines. And after a combat deployment lasting several months, they were removed from the front entirely.

When we caught wind of this, we were at a loss for words. Here we were, almost never granted any leave, forced to sortie nearly every day.

We were losing our most seasoned pilots like an overused comb. In fact, they were the first to perish. Inexperienced pilots were at greater risk of getting shot down and wasting precious aircraft, so our veteran pilots were called on first. Our superiors valued the planes more than our lives.

I am repeating myself again, but we had to fly over three hours one way to protect bombers in skies where the enemy lurked in ambush, only to make a three-hour-plus return journey, day in, day out. Our stamina and concentration levels inevitably deteriorated. One mistake and we were done for. It wasn't an easy world where you simply tried not to make the same mistake twice. Just once was all it took. "That single careless pitch was fatal," they sometimes say in pro baseball, and for fighter pilots it was literally fatal.

This is off the subject, but after the war I received quite the shock when I looked up records of German flying aces. At the top was Hartmann with 350 kills, and there were dozen others with over 200 kills each. Such numbers were unthinkable in the Imperial Navy. I think it's that they had the advantage of fighting over Germany. Their terrain greatly favored them. Even if they were shot down, they could parachute down to safety, or make an emergency landing in the case of engine failure. Hartmann had been shot down a number of times but parachuted each time. I believe the fact that they were intercepting was also big. They were going up against incoming hostile aircraft, so they could set up ambushes and didn't have to worry about conserving fuel. We were never given a second chance. Pilots like Tetsuzo Iwamoto and Hiroyoshi Nishizawa who were able to down over a hundred enemy aircraft each even under such circumstances were true masters.

Anyway, the latter half of '42 saw the start of an incredibly tough battle.

Replacements for lost aircraft were slow to arrive, as were fresh pilots to replace the men who died in action. Actually, the latter deficit was truly dire. With aircraft, at least, they could send them and that was that, but veteran pilots were irreplaceable. It took years to nurture expert pilots. Resupplying wasn't a possibility when it came to them.

One time Zeros were deployed to provide a screen for destroyers. I mentioned their "rat transportation" before, but even the speedy destroyers couldn't make the journey to Guadalcanal within nighttime hours. They had to make the approach while the sun was still in the sky, which allowed enemy aircraft to launch from Guadalcanal and attack them. Thus three Zeros were deployed from the base at Buin to provide cover. They protected the airspace over the ships, and a fresh flight of three Zeros relieved them when their fuel started to run low. However, the base at Buin was not equipped for night landings, so the replacement Zeros were to ditch in the ocean near the destroyers. In the rough seas, the three pilots lost their lives—all of them veteran with years of experience.

The crew of the destroyers risked their lives to get food to the starving soldiers on Guadalcanal, and in turn the pilots of Rabaul fought to the death to protect the ships.

The conflict over the tiny island in the South Pacific assumed the aspect of an all-out battle between Japan and the U.S. No matter how many blows we landed on the enemy, they kept sending out fresh forces. It was as if they had unlimited supplies.

I said earlier how I was floored by the sheer number of warships that I had seen anchored at Guadalcanal on my first mission there, but there was another spectacle I'll never forget. In September of 1942, thanks to an air raid and the brave fighting of our Zero pilots, we were able to make vast military gains. We shot down many enemy aircraft and destroyed many more before they could take off. When I glimpsed the airfield at Guadalcanal two days later, however, it had an equal number of planes. The sight made my hair stand on end. I feared we were battling an immortal monster.

That reminds me—of the time Flight Leader Miyabe machine-gunned an American who was parachuting down.

I think it happened on September 20th, two weeks into the Guadalcanal conflict. We were on our way back to Rabaul from an air raid when two Grummans jumped us. We must have been about 100 nautical miles from Guadalcanal. The Grummans abruptly emerged from the clouds above and swooped down to attack our formation. We were utterly taken by surprise. A Zero burst into flames before my eyes.

I immediately dove down to give chase, but they easily shook me off. A Zero, with its limited diving speed, couldn't keep up. *Damn it*, I thought, but there was nothing I could do.

Just then I saw a Zero in hot pursuit of a Grumman. It was Flight Leader Miyabe. He had caught on to the surprise attack and preemptively gone into a dive, hanging below. I saw his machine guns blazing and then the Grumman exploding.

The other Grumman pulled a 180 and went after the flight leader. This seemed to take him completely off-guard. Just when I thought they were headed for a mid-air collision, Flight Leader Miyabe dodged the enemy by a hair. The next instant, the Grumman caught fire. The pilot escaped from the falling aircraft, and I could see his parachute opening.

That did me good. Even so late in the game, I felt new admiration for my flight leader. But what happened next was shocking.

The flight leader's plane wheeled around, aimed its nose towards the escaping pilot, and fired. The bullets tore up the parachute, and the American pilot plummeted toward the sea along with his collapsed parachute.

Seeing this made disgust wash over me. *Why did he have to go and do that?* I thought. Sure, we had lost one of ours, but this was war, and it couldn't be helped. It didn't mean you had to open fire on a defenseless enemy pilot.

Many other aircrew must have witnessed the incident. When we returned to Rabaul, the formation leader immediately confronted Flight Leader Miyabe and yelled, "You bastard, don't you have a shred of samurai mercy?"

None of the other pilots said a word, but their eyes were filled with reproach for my flight leader. And as his wingman, I felt ashamed.

"Why take the life of an enemy when you've shot down his plane?"

"Yes, sir," my flight leader answered.

"We fighter pilots should be samurai. What you did was akin to skewering a fallen warrior with a bamboo spear. Don't ever do that again."

"Yes, sir."

Word of this exchange spread like wildfire through the unit. I overheard many pilots gossiping about what had happened. Most of the remarks amounted to "He's a damn disgrace to all of us."

Flight Seaman 1st Class Koyama, our third man, was also angry. He grumbled, "I don't want to be in his flight anymore."

"Don't talk nonsense," I said. "Do you have no idea how many times he's saved your life?"

"That's got nothing to do with this, Izaki. So you think what he did was right?"

"They killed one of ours right before our eyes. It's only natural to avenge a comrade."

"The flight leader did that by downing the guy's plane. I don't think there was any need to kill the pilot."

I was stumped as to how to respond.

Koyama had for some time been dissatisfied with Flight Leader Miyabe. Being called "weasel" behind his back by some other airmen was taking its toll.

A few days later, I worked up the courage to bring the matter up with the flight leader.

"Sir, there is something I would like to ask you."

"What is it?"

"Why did you shoot that parachute the other day, sir?"

The flight leader looked me right in the eye and said, "To kill the pilot."

To be honest, I was hoping to hear him say that he regretted his action. His words caught me off-balance.

"We are at war. In war, you kill the enemy."

"Yes, sir."

"The Americans have incredible industrial might. They can crank out fighters instantly. What we have to do is kill their pilots."

"Sir, yes sir. But—"

At this point the flight leader yelled, "I think of myself as a murderer!"

"Yes, sir!" I replied without thinking.

"I think the American fighter pilots are murderers, too. With every bomber that goes down, seven Japanese lose their lives. But if a bomber blows up one of their ships, many more American troops die. Their pilots murder our bomber crew to keep that from happening."

"Yes, sir." I had never seen the flight leader shouting like this, and in such a vehement tone.

"I do battle against aircraft, but I believe my true enemies are the pilots. If I could, I'd strafe them as they stood on the ground, rather than fight them in the air!"

"Yes, sir."

"That pilot was very skilled. He figured out our return route and hid patiently in a cloud. And when he pulled a 180, one of his bullets came through my windshield. If the shot had been just a foot in the wrong direction, it would have pierced my torso. He was formidable. Maybe he'd downed dozens of our planes. It was out of sheer luck that I won. If I'd let him return alive, he would have gone on to kill more Japanese. Maybe even myself."

So that's why, I thought. I felt like I'd realized for the first time that we were in a war. He wasn't whitewashing what our battles really were. In the end, we were all just killing each other. In war, the objective is to kill as many enemy soldiers as possible without getting killed yourself.

Even so, I had never seen the flight leader get so worked up before. Seeing him that way, I understood: Flight Leader Miyabe had suffered intense agony even as he opened fire on the parachuting pilot.

There's a surprising sequel to this tale.

That American pilot survived the ordeal—and I met him after the war, in 1970, at the WWII Air Show in St. Louis. Many American, Japanese, and German former fighter pilots were in attendance. The local newspaper gave the memorial ceremony major coverage, calling it a "Grand Reunion," and many Navy and Marine pilots who had served with Guadalcanal's Cactus Air Force were there.

A good number of the American pilots approached me to chat in a friendly manner. This was very odd, but the instant we met, it felt like greeting long-lost friends. I even met an ace who had downed more than twenty Japanese aircraft. In somber terms, he'd killed more than twenty of my compatriots, but for some reason I didn't feel an ounce of hatred or resentment. Perhaps it's true that time heals all wounds. Or perhaps it was because we'd fought like men in the skies. It seems they felt the same way about us.

They all said, "The Zeros' pilots were amazingly good."

I met a former Marine captain called Tony Bailey who had been stationed at Henderson Field in Guadalcanal. Tony was there from 1942 to 1943, meaning he'd fought on the same battlefield, during the same period.

We compared our log books and learned that he and I had fought on the same day seven times. And then we embraced. Isn't that funny?

But Tony had an odd story for me. He said that he had been shot down by a Zero once. He wanted to know if it was my doing by any chance.

When I pressed for details, he said that it had occurred on September 20, 1942. It was indeed the date of one of my missions.

The story blew my mind. That day, he and his wingman had lain in wait in the clouds to ambush Japanese aircraft regrouping on the way home. Just as Tony began his assault, however, a single Zero noticed them and proceeded to take out his wingman. Having witnessed his comrade's demise, Tony chose to strike back rather than flee. But he was fired on head-first, and his engine got hit. So he parachuted away from the falling aircraft.

I remember shivering from head to foot as he spoke.

"Were you that pilot?" he asked.

I shook my head no. Then I said, "I have a question for you, Tony. When you were parachuting down, were you fired on?"

"Yeah!" he exclaimed, spreading his arms wide. "How do you know about that?"

"Because I saw it. I thought you died."

"I thought I was a goner, too. But even with my parachute punctured, I was close enough to the surface and hit it before I could pick up the speed to die from the impact. I was very lucky."

"I'm so glad."

"Do you know who it was that shot at me?"

"It was my flight leader."

"Oh!" he cried out once again. "Is he still alive?"

"No, he died."

"Was he shot down?"

"No, he died in a kamikaze attack."

That instant, Tony's mouth fell open in astonishment. Then he muttered something quietly to himself. The interpreter didn't tell me what, but I could sense his mortification. Suddenly his face crumpled, and he began to weep.

"What was his name?"

"Kyuzo Miyabe."

Tony repeated the syllables to himself a number of times. Then he said, "I'd have loved to meet him."

"Don't you resent him?"

"Why would I resent him?"

"He fired on you as you parachuted down."

"It was war, and perfectly natural. We were still fighting. It's not as though he shot a POW."

Ah, I thought. "He said that you were a formidable pilot. And he clearly agonized over firing at you."

Tony lowered his eyes. "Miyabe was a true ace. I fought against Zeros many more times, but none of the pilots were that good."

"He was a respectable man."

Tony nodded many times as if to say, *I know.*

"Guadalcanal's American pilots were ferocious."

Tony shook his head. "It was only thanks to those Grummans that we won. No fighter was sturdier than a Wildcat. The only reason I'm here today is because of the armor plating behind the cockpit."

"I scored many hits on Grummans, but they kept going for the longest time."

"We were always terrified of Zeros. Back in '42, there weren't that many Japanese aircraft, but all the pilots were competent. Every time we intercepted them our planes ended up riddled with holes. We lost count of how many we had to scrap. It was like a fight where we had to take ten punches for each one we landed. But that one punch made a Zero go up in flames."

He was exactly right.

"Guadalcanal was the birthplace of many flying aces for our side. Me included," Tony said with a mischievous smile. "But all of us experienced being shot down by a Zero. Smith, Carl, Foss, Everton… Almost all of the aces that the Marine Corps boasted were downed at least once by a Zero. Carl, the pilot who took out Junichi Sasai, was himself downed by a Zero. We're only alive because we had the home advantage."

"Ah, Marion Carl, who took out Lieutenant JG Sasai, was shot down by a Zero once too?"

Tony nodded. "You Zero pilots were amazing. That's not just flattery. I know that because I returned from many missions with my fuselage filled with bullet holes. You had some true pilots."

I suddenly felt tears well up and spill down my face. He seemed shocked.

"If my comrades who died in Rabaul's skies could hear what you just said, they'd be overjoyed."

He nodded several times. "I lost many comrades myself. Maybe they're all up in heaven right now, telling jokes to each other."

I'd like to think so, I thought. What a sorrowful history we had— I and these good men whom I now faced had tried to kill one another.

Tony was a cheerful and sunny guy. "I have five grandkids, five!" he said, showing me a photo. I wonder if he's still alive and well…

By the way, Flight Seaman 1st Class Koyama, who had wanted to leave Miyabe Flight, died soon thereafter. One day in October, as our third plane, he ignored the flight leader's orders and pursued the enemy too far in the skies over Guadalcanal. While he managed to take out two Grummans, the mission would prove to be his last.

Our flight got separated from the rest of our formation, and the three of us made to head back towards Rabaul on our own. About an hour into the journey, Koyama pulled up alongside the flight leader and signaled that he was going back. I pulled up to his aircraft, too. Koyama indicated that he was running low on fuel and couldn't make it to base. Therefore he would return to Guadalcanal and conduct a suicide attack.

We fighter pilots—not only fighter pilots, but all IJN aviators, in fact—were taught to hurl ourselves against an enemy warship or base if the condition of our aircraft prevented us from completing the return journey. This was a must if our plane had been damaged over enemy territory. I personally witnessed many occasions where medium bombers damaged in combat crashed into the enemy airfield on Guadalcanal. Back then we thought that was the obvious choice. I, too, was ready to throw myself at one of their ships or their airfield if it came to that.

Thinking back on it now, the kamikaze special attack force may have arisen out of that fertile soil.

But at that moment, watching my comrade gesture that he was going to blow himself up because he didn't have enough fuel, I wondered if there really wasn't anything we could do. Koyama had been a year ahead of me at Yatabe, and we had practically eaten out of the same bowls. He was my closest friend at Rabaul.

I looked over to Flight Leader Miyabe, who was signaling with his hands as well.

We had radios, but they were entirely useless, all static and no words. So pilots had to rely on hand signs to communicate. At Pearl Harbor too, the attack forces used signal flares because they couldn't trust their radios.

How long can you last? Flight Leader Miyabe asked.

About 100 nautical miles, just short of Buin, Koyama responded.

One hundred nautical miles is about 180 kilometers.

Do your best to make it back there, the flight leader signed.

Roger, Koyama replied.

In an attempt to cheer him up, I got in pretty close and tapped his wing with my own. When he noticed, he made a fist as if he was threatening to punch me, and laughed. That made me laugh, too. Isn't it strange how people can laugh at times like that?

The flight leader gradually ascended. Aircraft use less fuel at higher altitudes because there is less resistance, and the air-fuel ratio in the engine is more efficient there. Also, if you run out of fuel at a high altitude, you have that much more of a gliding range. On the other hand, at such altitudes the temperature is very cold, so it's not a comfortable place for pilots to fly. And a rapid ascent will burn up a great deal of fuel.

Fully aware of these issues, the flight leader climbed slowly. He then gave detailed instructions regarding throttle and speed to Koyama, who seemed to be in high spirits. When I smiled at him, he smiled right back.

Our Zeros continued along their course back to Rabaul as if nothing was amiss. After a while, Bougainville Island came into view. *Just a little longer now,* I thought.

We continued the journey until we were about 30 nautical miles from the island. Koyama's Zero, which he'd assumed would fall 100 nautical miles short, was still in the air. Just a little further. If he could fly for another ten minutes, he would make it back alive.

I didn't think that Koyama was going to die. I couldn't believe that a man flying right next to me, smiling so happily, could die. Yet his time was running out.

Just as we were approaching Buin, Koyama's plane went into a descent.

Both the flight leader and I pursued him. Incredibly, even as we were descending, the flight leader didn't stop turning around in the cockpit. He was keeping a keen eye out for enemy aircraft.

On his way down, Koyama's propeller froze. His plane slowly fell and landed on the waves. It bobbed for a while. After a moment, Koyama got out of the cockpit, stood on the wing, and looked skyward. I circled above him, shouting out his name at the top of my lungs.

He must have been shouting, too. I saw him waving his white scarf with his mouth open, a smile on his face.

The nose of Koyama's plane soon dipped down under the waves. The Zero stood on its head, as it were, before starting to sink. Before it submerged completely, Koyama jumped off the wing into the ocean. I had heard that our lifejackets held out for seven hours. I wrapped my rations in my scarf and dropped them down to him.

Reluctant to leave, I kept on circling overhead.

Of course, I couldn't stay forever. My own plane was starting to run low on fuel. I wheeled around in one final, expansive circle, then banked. Koyama saluted from amidst the waves.

I pulled up my nose and departed from the spot. During that time, the flight leader had been waiting slightly overhead. Knowing him, he had probably been keeping an eye out in case any enemy aircraft suddenly appeared.

As soon as we landed at Buin, we alerted them to where Koyama had been forced to splash down. They immediately sent out a rescue seaplane, but it returned an hour later empty-handed. By the time they reached Koyama's last-known location, there'd been no sign of him. Instead, several sharks had been spotted in the area.

The news made me feel like a vise had clamped down on my chest. That Koyama, eaten by sharks? The pain he must have felt. The chagrin.

I recalled my last glimpse of him and how he'd been smiling. He'd fought so hard to keep his plane flying, yet lost his life just before he could reach safety. I couldn't get over it. If we had functioning radios, we could have called ahead for a rescue party. If only our fighters were equipped with telegraph machines like the bombers were... Such thoughts made my immense frustration all the worse.

On my way back to the barracks, my anger suddenly boiled up.

"Flight leader, sir," I said. "Why didn't you let Koyama go back and blow himself up?"

He stopped in his tracks.

"Surely Koyama would have been far happier dying in a blaze of glory than being eaten alive by sharks."

"At that point, there was still a chance he might survive."

"You really thought he might make it?"

"I wasn't sure. But if he kept flying, perhaps he would. If he blew himself up, he would die for sure."

"But there was only the slimmest chance. In which case, I wish he'd been permitted an end befitting a fighter pilot."

Tears of anguish were running down my face. Staring at his wingman, who was throwing a tantrum, the flight leader said, "Death can come at any time. It is important to endeavor to live."

"We won't survive this war anyways. If my plane gets damaged in battle, please allow me to blow myself up."

Flight Leader Miyabe suddenly grabbed me by the lapels. "Izaki!" he shouted. "Stop talking such garbage. You only have one life."

The ferocity of his reaction left me speechless.

"Don't you have family? Aren't there people back home who'll mourn your death? Or are you truly all alone in this world?" His eyes burned with rage. "Answer me, Izaki!"

"I have my mother and father back home in the country."

"Who else?!"

"And a younger brother, sir." As soon as I replied, the image of my five-year-old brother Taichi's face floated up in my mind.

"Wouldn't your family grieve for you if you died?!"

"They would, sir." I could see Taichi bawling. My own eyes filled with tears that signified something other than anguish.

"Then don't die, Izaki. Keep fighting to live no matter how much it pains you."

Flight Leader Miyabe released his grip on my uniform and headed off towards the barracks.

That was the first and last time that the flight leader berated me. His words settled in the deepest recesses of my heart.

I recalled those words a year later.

At that time, I had left Rabaul and was part of the crew of the aircraft carrier *Shokaku*. In 1944, during the Battle of the Philippine Sea, my fuel tank was pierced by a bullet during an intense battle with enemy fighters.

I was lucky that the hit hadn't ignited my fuel, but there was no way I would make it back to the carrier. To begin with, I was already surrounded by enemy aircraft, and they'd shoot me down sooner or later. These were new and powerful fighters, the Grumman F6F Hellcats which were even better than the F4Fs and against which Zeros were no match. Outnumbered to boot, it became increasingly obvious that there was no hope for victory. I'd certainly survived many a hard-fought battle, but I was beginning to think that my luck was running out.

I figured that since I was going to be shot down anyways, I might as well take one of them with me to the other side, and decided to fling myself at an enemy plane.

Suddenly, Flight Leader Miyabe's angry voice reverberated through my mind.

IZAKI!

I could hear his voice clearly.

Do you still not understand?!

At the same moment, I recalled Taichi's face.

The next instant, I went into a nosedive in an attempt to escape. Two Grummans gave chase. Their aircraft were capable of diving at much higher speeds. I made several evasive sharp turns, eventually coming very close to the ocean. I leveled out, skimming the surface as I flew. This prevented the enemy from taking aim at me from above, as they would strike the water. But the Grumman pilots were skilled too, and they stayed right on my tail and fired at me. I yelled, "How about this, then?" and descended until the edge of my propeller just grazed the water. One F6F crashed into the waves. The other stopped trying to stay on my tail and began gaining altitude. I held course, flying just above the ocean's surface. Over the next thirty minutes, the remaining Grumman followed me from overhead, but eventually he gave up, turned around, and flew away. I had finally shaken off all enemy aircraft.

But my luck was close to running out. I was very low on fuel.

I put my plane down on the ocean.

I jumped into the water. I figured I was about 20 nautical miles from Guam. My only hope of survival was to swim to shore. If I swam the wrong way, I would simply die. If my endurance failed me partway, I would die. And I would die if sharks attacked. But I was still alive. I had to fight to keep on living.

Pulling off my pants, I untied my loincloth and let its length trail out behind me in the water. I had been taught that sharks don't attack anything larger than them.

Somehow I swam for nine hours, finally reaching the shores of Guam. My lifejacket had failed at the seven-hour mark, after which I stripped naked and swam the rest of the way through will alone. I was mystified to discover such reserves of strength in myself.

What spurred me on each time I felt like giving up was my brother's face—Taichi crying and calling out, "Big brother! Big brother!"

But I think my true savior was Flight Leader Miyabe.

Let's get back to Rabaul.

I can't forget what the flight leader once said as he ran his hand over a Zero's wing: "I have a grievance against the men who created this aircraft."

I was shocked, since I thought the Zero was the greatest fighter in the world. "I'm sorry to contradict you, sir, but I think the Zero is an incredible fighter. Its flight range alone is—"

"Yes, of course, its range is impressive," he cut me off. "A single-seat fighter with a range of 1,800 nautical miles is unbelievable. It's amazing that it can stay airborne for eight hours straight."

"I think that's an excellent capability, sir."

"I had thought so, too, at one time. The Zero can fly far and wide across the vast Pacific Ocean. How excellent. When I was stationed on an aircraft carrier, I felt confident knowing I was riding a noble steed that could run a thousand miles. But..." He glanced around cautiously, making sure no one else was around before continuing, "That unique capability is what's tormenting us now. We fly out 560 nautical miles, do battle, and then fly back another 560 nautical miles. The only reason they could create such an unrealistic battle plan is the Zero's unique range."

I thought I understood what he was trying to say.

"Sure, it's great that this plane can fly for eight hours straight. But they never bothered to take the pilots into consideration. During those eight hours, a pilot can't let his guard down for even a moment. We're not civilian pilots. To spend eight hours flying in a combat situation never knowing when the enemy might attack is beyond the limits of anyone's normal physical endurance. We're not machines. We are humans, made of flesh and blood. Did the engineers who designed this aircraft never stop and think about the people who would be piloting it?"

I didn't have a response. He was right. Spending eight hours sitting in a cockpit went far beyond the limits of physical endurance. We were making up the difference by sheer force of will.

Now I can look back and see just how correct Miyabe-san was. Even today, when people talk about the Zero they extol its astounding flight range. Yet, precisely that range inspired appallingly reckless operations. After the war, an Air Self-Defense Force instructor told me that a fighter pilot's stamina and concentration lasted only about ninety minutes. If so, we had already lost our physical and mental acuity by the time we arrived at Guadalcanal after a three-hour flight. That instructor was talking about modern jet fighters, but I'm sure the conditions were similar for our propeller-powered Zeros.

I've said it before and I'll say it again: it was a really grueling battle.

The Guadalcanal Campaign ended in February of 1943. The conflict drew to a close after six months of intense fighting that started in August of '42.

Imperial General HQ had given up on recapturing *Ga* Island, and destroyers retrieved the 10,000-odd troops remaining there and retreated. Ship crew who saw the emaciated soldiers from "Starvation Island" were speechless.

The half-year Guadalcanal Campaign's casualties were atrocious. Five thousand troops had died in land battles. Fifteen thousand had died of starvation.

The IJN had also spilled great quantities of blood. Twenty-four warships sunk, 839 aircraft lost, and 2,362 crewmen killed in action. What a massive loss of life for a battle we ultimately lost. And by the time the campaign ended, the seasoned pilots, the jewels of the IJN, had mostly perished.

Looking back now, it was clear at that point that Japan would lose the war. Yet the fight against America would drag on for more than two years.

Even though we had lost Guadalcanal, the Solomon Islands proved to be an important battlefront where American and Japanese forces clashed.

That April, Admiral Isoroku Yamamoto announced Operation *I-Go*, a counteroffensive intended to destroy the enemy's air fleet. The plan was to send what little carrier-based aircraft and aircrew we had left to land bases around Rabaul in order to knock out the enemy's air power in an all-out attack.

Admiral Yamamoto came to Rabaul to helm the operation himself. The Combined Fleet's commander-in-chief deigned to speak directly to those of us on the front lines, raising our spirits.

Operation I-Go was successful, and we managed to complete our objectives in thirteen days instead of the projected fifteen. In exchange for our gains, we lost many more aircraft and crewmen.

But tragedy struck afterwards. The Type 1 land-based attack bomber transporting Admiral Yamamoto was shot down by enemy forces as he traveled from Rabaul to the forward base in Buin. Having broken all of the Japanese military codes they had intercepted, the Americans ambushed the admiral's plane. He had flown with a fighter escort, but the six Zeros were unable to foil the surprise attack launched by the enemy, which had lurked in the clouds.

The death of Admiral Yamamoto dealt an immeasurable blow to the Imperial Navy.

I also want you to know the tragedy that befell the six Zero pilots who'd failed to protect the admiral's aircraft. They were ordered to sortie daily much like they were being punished. In just four months, four of them died in combat, and a fifth lost his right hand. Only one, Flight Chief Petty Officer Shoichi Sugita, survived, having fought like a lion, leaving an impressive record of over a hundred kills. They say his fights were bloodcurdling, as if he were seeking vengeance for Admiral Yamamoto.

But in the final year of the war, he passed away at Kanoya Base in Kyushu. I was told about his last battle after the war had ended. That day, CPO Sugita went to board his fighter in order to ambush incoming fighters, but the enemy was already right on top of them. Ensign Sakai yelled, "It's too late! Get back!" Yes, the very same FPO1 Sakai who had made that miraculous return journey back from Guadalcanal was now an ensign with the 343rd Naval Air Group. Despite Ensign Sakai's attempt to hold him in check, Sugita bravely climbed into his Kawanishi N1K2 fighter and raced down the runway. Just as he took off, though, he was fired on by the enemy aircraft overhead and crashed into the runway.

I was assigned to the aircraft carrier *Shokaku* as part of an attempt to replenish its aircrew after devastating losses sustained from Operation I-Go. The *Shokaku* was a storied vessel that had fought since the attack on Pearl Harbor. She and her sister ship, the *Zuikaku*, were designated as part of the First Carrier Division, the core of the Mobile Task Force. Yet the force had lost its former might and faced a hopeless battle against its increasingly powerful American counterpart.

Flight Leader Miyabe remained at Rabaul. They had renamed the ranks for NCOs on down in November of the previous year, so Flight Petty Officer 1st Class Miyabe was now Flight Chief Petty Officer. Meanwhile, Flight Seaman 1st Class, my rank, became Flight Leading Seaman. At the same time, I was promoted to Flight Petty Officer 2nd Class, that is to say, from a sailor to a non-comm.

Even after the failed campaign to recapture Guadalcanal, Rabaul remained a strategic point in the South Pacific. In fact, it was our most important base, the focus of the enemy's counterstrike. By that time, American attack forces taking off from bases around New Guinea conducted raids on a near-daily basis. As the saying goes, it was hell to leave and hell to stay.

When I received orders to depart from Rabaul and join the crew of the *Shokaku*, I spoke with CPO Miyabe as we gazed out at Mt. Tavurvur.

"Izaki, don't die," he said.

"I won't."

"Even if the carrier sinks, don't just go and blow yourself up."

"As if I would. I've survived Rabaul for over a year. I won't die so soon. Besides, you've saved my life twice now, sir. If I were to give up too easily, that would be an insult to you."

CPO Miyabe laughed.

Just then Tavurvur belched up a great deal of volcanic smoke.

"It's pretty active today," he said.

"Today might be the last time I ever see that volcano."

CPO Miyabe didn't reply. I had always stared at that volcano until I got bored with it, but that day I realized I'd never see it again. So I stared hard, trying to burn its image into my head.

Even now I can close my eyes and see the shape of that mountain. This is getting off-topic a bit, but about fifty years after the war, it erupted, burying the nearby town and the airport in ash. Everything that served as a reminder of those years vanished. It's as if the volcano was trying to tell us to forget the war.

Ever since its conclusion, I've wanted to go back to Rabaul just once, but here I find myself never having had the chance. And, actually, I don't really regret it that much.

"My grandfather was a vassal of the Tokugawa shogunate," CPO Miyabe muttered all of a sudden. "When I was little, he often spoke of the olden days. Whenever he took me to Ueno, he always told me about the Battle of Ueno between the *Shogitai* defectors and the government forces. And his tales weren't limited to just Ueno. My grandfather told me all kinds of stories about the history of various places around Tokyo. It's so strange to think about. The Edo period feels like the world of raconteurs and plays, but back then my grandfather fought with the likes of Saigo Takamori." CPO Miyabe laughed as though bemused. "To my young mind, those tales sounded terrifying. My grandfather bore a scar from a bullet wound he'd received. 'Still have the bullet inside me,' he'd say."

"Oh, wow."

"He'd sure be surprised to learn that now his grandson is fighting the Americans," he laughed. "I wonder if I'll ever see the day where I'll tell stories about this war to my own grandchild. Basking in the sun on the porch, maybe I'd say, 'Your granddad once flew a fighter and fought the Americans'…"

Hearing him say this gave me an odd feeling. I couldn't picture the decades-far future he spoke of. But when I realized that such a day would someday come to pass, I was seized with a strange sensation.

"I wonder what sort of country Japan will be then," I said.

CPO Miyabe got a faraway look in his eyes. "Perhaps they, too, will feel like they're hearing fairytales, just as I did when my grandfather told me about the Edo period."

I tried to imagine it. Sitting on the porch in the early-afternoon sunlight. My grandchild coming up and begging for a story—and me turning to say, *A long time ago, Grandpa fought in a war on a tropical island...*

"I hope it'll have become a peaceful country," I mumbled without thinking, surprising myself. I found it hard to believe that such words had come from my own mouth. To think that I, a fighter pilot who risked my life in battle, fully prepared to die in the war, would say such a thing.

CPO Miyabe gave me a deep nod.

I took off from Rabaul very early the next morning. CPO Miyabe saw me off, waving his hat.

After taking off, I wheeled around once over the airfield. I could see CPO Miyabe yelling out to me, and his lips were forming the words: "Do. Not. Die." That was my final image of him.

I gave him a salute and left Rabaul.

I heard that Miyabe-san died a kamikaze.

I found out the year after the war ended. I cried. They were tears of regret. I thought in earnest that a nation who expended such a wonderful man in a kamikaze mission deserved to fall into ruin.

My sister had been weeping through the latter half of Izaki's story. He stared hard at her, his own eyes brimming with tears.

Then he said quietly, "To tell you the truth, I have terminal cancer."

I nodded.

"Half a year ago the doctors said I had three months left to live. Yet somehow I'm still here." Izaki looked right at us. "Now I know why I lived to see today. I was allowed to live to tell you all that. Miyabe-san said what he did before we parted ways at Rabaul so that I might someday."

Just then, Izaki's own grandson started crying. He wept aloud, completely unconcerned that he was in the presence of strangers. His mother and the nurse kept dabbing their eyes with their handkerchiefs, too.

Izaki gazed out the window at the sky. "Flight leader, your grandchildren have come to see me. They're both absolutely wonderful. Just like you, the lad is a fine young man. Can you see them, flight leader?"

Keiko pressed both hands to her eyes.

Izaki closed his and lay down on the bed. "Sorry, I'm a little tired."

"Are you all right?" asked the nurse, immediately on her feet.

"I'm fine. But I'll rest for a while."

The nurse gave us a meaningful look.

"Thank you very much, sir," I said, rising. But Izaki didn't seem to have heard me. He had wrung out every last drop of strength talking to us.

I wiped my tears away and placed a hand on my sister's shoulder. She nodded silently and stood up.

"He seems a bit tired. I'm going to have him get some rest," the nurse said.

Izaki was already asleep, his face very peaceful. I bowed deeply to Izaki's sleeping figure and left the hospital room.

When we reached the lobby, Suzuko and her son caught up with us.

"That was the first time I've ever heard my father talk about those times."

"I've never heard Grandpa tell such things," her son said, tears still streaming down his cheeks. "Gosh, Grandpa is so mean, never telling his own grandkid his stories. I'd love to have heard all that on a porch."

Tearfully, he turned to his mother.

"Mom. I'm sorry I've been so…"

The end of his sentence was unintelligible. Seeing her son in such a state, Suzuko wept as well.

"This has become a very precious day for us. Thank you both so much," she said, wiping at her face and bowing deeply. "It seems it's thanks to Miyabe-san that my father was able to survive the war and make it home. I was extremely moved by his story. Thank you so very much."

I was totally lost for words. All I could do was bow in return.

I felt ashamed, but I didn't know just why. I was just embarrassed.

What Izaki said at the end—*Just like you, the lad is a fine young man*—had pierced my heart.

My sister was silent the entire time until we left the hospital. I didn't say anything either. We went out onto the street.

After walking for a while, Keiko sighed and said, "Our grandfather was really a magnificent person."

"Definitely," I replied. "I think so, too."

"I wonder if he ever got to meet Mom. Or if he got to see Grandma again."

"I don't know. I can't imagine he was on the front the entire time…"

"Might we find out if we tried?"

I had no idea.

"I'm gonna seriously try," Keiko said.

"Hey, so you weren't serious until now?"

Keiko ignored me.

We parted ways at the entrance to the subway since the trains we needed to take went in opposite directions.

Before we parted, Keiko said, "I think Grandma was very happy to have been so loved by Grandfather Miyabe." I saw her eyes filling with tears once again. But before I could come up with a reply, she said, "See ya," and rushed down the stairs.

I thought over what Keiko had said. Had Grandma really been happy? Was she loved by our grandfather and therefore happy?

I couldn't say.

Chapter 6
The Nude Photo

"How's the research coming along?"

The day after we visited Izaki, my mother suddenly came home at dinnertime. I still hadn't told her what we'd learned about our grandfather. Keiko had asked me not to until we had a better grasp of the full picture. I agreed that we should especially avoid telling her about any criticism of him just yet.

However, I did tell her that I had met with three people in the past two weeks.

"That many! And did any of them remember my father?" she asked, her voice betraying her nervousness.

"Yeah, I learned all sorts of things. We're planning on telling you all the details once we've sorted them out. But Grandfather Miyabe seems to have, um, really loved you and Grandma."

Her eyes lit up with joy.

"Apparently, he told people that he couldn't die, for his wife's sake."

Mom pressed her lips together and looked up at the ceiling.

I continued, "And well, they said that he was a fearsomely skilled pilot who valued his life almost to the point of being cowardly."

"What a contradictory personality."

"What I don't understand is why someone who held his own life so dear joined the Navy in the first place. He even volunteered to become an aviator. Back then, flying was extremely dangerous, and many parents told their sons, 'Anything other than an airman.'"

"I don't think it's weird at all," Mom said, putting her chopsticks aside and looking straight at me. "It was probably just the rashness of youth. When you're a teenager, you've got an adventurous spirit and

155

do all sorts of dangerous things without batting an eye. If anything, it makes me happy to think that a youth like him started to value his life for our sake after getting married. He must have loved my mother and me."

Her voice caught at the end, and I saw a shine in her eyes. I tried to avoid looking at her, focusing instead on stuffing rice into my mouth.

"So the research is still ongoing?"

"Yep, there are several other people who remember him."

"Why, that's amazing."

It sure was. When we'd first started out on this project, I'd figured we'd be lucky to find even one person who remembered Kyuzo Miyabe. Yet we'd already met three. It almost felt like there was some mysterious force at work pulling strings behind the scenes to make things come together.

"Please keep at it," Mom said.

After dinner, I went into my room and thought once again about Grandfather Miyabe. He'd been a total stranger to me just two weeks earlier, but I felt like he was now standing behind me like a shadow, as though I could turn around and catch sight of him.

Three days later, I met up with Keiko. We were heading to Wakayama to visit the home of a former Imperial Navy aviation maintenance chief petty officer. It was a weekday, and Keiko canceled a job just so she could make the trip.

On the flight, I told Keiko what our mother had said a few days ago.

"I see. A man who was a risk-taker in his youth realized he should value his life after he fell in love with Grandma. That's wonderful."

I made a noncommittal noise in reply.

"Does it sound off to you?" she asked me.

"No, I understand how he might have come to value his life once he had Grandma. But him joining the military just because he was young and reckless? I'm not totally convinced."

"Why not?"

"I don't think that fits the image I have of Kyuzo Miyabe. It seems out of character. But maybe that's just my opinion. Heck, maybe he was just a gung-ho military youth."

"You don't want him to have been a gung-ho military youth."

"To be honest about it, no. What Takayama-san from the newspaper said has been snagging at my mind."

Keiko was silent.

"I wonder, was some part of him glad to be sacrificing his life for his country on his final mission as a kamikaze?"

"I doubt it. I don't think he was happy at all," Keiko declared. Then she added in a more subdued tone, "I think Takayama-san has it wrong."

Once we landed at Kansai International Airport, we got on a train to Kokawa Station in Wakayama Prefecture.

As soon as we emerged to the rotary outside, someone called out, "Are you the Saekis? I'm Nagai's son."

This was a well-tanned fifty-something man in work overalls. He had gone out of his way to meet us at the station in his car.

"My father told me about you. Coming all the way from Tokyo, you must be tired," he said with a smile as he drove along. "Yes, come to think of it, my father experienced war. Now he's a doddering old man, but amazingly enough, he fought against America when he was young. He said your grandfather was stationed with him at Rabaul?"

"That's right."

"I don't know how much the old man remembers, but I hope he can tell you some good stories."

"Thank you."

Former Chief Petty Officer Kiyotaka Nagai, Aviation Maintenance, lived in a farmhouse. It was old but fairly large, with a sizable garden out front sporting well-tended trees and shrubs.

Nagai was leaning on a cane, waiting for us.

"You all right, Dad?"

"Why do you ask?" the old man laughed.

"I've gotta do something at the agricultural co-op, so I'm heading out," his son said, then turned to us. "When you're ready to leave, call me on my cell and I'll drive you back to the station."

He drove away, and my sister and I were shown to a large

157

Japanese-style room that faced out south.

"I remember Miyabe-san very well," Nagai said. "We met at Rabaul. I worked on the Zero engines, as part of the ground crew."

Aircraft aren't like cars, where you can just turn a key in the ignition and start moving right away. Planes need constant maintenance. After a fixed number of flight hours, the plane's engine needs to be taken apart and given a full check and tune-up. With the Zeros, we gave their engines a major overhaul after 100 flight hours, I believe.

Rabaul was on a volcanic island, with Mount Hanabuki as we called it fuming all the time. The runway was always covered in ash. When aircraft took off, their wheels kicked up clouds of dust so thick you couldn't open your eyes.

First thing every morning, I used a palm branch to clear off the ash piled on the aircraft's wings. As you can guess, the fine particles also got into the engines, so the tune-ups were a real hassle. If the engines weren't properly maintained, the planes could stall out mid-flight and kill the pilots, so we spared no effort.

There was a leading seaman called Heisuke Kimura who'd enlisted the same year as me. One day, a Zero that he'd serviced ran into engine trouble, had to turn back, and ended up crashing into the ocean, killing the pilot. Kimura committed suicide by disemboweling himself. To be honest, I wouldn't have gone that far myself, but regarding engine maintenance I was the embodiment of seriousness. Even so, occasionally a plane that I was responsible for had to return right after takeoff because of engine problems. That always made me feel like a chump.

I was a mere mechanic, but I felt like I was participating in the battles fought by those Zeros. It pained me whenever one of my planes failed to return from a mission. It felt like I'd lost a child. Of course, it meant a pilot had died, too, so my sorrow was two-fold. I'd worry whether he'd lost a dogfight because the plane wasn't properly maintained or if he'd crashed into the sea on his way back because of engine failure. It'd make my chest ache like I was having a heart attack.

Rare was the day when all the pilots who sortied made it back to base. It was common for pilots who had laughed happily in the morning to have departed this world by nightfall. At first it came as such a shock that my dinner would stick in my throat. But after a while, I got used to it. Casualties were commonplace at Rabaul. Still, when a land-based bomber went down, it took the lives of seven men with it, so that was always sad. The bomber crews always flew as a team and liked to dub themselves the This-or-That Family. They all got along great with each other. And when they died, they went together, as a family. At Rabaul, we lost over a thousand bomber crewmen.

Looking back now, I feel sorry for the airmen. They were ordered to sortie almost every day to do battle at faraway Guadalcanal. The higher-ups were basically saying, "Go die."

They say the General Staff used to joke that airmen were "expendable goods," but I don't think they were kidding. Apparently, they called us maintenance crews "accessory equipment."

But the truth is that I wanted to be an aviator.

They were gallant and carefree and really cut a dashing figure. I would think, "Now that's what a man should be." At the time I was twenty by the old reckoning, only eighteen or nineteen by today's way of counting. I didn't fear death at all. What a brat, huh? Sure, I was afraid of air raids and dying, say, of illness. But getting killed in the skies fighting like a man was, you know, exactly what I wanted. Now I can look back and see how badly mistaken I was, but that's how I felt then. *If only I was in the interior, I could be taking the pilot-in-training test*, I lamented.

But if I had become an airman, I don't think I'd be alive today. So maybe it was for the best that I never got to be one.

This sounds petty, but the airmen got the good food. Compared to the meals we mechanics were served—well, theirs were delicious and nutritious beyond comparison. That made us all very jealous because we ground crew ate really poorly at Rabaul.

One thing the mechanics always looked forward to was hearing the reports of the aircrew returning from missions. I just loved hearing pilots say things like, "Today I shot down an x number of planes." I would always pester them to tell me about what had happened. Some pilots loved to talk, and they'd describe the air battles in great detail, gesturing with their hands for effect. As I listened, my heart would be aflutter with excitement. Listening to their stories made me feel like I was right there in the midst of battle.

Among the aviators there, Miyabe-san was something of an oddball.

How? I don't quite know how to put it, but he didn't seem to have a shred of that old bravado. He spoke politely and had the air of a well-bred salaryman in today's terms. He didn't seem anything like a fighter pilot. No matter how much I pestered him for battle stories, he never told me any.

There were some bad rumors whispered about him, too. Oh, what were they? Actually, I really don't remember it all too well...

No need to hold back? Well, okay, I think I remember hearing words like "coward" being used to describe him.

It's a fact that a number of airmen spoke of him in such a way. To be perfectly honest, I suspected that the rumors probably weren't far off the mark.

By that, I mean he rarely came back from a mission with bullet holes in his aircraft. No matter how skilled the pilot, his ride didn't come back unscathed all of the time. Especially on missions where you were escorting medium bombers, you tended to get hit. If you were guarding bombers, you were ordered to be their shield, literally if need be, so it was very difficult to come back without a single scratch. I think we lost many an excellent pilot thanks to that policy.

Yet Miyabe-san almost always came back with his aircraft totally clean, so at the very least he wasn't catching any bullets for the bombers. Which made me think the rumors might be true.

There was another thing that made me wonder if he was a coward. He never came back out of ammo. It meant he wasn't engaging in air combat all that much.

Of course, not every aviator in the Imperial Navy was a model warrior. There were some that just weren't up to snuff. For example, a pilot might brag on and on that he scored a kill that day, but afterwards, while tuning up his aircraft, I'd discover that his magazines were all full. Wow, you downed an enemy plane without firing a single shot? Was this like judo master Mifune's "air throw"?

It was pretty common for new pilots to come back with full magazines. In other words, they hadn't engaged. Newcomers were terribly nervous, so they couldn't even see the enemy on their first sortie, and participating in air battles simply meant darting around running away. Even so, first-timers were pretty lucky to come back at all. I say that like I was there, but this is all second-hand stuff I got from veteran pilots.

The fighters flown by the officers often came back with full magazines, too. This was because Naval Air Corps formation leaders had able NCO wingmen as bodyguards and often stayed at high altitudes, where they avoided combat and instead "directed" it. Back then, our aircraft radios were practically useless, so frankly, directing combat from on high was a bad joke.

In any case, in working on Miyabe-san's aircraft I came to the conclusion that he didn't do much fighting, that maybe what people said was true and he was extremely good at running away from fights.

And another thing. Well, this was just my personal feeling, but I found him irritating.

That's because he was very meddlesome when it came to airplane maintenance. "It doesn't feel right," he was always telling us ground crew, and what he really meant was, "Redo it." He was particularly sensitive about the engine. No, not just the engine—if he sensed anything was slightly off with the ailerons or some other part, he came to us. I thought maybe that side of him, too, was responsible for him being called a coward.

I mentioned before that standard operating procedure for Zero maintenance was to disassemble and tune their engines after 100 flight hours. But Miyabe-san would often ask for a full overhaul before it had reached 100 hours. He was so sensitive that he picked up on the tiniest change in the sound of his engine. If he detected even the slightest hint that something was off, he'd come right over to the mechanics' area, so there were many among the ground crew who openly despised him.

You know, it might seem like I'm contradicting myself, but Miyabe-san wasn't merely being oversensitive. A fairly high percentage of the times he came to us suggesting something was wrong with his engine, there would, in fact, be something faulty. Of course, this just made the mechanics resent him even more.

Yet he never forgot to express his appreciation to the ground crew. He would always say, "It's thanks to your diligent work that I'll be able to fight to my fullest."

Some badmouthed mechanics liked to mutter behind his back, "What 'to my fullest' when he won't fight at all?"

For some reason, Miyabe-san seemed to favor me. "When you work on my aircraft, I feel at ease, Nagai," he'd say.

Coming from him, it somehow made me very happy. I guess that's what people are like, huh?

To be honest, I was very confident in my skills as a mechanic, and it made me glad to have someone recognize them. In the Imperial Navy, it was very rare for an NCO to praise the work of the rank-and-file. So while I disliked Miyabe-san's cowardice, I liked him as a person.

Working on his plane was actually a breeze. That's because he never pushed it to its limits.

Airplanes are finely crafted machines, so we mechanics can tell right away if one has been handled harshly. For example, if a plane is taken into an excessive dive, the metal of the wings shows wrinkles or thin cracks. Or if the machine guns were continuously fired, they would overheat, resulting in malfunction. In some such cases, bullets from the plane's own guns had struck the propellers. The weapons were designed to fire through the gaps in the propellers, but if the barrels overheated, bullets could fire without being triggered and sometimes hit the propeller.

Miyabe-san's plane, however, always returned in great condition. It was pleasing to a mechanic to see an aircraft handled with such good care. The saying "Fine is the steed that survives intact" aptly described Miyabe-san for better or for worse.

Zeros were good planes, but starting in 1943, their quality began to deteriorate. While the changes were minor, their construction was shoddier than before. But it was something that we noticed because we were mechanics.

Surprisingly, Miyabe-san picked up on it, too.

"Doesn't the new Zeros' quality seem different?" he asked me one day while I was working on an engine.

Privately, I was astonished by his perceptiveness, but I couldn't find it in me to just tell him yes.

"Not particularly, sir," I said, standing at attention.

"Oh. Guess it was just my imagination," he conceded, bowing his head slightly.

I felt bad about my misleading reply. "Well, sir, now that you mention it, they seem to have been a little lenient during the manufacturing process compared to before, but it should in no way impact their flight performance."

"That's reassuring to hear."

"How did you notice, sir?"

Miyabe-san made a dubious face. "I can tell when I fly it."

I was impressed. "This is only a rumor, sir," I said, lowering my voice, "but I hear that we're running low on skilled factory hands. The Army is sending out more and more draft notices, and they're drafting even our best factory workers to become foot soldiers."

"Is that so."

"And the Zeros, as you know, are aircraft designed with an unusually high amount of aerodynamic lines. Not just on the outside, but the interior is made up of many intricate curves. Only the most skilled workers are able to cut such delicate curves with a lathe. Losing such workers must cause operations at the factories to suffer."

"I had no idea the Zeros were being crafted by such experts. Come to think of it, the Zero is indeed a beautiful plane." Miyabe-san touched the wing of the Zero. He whispered, "In war, the battle surely begins in the factories."

"Yes, sir. Getting just one aircraft in the air requires the efforts of many people," I said, deliberately referring to the maintenance crew personnel.

"I agree. The factory workers and the maintenance crew are extremely important."

I felt slightly abashed. "Not that it's my place to say, sir, but I think it's no easy task to replace such highly skilled craftsmen. Back in the interior, they're recruiting middle schoolers and ladies old and young to work in the factories instead. They're just not capable of doing the same work as top-notch factory hands."

"Which means that the manufacturing's only going to get worse from here on out?"

"It's possible, sir. But what scares me more is—" I broke off, instantly regretting what I had started to say.

"Tell me, Nagai."

"The engines, sir," I confessed.

"The engines also require skilled craftsmen, yes?"

"That's true, but I'm concerned about the attrition of the machine tools used to make the engines."

"The machine tools?"

"An engine is precision machinery, so you need machine tools that can accurately cut metal to a hundredth of a millimeter. Without them you can't make a good engine. If the tools wear out, our quality level will undoubtedly decline."

"The equipment isn't made in Japan, I take it."

I nodded in silence. This was something I had learned from an instructor while I was with a maintenance training unit. The instructor had previously worked in a factory that made aircraft engines, and he had high praise for the American-made equipment used there. He would often say, "Japan just doesn't have machine tools quite that good."

Miyabe-san sighed deeply in response. "So we're up against such a country in this war."

"The Sakae engines that power the Zeros are made in Japan, though. We use American equipment, but the people who created the outstanding engine are Japanese. And the Zero that carries the Sakae engine was also built by Japanese hands."

"But I'm sure the Americans will create an even better fighter eventually. If we want to make fighters that can stand up to them, we'll need engines even finer than the Sakaes, won't we?"

"Perhaps, sir. But I don't think even the Americans can readily make such an excellent fighter."

"I hope you're right, Nagai," Miyabe-san said uneasily.

Unfortunately, his fears came true. The Grumman F6F, a fighter that surpassed the Zero, first appeared in the skies over Rabaul in late '43.

Oh, you want to hear about Miyabe-san apart from the fighting? Hmm, well, there wasn't really much at Rabaul aside from the war.

Ah, I know. I just remembered something. He loved to play *go*. How did I ever forget?

We mechanics used to occupy ourselves during down time by playing *hanafuda* cards, *shoji* chess, and *go*. The ground crew's work was busiest immediately before and after sorties. Aside from then, however, we had a fair amount of free time. After lunch, during the afternoon nap time, troops from various crews who fancied *shogi* and *go* would come to play in the shade cast by the eaves of the mechanics' barracks. By '43, though, we would no longer have the time to spare for games.

But this was in the fall of '42. As usual, a number of mechanics were hanging out in front of the barracks playing park *go* when Lieutenant Commander Tsukino of Fleet HQ dropped by. In addition to the aviation units, Rabaul had a naval port that was home to many warships. There was also an Army garrison, so there were quite a lot of infantrymen around.

To us rank-and-file servicemen, a Fleet HQ lieutenant commander was like a deity, so his sudden presence made everyone freeze stiff with tension. But Lt. Cdr. Tsukino ordered us to be at ease, plopped down on a bit of grass, and began to watch the *go* players. After a few rounds, he picked out Chief Petty Officer Hashida, the strongest player amongst the maintenance crew, and asked him, "Mind if I challenge you to a round?"

Hashida was floored. The rest of us were stunned, too. Lower-ranking troops usually didn't even dare to speak to a lieutenant commander. Playing a game of *go* with one was unheard of. I remember Hashida looking around at the rest of us, his face ready to burst into tears.

We all found ourselves holding our breath. We couldn't joke around like we normally did, what with the lieutenant commander right there. We stood at attention even as we watched the games of *go*. Once more he told us to stand at ease.

"Rank doesn't matter when we're playing *go*. But, of course, that only lasts until the air-raid siren sounds."

Everyone laughed at that. In those days, we got occasional

air raids from Port Moresby. As soon as there was a report of incoming enemy aircraft, we ground crew started the engines of the Zeros so they could scramble. If our fighters couldn't launch in time to intercept the enemy, we had to hide them in bunkers, and the same went for any planes that weren't going up.

But just because the lieutenant commander told us to be at ease didn't mean we could bring ourselves to relax. "Well then," he said, looking around at us, "I order all of you to be at ease." And finally everyone sat down on stools or the bare earth.

After all this, you might expect that Tsukino was just a casual player. But that wasn't so. He was extremely strong and dealt a crushing defeat to CPO Hashida, the strongest player among the mechanics.

"Against the real pros, I take a handicap of two stones," the lieutenant commander said. Back then I didn't know just how advanced that meant he was, but after seeing him handily put the screws to Hashida, I could tell he was incredibly skilled.

After that day, the lieutenant commander would occasionally drop by to watch our park *go*. He would always bring steamed buns and such, which delighted us. On most occasions, he would simply watch, a smile on his face.

He was a *go* lover through and through and seemed to hold it in greater esteem than *shogi* chess.

On one occasion he said, "Apparently Admiral Yamamoto likes *shogi* a great deal, but knows nothing of *go*. If he knew how to play *go*, I think this war would've been fought very differently."

This was a very hazardous thing to say. It could easily be assumed that his comparison of *shoji* and *go* was meant as criticism of Admiral Yamamoto.

"If I may inquire, sir, how are *shoji* and *go* different?" someone asked.

"In chess, if you take the king, the game's over. No matter how weak your force is, no matter how badly you're losing, if you cut off the enemy boss's head, you win."

"Yes, sir."

"It's similar to Nobunaga Oda's tiny force of 2,000 troops crushing Yoshimoto Imagawa's 25,000-strong army. Under normal circumstances, 2,000 soldiers could never defeat a force of 25,000.

But take Imagawa's head and it's over. Chess is the same."

"And *go* is different, sir?"

He gave a small nod. "*Go* originated in ancient China. Since a *go* board has 361 points, the Chinese must have used it to augur the coming year, or something of the sort, before it became a war simulation. Surrounding a larger area of the board with one's stones than the opponent—it became a game where you tried to dominate the vast Chinese landmass, so to speak. *Go* is about countries seizing territory from one another."

"Is it also like fighting with the Americans over control of the Pacific?"

"Yes, you could say that. In the Russo-Japanese War, our Combined Fleet destroyed the Baltic Fleet and won the war. Ever since, the Combined Fleet has worked on the assumption that defeating the enemy's king—the main fleet—amounts to victory. But this current war isn't one that can be won by simply taking the enemy's king like in chess."

The unexpected weightiness of the lieutenant commander's words reverberated in our hearts. We were indeed fighting over the Pacific against the Americans and their formidable waves of materiel. It was apparent to all of us that winning would be no easy feat.

I looked at the *go* board before me. After the war I would develop a taste for the game, but at that time I was totally clueless. Even so, looking at the state of the match gave me a strange impression. The black and white stones scattered around the board started looking to me like islands dotting the Pacific Ocean. That odd feeling was what got me started playing *go* after the war.

Lt. Cdr. Tsukino muttered, "What a war Admiral Yamamoto has started."

I'm rambling on at length about this because, as I mentioned, Miyabe-san liked *go*, too, and I watched him play just once. His opponent was none other than Lt. Cdr. Tsukino.

That day, too, the lieutenant commander had dropped by the ground crew barracks to watch the men play *go*. He suddenly caught sight of Miyabe-san and said, "Hey, you bastard, do you play, too?"

The lieutenant commander must have not seen too many

airmen hanging out with mechanics. Yes. Miyabe-san, too, occasionally came over to watch our park *go*.

"I do, sir," he replied.

The lieutenant commander nodded. "All right, want to play a game?"

"Yes, sir. Thank you, sir," Miyabe-san said, bowing deeply and taking a seat. "I'd just like the first move," Miyabe-san said, drawing the black stones toward him.

We were astonished. Even with a handicap of two stones, let alone going first, Hashida, the best among the mechanics, was no match for Lt. Cdr. Tsukino.

But the officer didn't seem offended in the slightest as he reached out for a white stone.

The game began. At first, the lieutenant commander placed his stones quickly, while Miyabe-san's moves were more deliberate.

I wish I could explain exactly what happened on the board, but I only learned the game after the war was over. At that time, I couldn't understand much about the battle unfolding between them. However, sometime around the middle, the lieutenant commander suddenly began to think for a lot longer before placing a stone. Miyabe-san kept placing his at the same steady pace. After his opponent put down a stone, Miyabe-san tarried for a few moments, then slowly picked up a stone and placed it on the board so gently that it barely made a sound. It was nothing like when the mechanics played, slamming the stones loudly onto the board.

The lieutenant commander started letting out groans towards the end. We thought he might be losing. We'd have gone nuts over it if he did. We bore the lieutenant commander no ill will, but the prospect of an NCO besting an officer was incredibly thrilling even if it was just a game. Anticipation swelled among us.

Once the game was over and the tally was taken, Lt. Cdr. Tsukino had won by just one stone.

Everyone was quick to congratulate him on his victory, but at heart we were all very disappointed.

"Thank you very much, sir," Miyabe-san said, bowing low.

"No, no, I should be thanking you," the lieutenant commander replied in a hurry, bowing in return. Then, staring fixedly at the finished game board, he said, "What's your name, bastard?"

Miyabe-san stood up at attention and stated his name and rank.

"FPO1 Miyabe, huh? Might I ask you for a rematch?"

"Of course, sir."

Miyabe-san bowed deeply. The lieutenant commander smiled broadly, and this time he gathered the black stones on his side of the board. Everyone was stunned. You might already know this, but in *go* the better player takes white. Black goes first and has the advantage, and the white player needs to have the skills to overcome that initial disadvantage over the course of the game. Nowadays, in professional matches, the white player receives a handicap of six and a half stones, but back then there were no such rules.

"Oh, I don't know about that, sir," Miyabe-san said, trying to take a black stone.

"No, I'm black." The lieutenant commander stilled Miyabe-san's hand.

Miyabe-san had no choice but to draw the white stones to his side. But what happened next was even more surprising.

Lt. Cdr. Tsukino placed two black stones on the board. "I think even this isn't enough, but allow me one match thus."

"Understood, sir. If you'll suffer me," Miyabe-san agreed.

Lt. Cdr. Tsukino had boasted that he only needed a two-stone handicap against a pro, so for him to place two stones meant that Miyabe-san was practically a pro.

This game progressed differently from the first, with both of them taking their time before placing their stones.

The game ended halfway through when the lieutenant commander suddenly resigned. As I didn't know *go* back then, I had no idea why, but even the better players among the mechanics were cocking their heads, so I guess it seemed abrupt to the entire gallery. But Miyabe-san didn't seem particularly surprised and just silently bowed his head.

"I'm no match for you," the lieutenant commander said. "Petty Officer Miyabe, did you study *go* under an expert?"

"Yes, sir, I studied with Master Kensaku Segoe."

"Master Segoe… Go Seigen's mentor."

Everyone knew the name Go Seigen. A prodigy from China who'd stirred up excitement among *go* aficionados in prewar Japan, he was renowned even outside that world. There was even a *senryu*, a humorous haiku, that went, "Go Seigen, for whom the dancing girls secretly yearn." Dancing girls being young apprentice *geisha*, you see. I believe Go Seigen is still alive today. He's over ninety years old and still studying *go*.

It's only thanks to that day that I remember a name like Kensaku Segoe.

"So, did you intend to become a *go* expert?" Lt. Cdr. Tsukino asked.

"No, sir," Miyabe-san replied. "I had wanted to for a time, but my father forbade it."

"I see." The lieutenant commander didn't ask any more questions, instead picking up the stones on the board. "Thank you. This game was educational for me. If we get a chance for another match, I would like you to school me again."

Miyabe-san bowed deeply.

But they would never play another match.

Two weeks later, Lieutenant Commander Tsukino was transferred to fleet duty and boarded the destroyer *Ayanami*. He went down with her during the Second Naval Battle of Guadalcanal towards the end of that year.

After the lieutenant commander headed back towards the officers' quarters, Miyabe-san sat down on the root of a palm tree some distance from the barracks. I followed and sat down next to him.

"So you used to play *go* for real, PO1 Miyabe."

"My father liked to, and he made me at first. But I really took a shine to it, and by the time I started middle school, I wanted to become a professional player."

"Your father was opposed to it, sir?"

"He was a businessman and wanted me to follow in his footsteps. But I kept studying *go* even though my father objected. I took lessons with Master Segoe in secret. I couldn't afford the tuition, but the master kindly said I didn't need to pay. I took his word at face value."

"He sounds like a wonderful teacher."

"Well, as it turns out, my father had been paying my tuition to Master Segoe the whole time without telling me. My father's love for *go* was second to none, so while he didn't want me to go professional, he must have wanted me to get good at it."

"So what happened?"

"Soon after, he dabbled in stocks and his business went under. He owed a great deal of money to creditors, and our family ended up bankrupt. He said he needed to kill himself in order to satisfy his creditors, and hanged himself."

I realized that Miyabe-san had told me something very grave. Yet he continued to speak in a dispassionate tone.

"Our family that he left behind had a hard time of it. I had to drop out of middle school. My mother fell ill and soon passed away. In just half a year, I became entirely alone in the world. I had no money, no family, and no relations that I could turn to. I didn't know what else to do so I signed up with the Navy."

This was the first I'd heard of Miyabe-san's past.

"Master Segoe said to me, 'I'll look after you, so become my apprentice.' But he wasn't well-off, either, so I declined his offer. I figured if I failed to get into the Navy, I'd become an apprentice in some shop or another."

Incredible. Miyabe-san's no different than me, I thought. Most non-commissioned officers in the Navy were farmers' sons who'd left home to reduce the number of mouths that had to be fed. Unless you were the eldest, the son of a farmer typically had to choose between becoming an apprentice in a city or joining the military. Only a handful of kids were able to attend middle school. And in fact, many Naval Academy students weren't from affluent families, either. Military academies were free, so a good number of smart kids who couldn't afford regular high schools went there instead. Japan was really poor back then, and a class society to an extent that's hard even to imagine today.

Miyabe-san wasn't the younger son of a farmer. But due to family misfortune, like us, he'd had no choice but to join the military.

I, myself, was the third son of a tenant farmer. After graduating from an ordinary primary school, I went to work at a local soy sauce factory. When it went bankrupt, I found myself with nowhere to go. So I enlisted in the Navy. It's probably impossible for young people these days to imagine such a thing, but we joined the military just to keep ourselves fed.

"Are you going to try to become a pro after this war is over, sir?" I asked Miyabe-san.

He laughed. Perhaps he thought it was funny that I was assuming the war was going to end. "Impossible," he said. "I've lost too much precious time to become a professional."

"But if you work hard…"

"Becoming a professional is all about how much you can learn during your teens. I wasn't able to at all, and I'm already twenty-three. Even if the war were to end right now and I studied my head off, I'd never be able to go professional."

"That's a shame, sir."

"Not really," Miyabe-san shrugged off my sympathy. "When I was a kid, trivial things could upset or delight me. As a middle schooler, I really wrestled over whether to attend First Higher School or become a professional *go* player. And when both dreams were shattered, I was extremely distraught. But compared to the deaths of my parents, it was nothing."

He laughed. "Looking back now, even that wasn't such a big deal. We face more terrifying things on a regular basis in this war. Lots of men are dying every day. Just think of how many bereaved family members there are back home."

I couldn't bring myself to voice agreement. Death in battle was considered an honor, a joy. Nobody could publicly express sorrow over such deaths. Miyabe-san's words could quickly get him labeled "un-Japanese."

He noticed my perplexed expression and smiled, a little sadly. After a moment he said, "Do you know what my greatest dream is right now?"

"What is it, sir?"

"To survive this war and go home to my family."

I remember feeling incredibly disappointed by that statement. *Is that really something that an Imperial Navy fighter pilot should say? So the rumors that he's a coward are true,* I thought.

For me back then, "home" and "family" were things that you left behind, and my parents were people who supported my going out into the world. Wanting to go back struck me as unmanly. I hadn't even an inkling of the concept that being a man might mean protecting and taking care of family. I only understood after the war ended, when I was discharged from the service, got married, and set up house. Well, actually, I still didn't quite get it then. It wasn't until I had a child of my own that I saw that my life was not mine alone and that "family" is something a man carries on his back with all his might. Only then did I feel the true weight of Miyabe-san's wish to go back home to his family. How embarrassing.

I'm going to change the subject. Guess what my current favorite activity is?

It's go. We play easy-going games of go at the seniors' club. It's the highlight of my week. Too bad Miyabe-san can't play and teach me once.

Starting in the summer of '43, Rabaul suffered near-daily raids. The Lae airfield, once home to the stalwarts of the Tainan Air Corps, fell into enemy hands, other islands in the area were being recaptured, and Rabaul was in a very precarious position.

And towards the end of 1943, the Grumman F6Fs arrived on the scene. These new fighters were far more powerful than their F4F predecessors.

Once, I saw close up an F6F that had crashed at Rabaul and was dumbstruck. The fuselage was certainly intimidating, but the engine in particular was absolutely massive, a total monster. The impact of the crash had damaged it badly, but the chief mechanic estimated its output at 2,000 horsepower—double that of a Zero. The heavy armament and thick bulletproof armor enabled by that power were impressive.

Under the supervision of the chief mechanic, the whole crew disassembled and studied the engine. Even I could tell that it was very finely crafted. The chief just shook his head and said, "It'll be next to impossible to build such an engine in Japan."

The Grummans weren't the only superior fighters used by the enemy. There was also the Sikorsky, a cutting-edge fighter with a high-power engine and wings that resembled upside-down gulls. We mechanics felt like a new era was upon us.

The pilots in our air corps confirmed that the Americans' latest fighters were indeed excellent. Nevertheless, the Zero fighter pilots of

Rabaul kept bravely facing those sterling enemy aircraft.

At that point, we were no longer trying to invade Guadalcanal like before and mostly intercepting incoming enemy aircraft, so our fighter pilots had the geographical advantage in battle. They could engage in combat without worrying about running out of fuel or bullets. If worse came to worse, they could parachute out and still live. By then most pilots were wearing them into battle.

Even so, it was definitely not an easy situation. The cutting-edge F6Fs and Sikorskys were superior to the Zeros, and their numbers were just overwhelming. Some two hundred would show up for each air raid, and we could launch at most fifty Zeros to intercept them. No matter how many enemy planes we managed to shoot down, it barely seemed to hurt them, while replacement planes, not to mention pilots, were hard for us to come by.

Gradually the Zeros were driven to the brink.

In the span of a month, over half the roster of Zero fighter pilots had changed. Only a handful of the old guard, like Hiroyoshi Nishizawa and Tsutomu Iwai, remained. Nishizawa-san was renowned as the top flying ace in the Imperial Navy, and Iwai-san was a seasoned veteran, too. He was one of the original thirteen pilots back when the Zeros had first come into operation in 1940. He had survived a legendary air battle where they'd shot down all twenty-seven Chinese Air Force planes without suffering a single casualty. In later years, his students at the flight prep academy nicknamed him "the Zero fighter god," and his aerial combat skills were very nearly divine.

Both Nishizawa-san and Iwai-san said that the American fighters weren't so fearsome as long as you dodged their first strike, but only pilots like them could say that. They must have been confident they wouldn't be shot down once they got into a dogfight.

The famous Tetsuzo Iwamoto was also at Rabaul during that period, but he was based at Tobera Airfield, fairly far away from East Airfield where I was stationed. So, regrettably, I never had the chance to meet him though I'd heard he was a master to rival Nishizawa-san.

Another ever-present member of the Rabaul Air Corps was Miyabe-san. Looking back, I realize that it might have taken more than mere cowardice on his part to survive in those skies.

As I said before, starting in the latter half of '43 the Zeros' main mission at Rabaul was interception, and many American aircraft were shot down there.

Most of their pilots parachuted out. Where our Navy's men would try to blow themselves up on an enemy target, the Americans chose to float down to enemy territory. They weren't ashamed at all about becoming POWs. That came as a bit of a surprise because we'd been taught to shun the shame of captivity.

Once, our anti-aircraft artillery unit gunned down a B-17 bomber that had come to raid Rabaul. It crashed at the edge of the airfield. All the crewmembers had bailed, but their altitude was too low for the parachutes to fully deploy so they crashed into the sea or the island and died.

One crewmember, however, had fallen close to the airfield. The ground crew and airmen ran over to where he'd fallen to find he and his parachute had gotten caught in a tree. His body bore no signs of major injury, but he was no longer breathing.

We retrieved the dead pilot from the tree. Just then, someone started shouting and waving something in his hand. He was holding a photograph.

"The guy was carrying this with him into battle!"

He showed the rest of us. It was a photo of a naked white woman. Well, of her from the waist up. Those bared breasts gave me one hell of a shock. Not the fact that an American serviceman had such a thing on him, but the photo itself. I'd never seen one of a naked woman before.

For a brief moment, forgetting that I was on a battlefield, I gazed at the photo of the naked Caucasian woman. The others who had kicked up a fuss at first soon fell into a stony silence as they gazed at the photo too.

As it got passed around, it reached Miyabe-san. Like the others, he stared at it for a while in silence, but then he flipped it over, looked at the reverse side, and studied it intently. I foolishly thought to myself, *Oops, there was another one on the back!*

Miyabe-san slipped the photo into the breast pocket of the dead man's flight suit.

Another airman—I forget his name—reached out to take the

photo, but Miyabe-san yelled, "Leave it!" When the airman ignored him and stuck his hand into the pocket, Miyabe-san punched him. The other airman was stunned, but Miyabe-san seemed even more taken aback by his own action.

"I'm sorry," he said in a teary voice.

"What the hell is your damn problem?!" the airman yelled, his face turning red.

"That photo is of his wife." Miyabe-san's voice was strained. "It said, 'For my love.' So maybe it's his lover. In any case, they should be buried together."

The airman went silent. Miyabe-san apologized to him again, and then walked back to the airfield alone.

I looked at the dead pilot. He was young, not much older than twenty. The face of the woman in the photograph came back to me, vividly. Her expression had been slightly bashful and somewhat tense. She'd likely mustered all the courage she ever had to get the photo taken for her husband, who was going off to battle.

But he had just died on a tiny island in the South Pacific. His young wife, waiting for him to come home, didn't know yet. The photo would be buried along with him in the island's jungles...

I can recall that event very well, even now. I saw many corpses on the front lines, more than I could possibly count. Dead men, both friend and foe, many of whose images have faded. Yet for some reason, that particular day remains a very vivid recollection.

Afterwards, they must have notified his wife back on U.S. soil that her husband was dead. Disrespectful though it may sound, I sometimes wonder if her lovely breasts were ever fondled again. You might think I'm just being lewd, but that's not what it is for me.

How painful it must be to die like that, leaving a loved one behind.

The year after the war ended, I returned to the interior, and someone kindly bothered to find me a spouse. It's not that I was particularly keen on getting married, but my life was in order by then, and I figured I should settle down. She, too, was at an age where she wanted to settle down, which is probably why she agreed to the match. Of course, since we weren't dogs or cats, we must have at least not been turned off by each other at the arranged marriage meeting to decide to go ahead.

176

But I honestly don't remember exactly how I felt.

It wasn't until about a year into our marriage that the first stirrings of love came into the picture.

One night, I was just casually looking at my wife as she mended a tear in my trousers under a bare light bulb. I worked at a post office at the time, delivering mail each day on a bicycle. My wife was sewing like there was no tomorrow, and it was something I'd never paid attention to. I glanced down at the shirt I was wearing. There was a mended seam along the elbow. When I looked at it closely, each stitch looked perfect.

The instant I saw that, I felt an indescribable fondness for her well up. This woman who'd had no relations to take care of her, this woman of plain looks, this woman who mended tears and cooked meals, for me…

I was the first man she had known. Without thinking, I reached out and pulled her close. "Careful!" she let out a little cry. She was worried that her needle might prick my finger. I didn't care, and hugged her to me.

Then, for the first time, I called her by name. She looked surprised since this was so sudden, but bashfully replied, "Yes." Then and there, I fell in love with her.

And what do you think sprang to my mind just then? Don't be shocked—it was the dead American pilot and Miyabe-san putting the photo back into the pocket of his flight suit.

I made love to her. For some reason, like I'd gone mad. Later she told me that I was crying the whole time. I don't remember. She said that I did, so I guess I must have.

Our son was conceived that night. That fellow, who went to pick you up from the station. He might not seem like much, but he's now a town councilman.

How do I know he was conceived then? Because my wife said so. I guess she would be the one to know. My son became just as much of a treasure for me.

There was one other time that I cried upon remembering Miyabe-san. It happened when my son was in primary school, during the annual Sports Day competition. This was back in 1955. My wife and

I were sitting on a mat at the edge of the school's field and cheering on our son. Everyone was having a great time. Both the adults and the kids were laughing happily. Even when my son finished second from last in the footrace and started bawling, it delighted me to no end.

I looked around at the happy scene and was suddenly seized with a strange feeling. I felt like I'd accidentally slipped into another world. It hit me then—the country had been at war just ten years prior.

All the fathers laughing and smiling around me were once soldiers with rifles. They'd fought in China, in Indochina, on islands in the South Pacific. Just a decade ago, these office workers and business-men working hard for the sake of their families had fought for their country, their lives forfeit.

That's when I suddenly remembered Miyabe-san. Had he still been alive, he would have been partaking in a school event with his child just like me. Not a naval airman, not a Zero pilot, but a kind daddy cheering on his daughter as she raced around the schoolyard.

No, not just Miyabe-san. All the men gunned down in charges on Guadalcanal, the ones who fell in the jungles of Imphal, the officers and sailors who went down with the battleship *Yamato*... This joy had been stolen from all the countless men who were lost to that war.

The tears wouldn't stop. My wife got an odd look on her face but said nothing.

I stood up and walked to the edge of the schoolyard. I could still hear the happy shouts and cheers of the children behind me, and I was moved all over again.

I crouched down beside a large elm tree and cried and cried.

My sister had been sniffling by my side for some time by that point. As for me, my whole body was tense.

After a spell of silence, Nagai continued, "Towards the end of '43, it was clear that Rabaul could no longer serve as a military base, and all the pilots were withdrawn. Those of us who remained didn't even have any aircraft to send up against the enemy. Every day we dug tunnels in preparation for the anticipated land battle. But the Americans paid Rabaul no notice and instead headed straightaway to Saipan. Had they decided to attack Rabaul, I don't think I'd be here today. Cut off from the supply lines, the island was forgotten by both sides. I stayed there until the end of the war, but every day was such a struggle..."

It was all I could do to nod. Nagai spoke again.

"Luckily, though, I was allowed to live on. After the war, I worked my fingers to the bone. The joy of coming home alive taught me the joy of civilian work. I'm sure I'm not the only one. I think many men had a heartfelt appreciation of their lives and their work. No, not just men. Women too."

Nagai seemed to be savoring each word he uttered.

"After the war, Japan achieved a wonderful rebirth. But, Saeki-san, I believe that was thanks to all those men who brimmed with joy just to be living, working, and providing for their families. And that happiness came courtesy of the precious blood spilled by men like Miyabe-san."

Nagai wiped tears from his eyes.

My sister and I were both at a loss for words. The room fell silent.

"There's just one thing that really bothers me," Nagai said abruptly.

I asked what that might be.

Nagai folded his arms. "Miyabe-san valued his life above all else. He made choices that allowed him to survive even if it got him branded a coward." He cocked his head slightly. "Why on earth would someone like that volunteer to become a kamikaze? It's odd if you think about it."

Chapter 7
Total Lunacy

After the meeting with Nagai, I read all the books on the Pacific War that I could get my hands on. I wanted to learn how each of those battles had played out.

The more I read, the angrier I became. In most of the battles, the rank-and-file and non-commissioned officers were treated like they were disposable, like so many bullets. The high-ranking officers at Imperial HQ and the General Staff seemed to have never given a single thought to the lives of the troops. The brass never imagined that those infantrymen had families, people they loved. That's why they forbade them from surrendering, forbade them from getting captured, and compelled them to choose suicide and going out in a blaze of glory. Men who had exhausted themselves in battle were essentially ordered to just die.

The morning after Ichiki Expeditionary Force was annihilated at Guadalcanal, there were many wounded men lying on the beach. When American troops approached, the Japanese soldiers, even though they were barely able to move, mustered the last of their strength and fired at the enemy. Those who were out of bullets blew themselves up with hand grenades. The Americans had no choice but to roll over the wounded with their tanks. Such things happened again and again.

Airmen, too, were similarly forced to fight until they died. Pilots were instructed to blow themselves up against their targets if their planes were damaged and they couldn't make it back to base. For the most part, the graduates from the naval aviation training facilities and other programs became a list of war dead.

My grandfather had been a part of a grand generation. They

had fought bravely in the war, then rebuilt a homeland which had been reduced to ashes.

But there were several things I couldn't comprehend regarding the kamikazes. Some books stated they were all volunteers, while others said they had been forced to volunteer. Which had it been for my grandfather?

In any case, it was clear that my grandfather and others had neither the time nor the freedom to enjoy the prime of their lives.

Former Naval Lieutenant Junior Grade Masao Tanigawa was in a nursing home in Okayama Prefecture.

Keiko said she wanted to go with me to meet him. At some point, I had taken the lead for the project, and I was in charge of contacting the veterans' groups.

We traveled to Okayama on the bullet train.

"I've been meaning to tell you," I said as I took my seat, "that I'm planning to turn down Takayama-san's proposal to do a piece about us researching our grandfather."

Keiko nodded.

"He might take offense, but frankly, I don't like the idea of our grandfather being written up in some article."

"He'll understand," Keiko said, a subtle shadow passing over her features.

"Did something happen between you two?"

"Not really," she said, turning to look out the window. I could tell right away that she was lying. Keiko had never been able to mask her feelings, which is why I thought she was unsuited for a career in journalism.

"Did he say something?"

She shrugged in resignation. "He asked me to go out with him with marriage as the premise."

I stared at her in shock. But I couldn't tell from her expression if she was happy or not.

"Did you agree?"

Keiko shook her head. "I asked him to wait a little."

"Are you just teasing him?"

"Of course not. I'm not some kid. But if he's serious about

marrying me, I can't just give him a simple yes or no right away."

"So how do you really feel?"

"He's a good person, and he's supportive about my work. So… I guess I'd be okay with it." I opened my mouth to speak, but she cut me off. "I'm not discussing this anymore!"

"All right," I said. I closed my eyes to try and get some shut-eye, but I found myself oddly agitated by the possibility that my sister might finally get married. I couldn't tell if Takayama was right for Keiko. And anyway, it wasn't my call.

I occasionally cracked an eyelid to look at her, but she spent the whole time staring out the window. It was the profile of a thirty-year-old woman. Even though she's my sister, I thought she looked pretty.

Suddenly, I found myself remembering a scene from eight years ago.

Fujiki was doing his damnedest to comfort a sobbing Keiko. That was the day before Fujiki was to return to his hometown, the week after he'd taken us on that drive to Hakone. I had stopped by Grandpa's office and decided to head up to the roof deck for the first time in a while. There were a good number of potted plants on the roof, and I liked to hang out alone up there.

As I approached the door to the roof, I heard what sounded like a woman crying. Instead of barging through the door I crept over to the window and peered out onto the roof. I saw my sister, crouched down, sobbing. Fujiki stood next to her, a troubled expression on his face. He seemed to be saying something but I couldn't hear him. Each time he spoke, Keiko tearfully shook her head. At first I wondered if he had done something bad to her, but that didn't seem to be the case. Keiko was crying like a child throwing a tantrum. It was the first time I'd ever seen my headstrong sister crying like that. And I had never seen Fujiki wearing such a sorrowful expression, either. I carefully tiptoed back down the stairs.

I don't know what happened between them. But Keiko, who'd been in college at the time, had a crush on Fujiki that was more like a younger girl's.

The nursing home was in the suburbs of Okayama City, in an area lush with greenery right against the mountains. The building was an all-white modern construction, and at first I mistook it for a condominium complex. According to Keiko, who had done some research online, the nursing home charged tens of millions of yen on admittance but then took care of each resident until death.

We went to the office, told them we wanted to see Tanigawa-san, and were shown into a reception space that resembled a small conference room, with a large desk in the center.

After a while, a caretaker appeared pushing an old man in a wheelchair.

"I'm Tanigawa. You'll have to forgive me for staying seated," the old man said.

My sister and I introduced ourselves too.

"It's been years since I've had visitors," he said with a laugh.

The caretaker served us tea. Tanigawa held his teacup tenderly and quietly sipped at the tea.

"I've hardly ever discussed the war with anyone. I'd hate for people to think I was bragging, and I brook no pity or sympathy. Above all, I can't stand answering questions just to satisfy someone's idle curiosity. I'm sure many others who fought in that war feel the same way."

Keiko tried to say something, but Tanigawa motioned for her to be still.

"I know what you're going to say. Perhaps these stories should be passed on. Perhaps that is the duty of those of us who fought in the war. I think those who choose to talk about their wartime experiences are digging up a lot of painful things out of a sense of obligation."

He placed his teacup on the table. "I don't have a lot of time left. I've given much thought to it since my wife passed away, but I still don't know the answer. Perhaps my time will be up before I ever figure this out." Tanigawa looked me in the eye. "But today, I'll tell."

I fought alongside Miyabe as part of the 12th Air Fleet, based in Shanghai, China. He was an incredibly courageous and fearless fighter pilot. His skills in the cockpit were outstanding, and he was extraordinarily good at dogfighting. Once he locked on to an enemy aircraft, he never let go. One of the guys said, "That Miyabe's just like a snapping turtle."

Back then in Shanghai we had loads of masters in our ranks, like Sadaaki Akamatsu, Toshio Kuroiwa, and Kanichi Kashimura. Tetsuzo Iwamoto was also there, but compared to the others he was still wet behind the ears.

I got beaten up by Akamatsu-san fairly often. He was a force of nature born back in the Meiji era, and drinking made him wild. He had so many counts of alcohol-induced violence that he had his good-conduct badge taken away. Akamatsu-san continued to cause trouble even after the war and has a bad reputation, but he was a truly masterful pilot. He claimed 350 kills, which was actually a big fat lie, but his aerial combat skills were the real deal.

Kuroiwa-san was adept at one-on-one dogfights and famously handled a young Saburo Sakai like a child during a mock dogfight. He was discharged before the Pacific War and became a pilot at a private airline, but took on cargo transport duty during the war and died off the coast of the Malay Peninsula in 1944. Had he been flying a fighter instead, I'm sure he wouldn't have gotten shot down.

Kashimura-san was famous for making a return trip on just one wing, believe it or not. In an air battle over Nanchang, he lost one of the wings of his Type 96 carrier-based fighter, yet still managed to dexterously pilot the plane back to base. The newspapers published articles about his feat, and he became the most renowned naval pilot in the nation prior to World War II. His air combat skills were also exemplary, of course. I had him as an opponent in many mock dogfights, but I was no match. Yet, Kashimura-san, too, died in combat at Guadalcanal in 1943.

Even among such incredible pilots, Miyabe could hold his own. Even Akamatsu-san admitted, "He just might be a genius." At the same time, Kuroiwa-san once told him, "Stop being so reckless, or you'll be a goner no matter how many lives you have."

I was neither on particularly good or bad terms with Miyabe. We were the same age and joined the Navy around the same time, but Miyabe had become a trainee pilot before me, so he had more experience in the cockpit. Since he was obviously more skilled as well, there wasn't any sense of rivalry between us. But if you'll allow me to boast about one thing, before the Pacific War began, the overall skill level of us pilot trainees was very high. In my year, only fifty candidates out of eight thousand were accepted, and just over twenty made it to the end and became carrier pilots. We're talking about a 1 in 400 ratio. We were the chosen few, if I do say so myself.

In the spring of 1941, Miyabe and I were recalled to the interior and joined the crew of aircraft carriers. I was assigned to the *Soryu* and he to the *Akagi*, so although we were part of the same fleet and participated in the same operations for six months starting with Pearl Harbor, we never met during that time.

We ran riot, though. We were undefeated everywhere we went. That probably hurt us in the end. The higher-ups took to believing that we'd never lose no matter what.

Even so, we pilots never let down our guard. Why? Because we were always on the front lines of the conflict. While the Mobile Force enjoyed consecutive victories, it was impossible for us not to lose any pilots in the process. No matter how overwhelming the victory, there were always some planes that never made it back. We lost twenty-nine planes even at Pearl Harbor. So we always fought with everything we had. It was our own lives that would end if we got careless in the skies.

At Midway too, our Zero fighters shot down over a hundred enemy land- and carrier-based aircraft. Our losing that battle is on Nagumo, and also Genda.

After Midway, we aviators were summoned back to the interior and quarantined for about a month. We were issued a gag order about the four sunken aircraft carriers. There was a sense that if we dared to say anything, we would be court-martialed. It was so absurd. Why keep the truth from the people? What's worse, apparently the Navy didn't even tell the Army the full truth. I've heard the Army was just baffled that the Navy couldn't wrest control of the seas and skies despite being at an advantage, supposedly, against the Americans.

After that, I was assigned to a newly formed carrier air group. Most of the pilots not boarding a carrier were ordered to Rabaul.

I was part of the crew of the converted aircraft carrier *Hiyo* and participated in the Guadalcanal Campaign. We also fought in the Battle of the Santa Cruz Islands, which pushed us to the limit. We managed to sink the USS *Hornet* after several waves of attacks, but we lost a great number of battle-tested aviators, distinguished bomber aircrew in particular.

In the end, we failed to recapture Guadalcanal. During the half-year-long conflict, the majority of those who had survived Midway perished in the skies above the Solomon Islands. I think we lost about eighty percent of our most seasoned pilots there. It was an irrevocable blunder on the part of the Imperial Navy.

After six months working as a flight instructor in the interior, I was transferred to Kupang Base on Timor in Indonesia. From there, we repeatedly attacked Port Darwin, Australia.

At that point, though, the Americans already had complete hegemony in the southeast Pacific. Rabaul was bearing the brunt of America's counteroffensive. Attacking Australia under such circumstances was a howler.

They called Rabaul the Airmen's Graveyard, but by the latter half of '43, the surviving minority were all highly competent and withstood the American counterstrike quite well. After all, earlier they'd had to make the dangerous long-haul runs from Rabaul to Guadalcanal over 1,000 kilometers away, while now they were on the defense, intercepting incoming attacks. They could ambush the enemy on our own turf, so to speak.

Tetsuzo Iwamoto would have been at Rabaul at the time. Iwamoto-san was a flying ace with more kills than any other pilot in either the Japanese or American air forces in the Pacific theater. I believe he had over two hundred kills in the end.

Hiroyoshi Nishizawa was also there. He was temporarily transferred back to the interior, but I believe he returned to Rabaul in '43. Nishizawa was a master, possibly even better than Iwamoto. The American forces held him in high esteem, and reportedly there's a photo of him hanging in the halls of the U.S. Department of Defense. Pretty unique he was.

Tsutomu Iwai and Sadamu Komachi must have been at Rabaul, too. Komachi was young, but an expert pilot. In any case, while few in number, the pilots remaining there had virtuoso-like skills in the air. Those were not men who would be easily shot down. And Miyabe was amongst them.

Thanks to the efforts of those pilots, Rabaul held out, but they were far outnumbered. And since we had lost mastery over the seas, it became very difficult to replenish supplies, and eventually Rabaul became useless. As such, the Americans no longer needed to try and capture it. In the end, they succeeded in isolating Rabaul and hopping over to Saipan.

The American forces had lunged into our space swinging.

In early '44, I was transferred to the Philippines as part of the aircrew on the carrier *Zuikaku*, which had been deployed since Pearl Harbor. She had sunk the *Lexington* in the Battle of the Coral Sea and the *Hornet* in the South Pacific. She was a blessed warship that had never once suffered damage in battle. I felt lucky to be assigned to her. I figured that so long as I was on board that ship, I just might survive again. Military men are more superstitious than you might think.

Crewmembers were scraped together from disparate bases and assigned to aircraft carriers. That was how I had an unexpected reunion with a certain someone—Miyabe.

It was quite a surprise for both of us. Most of those who had survived the Sino-Japanese war had died in the Pacific, so to encounter an old war buddy at that point was truly thrilling.

Miyabe and I were never all that close before, but being reunited with him filled me with the joy of running into an old, dear friend. He seemed to feel the same way.

"So you're still alive, huh?"

"Glad to see you looking well, Tanigawa-san."

"Knock off the formal crap, we enlisted the same damn year. You're gonna make me feel awkward too. No honorifics."

Miyabe broke into a smile. "All right, Tanigawa."

After ten years of service, we'd both been promoted to flight chief petty officer of the fleet, which meant in the Imperial Navy nomenclature that we were warrant officers. Neither of us discussed the particulars of where or how we'd fought, but we were both fully aware of how great a feat it was to have survived to that point.

"Looks like it'll be an all-out battle," I said.

"It's gonna get real tough."

"We might not make it this time."

Miyabe tightened his lips in reply.

Facing the American Mobile Task Force, which had begun a counteroffensive, was our own Mobile Force of nine aircraft carriers, including the *Shokaku* and the *Zuikaku*, which had been deployed since Midway, and the newly built *Taiho*. Those three were the only "true" aircraft carriers, while the rest, smaller, were often reconstructed merchant ships. The Americans, however, kept pumping out large *Essex*-class carriers one after another. According to aerial observers' reports, the Americans had over a dozen carriers. The gap between our respective military might had stretched into a wide chasm. By the way, those *Essex*-class carriers were ridiculously resilient, and our side never managed to destroy even one of them.

But even when the enemy has the overwhelming advantage, you still have to fight. That's war.

What was heartening was the fact that the aircraft flown by the First Carrier Division comprised of the *Shokaku*, *Zuikaku*, and *Taiho* were all state-of-the-art. The fighters were cutting-edge Zero Model 52s, the dive bombers were the *Suisei* D4Y, and the attack bombers were the *Tenzan* B6N. Since we were at the point where the old Type 99s and Type 97s couldn't compete, having the latest models of aircraft on board was reassuring. The Suisei bombers were said to be faster than the enemy fighter planes, so we had high hopes that they would lend us much-needed striking power.

Moreover, the *Taiho* was a large-scale carrier on par with a 40,000-ton battleship, with an armor-plated flight deck able to withstand a dive-bombing with 500-kilo bombs.

"If we'd had the *Taiho* at Midway, we could've won," I said to Miyabe on the deck of the *Zuikaku* as I gazed at her in the distance. All four of the carriers we'd lost at Midway had been destroyed by 500-kilo bombs.

He laughed. "Haven't you got it backwards? If we hadn't lost at Midway, we'd never have made a powerful carrier like that."

"Yeah, I suppose."

"Personally, I'd rather we had planes with better protection."

I agreed. How many excellent pilots had been killed in action simply because their planes lacked bulletproof armor? I felt it was terribly unfair that a single stray bullet could take your life.

The Grumman F6F Hellcats could take 100 bullets from a 7.7-mm machine gun and still be entirely unfazed. When I was at Kupang Air Base, I once saw the wreckage of a downed Hellcat. I was amazed by how thick the steel plates covering the fuselage were. In particular, the bulletproof armor installed behind the pilot's seat was so thick that a 7.7 mm bullet could never pierce through.

The Americans really value the lives of their pilots, I thought enviously.

When they conducted air raids on us, they were always accompanied by submarines. It was to rescue any pilots that had to make an emergency landing in the water.

When I discussed this with Miyabe, he said, "If fallen pilots can be returned to the front lines, they can teach others lessons about why they failed."

"While if we fail just once, we're dead ducks."

"There's that, and they keep building up their collective experience, grooming more and more seasoned pilots."

"Even as our ranks of veteran pilots grow thin."

By that point, the skills of the American pilots were far and away superior to what they had been at the start of the war. Plus, the cutting-edge Hellcats and Sikorsky fighters surpassed the Zeros in performance. They flew those excellent aircraft in formation, skillfully coordinated by good radio communication. And to top it off, their sheer numbers overwhelmed us.

On our side, most of our pilots were young, with less than two years' experience. There was no way to cover up such a decline in skill. This became glaringly obvious when I watched them practice carrier takeoffs and landings off the coast of Tawi-Tawi in the Philippines. One after another, they failed to land on the carrier deck. Some crashed into the ship's stern, some flipped over on the flight deck, while others failed to rein in their momentum and skidded right off the bow. With every takeoff and landing practice, we lost a considerable number of aircraft and pilots—more than fifty of them all told. Just through landing training, we lost the equivalent of one carrier's fighting force.

"What the hell are we doing?" I asked Miyabe one time when

we found ourselves alone in the crew lounge. "How on earth are we supposed to wage war with kids who can't even nail down a carrier landing?"

He sat down in a chair and folded his arms. "They must've shortened the training period and sent inexperienced recruits right into combat. I recently asked a young pilot how many flight hours he had, and he said a hundred. You can't land on a carrier with just 100 hours under your belt."

"Hell, they can barely keep a plane in the air with just 100 hours." He nodded, and I continued, "By the time we struck Pearl Harbor, we all had over 1,000 hours each."

Miyabe closed his eyes. "So basically that means the First Carrier Division isn't anything near what it used to be."

It wasn't long before the carrier takeoff and landing drills were halted. It was clear that we'd only continue to lose more aircraft and pilots. Also, enemy submarines patrolled the waters just outside Tawi-Tawi's bay, so training there was extremely dangerous. While on the lookout for subs, warships followed a zigzag course through the waters, but during aircraft takeoffs and landings, carriers had to sail straight into the wind, making them an excellent target for submarine attacks.

Our fleet of destroyers were sorely lacking in anti-submarine capabilities. They were unable to halt the enemy rampaging under the waves. At times, the destroyers would be sunk by the subs they were supposed to be protecting us from. That's like the mice getting the cat. It was thanks to the other side's superior underwater equipment, their sonar and radar. Basically, it was a technological gap. And Command simply chose not to further expose their precious carriers to risk for the sake of mere landing drills.

The night of the decision to halt them, I asked Miyabe to join me on the flight deck.

"Halt their training, and then what?" I asked him.

A warm breeze swept across the deck. It was a typical evening in the tropics. We sat down on the deck.

Miyabe replied, "The brass probably thinks being able to take off will do. That's actually not too difficult, even for the new guys."

"Then the initial attack will be our only one."

He nodded. "They're betting everything on a single strike."

That put me into a black mood. Halting the drills was a severe blow to the aircrew. Training was the best way to maintain our edge. It's just like in sports, you see?

We were facing a decisive battle but couldn't fly for nearly a month.

In June of 1944, the Americans at last launched their fierce attack on Saipan.

Apparently this development had been wholly unforeseen by the General Staff. Our military had established many bases on Saipan and the islands in the Guam sector and had an impressive aggregate number of aircraft. The brass obviously assumed the Americans would never dare to attack. This could only be explained as negligence on their part.

The American Mobile Task Force sent an incredible number of aircraft to attack these bases, crushing our land-based aviation units and practically annihilating them.

But Saipan was one island that our military had to defend at all costs. We had captured Guadalcanal and Rabaul only after the war had begun, but Saipan was different. It had been under Japanese rule since before the war, and there were entire towns there where many civilian nationals lived. And if the Americans captured Saipan, their state-of-the-art B-29 bombers would be within striking distance of the Japanese mainland. That's why Saipan was within our military's critical defense zone.

As soon as the commander-in-chief of the Combined Fleet learned that the Americans had landed on Saipan, he immediately implemented Operation *A-Go*, a battle plan intended to wipe out the American Mobile Task Force.

The First Mobile Fleet, under the command of Vice Admiral Jisaburo Ozawa, headed to Saipan from Tawi-Tawi. Day after day, we sent out numerous scouting planes. This was in response to lessons learned from our defeat at Midway.

On the 18th, our recon planes finally discovered the American task force. It was nearly sundown by the time the discovery was made, and they were still too far off, so the attack had to wait for the following day.

By the next morning, the distance between our fleets had shrunk to 400 nautical miles. At that point, the Americans hadn't noticed our presence yet. This was a great chance for us. But actually, we wouldn't have minded even if they had discovered us, because our planes had longer flight ranges than American aircraft, and we could launch attacks from a greater distance. It was like we were a boxer with a longer reach.

This was Fleet Commander Ozawa's famous "out-of-range" battle tactic. If we launched attacks from a distance beyond the reach of the American forces, there was zero risk.

This sounds like an ideal strategy, but in the real world things are never so rosy. While it was true that there was no risk for our fleet, the same could not be said for the aviation units. It's no easy task for pilots to carry out an attack after flying 400 nautical miles. Four hundred nautical miles is about 700 kilometers. It would take over two hours flying over the ocean to reach enemy airspace. It would be one thing if the target was an unmoving land base like Hawaii, but the enemy was a speedy task force that could move up to 100 kilometers by the time our planes reached them. Which meant it wasn't a given that we would actually come upon them. Even though our most seasoned pilots led the way, if we chanced upon an ambush that broke up our formations, many of the aircraft would be incapable of reaching the enemy's fleet.

To make matters worse, most of the crew in the attack forces were rank novices. Sure, their morale was high. They had a far more powerful thirst for battle than their battle-weary senior counterparts. But spiritedness alone is meaningless once you're up in the air. There, the aircraft's performance limitations and the pilot's skills are all that matter.

When the attack was successfully over, crew who weren't confident about getting back to the carrier were to proceed to the land base on Guam to resupply. The orders were to then go back and attack the Americans again.

At any rate, the attack force launched.

The main mast of the flagship *Taiho* had run up the "Z" flag the day before. This was a signal flag of special significance that Combined

Fleet Commander-in-Chief Heihachiro Togo had used at the Battle of Tsushima during the Russo-Japanese War.

The Zebra flag, which hadn't been raised since the attack on Pearl Harbor, fluttered and flapped in the wind. "The fate of the Empire depends on this battle," indeed. The sight of it was bracing to the crew.

Early in the morning of June 19th, the Third Carrier Division launched the first attack wave. Next, the First Carrier Division launched a second attack wave. I sortied with the second wave, as part of the fighter escort for the Suisei bombers.

That day, our mobile force launched six attack waves with an impressive total of 400 aircraft. There had never been such a large attack force. This was on a scale even greater than that of Pearl Harbor. And all the aircraft deployed were state-of-the-art, from the Zero Model 52 to the Suisei dive bombers and Tenzan attack bombers.

But sadly, the pilots at the controls of those aircraft weren't the ones who had attacked Pearl Harbor. This became evident right after takeoff. Flying in a beautiful close-knit formation was beyond them! This was no longer the IJN air corps of the old days.

So how did it turn out? Exactly as you might imagine.

The Americans' advanced radar detected our incoming attack force while we were still 100 nautical miles out. What's surprising is that they could also gauge our altitude. I only learned all this after the war, mind you. To what extent Fleet Commander Ozawa and his staff were aware of the Americans' radar capabilities, I do not know. I'm afraid they had no idea. Meanwhile, we aircrew learned the hard way.

The Americans had launched all of their mobile task force's fighters to ambush our attack waves. While we thought we'd be dealing a surprise blow courtesy of our out-of-range tactic, we were the ones who suffered a nasty surprise instead.

Our formations were attacked from a higher altitude by more than twice as many enemy fighters. I managed to just barely escape the onslaught, but in the blink of an eye my wingmen became balls of flame and fell from the sky. I tried to lock onto a Grumman, but as soon as I tailed one, another came up right on my six-o'clock and fired at me. Taking down enemy aircraft was out of the question.

Our planes continued to drop like flies. The younger, less proficient pilots weren't even able to take evasive maneuvers, and one after another they fell prey to the enemy fighters.

You know what the American troops called this battle later? The Great Marianas Turkey Shoot. I don't really know what kind of bird a turkey is, but apparently it's so slow that even a child can shoot one. For the American fighter pilots, our aircraft were as easy to hit as turkeys that day.

While I had managed to elude the first bunch of enemy planes, there was a second one right behind them. The Americans had deployed multiple layers of fighters. In the end, most of our attack planes were shot down. Only a handful were able to break through the lines of interceptors.

Somehow, though, I was able to safeguard several Suisei dive bombers, and we made it to the skies above the American mobile task force. The Suiseis were fast, which likely helped them break through, but the Tenzans were slow, and I think most ended up getting shot down.

When we arrived above their fleet, I shivered. There was a whole herd of large-sized aircraft carriers, close to ten of them. The IJN had deployed only three fleet carriers, and here the Americans had three times as many. A difference in reach was totally meaningless. It was like a flyweight boxer trying to take on a heavyweight.

The American fleet was protected by a thick screen of innumerable aircraft. I gave up. I figured that my luck was about to run out. If I was going to die anyway, I hoped to help at least one of our bombers score a hit even if it meant sacrificing my own aircraft.

I took on the enemy fighters, very nearly hurling myself at them as they tried to attack the Suisei bombers. Perhaps it was my sheer fighting spirit that kept their machine-gun fire from touching the Suiseis. I clung fast by the bombers, driving away enemy fighters. I was totally prepared to put myself in the line of fire.

I saw the bombers nose down into the dive. The fleet sent up a furious volley of anti-aircraft fire. I had never before seen such an intense barrage. The sky turned black. The Suiseis dove down bravely through it all. *Hang in there*, I prayed. *Even if you're no more than a preying mantis against them, deal the enemy at least one slash! Even if it won't do a thing, land just one blow!*

But in the next instant, I witnessed something unbelievable. One after another, the Suisei bombers began spouting flames and falling from the sky. It was as though the Americans' anti-aircraft artillery were sniping at the Suiseis with scoped rifles. I stared in blank amazement at the falling bombers.

In the end, they'd done hardly anything to the enemy. I didn't know what to think anymore. A Hellcat approached me while I was in that state. I escaped by pure instinct. I was totally incapable of striking back, and it was all I could do to protect my own hide. They were like cats toying with mice, pouncing on me again and again. I would dodge one only to encounter another. I was fully occupied just evading enemy fire.

At long last, I escaped the airspace above the American ships, and no Hellcats gave chase. They had probably been tasked to defend the ships, first and foremost. Had they doggedly pursued me, I very likely would have been killed.

I decided to return to my home carrier. There wasn't a single friendly aircraft in sight. I considered heading to the base on Guam, but finally resolved to go back to the *Zuikaku*. This decision saved my life. The third attack wave that sortied after me failed to discover the enemy fleet, and instead of returning to their carriers flew to Guam, where they were ambushed by American fighters that shot down almost all of them.

Upon returning, I saw only one of our aircraft carriers. Both the *Taiho* and the *Shokaku* were nowhere to be seen, even though the enemy's attack force shouldn't have reached them yet.

I landed on the *Zuikaku* and headed to the flight captain to give my report. I stated that due to the Americans' interception most of the attack force was lost, and that as far as I could tell, the enemy had suffered almost no damage.

"Is that so," the flight captain said, then fell silent.

I asked a sailor as to the status of the *Taiho* and the *Shokaku*. He told me that American submarines had torpedoed and sunk both carriers. I felt all the strength drain from my whole body all at once. While we had devoted all our air power to a battle to no avail, two of our carriers had gone down…

A crushing defeat, I thought.

After a while, a lone Zero returned. It was Miyabe. He came back alone, without his wingmen. That was a given; no flight could have come back intact from that battle. His aircraft had suffered damage, sporting several bullet holes. A thoroughly exhausted Miyabe climbed out of the cockpit.

After he turned in his report, he saw me, which seemed to surprise him. His eyes seemed to say, "Good for you to have survived."

We went into the crew lounge. It was empty. Most of those who had sortied that day hadn't returned.

"We lost a hell of a lot of men," I said.

"Radar, probably. Seems like their radar technology has improved by leaps and bounds."

"Did you make it to their location?"

Miyabe nodded.

"Then you saw it?"

He paused and then said, "I did."

"Did you include it in your debriefing?"

"I did, but the flight captain and the staff didn't seem all that interested."

"Same with me. I tried to explain at length, but they just refused to pay it any particular attention."

"You have to see it to believe it."

"What on earth was that?"

Miyabe shook his head. "I don't know, but I do know that it's absolutely formidable. It might mean that we can't sink their carriers anymore."

We were discussing the Americans' anti-aircraft artillery, which had demonstrated an astoundingly high hit ratio against the bombers. It almost defied belief. I wondered if they hadn't developed some outrageous new weapon.

Our speculations later proved to be correct.

The Americans' secret new weapon was something called a "proximity fuze." Nicknamed "magic fuzes" or "VT fuzes," these were small radars in the nose of a shell. When an aircraft passed within a couple dozen meters of the shell, the fuze got tripped and detonated. It was a fearsome weapon.

This, too, I only learned years after the war had ended. Apparently, the U.S. military spent as much money developing these VT fuzes as they did on the Manhattan Project. The Manhattan Project produced the atomic bomb.

When I learned this, I realized that the basic thought processes of the American and Japanese militaries were completely different. VT fuzes were essentially defensive armaments, designed to protect their own side from enemy attacks. Such an approach would never have occurred to our military planners, who had focused purely on developing weapons that could be used in attacks on the enemy. The prime example of this way of thinking was our fighter planes: extremely long flight ranges, excellent air combat capabilities, and powerful 20-mm cannons, but totally deficient in armor...

The ideologies were fundamentally different. From the beginning, a complete contempt for human life permeated the Japanese military's thinking. That definitely had an impact on the kamikaze squadrons that were used in the twilight of the war.

At the time, the Imperial forces were totally unaware of the VT fuzes. Yet the Suisei bomber crew that survived the battle had instinctively figured out the mechanism.

"They explode right before your eyes. It seems like the shells are somehow made to blow up right when they get close to us," one of the Suisei bomber pilots who made it back told me. He'd served as a carrier-based bomber pilot since Pearl Harbor, which lent weight to his opinion.

But no matter what the pilots on the front lines said, the staff officers refused to believe in the existence of these mysterious new weapons and simply assumed that the enemy had stepped up their AA fire. However, even if they had acknowledged the existence of the VT fuzes, I don't think they'd have been able to work out effective countermeasures.

On the very first day of the Battle of the Philippine Sea, into which the Imperial Navy had poured its entire might, we lost over 300 aircraft and two treasured aircraft carriers. In mere hours, our Navy's fighting power had been nearly obliterated, while the Americans suffered negligible casualties.

On the second day, it was the American task force's turn to attack us as we tried to flee. An astonishing number of carrier-based aircraft descended upon our retreating fleet. I sortied as part of the intercepting force, but we were totally outnumbered and it was pointless. It took everything I had just to avoid getting shot down by the enemy escort. A dozen or so fighters could never hope to fend off hundreds of enemy bombers.

The *Zuikaku* was struck by a bomb and received minor damage. That was the first time that particular carrier was hit since the beginning of the war. Yet we somehow managed to escape after losing just the converted carrier *Hiyo* and two refueling ships.

I was forced to ditch my plane in the ocean and was rescued by a destroyer. I assumed Miyabe was rescued in a similar fashion.

Thus, in a battle where we'd staked everything, the Combined Fleet lost most of its military might, leaving it incapable of striking back at the troops that had landed on Saipan.

After that, most of the Imperial Army stationed on Saipan was annihilated, and many civilians died as well. Hundreds of Japanese threw themselves off of Banzai Cliff and plunged to their deaths. After the war, when I saw film footage taken by American troops showing all these Japanese jumping one after another from the cliff's edge, I wept uncontrollably. *Please forgive me*, I apologized over and over.

After returning to the interior from the Mariana Islands, the *Zuikaku* was docked for repairs. We aviators were temporarily transferred to various military bases for the time being. They granted us a short leave of absence. I don't remember which unit Miyabe was reassigned to after that, but I do remember the last conversation we had before our parting.

"I'll be seeing my family for the first time in a while," he said. "What are your plans, Tanigawa?"

"I've only got three days' leave, so if I go all the way home to Okayama that'll eat up all my time. I'll go back there when I get a longer break."

Miyabe thought quietly for a moment then said, "Is there no one you yearn to see?"

"You mean a woman?"

He nodded.

"Nah. The only women I can meet are comfort women."

"No one in your hometown?"

"Nope," I laughed. But then the face of a young girl unexpectedly sprang to mind. "Actually, there was one. A childhood friend. It was just an innocent thing, when we were kids. I'm sure she's long since married."

I felt a touch of melancholy. I was twenty-five at the time and had spent the last ten years in the Navy. I didn't know anything outside the world of the military. I had known no other adolescence.

That was all there was to my conversation with Miyabe, but it was the conversation that would change my life.

I was an instructor for a while at Kisarazu Base near Tokyo, but come autumn I was sent back to the front. It was to the Philippines.

When I received the orders, I was also granted a week-long leave thanks to the transport ship's schedule. I went back home for the first time in a long while. The townspeople gave me a warm welcome. They had considered me a local hero ever since I had participated in the attack on Pearl Harbor two years prior.

They asked me many questions about the status of the war, which put me in a bad spot. The official announcements made by IGHQ were utter baloney. But the townsfolk believed it, and tried to get me to tell them sensational stories. In the interior there was a surprising lack of urgency. While there were shortages of a fair number of mundane commodities, there hadn't yet been any attacks on the mainland, so the civilians on the home front weren't feeling the terror of war.

I couldn't spill my guts to these people about what had really happened at the Mariana Islands. Besides, I'd been ordered not to speak a word concerning our sea war situation during my leave.

Among the women who came to help out was a beautiful lady. It was Kae Shimada, whom I had known in primary school, the very woman I had told Miyabe about.

"Masao-san, you've become such a fine man," she said.

"You're too kind," I barely mustered a reply. I was still a virgin then. I had been invited many times to go to the military brothels, but the truth was that I'd never gone.

"Hard to believe you've become a hero of the nation, Masao-san," she said with a giggle.

"I can't believe it myself," I agreed solemnly, which made her laugh all the harder.

"There was that time when I made you cry."

"I remember."

That had been in the first grade. Kae had been a strong-willed girl, and one day we'd gotten into a quarrel over something trivial. She'd slapped me about the head until I cried. For a long while after, the memory of that incident made me feel humiliated. So it was very easy to recall.

"But now you're off shooting down American and British fighters."

"Yes."

"Thank you very much for all your hard work on behalf of the country." Kae placed her hands on the floor and bowed deeply. Then she left the parlor and didn't return.

All during the banquet, my head swam with thoughts of her. Maybe the alcohol was to blame. Towards the end of the evening I turned to the village mayor and asked, "Is Kae Shimada still single?"

"You've taken a liking to her, huh? A spinster, but the village beauty."

"Is she spoken for?"

"Not that I know of. Why, you want her?"

"Yes," I blurted out.

"All right, then," the mayor replied. That was all that was said.

The next day, while I was relaxing at home, the mayor and Kae's father came for a visit. They spoke to my father and elder brother, and it was decided on the spot that Kae and I would be wed. The rest progressed quickly, and a date was set two days from then for a private ceremony. I was scheduled to return to my post in three days.

I couldn't ask them at that point to please wait a minute. I made up my mind to go through with it.

Two days later, we were wed at my home. Kae and I hadn't been able to speak privately since the night of the banquet. By the time the ceremony was over and we were alone, it was very late.

"Please take good care of me," Kae said, giving me a deep bow.

"I ask the same of you," I replied, meekly lowering my head. I was nervous. I had never been so nervous, not even in the midst of battle. But I mustered up my resolve and said, "There's something I need to tell you, Kae-san."

"Yes."

"Imperial HQ says that Japan is winning the war, but in fact, we're losing."

Kae simply nodded. Her reaction made me realize that the village folk did not, in fact, believe the official announcements. Even without suffering air raids, they had sensed the worsening military situation.

"I return to my unit tomorrow. I don't know where they'll send me next. But if I'm sent back to the front, there's a chance I won't make it back alive."

"Yes."

"It's wrong of me to say this after we've gotten married, but I'm afraid I've done something unforgivable to you, all because I made a careless comment to the mayor. If I die in battle, you'll become a widow. If that happens, don't worry about my family and find yourself a new man."

"Won't you come home to me?"

"I can't make such a promise. So I don't want to take your virginity. That would be better for you in case I don't return and you have to remarry."

Kae listened carefully to every word. After a long while she said, "Why did you say that you wanted me?"

"Because I like you."

"Do you know why I agreed to marry you, Masao-san?"

"Why?"

"Because I like you too."

When she said this, I thought I'd happily die for Kae's sake.

I made love to her that night.

Now, what a bore I am to speak of this. Forgive me.

The next day, seen off by a crowd, I left Kae and my village. Three days after that, I left Japan once again.

The Americans' next target was Leyte Island in the Philippines. The Combined Fleet developed a plan for striking at the American forces trying to land on Leyte. It was codenamed *Shou-ichi-go*: Operation Victory One.

I was stationed at Mabalacat Base on Luzon.

Mabalacat, what a hateful sounding name. Well, the place's name itself shouldn't be faulted. But even now, just uttering the name of that town casts a dark shadow over my heart.

One evening sometime after I had arrived there, all aircrew from NCOs on down were assembled in front of the command center. The executive officer addressed us.

"There is only one reason we've gathered you all here. Japan is currently facing an unprecedented crisis. I am forced to admit that the current military situation is extremely severe. For that reason, we have decided to deal the Americans a death blow using special attacks."

I knew immediately what he was referring to. He was going to make us hurl ourselves at the enemy.

"However, as these attacks mean certain death, we have decided to only use volunteers for these units."

Tension filled the air. A heavy, stifling silence settled over the command center's environs.

"Volunteers, step forward!" barked an officer standing beside the XO.

Nobody moved. It wasn't that kind of proposal. The officer had said in effect, *Those who wish to die, speak up right now!* No one could possibly give an immediate reply. No matter how prepared we were to die in battle, this was an entirely different matter.

"Will you or will you not volunteer?!" another officer bellowed.

Several men stepped forward at that moment. Immediately, everyone else stepped forward, too, as if to keep pace. Before I'd even realized it, I, too, had conformed.

After the war, I read a book that had an account of this moment. It stated that when the officer asked for volunteers, we advanced one and all, begging to become a kamikaze. That stuff is all lies!

The truth was that it was an order made to sound like it wasn't an order. They didn't give us a chance to think about it at all. Out of habit from years of conditioning in the military, we reflexively submitted to our superior officers, more or less.

It was only after we returned to our barracks that the gravity of it sank into us. My first thoughts were of Kae. I thought I was going to be less than true to her. Kae's face came to me, not covered in tears, but hardened in anger. I remembered her face as she'd hit me when we were kids. I silently apologized to her over and over again.

I wrote my very first will then. I'd never bothered before. I don't remember what I wrote, except for the salutation: "To my beloved Kae-sama."

To be totally honest, I wasn't afraid of dying. No, I'm not putting on a front. Ever since Pearl Harbor, I'd thought of myself as a dead man walking. Many pilots far better than I had died already. I had participated in over a hundred air battles by that point, and the fuselage of my fighter had been scarred by enemy fire countless times. None of the shots had proven fatal, but in several cases, a couple dozen centimeters the wrong way would have sent me plunging down. Luck alone was the reason I was still alive. I had always thought that sooner or later I would follow my fallen comrades to the other side…

But being prepared to die on a mission and sortieing with death as the foregone conclusion are two very different things. Until then, even if the odds were very slim, I had gone into battle with a thin ray of hope that I'd live to tell the tale. Meanwhile, a special attack meant that not even luck could save you. Any effort to try and survive would prove useless. Taking off equaled death.

Yet, I had volunteered, so I had to keep my word and die like a man. The only thing that troubled me was thoughts of Kae. I bitterly regretted marrying her. At the same time, I didn't mind dying if it was to protect her.

In my recollection, it was after we'd volunteered that the First Air Fleet Commander Takijiro Onishi arrived at Mabalacat.

According to the history books, Fleet Commander Onishi came up with the idea of special attacks after arriving in Mabalacat, naming Lieutenant Yukio Seki captain of the first unit. But that can't be right. NCOs and airmen had been forced to volunteer beforehand. The decision to employ special attacks must have been made prior to the fleet commander's arrival on scene.

Soon thereafter, the names of the aircrew assigned to the special attack force were announced. Twenty-four men, with Lieutenant Seki their captain.

Frankly, I was very relieved to learn that my name wasn't on it. Of course, I was well aware that since I had volunteered, sooner or later I would become a kamikaze, but I was relieved all the same. And I hated myself for it.

I found myself at a loss for what to say to those who had been selected. I couldn't see them as pitiful or unfortunate, understand?

Not one of them grew pale. They were true samurai. I asked myself if I would be able to conduct myself so admirably if I were in their shoes. I'm sure many of us who weren't chosen wondered the same thing.

Fleet Commander Onishi delivered a speech to the members of the special attack force:

"Japan is in grave danger. Neither cabinet ministers, nor generals, nor the Chief of the General Staff can save her from this danger. Of course, neither can fleet commanders like myself. Only pure-hearted young men brimming with vitality such as you are able to undertake this task. I am making this request of you on behalf of one hundred million Japanese. I pray for your success. As you are all already gods who have given up your lives, you must be unburdened by desire. Your only regret must be that you can never know what gains you achieved by throwing yourself bodily at the enemy. I assure you that I will confirm them and that your accomplishments will be reported to the Emperor himself."

Onishi ended his comments, stepped down from the platform, and shook hands with each of the members.

The special attack force was named the "*Shinpu* Special Attack Force." The characters meaning "divine wind" were officially pronounced that way instead of *kamikaze*, though we came to use the latter reading. The units were named *Shikishima* (an old poetic name for Japan), *Yamato* (from "Yamato spirit" or the Japanese spirit), *Asahi* (morning sun), and *Yamazakura* (wild cherry blossoms).

These came from a *tanka* poem by the Edo-period classical scholar Norinaga Motoori:

Asked about the soul of Japan,
I would have to say that it is
Like wild cherry blossoms
Fragrant in the morning sun.

Around the same time, the Combined Fleet announced Operation Victory One, an all-out attempt to stop the Americans from invading the Philippines.

Japan's back was to the wall.

After capturing Saipan, the Americans' next target was the Philippines. If they managed to occupy the Philippines, our link to the southern territories would be completely severed. Petroleum and other resources would become unavailable. Hence the Imperial Army and Navy were prepared to defend the Philippines to the last.

The Combined Fleet deployed to strike at the American landing forces, with orders to wipe out the enemy's convoy of transports. To this end, the Combined Fleet hatched a daring plan: they would use the Mobile Fleet as a decoy to lure away the American carrier task force; a surface fleet headed by the battleships *Yamato* and *Musashi* would then charge into the Gulf of Leyte and send the American transport convoy to oblivion in one fell swoop. It was a desperate plan as in the proverb, "Let him slice your flesh while you sever his bone."

At the time, however, we base crew knew nothing about the overall situation and merely fought each battle as commanded.

The special attack was to provide support to the surface fleet as they stormed into Leyte Gulf. If the kamikazes managed to demolish the flight decks of American carriers, the enemy wouldn't be able to launch their ship-based aircraft. This would reduce the number of aerial attacks our fleet might face and facilitate its entry into the gulf.

If we'd had sufficient numbers of planes, land-based air corps could support the surface fleet or make a direct strike on the American task force. By then, however, our diminished strength in the air precluded any large-scale attacks.

It was under such circumstances that the kamikaze attack force was born.

206

The Shikishima Unit led by Lieutenant Yukio Seki first sortied on October 21st. But failing to discover the enemy, it returned to base. The unit sortied again the next day, yet returned once again after failing to make contact with the enemy.

I thought this was terribly cruel.

Lieutenant Seki was a newlywed. How heart-wrenching it must have been for him to leave her behind. Before his first sortie he'd told someone who was close to him, "I'm not dying for my country. I'm dying for my dear wife." I understand how he must have felt. I'm sure that all the other members, looking death in the eye, also considered what death meant to them, and departed on their mission having found peace only after a profound internal struggle.

Imagine how they must have felt returning to base. Having failed to spot their target, they were granted a short stay of execution—how that must have merely tormented them. How painful it must have been to live another night, when they'd sworn never to see a new day. Yet none of them, from Lieutenant Seki on down, betrayed even a hint of their anguish. Such men they were.

Then finally on their fourth sortie, they didn't return.

That day, the Shikishima Unit was escorted by four Zeros led by Flight Chief Petty Officer Nishizawa, who had been called up from Clark Air Base the day before. Yes, that Nishizawa, the famous ace of Rabaul. In addition to protecting the kamikaze unit, he was probably called up to assist in finding the enemy.

Lieutenant Seki's unit of five aircraft all succeeded in striking their targets, severely damaging three American escort carriers. We learned of the results of their mission by telegraph from the base on Cebu. The first kamikaze attack in history was a resounding success. CPO Nishizawa was the one to make the report, and it was very accurate. After the war, the U.S. stated that one ship was sunk and two others suffered heavy damage.

CPO Nishizawa hadn't just defended Shikishima Unit from hostile fighters and seen it dive through raging anti-aircraft fire. He'd also gunned down two Grumman F6Fs that were hot on his heels before making his way back to Cebu.

I heard this afterwards from aircrew stationed on Cebu, but

when CPO Nishizawa stepped out of the cockpit of his Zero, he had such an inordinately murderous aura about him that no one dared speak to him.

By the way, while the kamikaze attacks continued up to the end of the war, this first mission was the most successful. The element of surprise was probably the main reason, but I'm sure that having the greatest fighter pilot in the Navy providing support was immensely helpful as well. Ironically, it was the success of this mission that convinced the General Staff that kamikazes were its trump card.

Apparently, that night, Nishizawa muttered to a friend, "I will soon be following them to the other side."

He had lost his wingman to anti-aircraft fire during the mission—the very first time he'd lost anyone from his flight, we're told. He had sortied on hundreds of combat missions and gunned down more than a hundred enemy aircraft, and yet, never having lost anyone under his command was his greatest badge of honor. Only Saburo Sakai shared the distinction. Actually, since Nishizawa had served for over a year in that hellish place, Rabaul, without losing a single wingman, you could say he was even greater than Sakai.

Nishizawa's comment that he was soon to follow was probably in reference to Lieutenant Seki's Shikishima Unit, but perhaps he also had his fallen wingman in mind. And his premonition would come true.

The next day, as CPO Nishizawa made to return to Mabalacat, the base commander at Cebu told him to leave his Zero behind. Nishizawa and the two other pilots boarded an old Douglas transport plane bound for Mabalacat. It was shot down by an enemy fighter. It was an all-too-anticlimactic end for the man the American pilots feared as "the Devil of Rabaul."

How Nishizawa must have gnashed his teeth. The last flight of a man who'd never have been shot down flying a Zero was aboard a sluggish, unarmed transport plane.

And thus the greatest flying ace that the Imperial Navy produced died the day after the first kamikaze attack. He was just twenty-four years old.

Lieutenant Seki was heralded throughout Japan as a war hero. He had been the only child of a single mother. His bereaved mother was lionized as the woman who'd given birth to a god of war. But after the war, public opinion shifted and she was ostracized as the mother of a war criminal. She was forced into poverty, scraping by as a peddler, eventually finding employment as a cleaning woman at a grade school. She passed away one day in 1953, alone, in the janitor's room. They say her last words were, "At least allow Yukio a grave." That was the mood of postwar democracy: kamikazes who had perished for the country were like war criminals, and even erecting a stone for them was unforgivable. I've heard that the lieutenant's wife remarried after the war.

I should tell you about Operation Victory One, too. I'll preface this by saying that I didn't witness all of these events directly.

Around the same time that Shikishima Unit was repeatedly sortieing, the Central Force led by Admiral Kurita, on its way to Leyte, came under heavy fire from carrier-based enemy aircraft in the Sibuyan Sea. The Americans attacked in waves that resulted in damage to many ships, but they mostly focused on the battleship *Musashi*. The *Musashi*, sister ship to the famous *Yamato*, was the world's largest battleship and widely considered to be unsinkable. But after repeated attacks from hundreds of American aircraft, even the great *Musashi* was ready to rest in peace.

Meanwhile, the Northern Force comprised of aircraft carriers led by Vice Admiral Jisaburo Ozawa headed south towards Leyte in order to redirect the American mobile task force's attacks away from Kurita Fleet. Our carriers sent out a deluge of wireless messages to draw the enemy's attention and launched many recon planes.

Ozawa Fleet finally located its counterpart and sent out an attack force. It was not a "special" attack per se, but in essence very similar, as they would not be able to return. The carriers were lures, destined to be sunk, and the planes would be bereft of home ships. The pilots were instructed to go to various bases located in the Philippines if returning to the carriers proved too difficult in the aftermath of the attack, but this was a tall order for young aircrew unused to navigating over the vast Pacific. Besides, their surviving an onslaught of hostile interceptors from the mighty American carrier fleet was highly unlikely.

Indeed, most of the attack force was shot down by enemy fighters.

Yet Fleet Commander Ozawa's desperate operation accomplished its objective. The American carriers led by Halsey discovered Ozawa Fleet and mistook it for the main threat.

At that point, Kurita Fleet had made a temporary about-face, convincing Halsey that severe losses had forced it to retreat. Halsey chose not to pursue and instead headed in full force towards Ozawa Fleet.

Judging that it had been spotted by Halsey, Ozawa Fleet promptly turned north to lure Halsey away. Intent on striking the Japanese Mobile Force, Halsey gave chase.

He made the obvious choice. Ever since Pearl Harbor, the key players of most battles on the Pacific were aircraft carriers. In addition, Ozawa Fleet had the *Zuikaku*, the Combined Fleet's largest carrier. After achieving great military gains in the attack on Pearl Harbor, she had gone on to sink two U.S. carriers. To the Americans, the *Zuikaku* was a fearsome ship that had tormented them for the past three years.

I've heard that the American task force's assault was ferocious. Most of Ozawa Fleet went down, barely able to put up a fight. That storied ship in service since Pearl Harbor, until then the Combined Fleet's most blessed in battle, the *Zuikaku*, also sank at last, off Cape Engaño.

Yet Fleet Commander Ozawa's grand, daredevil operation was a success. Halsey was wholly taken in by the ploy and lured away, leaving the seas near Leyte wide open.

That is to say, freed from enemy aerial attacks, Kurita Fleet had turned back towards Leyte. Kurita Fleet had lost some ships, including the *Musashi*, to aerial and submarine attacks, and those that remained were damaged as well, but the world's most powerful ship, the *Yamato*, was still going strong, and a good number of other ships were still battle-worthy, too.

The American forces there, which consisted of six small escort carriers and seven destroyers, were thoroughly shocked when a Japanese fleet appeared off the coast of Samar Island. Throwing up a smokescreen, the destroyers launching torpedoes, they desperately tried to get away. Ozawa Fleet had managed to lure away the trusty Mobile Task Force, and the Americans who remained were prepared for utter annihilation, they say.

At last, the Japanese Navy's desperate plan to offer up flesh in order to sunder the enemy's bones bore fruit...

But then a miracle occurred for the Americans. Kurita Fleet abruptly reversed course.

This is the infamous incident that went down in history as "Kurita Fleet's mysterious about-face."

What on earth made Kurita Fleet reverse course? Various theories were postulated in later years, but the fleet commander himself passed away after the war without ever giving one word of explanation or justification.

What we do know is that he was unaware of the fact that Ozawa Fleet had successfully lured Halsey's task force far to the north of the Philippines. Perhaps the intensity of the aerial attacks made him think that the Americans were close at hand. Perhaps he assumed that if he were to charge into the Gulf of Leyte, his entire fleet would be destroyed.

There are no "ifs" in history. But it is pretty certain that if Kurita Fleet had pressed on, he could have wiped out the Americans' totally naked and defenseless transport convoy. There's no doubt their invasion of the Philippines would have suffered a massive setback. Heavy losses in both personnel and materiel might have forced them to spend more than a year restructuring their operation. At the very least, it would have thwarted the deaths of tens of thousands of Japanese soldiers in the following land battle on Leyte.

Kurita Fleet's withdrawal, however, wasted our final chance to deal a blow against the American forces. Ozawa Fleet's officers and sailors had died in vain. The *Musashi*, which had valiantly borne the brunt of the assault from U.S. attack aircraft, had sunk in Surigao Strait for nothing.

The Shikishima Unit's special attack came on the day after Kurita Fleet reversed course. But there was no chance for victory by then.

At first, the special attacks were meant to be specific to Operation

Victory One at Leyte. In order to support Kurita Fleet's advance into the gulf, pilots would daringly hurl themselves at American aircraft carriers' flight decks, render them inoperable, and prevent the enemy from launching attack planes—as a tactic exclusive to Leyte.

Yet even after Kurita Fleet's retreat and the failure of Operation Victory One, the special attacks didn't end.

They assumed a life of their own. Had our commanders gone insane?

Day after day special attack units took off from Mabalacat. For some reason or other, I was never called up to become a kamikaze and instead tasked as part of their fighter escort. Perhaps it was because I was one of the precious few veteran pilots, but even this was very dangerous. Baptized by the Japanese military's lethal tactic, the Americans cranked up their interception posture to frightening levels. There was no way an escort of a few fighters could fend off dozens of high-performance enemy planes lying in wait to pick off the kamikazes. Many of us died defending the kamikaze units. Even the veteran pilot Ensign Yoshimi Minami, who had served since the Sino-Japanese War, failed to return from one such mission.

Ensign Minami was a pilot with a long military career who had fought in many naval battles since the attack on Pearl Harbor. You could say he was the crown jewel of our navy's air corps. He climbed the ranks from NCO and was a wonderful human being, too. Kind and soft-spoken, he'd taught me the ropes in Shanghai. He'd been assigned to a carrier at Leyte Gulf, but having lost his mothership and after a hairbreadth escape, he made it back to the Philippines. From there his luck ran out, though, and he died escorting a kamikaze unit.

I resigned myself to meeting the same fate there.

Several days later, on the way back from a mission, I ran into engine trouble and was forced to land at Nichols Field. It was there that I happened to cross paths again with Miyabe. He had been on the *Zuikaku*, and after attacking the American task force, he'd landed at that base.

Miyabe was aware of the special attacks, too. The actions of Lieutenant Yukio Seki and his Shikishima Unit had been reported to the entire armed forces. No kamikazes had been launched from

Nichols Field, but the *esprit de corps* of the aircrew there had fallen to an all-time low.

More than a few books about the kamikazes written after the war claim that when the armed forces heard what Shikishima Unit had done, morale skyrocketed among the aviators. But this is decidedly untrue. Our morale was very clearly abysmal. Of course it was!

The day after I landed at Nichols Field, all the aircrew were assembled. Judging from the tense looks on the faces of the base commander and the squadron leader, I assumed our time had come. I'm sure the other guys thought so too.

After spouting some words about the unprecedented peril that Japan was facing, the base commander said, "All those who wish to volunteer for the Special Attack Force, step forward."

Everyone stepped forward. They had heard of the Shikishima Unit and already resigned themselves. I stepped forward, just as I had at Mabalacat. I couldn't suddenly refuse now.

Then I witnessed something unbelievable. One man hadn't moved, in fact. Miyabe.

The squadron leader turned crimson and bellowed on behalf of the base commander, "All volunteers, step forward!"

But Miyabe didn't budge. His face was ashen.

The squadron leader drew his saber and yelled again, "All volunteers step forward now!"

Miyabe was as immobile as a statue. The squadron leader's body shook with rage. "Flight Chief Petty Officer Miyabe!" he yelled. "Do you hold your life so dear?"

Miyabe was silent.

"Answer me, damn it!"

Miyabe very nearly shouted, "I do, sir!"

The squadron leader's mouth fell open in disbelief. "And you dare call yourself a member of the Imperial Navy?"

"Yes, sir," Miyabe said, loud and clear.

The squadron leader glanced at the base commander, who muttered, "Dismiss them."

An officer barked, "Dismissed!" The aircrew fell out of line and walked back to the barracks. No one spoke to Miyabe.

The next morning, there was no mission, but a strange mood had settled over the air contingent. The previous day's "volunteering" for special attacks weighed heavily on everyone's minds.

I invited Miyabe, and the two of us walked up a hill some distance from the airfield. Neither of us said anything.

Once we arrived atop the low hill, I sat down on a patch of grass. Miyabe sat down as well.

At last he said, "I absolutely refuse to volunteer for any special attack unit. I promised my wife to come home alive."

I nodded silently.

"It wasn't to die that I've fought until today," he said.

I couldn't manage a reply.

"No matter how severe the battle, I can fight like hell as long as there's even the slightest chance of survival. But I can't abide by any tactic that will result in my certain death."

Honestly speaking, I felt the same way.

But looking back now, out of the thousands of aircrew back then, how many dared say such a thing out loud? Miyabe's words revealed what really lay in the hearts of most of us. Yet, at the time, his words were frightening. They made me feel a bizarre, eerie sense of dread. I realize now that it was the fear of seeing my own self.

Miyabe suddenly asked, "Was that your first time volunteering, Tanigawa?"

"My second time. I first volunteered at Mabalacat."

"I have a wife," he said.

"So do I."

Miyabe looked stunned. I told him how I'd gotten married four days before leaving Japan.

"Do you love her?" he asked me.

I nodded without thinking. *Ah, so I do love her...*

"Then why did you volunteer to become a kamikaze?" he demanded.

"Because I'm an Imperial Navy pilot!" I shouted.

And then I burst into tears. That was the first time I'd cried since becoming a fighter pilot. Miyabe simply stared at me, saying nothing.

As I made to stand up, he said, "Listen to me very carefully,

Tanigawa. If you are ordered to fly as a kamikaze, find an island, any island, and just crash-land there."

I was astonished. Those were frightening words, most definitely worthy of a death sentence at a court-martial.

"Even if you die a kamikaze, it won't alter the state of the war one bit. But your death will hugely affect your wife's future."

An image of Kae floated up in my mind. "Don't say that. If I'm ordered to, I'll go, that's all."

Miyabe didn't reply.

Just then, a siren sounded, and moments later an explosion boomed in the distance. An enemy air raid.

We raced towards the bomb shelter. On the airfield, the maintenance crew were moving the aircraft into the bunkers. At that point, we no longer launched interceptors against air raids. Instead of sending the few airplanes we still had only to have them shot down by a massive formation of enemy aircraft, we'd resorted to preserving as many as possible. There were only a precious few battle-ready ones at Nichols Field.

But luck wasn't on our side that day. We were late in detecting the incoming fighters, and most of the aircraft on the ground were strafed. Nichols Field was left without a single operational aircraft. Soon thereafter, it was decided that the aviators there would be pulled back to the interior.

We boarded a transport plane that arrived from Clark Base, stopped over in Taiwan, then landed at Omura in Kyushu. We were ordered to rejoin our previous units.

I parted ways with Miyabe in Omura. I don't remember our final conversation, but I would never see him again.

After a stint as an instructor at Iwakuni, I served with the Yokosuka Air Corps to defend the mainland's skies. Beginning in March of 1945, a large number of kamikaze planes took off from southern Kyushu, headed for Okinawa. In the final days of the war, "All Planes Kamikaze" became the slogan. I've heard that they no longer asked for volunteers but ordered men into it.

I expected they would eventually call me up, but happily that day never came. I was at Misawa when the war ended. I only learned much later that Miyabe had died a kamikaze.

After the war ended and I returned to my village, everyone looked at me differently. I was like something unclean, and no one dared to approach me. They'd murmur behind my back, "He's a war criminal." One day, when I was walking along the riverbank, some children called out, "Here comes the war criminal!" and threw stones at me.

It was unbearable. The same people who had only yesterday cursed the British and the Americans as demons had done an about-face and now cried, "America, *banzai*!" and "Long live democracy!" And I, who had once been a local hero, was treated like some god of pestilence. My father had passed away, my brother had taken over the household, and Kae and I lived in the annex. My brother made it clear that he saw me as a burden.

Somehow a false rumor began circulating that all pilots who had participated in the attack on Pearl Harbor were going to be hanged as war criminals; and that any persons or villages sheltering them would face severe punishment. When I caught wind of this, I steeled myself for what was to come.

Then one day my brother offered me ten kilograms of rice as a farewell gift and told me to flee to Tokyo. It was a polite way of kicking me out. I took Kae with me, of course, and we left our hometown behind.

We arrived in Tokyo at the end of October. The place was a charred field in every direction. Kae and I stayed in a makeshift hut made out of tin sheets. I went out looking for work every day, but there was none to be had. We soon ran out of my brother's rice, and I ended up working as a day laborer just to eke out a living.

Things were really hard back then. The city was crawling with Occupation soldiers. The American troops walked with Japanese girls on their arms. It was hard to believe that just three months earlier I'd been engaging American fighter pilots in mortal combat.

We somehow managed not to starve back then only after Kae spotted a want-ad looking for people who could sew. They hired her and provided lodging on site. Kae and I shared a literal closet of a room, but compared to the tin hut, it was heaven.

The following year, thanks to the influence of a former superior in the Navy, I was hired as a temporary worker for the Waterworks

Bureau. But only a year later, I was fired during GHQ's purge. The Americans didn't want anyone associated with the previous regime to be in the public sector. After eleven years of service with the Navy, I had been discharged with the rank of lieutenant junior grade, and this had resulted in my being considered a career soldier. When Kae learned why I had been fired, she tried hard to console me.

"'Career soldier'? What a terrible term. As if those who risked their lives for the sake of the country were doing it for the money. It's unforgivable."

Nothing gave me greater joy than to hear such words. And I made a fresh resolve to devote my life to her.

I decided to go into business for myself. I tried my hand at all sorts of trades. I was deceived and betrayed countless times. People in the postwar years were entirely different from the prewar years. The night after a certain betrayal, I recalled my comrades who had fallen in battle and found myself wondering if they weren't the lucky ones. I envied them for not having to witness what had become of Japan.

Yet the chaos and destitution of the immediate postwar years was a short-term state of affairs. Many Japanese showed compassion and warm-heartedness. Some tried to help others, even though staying alive themselves was almost all they could do. I believe that was why my wife and I survived that miserable period. I was eventually able to own a modest building in Tokyo only thanks to many kindnesses.

It wasn't until many years later that Japanese truly changed.

Japan became a democracy, a peaceful society. We entered a period of rapid economic growth and enjoyed freedom and material wealth. But that caused us to lose something important. Postwar democracy and prosperity robbed the Japanese people of "morals"— I think.

Nowadays, the streets are filled with people who only care for themselves. It wasn't like that sixty years ago.

Perhaps I've simply lived for too long.

The reception room that had been alight with the setting sun was now dark.

I felt that far more time had passed than the few hours that Tanigawa had spent talking. He'd looked like a young man as he spoke, a youth who fairly sparkled with fearlessness. But now there was just a skinny old man in a wheelchair.

I looked at his bony arms. They seemed so fragile. Once, those arms had handily commanded a Zero fighter fleeting through the skies, engaging in battle. The passage of sixty years made my chest feel tight.

"Even now I sometimes wonder if what I saw back at Nichols Field actually happened," Tanigawa said softly, "or if I just dreamed it."

"You mean how our grandfather refused to volunteer for the special attack?"

"Since it wasn't an order, he couldn't be accused of insubordination. But that's what it was."

"Insubordination?"

"Yes, disobeying orders. In the military it was an offense punishable by death."

I let out a groan. What a man my grandfather had been.

"But there's something I don't understand. When Miyabe was ordered to become a kamikaze at the very tail end of the war, why didn't he make an emergency landing somewhere? Why did the very man who'd urged me to abandon the mission and land somewhere safe go off and blow himself up?" Tanigawa folded his arms. "A good many veteran pilots were sent out to perform special attacks at Leyte, but I think that was due to the chaos and confusion. True, while Ensign Minami wasn't a kamikaze himself, after sortieing from Ozawa Fleet, attacking the American task force, and making it to Echague Base on Luzon, he was tasked with the unforgiving duty of escorting kamikazes, which cost him his life."

"So he, too, died conducting a special attack, in effect."

Tanigawa nodded. "I also heard that Ensign Tsutomu Iwai and others from Ozawa Fleet who flew to the Philippines were nearly forced into becoming kamikazes. But by the time of the Okinawa Special Attacks starting in March of '43, they had stopped using veteran pilots as kamikazes. They needed experienced pilots as instructors and to defend the mainland."

"So that means that most kamikaze pilots were very young."

"The majority of special attacks took place during the Battle of Okinawa in the final year of the conflict. Most were student reservists or very young airmen. I thought it was a mistake to use veteran pilots as kamikazes. Of course, the lives of young pilots were just as valuable as those of their seniors, and I'm not saying it was perfectly fine to send student reservists off to die. But I just can't forgive the higher-ups for letting Minami-san get killed."

Tanigawa's voice rose as he said, "Those men swore to follow behind and ordered so many subordinates into kamikaze units—how abominable that once the war was over, they coolly decided to go on living."

He slammed the desk, rattling the ashtray. I jumped.

"Sorry. Got a bit worked up there."

"It's fine, sir."

Tanigawa pulled a medicine bottle out of his breast pocket and put a pill in his mouth. My sister stood up, walked over to the sink, and filled a cup with water, then handed it to him.

"Thank you, young lady." Tanigawa took the cup and washed down the pill. After a moment he said, "I just don't understand why Miyabe didn't ditch someplace. He had the skills to do so."

"Were there pilots who did?"

Tanigawa's features briefly clouded. "Some kamikazes returned saying that they'd failed to make contact with the enemy or had engine trouble."

"Isn't that—" Keiko began, but Tanigawa firmly shook his head.

"I don't know if it was intentional. But there were such pilots."

Silence filled the room.

I opened my mouth. "My grandfather was listed as having died on the seas near Okinawa. Supposing he had run into engine trouble, where could he have landed in that area?"

"Kikaijima Island," Tanigawa replied instantly. "Kamikazes who had mechanical issues preventing them from completing their mission after taking off from southern Kyushu were to land there."

"Ah."

"But towards the end of the war the Americans controlled the airspace over Kikaijima too, so perhaps even Miyabe couldn't pull it off with a heavy load of ordnance."

I nodded.

"In any case, this all happened sixty years ago. We have no way of knowing the truth."

Tanigawa heaved a sigh. He reached out and flicked the switch on the wall and the fluorescent lights blinked on, brightening the dark room. He slowly pulled a single photograph from his pocket.

"This is my wife. She passed away five years ago. She was incredibly devoted. When I returned to my hometown after being discharged, she started bawling the moment she saw me. She was a woman of iron will. I never saw her cry before nor since." Tanigawa's eyes shone faintly with tears. "Had Miyabe not said to me what he did, we might never have spent our lives together."

"You really loved each other," Keiko said.

He nodded. "We never had children, but we were very happy."

After we walked out of the nursing home, I noticed Keiko dabbing at her eyes with a tissue.

"I'm frustrated," she said. "Grandfather made sure everyone else was happy, then went off and died himself. How is that possible? It's just not fair."

"It's not like he was the only one. Three million people died in the war. Or just counting the men in uniform, two million and three hundred thousand. Grandfather was just one of millions."

Keiko fell silent. She didn't utter a word during the entire taxi ride.

We got out at the train station. As we were heading towards the platform, she suddenly snapped, "You said before that Grandfather was just one in 2.3 million war dead. But to Grandma, he was her dear husband. And he was Mom's father, her only one."

"And just as he was Grandma's one and only husband at the time, all the other 2.3 million who died meant everything to those they left behind."

Keiko gave me a surprised look.

"You might laugh at me for saying this, but right now I'm feeling the sorrow of all those people who died in the war."

Keiko nodded gravely. "I'm not laughing."

We were silent on the bullet train.

Keiko seemed to be lost in thought, and I pondered on our conversation with Tanigawa. When I closed my eyes, I felt like I could see my grandfather. But it was hazy, like a mirage, and I wasn't able to capture a clear image of him.

Sometime after passing New Osaka Station, my sister broke her silence. "Listening to people who fought in the war, it makes me feel the rank and file were really treated like they were expendable."

I nodded.

She continued, "They figured they'd always have a fresh supply of men if they just sent out draft notices. Apparently, officers used to tell soldiers that horses were more valuable than them. That they were 'penny postcards' that were easily replaceable."

"Penny postcards?"

"The postage on a draft notice was a penny back then. So to the higher-ups, Army soldiers, Navy sailors, and pilots were worth just a penny each. And they could afford to buy as many as they wanted."

"And yet the recruits all fought bravely for the sake of their country."

My sister nodded ruefully. After another stretch of silence she said, "Can I discuss something with you?"

"Sure."

"I've been doing all sorts of research about the war, and there's something I've realized as a result."

"What's that?"

"The timidity of the admiral class."

"Wasn't the Imperial military always pushing it though?"

"It wasn't that they were pushing it. So many of the operations were just foolhardy and suicidal. From Guadalcanal to New Guinea to the Battle of the Philippine Sea to the Battle of Leyte Gulf—it's all the same. The famous Battle of Imphal in India, too. What we mustn't forget, on the other hand, is that Imperial General HQ and the General Staff who hatched those operations could rest easy knowing there was absolutely no risk to their own lives."

"So the higher-ups could come up with all sorts of rash plans if all they were going to lose were rank-and-file soldiers."

"Exactly. But when they were commanding on the front and faced the possibility of their own deaths, they became extremely timid. Even when they were winning, they feared counterattacks and were quick to retreat."

"I see."

"I don't know whether it should be called timidity, or caution, but take the attack on Pearl Harbor. The field officers urged a third wave of attacks, but Fleet Commander Nagumo chose to turn tail as fast as he could. At the battle of the Coral Sea, after sinking the USS *Lexington*, Fleet Commander Inoue pulled back the landing troops that were sent to invade Port Moresby, despite the fact that that operation had been in support of the landing. And during the first battle of the Solomon Seas in the early stages of the Guadalcanal Campaign, Fleet Commander Mikawa withdrew after defeating the enemy fleet, choosing not to pursue the American transport convoy even though the original goal of the operation was its destruction. Had they taken the opportunity to sink the transport ships, they might have prevented the later calamity on Guadalcanal. Halsey supposedly said that there were quite a number of battles where he'd have been done in if the Japanese forces had given just one more push. The foremost example of that is Kurita Fleet reversing course in the Battle of Leyte Gulf, like we just heard."

I was stunned to hear such a detailed analysis of the war from Keiko. *She must have read a ton of books*, I thought.

"So why were there so many weak-willed men in the military?" I asked.

"I'm sure it comes down to each person's character, but in the Navy's case, I think too many admirals were like that. So maybe there was a structural issue."

"What do you mean?"

"The admirals were the elite. The most gifted officers, graduates of the Naval Academy, were further handpicked for the Naval War College, which future admirals attended. These were the elite among the elite, so to speak. This is just my personal opinion, but I think their timidity was a result of their elite status. I can't help but feel they were constantly thinking about their own careers."

"Their careers? In the middle of a war?"

"I might be reading too much into it, but there are just too many instances. Researching individual battles, I feel that they prioritized not making any major mistake instead of focusing on destroying the enemy. Remember what Izaki-san said, for example. In the assessment for awarding medals to fleet commanders, sinking a warship earned the most points, while destroying dry docks, oil reserve tanks, and transport convoys didn't amount to much. So they always put off such targets."

"But that doesn't mean they were only thinking of their careers."

"Well, sure, I could be overthinking it. But these elites who entered the Naval Academy in their mid-teens, who fought their way through fierce competition, who went on to live the cutthroat competition of the small world called the Imperial Navy—is it so unnatural to think that they were saturated from head to toe with the desire to climb the ranks? That drive must have been especially strong among the admiral class, the very best students… During the Pacific War, all the fleet commanders were over fifty, and actually, the Navy hadn't engaged in naval battles for nearly forty years, not since the Russo-Japanese war. In other words, since joining the Navy and until the Pacific War began, they didn't experience actual combat and spent their lives competing for promotions within the Navy."

Wow, I thought. While I was surprised by Keiko's unexpected breadth and depth of knowledge, what was even more impressive was her keen insight.

"When I researched what the Navy was like back then, I realized something," she continued. "Your promotion order in the Imperial Navy was basically determined by your Naval Academy standing, which they called the 'hammock number.'"

"So your ranking at graduation essentially decided the rest of your career."

"Right. The best test-takers are the ones who got ahead. Just like with bureaucrats today. So long as you avoid any major mistakes, you continue to get promoted. This might be going too far, but I think star students who excel at written exams might be great at playing by the book, but fragile in situations that aren't covered by it. Also, they don't imagine they could be wrong."

I leaned forward, pulling away from the seat's backrest. "So the commanding officers that always had to react to unpredictable situations were chosen on the basis of written exams."

"It might have had something to do with the Imperial Navy's fragility."

I nodded deeply. "What about the Americans?"

"I haven't really done much in-depth research yet, but in terms of one's career, it was the same in America. Naval Academy graduation rankings had a lot to do with it. But that was only true during peacetime. During wars, the best combat commanders were given exceptional promotions. Pacific Fleet Commander-in-Chief Nimitz leapfrogged over dozens of men. Of course, they had to take responsibility for failures, too. Admiral Kimmel, who had held that position, was relieved of his command and demoted to rear admiral after the attack on Pearl Harbor wiped out the fleet there. It's difficult to say whether Kimmel was to blame for the thrashing they took at Pearl Harbor, but apparently the U.S. military was very clear about assigning responsibility. Also, there seems to have been few, if any, timid commanders in the American Navy. They were all surprisingly aggressive."

Just how much research have you done? I wondered. She had always been the type to become engrossed in a subject that snagged her attention, but even so, she seemed especially intent on digging up info for this project. She'd always been pretty smart.

"I see. So that could be the key to America's strength."

"I was talking about the Imperial Navy just now, but it seems to have been the same with the Imperial Army. Apparently, the prewar Army and Navy War Colleges were harder to get into than Tokyo University in some ways. Just being selected from among the officers to take the entrance exam earned you a listing in the official gazette, so it must have been incredibly difficult. I'm bothering to tell you all this because the more research I do on Japan's former military, the more it seems to have in common with our current bureaucratic system."

I looked at my sister again. Maybe I'd failed to get what she was about for the longest time. "I've been doing some research into the military back then, too, and realized something myself," I offered.

"Oh?"

"You touched on this—how the senior officers in the Imperial

Navy skirted accountability. Even if an operation ended in failure, they weren't penalized for it. Take Fleet Commander Nagumo, who made a serious judgment error at Midway and lost four aircraft carriers. Or General Staff Chief Fukutome, who allowed important operational documents to fall into the hands of the American military when he got captured by anti-Japanese guerrillas before the Battle of the Philippine Sea. Vice Admiral Fukutome was taken prisoner, but the brass let him off the hook. Had he been a common soldier, there'd have been hell to pay."

"They ordered the rank and file to kill themselves rather than be captured, but turned a blind eye when it was one of them."

"It was common practice in the Army as well not to hold the top elite liable. Masanobu Tsuji was never taken to task for his repeated foolish operations on Guadalcanal. Lieutenant General Mutaguchi was never officially made to take responsibility for his unbelievably stupid Imphal operation that resulted in some thirty thousand soldiers dying of starvation. By the way, before the War in the Pacific ever began, Tsuji's inept plans during the Nomonhan Incident had led to massive casualties, but he wasn't held accountable and just continued to rise through the ranks. In his stead, field officers were forced to take the blame, and many regimental commanders were coerced into committing suicide."

"How awful!"

"If Tsuji and other senior general staff had been made to take the fall for Nomonhan, it might have prevented the later tragedies on Guadalcanal from ever happening."

Keiko grimaced in irritation. "But why were they let off the hook?"

"I'm not too clear on that point," I said. "But my feeling is that they'd turned into bureaucracies."

Keiko nodded. "I see—they were able to shirk responsibility because the elite all covered up for each other. Making a fuss about their peers' failure might come back to bite them later when they screwed up."

"I think that definitely was the case. Division Commander Ko-toku Sato, who pulled back his troops against Mutaguchi's orders during the Battle of Imphal, never faced a court-martial. They ruled it a mental breakdown and let him off the hook. Had a court-martial taken place, they'd have had to assess Mutaguchi's blame as the operation's commander. So to cover for Mutaguchi, they declared Sato mentally unfit to stand trial. Court-martial proceedings might touch on their own accountability as senior IGHQ staff since they'd green-lighted Mutaguchi's operation. By the way, Lieutenant General Kawabe, who was the one who approved Mutaguchi's Imphal operation as his superior, became a full general."

"That sucks," Keiko muttered. "The regular troops had to risk their lives fighting for such people?"

"Speaking of responsibility, remember what Ito-san told us? Commander-in-Chief Isoroku Yamamoto left for Pearl Harbor with the parting words, 'Make sure this won't be a sneak attack,' but it did, in fact, end up being a nasty surprise attack thanks to the laxness of the embassy staff in Washington, who delayed in delivering the declaration of war. That story kept bugging me, so I did some research and found that no one was made to take any blame after the war."

"The higher-ups had been at a party the night before, right?"

"Yeah, they drank the night away at a farewell party and were late getting to work the next day, a Sunday. The day before, they'd received a 'Memorandum to the U.S. Government,' an extremely high-priority thirteen-part cable from the Ministry of Foreign Affairs, yet they didn't bother typing it up and went partying. When they saw the telegram declaring war that arrived the next morning, they panicked and started to type out the memorandum first. It took them forever, and by the time they delivered the cable to Secretary of State Hull, the attack on Pearl Harbor had already commenced. The declaration of war itself was only eight lines long."

"They should have been dismissed from the civil service."

"Or worse. Thanks to their screw-up, Japanese suffered the unbearable stigma of being 'a race of people who stoop to vile sneak attacks.' That was huge, you know? About America having dropped the atomic bomb, for instance, there are views that 'those vile Japanese got exactly what they deserved.' After 9/11, their mass media compared the terrorist attacks to Pearl Harbor, or so I've heard. Yet not one of the embassy higher-ups was held accountable for an inexcusable failure that besmirched Japan as a country. A certain career diplomat even tried to pin the blame on a non-career telegraph worker who had, in fact, offered to stay overnight. The very same man who'd said, 'That won't be necessary' and sent him home turned around after the war and tried to blame it on the poor fellow."

Keiko sighed.

"So in the end, not only did the high-ranking diplomats all wash their hands of the whole matter, but a few of them went on to become the ministry's undersecretary after the war. Had they been thoroughly taken to task back then, we might have avoided the 'vile race' stigma and won back some honor. Americans might have said, 'Ah, so it wasn't meant to be undeclared.' But even to this day, the Ministry of Foreign Affairs hasn't officially admitted its error, and globally speaking, people still think of the surprise attack on Pearl Harbor as a sneak attack."

Keiko pressed her hands to her forehead. "Just what sort of country is Japan, anyway?"

I had no answer for such a question. I'm sure she wasn't really expecting one. I said, "Learning about the military and some bureaucrats back then puts me into a dark mood, but nameless people gave it their all as always. I think this country was and is carried on their backs. I think the NCOs and enlisted men truly fought hard. Setting aside whether fighting well in a war is such a good thing, they carried out their duties to the fullest."

"They all fought as best they could for the sake of the country." Keiko turned to look out the window into the darkness outside. Her reflection in the glass showed a grim expression. With a sigh she said, "I think Hasegawa-san, who'd lost his arm, understandably felt some deep-seated resentment."

"He couldn't bear a grudge towards his country, so he must have transferred it onto our grandfather instead."

"I'm sure people were very cold to him, too. Far from expressing gratitude to him for his sacrifices, they might have seen his having lost an arm as just punishment for a career soldier."

I nodded. "So forgive him for speaking ill of Grandfather Miyabe."

"I know." Keiko cracked a small smile, but then her expression darkened again. "At any rate, the higher-ups in the Japanese military really thought of the troops as nothing more than tools."

"And the prime example of that was the kamikazes."

I imagined my grandfather's chagrin and closed my eyes.

Chapter 8
Cherry Blossoms

A few days later, I called my sister's cell. "Hey, I just got in touch with someone who was in a kamikaze unit."

Keiko made a surprised sound.

"He says he knew Grandfather," I added.

But her response was wholly unexpected. She didn't want to come.

"Why not?"

She didn't reply.

"Don't you want to hear from someone who was actually in one?"

"I do. But then again, I can't bear listening to more sad stories about our grandfather," she fumed. "I did some research on the kamikazes on my own. It was so painful that I had to stop reading."

"I understand."

"The former kamikaze guy might talk about when Grandfather was sent out. I won't be able to take it. I mean, can *you* sit there calmly if he does, Kentaro?"

"Well, of course it'd be hard for me to hear," I said. "But I feel like there's something at work that's bringing us together. This person called Kyuzo Miyabe, who went unknown for sixty years, is beginning to show himself to me now."

I heard Keiko swallow her breath.

"I think it's something of a miracle. I can't help but feel like it was a turn of the wheel of fortune that we started this research project now, just when all those people who fought in the war are departing from the stage of history. Had it been even five years later, I think Kyuzo Miyabe would have quietly passed into time. That's why I feel like I ought to hear from everyone who once knew him."

After a moment, Keiko said, "Gee, you've really changed,

Kentaro."

"I do see how you might find it too painful. It's not like I don't feel that way at all. Anyway, I'll go by myself this time."

Keiko fell silent.

"Have you said yes to Takayama-san yet?" I asked my sister, who was in the passenger's seat as I drove along. Former Ensign Masao Okabe's house was located in Narita, Chiba Prefecture, a little east of Tokyo, so I'd borrowed Mom's car.

"Not yet, but I'm planning on saying yes." The day before, Keiko had called to say that she'd changed her mind and that she'd come after all.

After turning onto the expressway I said, "Weren't you actually in love with Fujiki-san, sis?"

Keiko looked at me in astonishment.

"I can tell you this now. Totally by accident, I saw you crying next to him that one time."

Keiko didn't say anything. A gulf of silence opened up between us. I turned up the A/C.

"Can you listen without laughing at me? It's true, I had a crush on Fujiki-san. My dream was that he'd pass the bar exam and marry me. So it was a shock when I heard that he was giving up on the bar and moving back home. I had just gotten a job, so I begged him not to leave."

"Were you two seeing each other?"

She shook her head. "We'd never even held hands, he'd never confessed any feelings for me, and we'd never gone out on a date. So we weren't lovers or anything."

"Oh, I see."

"It wouldn't be an exaggeration to say that my tears were my confession of love." Keiko gave a slightly sad smile. "But he left. And he never asked me to go with him or to wait for him."

Of course not. Fujiki would never, I thought. He wasn't the type to demand that of her when it was clear that his life wouldn't be rosy.

"Do you regret it?"

"Regret? Why would I? I think I made the right decision. I'm glad he didn't ask me to move with him to the countryside. I was just a kid back then, so I might have turned down my job offer and gone with him." She laughed out loud at that. "Did you know that his ironworks is doing pretty poorly?"

I nodded.

"If I'd married him, I'd have struggled terribly." She pulled a pack of cigarettes from her handbag and lit one.

I was a little surprised. "You've started smoking?"

"Never in front of Mom, though." She cracked the window, letting in a stream of hot air. "By the way, Fujiki-san called me yesterday. He asked me to marry him."

For a moment this didn't even register.

"I wrote him a letter recently, saying that I might get married. The first letter I'd ever written to him. Ten days later, he called me."

"What the hell are you thinking?!" I shouted at her.

She flinched in shock. I realized I was coming up fast on the car ahead of me and hurriedly slammed on the brakes.

"Are you just trying to get revenge on him for leaving you?"

"I'm not thinking about revenge at all. I just wanted to get closure. Stop yelling at me and watch the darn road!"

"And how did you answer him?!"

"I turned him down, of course."

I moved into the passing lane and stepped on the gas. Keiko fell quiet. I thought about how Fujiki must be feeling, and my chest tightened.

Neither of us spoke a word again until we turned off the expressway.

Former Ensign Masao Okabe had served four terms as a member of Chiba's prefectural assembly. Before that, he had spent many years on the prefecture's board of education. When I first learned of his career, I was surprised that a former kamikaze had become an assemblyman. But on further thought, it wasn't the slightest bit strange. Back then, all young men had served in the military, and most of those who bore postwar Japan on their shoulders were former soldiers. So it wasn't so bizarre that there were former kamikazes among them.

Okabe lived in a quiet residential neighborhood in Narita. His was a small, snug house, not at all what one might expect of a former four-term prefectural assemblyman.

"Pretty ordinary house," Keiko said, echoing my thoughts.

I pressed the buzzer to the side of the doorway. The door immediately opened, revealing the face of an elderly man of small stature.

The ex-kamikaze was totally bald. He smiled broadly, giving a very affable impression. I had pictured a more imposing man since he'd been a local politician, and I felt silly for having been on guard.

"My wife is at the community center teaching flower arrangement today, so I can't really offer you much," Okabe said as he led us into a Japanese-style room. "We're just two old folks living here, so I'm not too sure what I should serve to you young people." He brought out some cider.

"Please, don't trouble yourself, sir," I said.

I couldn't reconcile the image of a kamikaze pilot with the diminutive old man seated before us. But to be fair, I hadn't really had any set image in my mind as to what a kamikaze should look like.

"Miyabe-san was a truly outstanding instructor," Okabe suddenly started in.

"By 'instructor' you mean?"

"An instructor at an air training unit. Even though they were all teaching us, officers were called 'instructing officers' and NCOs were called 'instructing staff.' The military was very stratified, even in ways like that."

"I didn't know that our grandfather had worked as an instructor."

"Miyabe-san came to teach at the Tsukuba Air Training Unit at the start of 1945."

I was a flight student reservist. Student reservists were basically officers who came from colleges. The Imperial Navy had previously accepted a small number of student reservists, but starting in 1943 they sought a large number of us.

Unlike nowadays, not everyone was able to attend college. I doubt even one out of a hundred did. College students were members of an exclusive elite, which is why the military didn't try to force us into service at first. But by '43, the progress of the war had taken a turn for the worse, and they couldn't be so lenient. That was the year we were defeated at Guadalcanal and Admiral Isoroku Yamamoto was killed.

Collegians and high school students of the old system who had until then been exempted from conscription were drafted under the student mobilization order. Except for those majoring in the sciences, all college students were now subject to the draft. I thought then that Japan had entered an age where every citizen was a soldier.

Many of us college students had been uncomfortable about our deferrals. We wondered whether it was really appropriate for us to be cooling our heels in class while soldiers our age were out there dying every day. Of course there were some who had enrolled in college specifically to escape military service. For instance, some professional baseball players enrolled in night classes to avoid the draft. But most college students didn't relish their privileged status.

The first student mobilization in 1943 produced over a hundred thousand student soldiers. They said that colleges across the country had gone empty. In October, a send-off rally for the newly tapped students was held at Meiji Jingu Gaien Stadium. As a cool rain fell, fifty thousand female students saw off a procession of half as many student troops.

Ah, the irony of fate. Most of the pilots in the special attack units were selected from that year's recruits. This was because both the Navy and the Army selected a great number of flight trainees from the student pool.

Piloting an aircraft isn't as easy as driving a car. There are many things one must learn before ever getting into the cockpit. And so, before the war, the pilots in training and those who attended the flight prep program were all brilliant kids who'd passed highly competitive exams. The military believed that the air corps required such standout personnel. Since college students had a wealth of knowledge and high intelligence, we offered some fine material to quickly dress up as pilots. Thus, after intensive training, we became for-kamikaze aviators. Over 4,400 men died as kamikazes, and nearly half of them were flight student reservists.

Those chosen to become pilots from among the students culled that year, the 13th class of reservists, would make up the bulk of the IJN's special attack units. I belonged to the 14th class, mobilized the following year. Many members of my class, too, were selected to become kamikazes.

By the way, the generally accepted story is that the first kamikaze unit was Lieutenant Seki's Shikishima Unit deployed at Leyte Gulf, but, in fact, the very first one was Lieutenant Junior Grade Kofu Kuno of the Yamato Unit, also formed for Leyte. Lieutenant Kuno came from the 11th class of student reservists.

Lt. Seki's Shikishima Unit struck on October 25th, but Lt. Kuno's Yamato Unit made its charge on the 21st. On that day, both units failed to make contact with the enemy and all aircraft turned back, except Lt. Kuno, who kept flying and searching for the enemy and never returned to base.

So in truth Lt. Kuno was the very first kamikaze, but he was never honored as such. Partly because they couldn't confirm his results; another major reason was that he'd been a reserve officer. The Navy naturally wanted the credit of "first kamikaze" bestowed on a Naval Academy graduate, so they announced that Lt. Seki had become the first kamikaze. This fact should make it pretty clear how much they valued their own academy's officers and made light of us student reservists.

Even so, a great number of reservists of the 13th and 14th classes were turned into aviators for special attack purposes.

It was rare for a veteran pilot to be sent out as a kamikaze. In the Philippines theater in 1944, a number of seasoned pilots were ordered to become kamikazes, but that no longer happened in the Battle of Okinawa the following year. Because most of the old guard who had served since the start of the war had died out by that point, highly skilled veteran pilots had become precious to the military.

The battle-tested aviators mostly defended the mainland or deployed to escort the kamikazes. Either that or they served as flight instructors. As I've said many times, it was the expendable student reservists and boy pilots from the prep program who were picked to be kamikazes.

I became a flight student reservist in May of 1944, as a member of the 14th class. Lieutenant Seki's Shikishima Unit's deployment would come half a year later. But I'm sure the Navy was already seriously considering the option of using special attack units at that point. I think they had already decided to use the 13th and 14th classes as kamikaze pilots. But of course, we had no way of knowing.

We weren't taught anything about dogfighting or bombing methods, probably because such lessons would have been completely pointless given that all we were meant to do was load ourselves up with explosives and crash into enemy ships.

Flight training was incredibly rigorous. Since we had to complete training that normally took two or three years in less than one year, both instructors and students were frantic. The military wanted us students to be able to fly as soon as possible for use as kamikazes.

But the instructing staff were non-commissioned officers, and they were very conscientious. Since a cadet's status fell between commissioned officers and non-comms, we outranked most of our teachers. Once we completed training, we were immediately made ensigns, that is to say, commissioned officers, even without any actual experience in battle. For a rank-and-file enlisted serviceman to rise to commissioned status took over a decade. When you stop to think about it, that was pretty irrational.

In the flight training units, too, the student reservists had a higher rank than most of those who taught them, which was definitely awkward for both sides. I think the instructing staff felt they had to stand on ceremony with us. Even if they wanted to be strict or stern, the difference in rank prevented them from doing so. But in any case, we were being trained for use in kamikaze attacks, so perhaps it wouldn't have made any difference.

Meanwhile, ignorant of our fates as kamikazes, we threw ourselves into the training, wanting to become full-fledged pilots as soon as we could. We were chafing to go off and shoot enemy aircraft out of the sky. How ludicrous.

We learned of Shikishima Unit's fate in October of '44. And after that we heard news of continuous launches of special attack units in the Philippines, which made us begin to wonder if we were to follow in their footsteps.

Miyabe-san arrived as an instructing officer towards the end of our training period. I believe it was in the beginning of 1945.

I clearly remember my first impression of him like it was only yesterday. His whole being gave off a strange sort of aura. There were several members of the Tsukuba Air Unit that had transferred there from the front lines, and, having survived many life-or-death situations, they all seemed intimidating. Miyabe-san, too, had that special air about him.

Strangely, the more intense fighting someone had seen, the less inclined they were to discuss the war, while those with little experience in battle tended to act like they were the authority on what the front lines were like. Miyabe-san, too, rarely spoke of his experiences in battle. He wasn't the type to talk of glory or brag about his exploits.

Instructing Officer Miyabe's rank was ensign, but he always spoke very politely to us. The few instructing officers there who had graduated from the Naval Academy tended to speak very rudely and yelled at us as a matter of course. But Miyabe-san never once raised his voice when speaking to a student. While he was technically an ensign, he was a so-called "special duty officer," treated as a notch below an officer who had graduated from the Naval Academy. Once, I witnessed a young ensign from the Naval Academy chewing out an SDO lieutenant junior grade. Such were the ways of the military.

The student aviators who had graduated before us were branded "reserve officers" or "spares" and considered one rung below those who had attended the Naval Academy, too, so we were sympathetic towards the SDOs. But the non-comms must have thought of us as belonging to a privileged class.

While Miyabe-san was very polite, he was an extremely strict instructor. He was infamous for not readily giving passing marks to his students. Where other staff would give us qualifying marks, it was extremely common for him to give out F's.

Therefore, he wasn't popular with many students, me included.

"I'm sure to someone who's just back from the front, our flying skills are pretty bad. But that attitude is even nastier than bragging about war experiences."

"I bet he doesn't like the fact that we're officer candidates, but why harass us in this way?"

I also sensed something obstinate in Miyabe-san's methods. I thought that maybe what someone had said was right on the mark: he was probably unhappy with the fact that we were graduating right into the rank of ensign with hardly any effort at all, while it had taken him over a decade of work to get there. I could understand such feelings, but it was not our fault.

After Miyabe-san began instructing us, there was supposedly scant progress in our training. Finally, a group of students complained about him to a more senior instructing officer.

The next day, when Miyabe-san drilled us on in-flight turning, he failed every one of us. I could understand giving a majority of students F's, but to fail everyone seemed like it was just plain harassment.

Again we complained to the senior instructor, but Miyabe-san's attitude didn't change one bit. He continued to fail most of his students. Our hearts almost went out to our nemesis, because here was a man made of incredibly stubborn stuff. Eventually, he was relieved of his duties as an instructor.

However, they were short of teachers, and Miyabe-san was quickly reinstated. But he was limited to carrying out in-flight training only, and it was another instructor's duty to grade our practical skills. This was probably an order from above.

The arrangement clearly had an effect on Miyabe-san. Well, of course. A *sensei* who can't mark his pupils is, after all, not a real *sensei* at all. The situation had probably greatly wounded his pride. From that point on, his instructing style became even more meticulous. *Serves you right*, we thought to ourselves.

However, he was obviously disgusted whenever he said, "You have improved some," which irked us to no end.

One day after I had completed a turning drill, Miyabe-san said, "You've made progress." But I could see on his face that his words weren't sincere. I felt that my performance had at least been adequate. Quite irritated, I suddenly found myself saying, "Instructing Officer Miyabe, are you really that dissatisfied with the fact that I have improved?"

He looked stunned. "No, of course not. If I have given you that impression, then the blame is entirely mine," he replied and deeply bowed his head.

His attitude struck me as a mere hypocritical courtesy. "If that's the case, then why can't you look even a tiny bit happy about my progress?"

Instructor Miyabe fell silent.

"Or are you really thinking that I'm totally hopeless?"

He didn't reply.

"Well? Or are you, in fact, just being spiteful?"

"To be perfectly honest, Flight Student Okabe," he said, "I think your flying skills will not be worth a damn in combat."

I felt myself flush red. "How…on what grounds?" was all I could manage.

"Flight Student Okabe, if you were to go to the front right now, you would almost certainly be shot down."

I wanted to object, but I couldn't think of a single thing to say.

"I do not continue to fail everyone out of mere spite. I have seen too many pilots lose their lives in battle. Many men more skilled than me with longer military careers have been shot out of the sky. The Zero is no longer the invincible fighter it once was. The other side now has excellent aircraft, and their sheer numbers are overwhelming. Battles are severe and unforgiving. Do you think I am just blowing wind about the front lines?"

"Um…no."

"At the Mariana Islands, and at Leyte, many young pilots were sent into battle before they had acquired sufficient experience or training. Most died on their very first mission."

Instructor Miyabe spoke in a matter-of-fact tone. I couldn't come up with any reply.

"I have mentioned my concerns to the squadron leader, but he was deaf to my words. In fact, he ordered me to give passing marks to all students except in the case of an extreme blunder. He said that great skill didn't matter anymore because they're short on pilots and want as many fresh ones as they can get as soon as possible."

I nodded.

"As I instruct such excellent young men as yourselves, I honestly find myself thinking that you should not be made pilots. I think you all can and should do something better with your lives, more magnificent work than that. If I had any say in the matter, I would not send any of you to your deaths."

Instructor Miyabe's words lodged in my heart and stayed with me all through the postwar years. Whenever I was having a hard time at work, those words came back to me.

"That was terribly impudent of me." Instructor Miyabe bowed his head and then turned and walked towards his quarters.

I was ashamed. I'd judged him in such a shallow manner, and I couldn't forgive myself for it.

I completed the pilot curriculum at the end of February. The short training had taken less than a year to finish. The old Preparatory Flight Training Program would have taken more than two years to complete, so it was patently obvious that ours had merely been a crash course.

That night I was handed a single sheet of paper. On it was written the question: "Do you volunteer for the Special Attack Force?" And I was ordered to submit an answer by the following day.

This is it then, I thought. But the shock of actually receiving that sheet of paper was far greater than whatever resolve I'd been able to muster.

I had been prepared to die from the moment I joined the training unit as a student reservist. This was something I had discussed many times with classmates that I was friendly with. But we had meant dying after giving our all in battle. Volunteering for a special attack unit and certain demise was something altogether beyond what I had been prepared for.

But we'd known that they'd started using kamikazes the previous year, so I wasn't totally panicked in face of the volunteer form. Shikishima Unit's actions at Leyte Gulf in the fall of '44 had been announced with great fanfare by the papers and such. The media and Imperial General HQ had continued to issue news on kamikaze units for days on end. So I had kept the possibility of this happening in the back of my mind.

—Was I shocked by reports of the first kamikaze attack? Not

really, to be frank. It did make me gird up.

By that time, I think I'd become desensitized with regards to death. It had become common to see the phrase "shattered jewels" in newspaper columns. What did "shattered jewels" really mean? Annihilation. It meant that all members of a unit had died in combat. They replaced "annihilation" with "shattered jewels" to paper over the sheer calamity of it. Back then, the Japanese military used such rephrasings on all sorts of matters. They referred to the mass evacuations from the cities to the countryside as "dispersals," and retreating on the battlefield was "advancing upon turning." But I think "shattered jewels" is the worst example because the intent was to disguise death as something beautiful. Eventually, the press bandied about the phrase "100 million shattered jewels"—a call for the entire nation's all-out fight to the death.

After seeing news reports of so many deaths day in and day out, I began to think of life as something quite insignificant and transient. As thousands of soldiers were dying on the front lines each day, the thought of a dozen or so kamikaze pilots sortieing to their certain demise didn't seem all that shocking.

But once I found myself in their shoes, my perception of the situation completely shifted. People are so very self-centered, as you know.

I thought of my parents—my mother and father who had doted on me like nothing else. And I thought of my little sister, ten years my junior. While my parents would be able to bear my death, my sister would no doubt weep inconsolably. She loved me more than anyone else. "I love you the best, big brother. I love you even more than Mom or Dad," she liked to say.

The truth is, my sister was mentally disabled, though not acutely. Like many such children, she was exceedingly innocent, never mistrustful of anyone, which made her all the more pitiable and endearing.

Had I had a girlfriend or wife, things might have been different. But thankfully I was single back then. I didn't even have someone I admired in secret. So at the time, I was only concerned for my family.

I thought that my parents would be able to bear up. They would even pardon me for failing in my filial duty. Perhaps they would feel pride over their son having given his life to defend the home-land. But I was filled with remorse for my sister. There would be no one left to care for her once my folks passed away, and I couldn't get over that.

I don't remember how I actually made up my mind with the volunteer form staring me in the face. I don't really remember a thing now as to whether I made the decision with some deep-seated mental resolve or what.

Near dawn, I finally checked the box next to the "I volunteer" option. I think I was driven by the sense that many if not all of the others would be volunteering. I didn't want to become the only coward. I remember taking care to keep my hand steady when I wrote down my name. I was worried about such things even at that juncture.

All of the flight students elected to volunteer. But later I did hear that some had originally checked "I do not volunteer." Those reserves had been individually called up by the officers and persuaded to change their answers. "Persuasion" by one's superiors in the military back then was essentially the same as being ordered to do something. It was virtually impossible to disobey.

Do you think we were wimps? I don't expect people born and raised breathing freedom to be able to understand. But really, even nowadays, how many people at work do you think are actually capable of sticking their necks out and boldly saying "no" to their superiors? We "volunteers" were faced with a far more severe situation back then.

When I heard that some had initially chosen not to volunteer, all I thought was that since we were going to be coerced into doing it anyway, they should've just consented from the start.

Now I'm convinced, though—the men who initially refused to volunteer were truly admirable. The ones who made completely unfettered choices about a matter of life and death, according to their own will and nothing else, were the real men. Looking back, had more Japanese people, including myself, been made of such stuff, we could have ended the war much sooner.

The ones who convinced those men to change their answers might not have been superior officers but their fellow reserves. To be sure, none of us were happy with the idea of going to our deaths. But back then, there simply was no alternative. The military would never have forgiven us for refusing to volunteer for the kamikaze units. Indeed, there were rumors to that effect. Pilots from other training units who had stubbornly refused were shipped off to join the ground troops fighting on the front lines or were deployed in suicidal battles. They were only rumors, so we had no way of knowing how much, if any of it, was true. But for those of us in that era, it was sufficiently close enough to the truth to believe.

The military thought nothing of the lives of the troops. I said earlier that 4,400 young lives were lost in kamikaze attacks. But a single mission of the Surface Special Attack Force led by the battleship *Yamato* during the Battle of Okinawa saw the loss of nearly as many lives.

The *Yamato*'s sortie was a desperate effort. The preposterous plan was for the ship to be beached on Okinawa and used as a land-based gun battery against invading American troops. Of course, such a plan of action was doomed to fail. A single battleship with no air cover and just a handful of escort ships had practically no chance of actually making it to Okinawa.

Essentially, the *Yamato* was turned into a kamikaze unit that took the lives of her entire 3,300-man crew plus those of smaller vessels along with her. The staff officers who had come up with that plan didn't care a farthing about the lives of those men. Maybe they were incapable of imagining that the 3,300 were all human beings with families, mothers and fathers, wives, children, and siblings. Even in a battle they knew they would lose, the higher-ups couldn't just stand by, so they used the *Yamato* and several light cruisers and destroyers and thousands of crew members in a "special attack" to save face with a bold gesture.

The General Staff and the Combined Fleet admirals who drew up a flimsy battle plan which would sacrifice the *Yamato*, the pride of the Combined Fleet, would obviously not hesitate to throw away the lives of student reservists as kamikazes. In the best-case scenario, a warship could be sunk at the cost of only one man and one plane. They likely thought it couldn't be helped that dozens of aircraft and pilots would be lost for the sake of one such strike hitting its target.

By the way, even when you volunteered to become a kamikaze, you weren't immediately shipped off. Making us volunteer for special attacks was merely a premise, an element of process for the military. Once you volunteered, you were put into the pool of special-attack personnel from which the higher-ups could freely select when and who to send on kamikaze missions.

Even after we had graduated and been commissioned as officers, we were put through continued drills. At that time, though, while there were enough warm bodies for the kamikaze units, there weren't enough aircraft. And not just aircraft—we didn't have enough fuel, either, which interfered with our training.

It was around that time that the Okinawa Special Attack Operation began.

From March of 1945, kamikaze planes took off from bases in Kyushu almost every day to strike against the U.S. fleet in the seas around Okinawa. There was a media blitz concerning those attacks.

One day in April, there was an announcement: sixteen members of my 14th class of reserve officers had been named as special attack personnel. I was not on the list. Those selected were all our class's top pilots.

My best friend, Yoshio Takahashi, was among those called up. We had been in the same year at Keio University. He loved literature and hoped to become a scholar of Japanese lit. He was also a third-rank judo wrestler of the *Kodokan* School. He cut a stately figure, standing nearly six feet, the very picture of excellence in both mind and body.

There was one incident between us that I'll never forget.

Once, when he was over at my house for a visit, my sister came home in tears. According to a girl from the neighborhood who was with her, some middle schoolers had teased her, called her "retard," and then slapped her about the face until she started crying. Even before then, she'd been laughed at and teased for her disability, to my great irritation, but this time I'd had enough. Getting slapped around because she was mentally disabled?

I asked the neighbor girl which school those kids were from.

Then, when I turned around, I saw something that floored me.

Takahashi was petting my sister's head and sobbing himself.

"You poor thing, you poor thing, Kazuko-chan. You didn't do anything to deserve that," he said, tears streaming down his face.

Takahashi's kindness towards her pierced my heart. I felt like I could do anything for the man.

And now, he'd been called up to be a kamikaze.

"Trade places with me," I begged him.

"Don't be stupid, Okabe," Takahashi laughed.

"Please, let me go in your place."

"Nope."

"Trade with me, damn it!" I yelled, grabbing him by the lapels.

"Hell no!" he bellowed right back.

"Trade with me, Takahashi," I said, trying to push him over.

"Like I would," he said, then sent me sprawling.

I got up and wrapped my arms around his waist, but he had no trouble flinging me off. As I stood up and tackled him again, I was crying. Seeing me in such a state was making him cry, too, but he continued to fling me away.

At long last I had used up all my strength and lay prone, weeping.

"Okabe, *you* survive. For Kazuko's sake, you can't die," Takahashi said, embracing me about the shoulders. He was still in tears.

We weren't the only men to cry that day. At night, after getting drunk, those who hadn't been selected wailed aloud and begged those who'd been chosen to let them go in their stead, though it wasn't an option. Some guys even went and pled with the flight commander in tears to be allowed to go on a special attack.

Both the chosen and the unchosen cried that night.

Starting the next day, the chosen sixteen began flight training with high-octane aviation fuel, the type used in actual combat. They were, quite literally, training to die.

Even so, Takahashi and the other reserve officers were magnificent.

Being selected for a kamikaze unit was akin to being handed a death warrant. But those men never betrayed any hint of fear to the rest of us. They never even looked gloomy. If anything, they acted downright cheerful.

Of course, that couldn't have been a reflection of their true states. It was for us that they showed us smiles. Facing death and still considering the feelings of friends they'd be leaving behind— how amazing those men were.

Their instructing officer was Miyabe-san. Of course, he was aware that Takahashi and others had been selected for special attack units.

One day, in reference to Instructor Miyabe, Takahashi said to me, "He actually has a real heart, you know."

I asked him what he meant by that.

"It's just too painful for him to teach us, I can tell. It pains him to send us off to die."

"Really?"

"And it's painful for me to see him look so pained."

I told him what Instructor Miyabe had once said to me. Takahashi nodded in understanding. "That's the sort of person he is," my friend mumbled.

Then he added, "It's just a rumor, but I heard that he refused to become a kamikaze back in the Philippines."

That came as a surprise to me.

"It's probably true, too," Takahashi said. "I really have a lot of respect for him."

There was nothing I could say.

It was with a sad expression that my friend declared, "We're wimps."

At the beginning of May, Takahashi and others headed to Kokubu Airfield in Kyushu. There weren't enough planes, so of the sixteen chosen pilots, only eleven took off in Zero fighters. Instructor Miyabe would guide the formation.

Before leaving, Takahashi told me, "So I'm off." When I couldn't manage a reply, he said, "Wipe that look off your face," and gave me a big smile. His sunny expression was almost dazzling.

Then he ran off towards the airstrip.

I later learned that all eleven of the pilots who took off that day were dead within a month.

Instructor Miyabe stayed at Kokubu and apparently sortied numerous times, as a fighter escort to special attack units. I've heard that he, himself, died as a kamikaze right before the end of the war.

After that, I was transferred to Konoike Air Base in Ibaraki Prefecture where I became an *Ohka* pilot.

Do you know about the *Ohka*, written with the characters for "sakura" and "flower"? They were rocket bombs piloted by humans.

No, these weren't airplanes. They were bombs, pure and simple. They couldn't take off on their own, nor could they land. They couldn't even turn, they just glided straight through the air. The Ohkas would be suspended underneath a Type 1 land-based attack bomber and then released towards a hostile ship—as human rockets.

Amazing, isn't it, that such inhumane weapons were even built.

For the training, all we did was practice nose-dives. Swooping straight down towards the target from a high altitude was all there was to it. We used Zeros to practice diving.

We got just one practice flight in an Ohka. Since they didn't come equipped with landing gear, they were fitted with skids instead. After diving at a terrifying speed from a high altitude, you leveled out close to the ground then touched down on the runway. If you successfully landed, you were given an "A" grade, listed as an Ohka pilot, and shipped off to Kyushu with no time to spare.

Hm? What if you failed to land properly? You died.

Many pilots met that fate. Some couldn't pull out of the dive and go into level flight, some overshot the runway and crashed into the embankment, some had broken skids and burst into flames from the friction, some simply crashed because the rocket propulsion mechanism had malfunctioned...

That training was beyond terrifying. I went through it. I'll never forget the fear.

I went weak at the knees when I had to transfer from the mother plane to the Ohka. The Type 1's belly opened up, and in the face of wind pressure strong enough to blow me away, I had to jump into the cockpit of the Ohka suspended underneath. Of course, there was no lifeline or anything like that. If some accident or malfunction occurred and the Ohka fell, I would be a goner.

But that fear was nothing compared to what I felt when I went into the dive. The instant the Ohka was cut loose from the mother plane, it fell about 300 meters at an incredible speed. The powerful negative g-force made all the blood in my body race to my head. It felt ready to pop open. My guts felt like they were being squeezed out of my mouth. Doing my best not to lose consciousness, I had to pull the control stick with all my might, aiming the gliding rocket towards the airfield. Once close to the ground, I had to pull even harder to bring the rocket into level flight. This caused yet another unimaginably intense g-force, and my vision blacked out briefly. I felt like I was on the verge of passing out. It's possible that my friends who'd failed to pull out of the dive had in fact fainted at that point. The Ohka landed with a tremendous impact, like my whole body had been slammed against the pavement.

I've lived for eighty years, but I have never experienced anything more terrifying than that. Of course, the fear of the kamikazes who actually crashed into enemy ships must have been even greater.

In July, I was transferred to Omura Base in Nagasaki as an Ohka pilot. By then the military bases at Kagoshima, Miyazaki, and other areas in southern Kyushu had suffered damage from air raids and were barely functional. They were being used exclusively as staging grounds for kamikaze missions.

I thought I actually saw Instructor Miyabe at Omura, but I don't remember whether or not we spoke. My memory of those days is hazy like it was all some dream. I do recall that each morning that my name was not on the list of pilots selected for that day's mission, I felt I had been given an extra day to live.

Fortunately, the war ended before I was ordered to sortie.

How did I feel when the war ended? I was certainly relieved. But at the same time, I felt like I hadn't made it in time. I felt guilty that I alone had survived and that I couldn't ever face my many friends who hadn't.

Those feelings never faded—they still haven't, even now.

Silence reigned over us. Cicadas buzzed in the distance.

"Whoever invented the Ohka was a monster!" Keiko said in a tear-choked voice.

Okabe nodded deeply. "Part of the base at Konoike where we trained is now a memorial park, Kashima Ohka Park. They say there's even a real one on display there. But I never want to see another Ohka as long as I live."

"I can understand that," I said.

"But about ten years ago I saw one by accident. On a trip to America, I saw one on display at the Smithsonian. It was suspended from the ceiling. I remember being stunned to see just how small it was. What was even more shocking was to see what they called it. Do you know what they called it? The 'Baka' Bomb."

"'Baka' Bomb?" my sister parroted.

"Yes, the Idiot Bomb. Even though my son and his wife were standing right next to me, I wept out loud. I was so mortified, so miserable... No matter how long I cried, the tears just wouldn't stop. But in fact, 'idiot' was the perfect term. The kamikaze tactic cooked up by the insane Japanese military was truly the most idiotic battle plan in the history of the world. That wasn't the only reason for my tears, though. I just felt so sorry, so very sorry for Takahashi and all the others who had died in such an idiotic operation."

Okabe's face suddenly crumpled, and tears spilled from his eyes. His vexation and regret began to affect me. I was pretty shocked by "baka" too, as if they were putting down my grandfather as an idiot.

"Over 150 Ohka pilots died as part of the Divine Thunder Unit, formed around the Ohkas, and a total of 800 men for the unit as a whole. The crew of the Type 1 bombers that ferried the Ohkas are included in that number."

"So the mother planes were shot down too?"

"Exactly," Okabe replied. "An Ohka weighed two tons. With that kind of freight the Type 1 planes flied so slowly that they were practically asking to be shot down. The Ohka's range was at best 30 kilometers, and there wasn't one chance in a hundred for the mother planes to break through the enemy's line of interceptors to within 30 kilometers of their warships. Whoever invented the Ohka was totally ignorant of the realities of aerial warfare.

"The first Ohka attack was launched in March of '45 with eighteen Type 1 bombers hauling fifteen Ohkas, and every last aircraft was shot down by American fighters. The leader of the Divine Thunder Unit, Lieutenant Commander Goro Nonaka, thoroughly opposed such an imprudent operation, but his superior, Admiral Matome Ugaki, overruled him. Lieutenant Commander Nonaka then asked for a fighter escort of seventy Zeros, but was only allotted thirty. He couldn't bring himself to send off his subordinates alone on a mission that was nearly impossible to survive, so he led the formation himself."

"Ahhh," my sister voiced.

"Everyone who knew Lt. Cdr. Nonaka has said that he was a truly wonderful superior. He was a big-hearted man who cared very much for his troops and liked to say, 'C'mon guys, let's give 'r a go!' His unit was referred to as the Nonaka Family, and his men loved him like he was their daddy."

"He sounds like an extraordinary person."

"Given his position he didn't need to sortie. He participated in that mission because he couldn't stand by idly as his men went to their deaths, but possibly also to impress upon his superiors that it was an idiotic idea."

"He was a true officer."

Okabe nodded. "But even though the Nonaka Family was utterly wiped out, the Divide Thunder Unit sortied with Ohkas many more times after that. As could be expected, almost none of them ever managed to reach the enemy ships and were shot down along with their mother planes. And thus the unit saw a staggering eight hundred casualties."

Silence reigned among the three of us again. After a while, Keiko said, "Okabe-san, how were you able to accept being in a special attack unit?"

"What do you mean by 'accept'?"

"How were you able to accept your own death, in the context of a special attack?"

"That's a tough question." Okabe folded his arms.

"I think it's impossible to accept one's death in the absence of some sublime purpose that transcends it. Okabe-san, what was that sublime purpose in your case?"

Keiko's question was unexpected. It might have been something she'd prepared in advance.

Okabe was silent for a while, but he finally opened his mouth. "This might sound like I am just trying to put up a good front, but I thought that I would gladly offer up my life if my dying could protect my family."

"Did you really think that by dying you could keep your family safe?"

Okabe stared at Keiko. "Are you trying to say that the kamikazes died in vain?"

"Not at all," Keiko said, shaking her head hastily.

"Okay, then may I change the subject somewhat?" he asked.

"Please do, sir."

"America is a free country that values the lives of its citizens more than any other nation. Yet the same America fought against Nazi Germany in World War II in order to protect that freedom. In 1943, B-17 bombers were deployed numerous times to bomb the Germans' war plants, in broad daylight with no fighter escort. They didn't have a fighter escort because back then America didn't have fighters capable of flying such long distances. And they carried out the raid in broad daylight because they wouldn't be able to sight the plants at night."

"I follow you, sir."

"This was a very dangerous mission. On each sortie, the B-17s met with intense resistance from the Luftwaffe, and each time more than forty percent of the bombers failed to return. They say no aircrew survived four missions. Even so, in order to defeat Hitler and Nazism, the American military continued the daylight raids. And the American pilots bravely flew into German airspace. Over five thousand B-17 crewmembers were killed in action. That's actually a thousand more than our Special Attack Force dead."

"That many?"

"Such is war. Just as the Americans risked their lives fighting so their homeland could claim victory, we too put our lives on the line. Even if we were to die, we didn't think it was meaningless as long as we were protecting our homeland and our families. We went into battle believing that to be true. I know that you who were born and raised in the peaceful postwar era can't possibly comprehend what that was like, but we really believed that as we fought. Otherwise, how could anyone go to his death as a kamikaze? How could anyone give his life if he thought his death would have no meaning or value? I'd rather die first than tell my late friends, 'Your deaths were in vain.'"

Keiko was silent. An oppressive tension filled the room. Okabe was the one to break it.

"Even so, I disapprove of the special attacks. I absolutely disapprove," he said in a very firm tone. "There was no hope of surviving a kamikaze mission. While the American B-17 bombers had a huge number of casualties, there was still a chance that they would make it back alive, which allowed them to be courageous. It wasn't an operation that was guaranteed to kill them.

"This is what I heard from someone after the war, but Fifth Air Fleet Commander Matome Ugaki, who had advocated for all planes to become kamikazes, went to each of the special attack pilots before they sortied and shook their hands, weeping as he spoke words of encouragement. And then he asked, 'Does anyone have any questions?' A veteran aviator who had served since Midway took up the offer and said, 'If I score a hit on an enemy ship with my bomb, am I allowed to return, sir?' Fleet Commander Ugaki had the gall to tell him, 'No, you don't.'"

"What?" I said, unable to check my disbelief.

"That's the truth about the special attacks. The tactic wasn't about winning. Pilots hurling themselves at the enemy was its very purpose. And by the latter half of the Battle of Okinawa, volunteering was out—they simply ordered you to do it."

Chapter 9
Kamikaze Attack

We met Former Navy Lieutenant Junior Grade Takanori Takeda at a hotel in Shirogane, Tokyo. He had reserved a hotel room just for our meeting.

What I found surprising was that Takeda had been the president of a large corporation that even I knew about, one listed in the First Section of the Tokyo Stock Exchange. Keiko, too, said that she had heard his name before. He had been a student at Tokyo University when he had joined the flight student reservists, and after the war he had gone back to college, gone on to graduate school, and then joined a company. He had served in the vanguard of Japan's postwar economic recovery.

Initially, I felt it was a bit strange that a former kamikaze pilot would turn into a corporate bigwig. But in terms of Takeda's own career, it seemed that the short year-plus he'd spent in the Navy was the exception to the rule.

My sister and I were supposed to meet up in the lobby before going to his room, but Keiko emailed saying she was running late.

I phoned up to Takeda's room. Soon thereafter, he and his wife came down to the lobby.

"I'm Takeda," the man said in a firm voice. He was tall, with white hair and a matching moustache above his lip. "Dandy" would have been an appropriate description, and he looked far younger than an octogenarian.

"I'm Kentaro Saeki, Kyuzo Miyabe's grandson. My sister's running late, I'm afraid. Thank you very much for going to the trouble of reserving a hotel room, sir."

"Oh, it was nothing. It just happened to overlap with a getaway we'd already planned. We haven't gotten out of the house for a while, so this was a perfect opportunity for us." Takeda glanced at his wife and laughed. "Why don't we have some tea or something while we wait for your sister?"

We went into the lounge area, sat at a table, and were placing our orders just as Keiko arrived—surprisingly, with Takayama in tow.

"Takayama-san said he was really interested in hearing what you have to say, sir. So he was hoping to join us today."

Takeda, instead of replying, turned to look at me.

"That's going to be a problem, Keiko," I said. "This is a private discussion. It has nothing whatsoever to do with Takayama-san."

Keiko looked troubled, but I was not going to bend on this point even if she begged.

"It's fine. Please, have a seat," Takeda said.

"Much obliged, sir," Takayama said with a polite bow of his head. He sat down, then handed a business card to Takeda and introduced himself.

"A reporter," Takeda muttered as he read the business card. His expression briefly clouded over.

"This isn't an interview. I simply wish to be present during a personal discussion, if you'd please be so kind." Takayama bowed deeply.

Takeda nodded silently. "We'll talk later, in our room."

Takayama and Keiko placed their drink orders with the waiter.

"However, as I said on the phone, I will not discuss myself or the kamikaze units. I will only discuss my memories of Kyuzo Miyabe," Takeda said, adding milk to his black tea.

Takayama suddenly opened his mouth. "Why are you unwilling to talk about the kamikazes, sir?" Takeda turned towards him. "I'm very interested in the fact that you were a kamikaze pilot yourself, Takeda-san."

"I was not a kamikaze pilot. I received flight training and was merely put in that standby pool. Kamikaze pilots were those who were selected to actually sortie in a special attack unit."

"This may be audacious of me, but I think it would be incredibly valuable for someone like you to talk about your kamikaze experience."

"I do not want to discuss such things, especially with the likes of you."

"Why not?"

Takeda heaved a deep sigh, then looked Takayama squarely in the eye. "Because I don't trust your newspaper."

Takayama's expression stiffened.

"After the war, your newspaper changed your tune to gain popularity. You denied everything prewar to pander to the masses. You robbed the people of patriotism."

"We examined prewar excesses and repudiated war and armies. We corrected people's crooked patriotism. For the sake of peace."

"I'll thank you to not throw around the word 'peace' so flippantly."

Takayama's expression shifted at Takeda's words. After a heavy silence, Takayama said, "Then, please allow me to ask one question. Were the kamikaze pilots selected from a pool of special attack personnel?"

"Yes."

"And was the pool comprised of volunteers?"

"That's how it was, yes."

"Which means that you volunteered. Correct?"

Takeda didn't reply and took a sip of his tea.

"So doesn't that mean that there was a time when you yourself were an ardent patriot?"

Takeda's hand froze as it held the teacup.

Takayama plowed ahead. "After the war, you became a great corporate warrior. But even you were once a patriot, and I can't help but be terribly interested in that. Back then, the whole populace, even people like you, were utterly brainwashed."

Takeda put his cup back on the saucer, striking the spoon with a loud clatter as he did. "I was a patriot, but I hadn't been brainwashed. Nor were my comrades who died."

"I think the kamikaze pilots were all brainwashed, at least temporarily. That's not their fault, of course. The blame lies with the era and the military establishment. And I think that after the war, people were deprogrammed, which is why Japan became a democracy and was able to achieve such an impressive recovery."

"Give me a break," Takeda muttered.

Takayama didn't relent. "I think the use of special attack units was an act of terrorism. In fact, I'd go so far as to say that the kamikaze pilots themselves were terrorists of a sort. You can conclude as much from what they wrote in the wills they left behind. They weren't lamenting the fact that they had to throw away their lives for their country. Actually, they were proud to do it. Proud to serve their country, proud to die a noble death for their country. You even get a whiff of heroism."

"Shut up!" Takeda yelled. The waiter spun around, alarmed. "Stop talking like you know everything! We weren't brainwashed. Nothing of the sort."

"But I think it's evident from reading the wills of the kamikaze pilots that they had the mindset of martyrs."

"You jackass! You really think that the kamikaze pilots were expressing their true feelings in those wills?" Takeda shouted, his face turning bright crimson. Other patrons in the lounge turned to stare, but he was totally oblivious. "Back then, our written correspondence was subject to inspection by superior officers before it could be sent out. Not infrequently, even our diaries and wills were read. Criticism of the war or the military was absolutely not permitted, as was even any hint of weakness unbecoming of a military man. Under such strict constraints, the kamikaze pilots had no choice but to express their feelings in between the lines. If you wanted to, you could glean them. Don't be deceived by phrases like 'serving the nation' or 'loyalty.' You really think they were happy to die just because they wrote as much? And you call yourself a reporter. Don't you have any imagination at all? Hell, do you even have a human heart?"

Takeda's voice was trembling with anger. His wife gently placed a hand on his arm.

Takayama defiantly leaned forward. "Then, if they weren't happy to be going off to their deaths, why did they bother to write that they were?"

"Do you really expect them to have written things like 'I don't want to die! And I'm so sad about it!' in the last letters to the poor families they were leaving behind? Can't you even imagine how much their parents would have suffered if they did? How painful it would have been to learn that the sons that they had raised with such loving care had died tormented? Can't you understand that when faced with their deaths, they at least wanted their parents to think that they'd gone to their deaths with clear hearts and minds?"

Takeda hollered, "Even if they couldn't be honest and say that they didn't want to die, their loving families could tell. How? Because most of those wills express boundless appreciation for loved ones. How could anyone who was actually happy to go off and die write such letters brimming with love?"

Takeda was in tears. Even the waiter had been staring at him for some time.

"You call yourself a reporter? Yet you're incapable of reading between the lines written by men doing their damnedest to suppress the chaos in their hearts, in the precious few hours they had left, to say something to their families?"

In response to Takeda's tearful speech, a cool smile crept up Takayama's face. "I take sentences at face value. That's how the written word works. On the day of their sortie, some pilots wrote that 'Today is a day of tremendous joy.' Some expressed delight at the prospect of sacrificing their lives for the sake of the Emperor. Many, many kamikazes wrote very similar things. Their sentiments are the same as those terrorists who style themselves martyrs."

"You dumbass!" Takeda slapped his open hand onto the table, rattling the china. The waiter took an instinctive step forward. Everyone sitting nearby had been staring at our table for quite some time. "Terrorists? Stop spewing that garbage. Terrorists massacre ordinary civilians. They target the lives of innocent people. That's why the attacks on the Twin Towers are considered an act of terrorism. Yes or no?"

"Yes. Those were terrorists."

"The targets of our kamikaze units were not buildings where innocent civilians lived or worked. We targeted aircraft carriers loaded with bombers and fighters. The American carriers launched aircraft that conducted raids on our mainland, indiscriminately bombing and strafing ordinary citizens. Are you really trying to tell me the American military were just innocent people?"

Takayama was momentarily lost for an answer. Takeda continued, "An aircraft carrier is a terrifying weapon capable of mass murder. We targeted our attacks on those extremely powerful killing machines. Plus, the kamikazes sortied in planes of inferior performance, fitted with heavy ordnance, with only a very minimal fighter escort. They were attacked by several times their number of enemy fighters; and if they somehow managed to evade those attacks, they then faced an intense barrage of anti-aircraft fire. That is in no way the same as flying into those defenseless World Trade Center buildings!"

"But you have to admit that they share a common aspect in that both groups were willing to give up their lives for their bel—"

"Shut up!" Takeda cut him off. "Despite your being totally ignorant of where you stand in the world at large, you act like you're a champion of justice or something. You know what, I think it was the media that caused that war. After the Russo-Japanese War, when the Portsmouth Peace Talks convened, many newspapers expressed intense anger over the terms. 'Why should we Japanese swallow such lousy conditions?' they all argued on their pages. Many people were riled up by such articles, and anti-government riots erupted all across the country. They set fire to the Hibiya Public Hall, and Jutaro Komura, who signed the peace treaty with Russia, was subjected to nationwide censure. The only antiwar paper then was Soho Tokutomi's *Kokumin Shinbun*, and their offices were set on fire, too."

"But that was—" Takayama tried to get in a word, but Takeda kept on talking.

"I think that series of events was a watershed moment for Japan. After that, most of the population started to applaud the idea of going to war.

"And then the 'May 15 Incident' happened. In objection to the political leadership, which was swerving from the invasion track and heading toward accepting arms control, young military officers assassinated the prime minister. He tried to reason with them, but they answered, 'Dialogue is useless' and shot him. If that wasn't a military *coup d'état*, then what was it?

"Yet most newspapers heralded those youths as heroes and advocated for reduced sentences. Stirred up by the media, the people became caught up in a movement to extenuate the punishment, sending over 70,000 petitions to the court. Influenced by the public's opinion, the court handed down extremely light sentences to the perpetrators. It's said that the abnormal commutation gave rise to the February 26 Incident and the rise of Japanese militarism. Even now, there's still a tendency in the media to treat the ringleaders of the February 26 Incident as warriors with beautiful hearts full of patriotism. It's a sign of how powerful the prevailing opinion was at the time. After that, no one dared to oppose the excesses of the military, and I mean every politician and journalist. Japan became entirely militaristic, and by the time people started to realize that it wasn't such a good idea, it was far too late to do anything about it. And who was responsible for turning the military establishment into such a monster? The newspapers and the populace that the media riled up."

"To be sure, journalists erred before the war. But that ceased to be the case after the war. We rectified that crazed patriotism," Takayama said, his pride evident.

Mrs. Takeda once again placed a gentling hand on her husband's arm. He looked at her and gave a small nod. When he spoke again, his voice was just above a whisper.

"Most of the newspapers after the war argued that the citizenry must cast off their patriotism, even going as far as to suggest that loving one's country was a crime. While that might appear on first glance to be the exact opposite of what the media supported before the war, their attitude that they knew what was just and that they had to educate the witless masses was the same. And what was the result? No other nation has produced as many sell-out politicians and intellectuals who disdain their own country just to curry favor with our neighbors."

He faced Takayama head-on and said in a clear voice, "I won't ask about your political views, but I insist you stop discussing the kamikaze pilots from some inane ideological viewpoint. If you're incapable of reading between the lines to glean the intended meaning of words written by men who were prepared for death and who did their utmost to express their love for the families and the country they were about to leave behind, then I cannot call you a journalist."

In response, Takayama crossed his arms and arched back, unfazed. "No matter how much you try and gloss it over, most kamikazes were terrorists."

Takeda stared fixedly at him. Then he said very quietly, "People like you are just all words and no action. Get out of my sight."

"Understood. I'll be taking my leave." Takayama stood up, a glum look on his face. Keiko looked lost for a moment but immediately got up and followed him.

"Aren't you going to leave, too?" Takeda asked me.

"My grandfather died a kamikaze, sir."

"Ah, that's right. You're Miyabe-san's grandson."

"Yes, sir. But I don't know anything about how he died. He didn't leave a will or anything. Listening to you, sir, I feel like I get at least some of the suffering that he endured."

Takeda slowly shook his head. "Only kamikaze pilots really understood their own suffering. There was a world of difference, a massive chasm, between us in the reserve pool and those who were selected."

Just then, Keiko came back to join us. "Takayama-san has left. Will you allow me to stay and listen to your story, sir?"

"I don't mind, so long as you intend to actually hear me out with an open mind."

"Yes, I indeed do, sir," Keiko replied.

Takeda nodded. "Let's change the scene," he said, standing.

A few minutes later we were inside Takeda's room. It was my first time inside a top-class hotel suite. Mrs. Takeda poured us green tea from a set in the room. It was very good tea. Takeda sipped at his in silence, clearly attempting to calm his agitated heart. We drank ours quietly.

After a while Takeda spoke. "Before I talk about Miyabe-san, there's something else I need to tell you."

After the war, kamikaze pilots were both praised and censured. While sometimes they were extolled as heroes who sacrificed their lives for the country, at other times they were reviled as warped, fanatical nationalists.

Neither was accurate. The kamikaze pilots were neither heroes nor madmen. They accepted their inescapable fate, and struggled to turn their all-too-brief lives into something meaningful. I observed them close at hand. They thought of their families, and about their country. They weren't fools. And they knew the plan to use kamikazes was hopeless in turning the tide of the war.

They weren't like the fanatical young officers of the February 26 Incident. They weren't drunk on the heroism of dying a glorious death. Some may have adopted that sort of mindset in order to accept their fate. But even if there had been such pilots, who could blame them? They were faced with the very difficult-to-digest fact that they were about to die. So what if they dressed up in some bravado in an attempt to come to terms with their death and to seek refuge from their fears?

There wasn't a single pilot, not one, who went to pieces upon learning that he had been selected to become a kamikaze. Of course, none of them cried or made a fuss before they left on their missions, either. In fact, many of them smiled before climbing into the cockpit. They weren't just putting up a brave front. Their hearts had become free and clear.

I've heard that many death-row inmates scream and cry on the day of their execution. Some even can't stand or walk on their own, and the guards have to practically drag them to the execution chamber. Even though they're being punished for their own heinous deeds, they're miserably incapable of accepting their fate.

Among those who stand opposed to the death penalty are some who say that the psychological terror is cruel. That's probably accurate. I think it's unimaginably terrifying to be told, "We're going to kill you," and then spend the rest of your life wondering when the day will come. That morning, when the door opens and they come for you, you know it's your time to die. If they don't come, then you've been allowed to see another day, which only prolongs the fear. Until the day comes, the torture continues. It's the pain of purgatory.

It was similar for those pilots the moment they were selected from the pool of reserves to become kamikazes. If their name was listed on the blackboard in the morning, then their time had come. If their name wasn't listed, they had been given another day to live. They didn't know when that day would come. The day their name was listed, their lives were over. They wouldn't see their loved ones ever again, and they would never be able to do the things they wanted to do with their lives. Their future was to be broken off in just a few hours' time. How terrifying that must have been for them. No matter how hard I try to imagine it, I'm sure the reality was far more horrible.

And yet they calmly accepted it. I saw off many a friend who gave me a smile before departing. How much internal conflict did they have to overcome to get to such a place? If you can't imagine it, you aren't qualified to discuss those men. That's why I said that the kamikazes and the reserve pool pilots were totally different.

It goes without saying that even those of us in the reserve pool felt like we were going to die. We had resolved to go in a manly way when our names came up. But I think there was a big difference between those actually placed in those circumstances and those yet to be chosen.

There wasn't a single man among us who wanted to give his life for the Emperor.

After the war, many intellectuals wrote that before the war most Japanese revered the Emperor as a living god. What garbage. No one did. Even the young officers who had seized the reins of the military didn't believe anything of the sort.

I'm repeating myself here, but the ones responsible for turning Japan into that kind of country were the journalists.

Before the war, the newspapers would simply print verbatim the announcements from Imperial General HQ, writing article after article of propaganda. And after the war when the American GHQ took over the country, the newspapers followed GHQ's orders and ran articles heralding democracy and decrying prewar Japan as a country of unenlightened fools. They wrote as though the entire population was ignorant and below them. The journalists believed themselves to be the arbiters of justice, and their condescension towards the masses makes me sick to my stomach.

Sorry, I wandered off topic.

It's useless to complain about such things at this point in time. But listening to that reporter just now reminded me of a typical commissioned officer in the military back then. The type that places blind faith in their organization, never attempting to think for themselves, always believing their actions to be correct, paying absolute loyalty to the organization they serve.

Many of those who commanded kamikaze operations were that type of officer. They would say, "You aren't the only ones who are going off to die. I'll be following you without fail." But barely any of those officers actually followed their men as promised. Once the war ended, they all feigned ignorance, acting like they had no responsibility whatsoever. Even worse, a good number said things like, "The kamikazes were all volunteers. They all gave their lives for the country out of the pureness of their hearts." They were shirking responsibility by flattering the kamikazes. Or maybe they were attempting to lessen the pangs of their consciences. In any case, it was because of this sophistry that the kamikazes became the subject of public criticism after the war.

I said that there were almost no officers that followed the kamikazes into death. But Vice Admiral Takijiro Onishi, the "Father of Special Attacks," committed *seppuku* the day after Japan surrendered. More than a few people interpreted his suicide as a noble act, calling it Onishi's atonement. But I don't think it was noble in the slightest. How is the suicide of one old man sufficient atonement for stealing the futures of so many young men?

Even if I ever ceded that it was a desperate but necessary tactic for the Battle of Leyte, special attacks were altogether pointless from the Battle of Okinawa on. If he had the courage to die, then why didn't he say, "I oppose special attacks even at the cost of my life," and disembowel himself then?

They say that Vice Admiral Onishi proposed and adopted kamikaze tactics in October 1944. But was that true? Onishi, himself, once called the special attacks "heresy for any commander."

The Navy started to deploy other suicide weapons, the *Kaitens* and *Ohkas*, towards the end of 1944. But they had been in development since the beginning of that year. Such weapons would never have been developed had the military not already mapped out that course of action, which leads me to believe that Vice Admiral Onishi was just made into a scapegoat. He never attempted to make any excuses. It's likely he died shielding many others who'd been involved.

If he was going to shield anyone, I wish it'd been all those young men.

The *Kaiten* was a human torpedo. A modern torpedo is guided by computers, so even if the target tries to escape it can still give pursuit and score a hit. With the Kaiten, humans played the role of those computers. No other country's military would ever have come up with that.

It's possible that the groundwork for the kamikazes existed within the Navy since the very start. Type A submarines were deployed in special attacks on Pearl Harbor at the outset of the war.

Type A subs were midget submarines with two-man crews. For Pearl Harbor, they were loaded onto full-size submarines and carried close to the Hawaiian shore, then launched into the harbor. But there was little hope of small subs making it into a heavily guarded U.S. naval port. Even if they managed to succeed in their mission, it was impossible for the crew to then escape and be recovered by the mother submarine waiting off shore. In other words, this tactic was essentially the same as the kamikaze forces. The ten crewmembers that sortied knew full well there was no hope of them returning alive. And indeed, all five Type A subs never made it back. I think that was the point when the fate of the future special attack units was sealed.

This is a digression, but during that mission one of the Type A subs ran aground at the mouth of the harbor, and one of her crew was taken prisoner. Imperial General HQ sang the praises of the nine others who had fallen in combat, proclaiming them war gods, and totally ignored Ensign Sakamaki, who had been captured. Even so, Ensign Sakamaki's name became known to the public. Stones were thrown at his parents' house, and abusive letters poured in from all over the country. "Why didn't that damn unpatriotic guy kill himself?" and all that.

An essential navigational instrument, the gyrocompass, was malfunctioning on Ensign Sakamaki's sub. The captain of his mother sub asked, "What do you plan to do?" Ensign Sakamaki apparently replied, "It's a go, sir." There was no military man then who could refuse to embark on a mission when asked that by a superior officer. Why didn't the captain simply cancel his sortie? Due to the faulty gyrocompass, Ensign Sakamaki was unable to properly direct the sub, miscalculated his position, and ran aground. His crewmate died.

In stark contrast to Ensign Sakamaki, who was branded as unpatriotic, local villagers and children thronged the houses of the nine dead men, praising them as heroes. But after the war, the villagers abruptly reversed their opinions and frowned upon their families as ones that had produced war criminals.

There is nothing that puts me in a fouler mood than stories like this.

There's an endless supply of infuriating people and events concerning the kamikazes, but, in particular, I will never find it in me to forgive the commander of the Fifth Air Fleet, Matome Ugaki. Once he learned that the war was over, he sought out a place to die and took along seventeen of his subordinates, young men who didn't need to perish, on a final suicide mission. "If he wanted to die, I wish he'd done it alone." That's what the father of Lieutenant Nakatsuru, one of the subordinates, said, and I wholeheartedly agree with him.

But there's someone we mustn't forget: Lieutenant Commander Tadashi Minobe, who stridently opposed the use of kamikazes.

In February 1945, over eighty military commanders convened a council at Kisarazu to discuss the Combined Fleet's battle strategy for Okinawa. There, Lt. Cdr. Minobe expressed unambiguous opposition to the presiding general staff officer's announcement of a full-force kamikaze operation.

The military had been imprinted with the concept that an order from a superior officer was an order from the Emperor himself. Those who disobeyed orders could be executed after a court-martial. Yet Lt. Cdr. Minobe defied death and voiced steadfast opposition. When his superiors yelled themselves red in the face at him, he retorted, "Is there anyone gathered here today who is ready to charge in?" Then he said, "And it is preposterous to order kamikaze missions using training aircraft. If you think that I am lying, try getting into the cockpit of one and carrying out an attack. I will easily shoot each and every one of you down with a Zero."

After the war, when I learned of what he had said, I was deeply impressed that such a brave officer had existed in the Imperial

Navy. Had there been just a few more men like him present at that council, the plan to use kamikazes at Okinawa might never have been enacted.

I blame the negligence of journalists for the fact that most Japanese have never even heard the name Tadashi Minobe.

—Why isn't he well-known?

I think that has to do with his postwar career as an officer of the Self-Defense Force. Progressive journalists who considered the SDF to be evil were probably unwilling to praise its senior officers. Moreover, ultimately, Minobe did not totally oppose the use of kamikazes. After the war he said, "In the absence of any other effective course of action, a special attack is inevitable." Perhaps they considered this statement to be an affirmation of kamikaze tactics. Yet Lt. Cdr. Minobe never sent a single pilot in his squadron off on a special attack.

I've heard that his name is held in higher regard overseas than in Japan. That's unfortunate. Tadashi Minobe was one of the truly magnificent Japanese of that period. I don't think he should be forgotten.

Lieutenant Commander Saburo Shindo was another exemplary fighter squadron commander. Shindo was the CO of the squadron of thirteen Zero fighters when the aircraft made its spectacular debut over mainland China. He went on to serve in Rabaul, fought at the Mariana Islands and Leyte Gulf, then became the commander of the 203rd Air Unit in Kagoshima in the final year of the war. Even as the "All Planes Kamikaze" call came from the brass, Shindo did not deploy a single special attack.

Lieutenant Commander Kiyokuma Okajima of the 303rd Combat Flight Unit also staunchly refused to send out any kamikazes, whatsoever, even after command branded him a traitor to his country.

So, even among the Naval Academy graduates, there were some fine, upstanding officers. Unfortunately, though, their numbers were disappointingly few.

Anyway, let me tell you about Miyabe-san.

He was an excellent instructor. Many of the student reservists adored him. His gentle bearing and polite manner of speech were entirely unexpected of a military man of that era. Even so, there was something indescribably intimidating about him. We often said among ourselves that he was what they called a professional.

We never did any mock air battles because all of us student reservists were intended to be used on kamikaze missions.

On the day our training ended, we were forced to fill out a Special Attack Force volunteer form. It was a direct order masquerading as an opportunity. Because of this, those in command were later able to get away with saying that "They all became kamikazes of their own volition," and even sixty years later, men like that journalist insist on echoing the lie.

Let me be very clear. Except for a small number of exceptions, the special attack pilots were ordered into it. I don't want to tell you about the pain and inner anguish we felt when we checked the "I volunteer" box on the form. Even if I told you, I don't think you'd fully understand.

After we graduated from flight school and were commissioned with the rank of ensign, we weren't immediately deployed. Instead, we underwent continued flight training. Around that time, there was a shortage of aircraft fuel, and we'd barely been able to practice as flight students.

Even during the continued training, what we flew were either biplane trainers that we called "red dragonflies" or the old Type 96 carrier-based fighter. Training aircraft were fueled with crude gasoline, oil derived from pine tree roots, or ethyl alcohol. I heard later on that even actual combat aircraft weren't using high-octane fuel.

This is getting off topic a bit, but after the war the Americans ran various flight tests on Japanese fighters. When they fueled an Army Type 4 fighter with U.S. military-grade high-octane gasoline, they found that it indicated performance levels superior to that of a P-51 Mustang. The P-51 was considered the most powerful fighter of WWII. When I heard of this, it really sank in that winning a war is all about comprehensive strength. Even if you have one or two superior elements, that doesn't mean much in the end.

Still we persevered. We thought that if our poor abilities might aid the country, we would volunteer. We were willing to sacrifice our lives to protect our homeland. Are such thoughts really fanatical nationalism?

Once I became a kamikaze reserve, I piloted my first Zero. I was stunned by its performance, which was on a different level from the trainers I'd flown up until then. I was thrilled and deeply moved to be sitting in the cockpit of the fighter that was out there gunning down American aircraft.

But our training in the Zeros was limited only to diving. That was what kamikaze training consisted of. Carry a bomb and fling yourself at an enemy ship—we were practicing how to die. Yet we tackled it in earnest.

Why? That's just how people are.

One day, during drills for pulling out of a steep dive, for the first time even I thought I'd done quite well. After the training session, I approached Instructor Miyabe on the airfield and said, "I did pretty well today, don't you think, sir?"

"I was surprised. That was extremely well executed," he said with a smile.

"Really?"

"Yes, really. I'm not flattering you. You're all excellent, yourself included, Takeda-san. I can see why the Navy wanted to turn so many college students into pilots. But..." The smile faded from his face. "Those who become good pilots are immediately shipped off to the front."

I understood what he was saying. At the front, we would be made into kamikazes.

Instructor Miyabe continued. "When I trained to be a pilot, the lessons were on how to survive. How to best shoot down an enemy fighter, how best to escape an attack. All fighter pilots should be given such training. But the situation is different for you. You're only being trained on how to die. What's more, the best ones get sent out first. In such a case, never improving would be better."

I didn't know how to respond.

"Japan needs you all. When this war is over, this country is going to need people like you," Instructor Miyabe declared.

Today, I firmly believe that it was Miyabe-san that Japan needed for its future. He was the one who should never have died.

"Is the war going to end, sir?"

"It will. And soon."

"Will we win, sir?"

He laughed. It was a decidedly sad sort of laugh. "That, I don't know," he said. "I have fought the Americans in the Pacific since Pearl Harbor. They are frighteningly strong."

"In terms of materiel, sir?"

"Not just that. They are superior to our forces in every way."

"What about the Zeros?"

"At the start of the war, the Zero was invincible. I thought that as long as I was in a Zero, I would never lose. But in the latter half of '43, the Americans finally started deploying fighters that are better than the Zero. The Grumman F6Fs and the Sikorskys significantly outperform the Zero."

His statement was earth-shattering. We had been taught that the Zero, the most powerful fighter in the world, was so dominant it could smash any and all enemy fighters.

"The Zero has fought for way too long," Instructor Miyabe said. "It has fought in the vanguard for five years, since the Sino-Japanese War. They've made countless minor revisions to it, but there has never been any dramatic improvement in performance. The tragedy of the Zero is that they never developed new aircraft that could succeed it. Once, the planes were unrivaled warriors, but now they're a bunch of…old-timers."

The image of the plane as he spoke of it overlapped with him in my eyes. I found myself wondering if the Zero wasn't an avatar of the instructing officer himself.

Day by day, the state of the war worsened, yet every day we kept on throwing ourselves into training, at considerable risk to our lives. If you made a split-second error in a nose-dive, you were a goner. In fact, more than a few flight students were killed in training accidents.

My best friend, Ito, died that way. He failed to pull up the nose of his aircraft during a diving drill and crashed into the ground. He was a very bright, cheerful guy, popular with everyone. He was great at reciting old comical limericks, and after a tough day of training when everyone was feeling depressed, he would amuse us with his wonderful voice. He died right before my eyes. "Shock" can't come close to describing what I felt.

Miyabe-san was the instructor at that time. When he got out of his plane, his face was white as a sheet.

That night, all the students were made to line up. A junior-grade lieutenant, a Naval Academy graduate, screamed at us in a hysterical voice. "I don't think I need to tell you that there was a fatal accident here today!" We thought he was about to offer condolences. What he actually said next was wholly unexpected.

"The reservist officer who died today lacked spirit. How could such a man fight a real battle?!" the JG screamed at us, striking the ferrule of his saber cover against the ground. By going out of his way to refer to Ito as a "reservist officer," he made it clear that he held us all in contempt.

"Anyone who dies in training is a disgrace to the military. How dare he ruin a precious airplane? All of you had better make damn sure it never happens again."

In our hearts, we were all shedding bitter tears. Was this war? Was this the military? I learned that a man's life was worth less than an aircraft for them.

It happened then. "Sir!" Instructor Miyabe said. "The late Ensign Ito was an upstanding young man. He was no disgrace to the military."

The phrase "the air froze solid" was created for moments like that.

The JG's face went bright red as he trembled with rage. "You damn bastard!" He jumped down from the dais and threw a punch at Instructor Miyabe, who held his ground and withstood the blow. The JG struck again. Blood spurted from Instructor Miyabe's nose and mouth, but he remained standing.

The JG was short. Even though he was throwing punches with all his might, he couldn't knock down our instructor, who stood looking down his bleeding nose at the smaller man. The JG's face scrunched like he was going to cry.

"Ensign Ito was a fine man, sir!" Instructor Miyabe bellowed as loud as the JG.

He gave a jolt. "For an SDO, you are one insolent bastard!" With this, he punched the instructor once more, then spun on his heels and marched towards the barracks. The squadron leader, looking a bit perturbed, said, "Dismissed," and we fell out of line.

The damage to Instructor Miyabe's face was fairly severe. His lips were split in several places and blood was running down his face from a cut above his eye.

We were all extremely moved. In our hearts, we all thanked him for defending Ito's honor.

It was then that a thought occurred to me. *If I can protect this man by becoming a kamikaze, then so be it.*

I wasn't the only one who felt that way. One guy actually risked his life to save Instructor Miyabe, in fact.

This happened right after Ito's death. Instructor Miyabe was leading three reserve officers through a diving drill. Then, as he was flying along at low altitude, four Sikorskys came through a gap in the clouds behind him and attacked.

The air raid siren didn't sound. The fighters were probably launched from an aircraft carrier in the nearby seas to recon in force. By that point, it wasn't rare for carrier-based planes to conduct open raids on the mainland. By the time the lookout realized their presence, the fighters were already at low altitude.

Instructor Miyabe had completely let his guard down. Unaware of the approaching enemy planes, he was flying along intently watching over a student's aircraft that had just gone into a dive.

The Sikorskys rapidly closed the gap. We shouted as loudly as we could, but there was no way our voices would reach the instructor's plane.

Just then, the Zero of a student reservist who was climbing, having already completed the diving drill, went screaming between Instructor Miyabe's plane and the approaching Sikorskys. Since the machine guns of the reserve officer's training Zero were unloaded, he couldn't fire on the enemy fighters. Even so, his single-minded desire to rescue Instructor Miyabe led him to essentially throw himself headlong at the attacking aircraft.

Two of the four Sikorskys broke away to avoid the trainer plane, but the remaining pair were unfazed in their pursuit. The lead fighter opened fire. It was then that Instructor Miyabe finally noticed and rolled away, but he seemed to be too late.

The reserve officer's Zero took on the bullets from the Sikorsky. Instructor Miyabe dodged and then fired on the Sikorskys from below. One of them was immediately engulfed in flames.

The other Sikorsky attempted to flee by making a turn and climbing, but Instructor Miyabe was right on his tail. As this was a low-altitude fight, the enemy had no way to employ their favored battle tactic of diving to escape.

The American fighter suddenly pulled a 180 and headed right towards the instructor. Immediately after the two passed each other, the enemy plane's nose turned down and it started to fall. The pilot didn't parachute away. He must have been shot in the cockpit through the front windshield. The two other Sikorskys pulled back, retreating high into the sky. Perhaps they were attempting to goad us into pursuing them, but we made no move to follow.

Instructor Miyabe assembled the remaining student planes in the sky, then after a thorough check of the surrounding airspace, allowed them to land. He was the last to touch down. My spine froze when I saw the state of his aircraft—both wings and the fuselage were riddled with bullet holes. I found out afterwards that there'd been a bullet mark just one centimeter away from the fuel tank in one of the wings. Had the bullet struck the tank, no doubt his plane would have gone up in flames.

"I was careless." Instructor Miyabe's voice was trembling. His face was ashen. "Who was it that came to my rescue?"

The cockpit of the reserve officer who had shielded him had received gunfire head-on. The windshield had been pulverized, and the instrument panel smashed to pieces. The pilot himself had been struck, but miraculously the injury wasn't fatal.

Instructor Miyabe ran over to the student as he was carried away on a stretcher.

"Why did you do something so foolish?"

The student, lying on his side on the stretcher, raised his bloodied face. "Sir, you made it."

"Why were you so reckless back there?"

"Japan needs you, Instructor Miyabe. You must not die."

My heart filled to bursting on hearing his words. I was painfully aware of how he felt. He was ready to die for Instructor Miyabe's sake. I felt the exact same.

At any rate, the only word to describe his combat skills was "incredible." He had shot down the far superior Sikorsky fighters in the twinkling of an eye. *The jewel in the crown of the Imperial Navy*, I thought.

Yet the Navy didn't allow him to survive the war.

Soon afterwards, he was transferred along with a number of reserve officers to a base on Kyushu.

I later heard that every last one of the reserve officers died in kamikaze attacks.

Not long after I, too, received orders to go to Kyushu.

I arrived at Kokubu Base in Kagoshima. *Looks like my time is up*, I thought. But I wasn't immediately ordered on a kamikaze mission. I was put on standby as part of the kamikaze pilot pool. Other kamikaze pilots sortied in the Zeros we had brought with us.

At the time, near-daily kamikaze missions were launched from Kokubu Base. I saw off many friends there. I always thought my number would be up next. I wrote a will addressed to my parents. I wished for a chance to see them just one more time before I died, but I knew there was no way for that wish to be granted.

After the Battle of Okinawa, Kokubu Base was attacked multiple times by the Americans. We lost a great many aircraft to bombs and ground strafing. I was among those ordered to join the Usa Air Group in nearby Oita Prefecture.

As I was leaving the base, an elderly couple called out to me. They asked after the whereabouts of a certain reserve officer. I explained to them that the ensign had sortied on a kamikaze mission a few days prior. Upon hearing this, the man bowed deeply and the woman crouched down on the ground.

"We're his parents," the man said. "We'd heard he was at Kokubu so we came here, but it seems we're too late," he lamented.

"He gave us a brilliant smile before he sortied, sir. He flew off, and gave his life like a man."

"Thank you very much. That puts my mind at ease," the ensign's father said. But the mother, still crouching, let out a sob. "He was our only son," the man told me unbidden. Then he wrapped his arms around his wife's shoulders and hauled her up, bowed once more to me, and walked away from the base.

This was not an uncommon sight at Kokubu Base.

Pilots were forbidden from telling their families that they were departing on a kamikaze mission. Friends of the selected pilots would ask someone outside the base to send letters to the soon-to-be-bereaved families. But it was very rare for them to make it to the base before the pilots sortied. Many family members would arrive after the mission only to have to return home in grief.

I also saw young wives who learned of their husband's death at the base. I saw this over and over again at both Kokubu and Usa. Some were so grief-stricken and devastated that their legs failed them. When I saw them, I was thankful that I hadn't gotten married myself. At the same time, I felt sorry for myself since I'd be dying without ever having found a woman's love.

At Usa, I was once again assigned to the special attack pool. Those who were called up were sent to their deaths.

How did I feel back then? I'm sure I was terrified, but I don't really remember anything much.

But I do remember quite clearly the heartbreaking sorrow at having to say farewell to my friends. No matter how hard I try, I can't manage to forget that sadness.

I never saw Instructor Miyabe again, at either Kokubu or Usa.

Silence filled the room for some time.

Mrs. Takeda was the first to speak. "This is the first time I've heard you talk about the special attacks."

Takeda nodded deeply. "I never spoke to anyone about these experiences. I figured that even if I told someone they wouldn't understand. And the thought of unnecessary misunderstandings arising due to my not having a way with words was unbearable."

"Did you think that about me, too?"

He shook his head. "I wanted to try talking about it many times, but I wasn't able to, not until today. While I wanted you to understand my pain and sadness, on the other hand I never wanted you of all people to learn such horrible things."

"I, too, kept something from you all these years," Mrs. Takeda said, looking her husband in the eye. "It was in 1950, wasn't it, that we met through work and married. There was some talk that you had been a kamikaze, but I couldn't even imagine it to be true. You were always so cheerful and full of smiles at work."

Takeda nodded.

"You didn't tell me about the special attack units before we married. And once we were married, I was surprised to discover that you had nightmares every night. You would suddenly groan in torment, your face looking ghastly, like nothing I ever saw during your waking hours… And occasionally you would scream out. When I saw you like that, I wondered, *What horrible things has my man gone through?* And I wouldn't be able to stop myself from crying."

"I didn't know that," Takeda said. "Why didn't you ever tell me?"

"What good would it have done to tell you? There was no way for me to help carry your burden. You did that for more than ten years, until it finally subsided around the time our eldest was in middle school. It was only when I saw you sleeping peacefully that I thought you'd come home from the front at last."

"Thank you, dear," Takeda said in a small voice, placing his hand over his wife's.

Just before we parted, Takeda said, "Miyabe-san was a wonderful man. I only spent a few months in his presence, but I think he was a truly phenomenal person."

"Thank you very much, sir."

"He's the one who really should have survived the war."

"It is very kind of you to say that."

Takeda's expression became stiff. "As he was climbing into the cockpit of the Zero to fly to Kyushu, I wished him good luck."

"Yes?"

"He suddenly got this terrifying look on his face and said, 'I absolutely will not die.' I saw this tremendous obsession with life in his eyes. I thought there was no way he would ever die."

"But the war wouldn't let him live," I said.

"Not the war," Keiko said sharply. "Our grandfather was killed by the Navy."

Takeda nodded. "You might be correct. It probably was the Navy that killed him."

Chapter 10
Fighting Demon

"That guy was doomed to die," former Flight Chief Petty Officer Kaizan Kageura said, his eyes boring into mine. "I know that he wanted to come out of the war alive. But it was he, himself, who cut off any chance of that wish being fulfilled."

My heart pounded violently. I tried to glean Kageura's feelings from his face, but he was expressionless, unreadable.

Kaizan Kageura was a former *yakuza* gangster. He lived in Nakano, a quiet residential district a little west of Shinjuku, but there was no nameplate on the front gate, and the wall surrounding the property was dotted with numerous security cameras. He claimed to be retired, but even so, I felt trepidation over visiting him at home. Keiko had said that she wanted to come with me, but I wasn't keen on the idea of bringing her to the home of someone whose criminal record included murder.

When I pressed the buzzer on the intercom, a young man with a shaved head appeared. His speech was very polite, but his eyes were hawk-like. After I stated my name and the purpose of my visit, he led me through to a sitting room.

The sitting room was decidedly not extravagant, but the walls and ceiling appeared to be made from fine materials. The room lacked any sort of furnishings.

Kageura was a tall man. He was supposed to be seventy-nine, but he looked younger than his years. His hair was thinning, but his complexion and poise made him appear to be around sixty.

The young man who had answered the door remained standing behind Kageura. Perhaps he was something like a bodyguard.

"So you're Miyabe's grandkid," Kageura said without a trace of a smile. His voice was low and subdued, yet imposing.

Feeling a bit overawed, I repeated the purpose of my visit.

After I had gone over everything, Kageura said, "I despised him."

I nodded wordlessly. I had sensed as much when we spoke on the phone. Since I no longer found it baffling that some of his former comrades might hate my grandfather, having someone tell me as much to my face didn't faze me anymore.

"The war is over sixty years in the past. I've forgotten about most of the people I met back then. Yet I can recall that guy very well. Hmm, how strange."

I hated Miyabe's guts. I thought he was entirely disgusting.

I vividly remember when he departed as a kamikaze. I was one of the fighter escorts that day.

Sorry to say I didn't witness his last moments. After the Battle of Okinawa, most kamikazes failed to reach the American fleet because there were squadrons of enemy fighters three layers deep lying in wait far ahead of their task force. There was no way planes loaded down with heavy ordnance could make it to the enemy's fleet. On many occasions, even the nimble escorting fighters failed to return to base from their missions. Most were probably taken out by the other side's fighters.

As I've been saying, I loathed him from the bottom of my heart.

Why? No particular reason. There must be people in your own life that you just don't get along with. Someone whose very presence you find exceedingly aggravating. For me, that guy was Miyabe.

He treasured a photo of his wife and kid. You might want to say that young people these days are all like that, and I won't quibble with you on that. Modern society is all lukewarm. If some weakling of a salaryman who relies entirely on his company keeps a photo of his wife and child tucked inside his commuter-pass holder, that's actually kinda cute. But sixty years ago, things were different. We were putting our lives on the line.

Even today, people commonly bandy about phrases like "on my life," but it's nothing more than words. It's just a flashier version of

"I'll do my best." Don't make me laugh. I'd love to give them a lesson, about what it really means to risk your life. Back then, we were literally putting our lives on the line.

And yet back there in the thick of war, he was like some modern salaryman gazing at that photograph and spouting crap like, "I wanna survive this war and go home." Imagine risking your life in combat every day and hearing that nonsense from some fellow next to you.

—Did I ever actually hear him say that? True, I don't have any precise recollection. But even if he didn't say it out loud, it was obvious to everyone that he was thinking that all the time.

I graduated from the Preparatory Flight Training Program in Kasumigaura in early 1943.

I was first stationed in Taiwan, and then transferred to the Philippines. From there I was sent to Java, and then on to Balikpapan on Borneo. It was already clear at that point that the tide of the war was turning against us. But I didn't give a damn. I simply focused on carrying out my duty as a fighter pilot. And what was that duty? Shooting down as many enemy aircraft as possible.

I was lucky to see my first action at Balikpapan. There was an oilfield there, which meant an abundance of fuel, so we could train to our heart's content. I'm sure that was how I was able to polish my piloting skills.

In my first sortie at Balikpapan, I shot down an enemy fighter— a Spitfire. Many of my former classmates who'd arrived from Japan with me lost their lives during their first air battle. Guys who arrived later met the same fate. It was as though they were showing up just to die. Rare was the pilot who survived three dogfights. The enemy had fighters that could outperform the Zero and their pilots were more skilled. Plus, they had radar, and their sheer numbers were overwhelming. Even veteran pilots had a hard time staying alive in that theater.

It was under such circumstances that I sortied four times in the first week and shot down two aircraft. Everyone's attitude towards me changed, noticeably. I don't mean to brag, but I was a gifted fighter pilot. In the first six months, I downed about ten enemy aircraft if I include unconfirmed kills.

I was sent to Rabaul in the fall of '43.

By that point, Rabaul was no longer the home of the glorious Rabaul Air Corps. The Americans were recapturing the surrounding islands one after another, and we were forced into a defensive stance. A transfer to Rabaul was considered a one-way ticket.

Air raids would continue for days on a tremendous scale. Nearly every day, formations ranging from 150 to 200 fighters and bombers would conduct raids on us. Some days there were as many as 300 aircraft. We had a mere fifty fighters. We were mostly just intercepting the enemy, which actually agreed with me. Frankly, I hated escorting the slowpoke bombers. It was like a ball and chain. But in an ambush, I was free to engage with the enemy. *I like it here*, I thought.

When you're intercepting, whoever's faster wins. As soon as there's a report of incoming enemy aircraft, the pilots ran at full tilt towards their fighters. The ground crew would start the engines, and we'd jump into the cockpits then head up into the skies.

I never took on their large aircraft. My targets were always fighters. We interceptors were supposedly tasked with shooting down bombers that invaded the airspace over the base, but I didn't care. I fought the way I wanted to.

The American fighters were sturdily built. A 7.7-mm machine gun couldn't take them down. The 20-mm cannons could, but their initial velocity was slow and their range was short, which meant they rarely struck their targets. Even so, I easily managed kills using the cannons.

How? By leading the target. It's a technique where you fire at an enemy aircraft that's not yet in your sights.

Here's how it is. Airplanes move at blazing speeds. In a dogfight, your aircraft, too, is slicing through the air. So even if you manage to get the enemy in your sights and pull the trigger, the bullets drift or drop and rarely hit the target. That's why you have to take aim at the expected trajectory of the aircraft, at open space, and fire there. That way, the enemy will fly into the path of your bullets.

Nobody taught us these things during flight training. In fact, I wonder if there were very many seasoned pilots who used that technique. It was kind of like a trick shot, and, if I say so myself, I was naturally gifted at it. I've heard that Germany's Marseille was a master at deflection shooting, that's to say, leading the target.

I drilled at it every damn day. I was always practicing plucking flies out of midair with my hands. After countless efforts, I was able to nab them with near certainty. My special talent gained a measure of notoriety within my unit. Everyone tried their hands at it, but hardly anyone succeeded.

I scored over twenty kills at Rabaul.

There aren't any official records, because by that time the Navy didn't acknowledge individual kills. Kills were credited to the unit as a whole. How very Japanese that was. They tried to erase any hint of individual achievement.

I suspect the reason the Navy stopped recognizing individual kill records was that such stats would reveal who kicked ass and who sucked. That'd be enough to make any incompetent commissioned officer uncomfortable, huh?

Formations were always led into combat by commissioned officers, regardless of skill level. Some of them were good, but that was very rare. Most Naval Academy-trained formation leaders were inexperienced and incompetent. There were many times when a leader's lame decision resulted in the entire formation getting into a jam. I myself was faced with such danger many times. But in the military, a superior officer's orders are absolute. Even if we knew it was dangerous to fly in a certain direction, if the formation leader flew that way we had no choice but to follow. And just as expected, we would be attacked by enemy aircraft lying in wait.

Had they made individual kill records public, it would have been painfully obvious that incompetent commanders were leading highly capable non-comms into battle.

Apparently things were different in the U.S. military. All their pilots were commissioned officers, and those with superior skills headed their formations. Individual kill scores were made public, and pilots were openly lauded for their achievements. All their pilots would excitedly rush into battle, eager to raise their own scores. If a pair of pilots shot down one aircraft, they would each receive 0.5 points. Isn't that so very American? That encouraged pilots to hustle even when they had to work in tandem. Those guys went all in. You can't win a fight otherwise.

The Imperial Navy was nothing like that. No matter how

excellent an aviator, an NCO was never made a unit commander. At best, he could become a flight leader. My rank then was Flight Seaman 1st Class, the third rank from the bottom. No matter how many enemy aircraft I shot down, my advancement up the ranks was never fast-tracked. The IJN was designed to never allow individuals to stand out.

Yet, there were some who triumphantly defied the policy. Tetsuzo Iwamoto just went ahead and painted the number of kills on the fuselage of his beloved plane. His ride was thus covered in cherry blossoms, one for each kill. From a distance, that whole section looked to be of a different color.

In person, he looked like a lackluster middle-aged fellow. But once he flew off into the sky he and his aircraft sparkled. He called himself "a penniless *ronin* of the big wide world." An oddball.

Hiroyoshi Nishizawa, too. When the pilot of a *Gekkou*, a new-model night fighter, downed a B-17 and was presented a saber to commemorate his exploit, Nishizawa is said to have audibly wisecracked, "I wonder how many kills it'd take for me to get one of those." Nishizawa was a quiet man, but he exuded an indescribable vibe. He wasn't the type to ever brag about his kill number. I think he made that remark because he was frustrated that the Zero pilots, constantly on the front lines, were rarely rewarded for their service. He was indeed another fine blade in the IJN's arsenal. Yet they shipped him off to the Philippines on a troop transport and let that precious gem slip through their fingers. So stupid!

I didn't mark up my plane to record my kills, but I remembered every single aircraft that I'd downed. I didn't care if no one else knew, so long as I did. I kept a mental tally of each time I shot down an aircraft. I meant to eventually reach a hundred, even two hundred. They said back then that Nishizawa and Iwamoto each had over a hundred kills, and I wanted to rival them. They were stalwarts who had served since the Sino-Japanese War. They had spent years building up their kill records. I was a total greenhorn. But I always thought, *Someday I'll catch up to them…*

Since there were no official records at that time, the only way to confirm someone's kill number was to hear it from the pilot himself. The numbers that Nishizawa and Iwamoto mentioned to close friends spread from person to person. Since everyone accepted that those two aces could have easily made so many kills, the rumored numbers grew legs. You could try to exaggerate, but everyone knew your skill level. Lies didn't pass in that world.

I loved to dogfight. It was in the skies that I felt the most alive. If an enemy shot me down, I'd have no regrets.

After the war I became a yakuza. Not that I looked up to them. In fact, I looked down on men who ganged up and relied on violence, more than anything else. But after the war, my fast living resulted in me getting dragged into that world. After roaming about in search of a place to hang it all up, I found that I had become an outlaw.

I've committed murder, too. I was sent to prison many times. My life was threatened many times. Yet by the devil's luck, I've survived to this age. Compared to the battles we waged in the skies back then, giving and taking lives down here is like child's play. Some issues can be resolved with money, and some lives can be saved with bodyguards.

There were no compromises in the sky, though. The tiniest mistake could get you killed. But if the enemy's skills exceeded my own, I was willing to go down like a man.

To be sure, the other side had superior fighters, but they used simple hit-and-run tactics when attacking. So long as you could dodge their first strike, there wasn't much left to fear. They rarely engaged in one-on-one dogfights. While the Zero was getting on in years, they were well aware of its terrifying fighting prowess.

I would lure the enemy into dogfights. If one of them attacked, I would purposely flee downwards, which was the more dangerous route, and get him to give chase. In that scenario, it was important to get him to shift his longitudinal axis line—the direction the nose of the plane is pointing towards. Machine guns fire along that trajectory. So if that line is angled away from you, no matter how many bullets are fired they won't strike you. Just when he thinks he can lock onto you and shoot you down, he's right where you want him. Pull your nose up, and then drag him into a contest of lateral turns. By the time he thinks, *Oh, shit*, it's already too late. After the first turn, I'm up right on his tail and open fire with my machine guns. I downed dozens of planes that way.

I think there were very few Zero pilots who did things like that. Iwamoto, for instance, almost never engaged in dogfights. He was a hit-and-run genius. He'd spot an unfriendly before anyone else, sneak up behind him, deal him a blow from diagonally above, and then make a clean getaway, just like the Americans preferred to do. He also made a habit of targeting solo aircraft. In an ambush, instead of engaging right away he would wait until they drew back, and then cut them down from behind. It was like he was a master of the quick draw. He was the mirror opposite of Nishizawa, who was adept at orthodox dogfighting. Come to think of it, Iwamoto was like a man possessed by the spirit of aerial battle. He dedicated his life to sending enemy aircraft to oblivion. I, too, gave my all to air battles, but I didn't become a fighter pilot until 1943. By that point, Iwamoto had already seen five years of combat.

If Nishizawa was a fine *Masamune* sword, then Iwamoto was the enchanted blade *Muramasa*. Of course, this is my own interpretation, but I don't think it's far off the mark.

Legend has it that wielding the enchanted Muramasa transforms you into a terrifying slaughterer. Perhaps the Zero was Iwamoto's Muramasa. He was never able to blend into postwar society, and people eventually forgot him. I hear he died in obscurity of complications from battle injuries. Maybe postwar Japan was no longer a world where flying aces could live.

I didn't fight for the sake of my country or for my fellow countrymen. Not even for my family. And certainly not for the Emperor—no, absolutely not.

I have no relatives, so I was never fighting for anyone else's sake.

I was born a bastard. My mother was some guy's mistress. She'd lost her own mother when she was a child. Her father died when she was fifteen. She probably became a kept woman just to survive. Her keeper, my father, was an up-and-coming trader. My mother died the year I started middle school, and he took me in.

In his large home lived his wife and my older half-brothers. They always looked at me as if I was a piece of filth. My father never gave me any affection, either, or even his surname. If anything, he made it clear that he considered me a parasite. He, himself, had been adopted into his wife's family and was totally spineless, never able to stand up to his wife. He deserved nothing but scorn.

The attack on Pearl Harbor took place when I was in my fifth year of middle school. The following year, when I graduated, I sat for the Preparatory Flight Training Program. It had begun accepting large numbers of applicants since the start of hostilities with the U.S., which is why a bad student like me passed.

From that point, I never saw my family again. Well, they weren't my family to begin with.

Once I became a pilot, I decided to live my life as a *bushi*, a warrior. It was my mother's word. Her grandfather had been a vassal of the Nagaoka Clan and had died in the Boshin War. His son had been branded a traitor after the Meiji Restoration and had endured terrible hardship. He died destitute, leaving behind a fifteen-year-old daughter.

When I was a child my mother often said to me, "Samurai blood flows through your veins. Live proudly as a *bushi*."

So for me, that war existed for my sake. I never fought for anyone else. It was for myself that I fought.

Just as Musashi Miyamoto fought purely for the sake of his swordsmanship, I fought as a mere fighter pilot.

I didn't have any friends, either. I'd been friendless ever since I was little. What is friendship, anyways? Huddling together? Friendship in our society just means you hang out or go drinking together. I've never felt that I wanted such a relationship, not once.

My wife? I don't have one. Never been married, not in my whole life. Of course, I don't have any kids.

There've been women, though. I never wanted for female company. I even lived with one for a time. That was all after the war. During the war I never had a lover, never longed for anyone back home. Out on the front lines I was only concerned with fighting. I lost my virginity after the war to a streetwalker.

Never wanted kids. Since I don't have any siblings, the Kageura line will end when I die.

But so what? Children are merely a consolation. Men who can't recognize any other proof of their own existence have kids and treasure them for the rest of their lives.

I chose not to have kids. I knocked up several women, but I made them get abortions each time. When I was forty, on a friend's suggestion I got a vasectomy. That was a huge relief. I thought, *Finally I'm free of shackles.* Somehow it made me feel like I was ready for death at any time. I should've had it done much sooner.

I figured as soon as you have kids, you can no longer live like a true man. Same thing with taking a wife, of course. Women are nothing more than playmates in this fleeting life. There was one woman that I lived with for years. But I never fell in love with any, not once. And I don't think any of them ever loved me.

But Miyabe, even in the midst of a life-or-death struggle, thought of his family more than anything else. Does a *bushi* clashing swords on the battlefield spare a thought for his family? I can't forgive a man who deemed his wife and child most important when the fate of the nation was at stake.

Even so, had he been a wimp, I could have just laughed at him. The thing that I couldn't tolerate one bit was all the talk about him being such an outstanding fighter pilot.

He thought of nothing more than his family while fighting, and yet he excelled at aerial combat. Why couldn't I forgive that? All I can say is that I was still young.

While all of us were putting our life on the line, he alone thought of his wife and child and engaged in combat on the side, so to speak. And yet his skills were supposedly better than everyone else's. I couldn't stand it.

It's not that I ever saw him in action myself, but many veteran pilots including Nishizawa all held him in high regard. His kill score was a total mystery, though. The rumors were all over the place. Some said he'd downed nearly a hundred; others thought the number was closer to a dozen. This was due to the fact that he hardly ever stated kills when he was debriefed. Kills were only considered confirmed if you succeeded in blowing up an enemy aircraft in midair or witnessed the pilot bailing, or if the aircraft crashed into the ocean. Aside from those cases, if you could only report that you saw the aircraft falling or that it began to spout fire, the kill was considered "unconfirmed."

Most of Miyabe's kills seemed to fall into that category.

One day, I asked him point-blank: "Flight CPO Miyabe, how many kills do you have?"

"I do not remember," he replied without drama. His manner of speech was excessively polite. He spoke to someone even three ranks below him as if he were addressing a superior officer. That only added fuel to my anger.

"The guys are spreading all kinds of rumors," I persisted. "Some say ten, others say a hundred. So what's the real number?"

"I think that I might have shot down more than ten."

This answer was a surprise. I was hoping to estimate the number through his response. If he'd laughed it off, it meant his kill total wasn't all that impressive. If he'd given an outsized number, he was nothing more than a braggart. Yet his response was neither of these.

And then he said, "No matter how many of their aircraft I shoot down, if they shoot me down just once, I'm done for."

I was momentarily lost for words.

He continued, "It's important to the air corps to know how many enemy aircraft were taken out. War is about inflicting losses on each other. If our losses are small and their losses are large, HQ considers that a win. If we lose only one aircraft and they lose ten, then it's a major victory. But what if that one aircraft is yours?"

His question left me bewildered. "I fight my own battles," I said.

Miyabe laughed. "I feel the same way. So instead of focusing on how many aircraft I downed, I fight desperately to avoid getting shot down."

I felt like he was laughing at me. I had always considered air battles to be like fights between master swordsmen. I wasn't the slightest bit afraid of dying. If I'd fought with every esoteric technique available to me, then losing was fine. Miyabe's words directly opposed my kind of resolve.

"But—" I started to say when Miyabe suddenly grasped my shoulder.

"Flight Seaman 1st Class Kageura, you seem to fancy yourself a Musashi Miyamoto, but remember that Musashi did plenty of running away in his time. And another thing: Musashi never challenged an opponent that he couldn't beat. Is that not the innermost secret of a top swordsman?"

I could feel my face heat up. I was sure he was making fun of the phrase I'd drawn on my scarf—*The Sword and Zen are One*—and telling me that I seemed childish to him. It was Musashi Miyamoto who had said that.

After Miyabe left, I tore my scarf to shreds, tears of chagrin rolling down my face. I swore I'd become a better fighter pilot than Miyabe.

My hatred of Miyabe wasn't some half-baked thing. Whether I slept or I was awake, my mind was always filled with thoughts of him. Sometimes he appeared in my dreams. On some occasions, I would spring out of bed in the middle of the night covered in sweat, Miyabe's laughter still ringing in my ears.

One day I said to him, "Flight CPO Miyabe, I have a request."

"What is it?" he asked, his expression typically dispassionate.

"I would like for us to engage in a mock dogfight, sir."

"That isn't necessary. You are a very skilled pilot, Kageura."

"I have heard that you are unparalleled when it comes to mock dogfights. Please, I ask for your instruction, sir."

"A mock battle is nothing more than a practice run. It's not a real fight. You are much better than I when it comes to actual combat."

"Please, sir!"

"We are on the front lines. We currently do not have the time or resources to spare on such a thing. And HQ won't allow it."

I fell to my knees and begged, "Please!"

"No!" Miyabe said sharply, and quickly walked away.

I had never been more humiliated in my life. And in the sixty years I've lived since then, I have never tasted such mortification. I was on the verge of launching myself at him. If there hadn't been several mechanics looking on from a short distance away, I might have done so.

For the next few days, I was obsessed with the idea of dogfighting Miyabe. *If only I were with the American forces—then I could dogfight him,* I even thought.

Several days later, as I was racing towards my fighter in order to intercept incoming aircraft, I caught sight of Miyabe next to me. In order to make myself heard over the roar of the engines, I shouted, "Flight CPO Miyabe, after today's defensive action, please fight a mock battle with me!"

Miyabe, not even looking in my direction as he ran, said no.

"I'll do it even if you don't," I shouted.

Miyabe glanced at me. His expression was filled with an intensity I'd never seen until then. Then, without a word of reply, he ran off towards his plane.

That day, we had to fend off attacks from 30 B-17s and about 150 Grummans. Forty Zeros went up to intercept them. We were overwhelmingly outnumbered, but we had the advantage of fighting above our own base.

They began bombing from an altitude of 3,000 meters. We assaulted the enemy aircraft after they had finished, and the Grummans tried to prevent us. I dropped down, feigning to escape, inviting the enemy to pursue me. One took the bait. I immediately pulled up and engaged him in a dogfight. He was right on my six o'clock. I made a sharp turn and ended up behind him. In a panic, he dove down and tried to break away—just what I had hoped for. I fired my 20-mm cannons towards the direction he was fleeing. He flew right into the stream of my bullets, as if drawn there. Yellow flames spouted from his plane. I caught a glimpse of the pilot parachuting away, then immediately sought out my next target.

I saw two of our birds attacking a B-17. I pulled up and headed in their direction, not to aid in their assault but to pick off a Grumman that was attacking the Zeros.

I flew up behind the Grumman, which was bathing a Zero from the rear with bullets, and opened fire with both my 20-mm and 7.7-mm guns. The Grumman fell away, but so did the Zero under attack. The B-17, meanwhile, escaped.

The interception lasted for just over ten minutes. The many large ripples on the surface of the ocean far below indicated where aircraft had crashed. I couldn't tell which side had taken greater casualties.

There were no friendlies around me.

Then, just as I was about to head back to Rabaul, I spotted a single Zero below me. It was Miyabe's. I made my decision.

I immediately went into a dive and came up behind him. At

about 1,000 meters, I fired at his plane. There was no chance of hitting him at that distance. It was merely my way of signaling that I wanted to start a mock dogfight.

Miyabe nosed up and turned towards me. For a split second, we were facing each other, but our planes were too close. We passed by one another and quickly put 2,000 meters between us. Then we both made wide turns and faced each other again, understanding each other without words.

Miyabe had responded to the mock battle challenge. We were at the same altitude, so this would be an even match.

We both closed the distance. I made a wide left turn, attempting to get behind him. He made a similar turn. Our aircraft drew closer and closer together as we chased each other. This was a proper dog-fight, as the nickname comes from two dogs going in circles, nipping at each other's tails.

We both dipped our wings down, continuing to turn sharply. We twisted through the air like pestles sliding inside a mortar. I felt an immense g-force all over my body, like my innards and eyeballs were being crushed. If you've never experienced the pain of g-forces, I'm sure it's very difficult to understand. It's so intense you feel like you're dying. Just imagine large stones weighing several hundred kilos on top of your body, if that makes sense. If you haven't built up your dorsal and abdominal muscles, it can snap your spine. Your facial muscles are yanked backwards, making you look inhuman. Your eyeballs are forcefully pushed back, making your eye sockets look sunken, like a bare skull. Your field of vision narrows sharply, like you're looking down the wrong end of a telescope. The instant you cry uncle to the anguish of the g-force, you've lost the battle.

Even if this was just a mock dogfight, I was determined not to stop turning. I didn't care if I died. I screamed out in pain, but I kept my eyes fixed on Miyabe above the crown of my head and didn't ease up on the control stick even by an inch.

Suddenly he stopped turning and transitioned into level flight. *Damn, I win!* I thought, and turned onto his tail. His plane was slowly drawing towards my crosshairs, but then in the next instant he went into a loop. To pull a loop from an inferior position and at reduced speed like that was akin to suicide. I followed him. I kept my eyes locked on him overhead as I pulled on the stick. The moment I came out of the loop, he'd be right in my sights. Then his life would be in my hands...

Then the unbelievable happened. His plane had vanished. Not only was he not in my sights, he was nowhere to be seen in my entire range of vision.

As I continued to loop, I turned and twisted my head, looking for him. His aircraft was gone. I instinctively went into a steep dive. It was then that I felt a chill shudder down my spine, and I turned around to look—he was right behind me.

I can't forget the shock I felt at that moment, even now. After the war, I got into many fights where my life was at stake, and it wasn't just once or twice that I thought I was a goner. But I never again felt the fear that I experienced back then with Miyabe.

He was so close that our planes were nearly touching. He didn't need his gun sights or anything. All he had to do was pull the trigger and my Zero would be blown away. He'd won, no question about it. I felt like I was about to lose my mind. I was in a state of *panic*, to use a foreign word as we've come to do.

After he saw me turn around and look at him, he increased his speed and pulled up alongside me, then passed me by. Just then, his plane entered my sights. It happened in the blink of an eye.

I pulled the damn trigger...

I won't make excuses for myself.

I did something that one must never do. It was as though, after fighting a *kendo* match with bamboo swords and losing, I had cut down my opponent with a real sword the minute his back was turned.

I hated him. And he had thoroughly beaten me. Did I leap without thinking at the first opportunity to shoot him down? It would be a fair accusation. I have to accept the label of "coward" if you wish to call me that.

But what really stunned me was what happened the next moment. The tracer bullets that I had fired arced away as if spooked by his plane, which was in my sights. I felt like I was trapped in a nightmare. Had I been dragged into some sorcerous realm? Was he a demon?

He rapidly swung through the air and once again came up behind me. I didn't turn around this time. I didn't even think about trying to escape. I wanted to be shot down by Miyabe. From the second I fired on him, my life no longer had any value, whatsoever. I would have been perfectly satisfied with him shooting me down. It was my dream to die at the hands of a true fighter pilot. It didn't matter whether the pilot was American or Japanese.

But Miyabe didn't open fire.

"Shoot, damn it!" I yelled. "Fire! Shoot me!" I shouted at the top of my lungs.

Once I realized that he had no intention of doing so, I banked hard then dropped into a dive. My only choice was to blow myself up in that case. Yet once again something incredible occurred. Miyabe raced ahead of me, cutting across my flight path. I had to turn sharply in order to avoid a collision. He opened up his windshield and signaled with his hand to stop.

As soon as I saw his signal, I lost the will to blow myself up. From my cockpit I signed back, "Roger." Self-destructing in such a way was for cowards. I would go back to the airfield, confess to everyone in the unit that I had fired on Miyabe, and then commit *seppuku*. I had no intention of apologizing to him; it wasn't the sort of thing that could be settled with a simple apology. What would saying "sorry" accomplish? Instead I meant to go ahead and express my feelings by disemboweling myself.

After touching down on the runway and climbing down from the cockpit, I was heading towards the command post when Miyabe, who had landed after me, came running up.

"Listen, don't tell anyone. That's an order!" he said, a ferocious expression on his face. "You fired on me, but I'm still alive. So there's nothing to report." Then he added, "Don't throw your life away."

He understood. He understood everything I was feeling. My resolve to commit suicide wilted in my heart. And I didn't die.

Do you think me a coward? I think my grandfather would have done it—sliced a cross into his abdomen, without relying on an aide to cut off his head, either. So why did I not go through with it?

Because I felt like he still held my life in his hands.

And what was that damn maneuver he had pulled?

The answer came to me immediately: a left-turn corkscrew loop, a move considered a secret technique among the Imperial Navy's fighter pilots. With an aircraft locked on your tail, you quickly kicked in hard left rudder at the peak of your loop and got on the other aircraft's tail.

I'd heard about it a number of times back in training, but none of our instructors could do it. One of them had seen it just once, though. A seasoned pilot serving since the Sino-Japanese War had pulled it off in a mock battle. "His plane vanished into thin air. It was like a magic trick." The instructor had also said, "Virtually none of the Naval Air Corps' surviving pilots can do it."

Miyabe had pulled that very same maneuver on me. The technique was truly divine. I could scarcely believe airplanes could actually move in such a way.

But what surprised me even more was what had happened next. I'd had him squarely in my sights, yet my bullets had missed. Again, I soon figured out why—my plane had been slipping.

It's difficult to explain. Basically, he wasn't flying straight forward.

The first thing we pilots learn is how to fly straight and level. Beginners will typically have their aircraft inadvertently angled to one side. That's referred to as "slipping," and it gets thoroughly hammered out of flight students before anything else. It's a basic part of flying. If your aircraft is slipping, then there's no way your bullets will strike their target. A bomber's bombs will absolutely miss, too, and so will a torpedo attacker's torpedo. So straight and level flight is drilled into your head.

When he had cut ahead of me, Miyabe had purposely made his aircraft slip. I'd instinctively jumped on his tail. But when I chased directly after him, inadvertently I was slipping as well.

Do you see? My plane is right behind his. Two Zeros lined up one behind the other as they fly. Yet in fact both aircraft are sliding together. I opened fire under such conditions. And of course, the bullets arced away.

He hadn't gone in front of me by accident. He'd tested me.

I realized then how he had managed to survive from Pearl Harbor up to that point. There was no way the Americans could shoot down a pilot with such skills. It was as though he was an *Asura*, a fighting demon.

I was knocked flat by an immense sense of defeat. Not only had I lost the dogfight, I had failed his test, too. When I put it all together, a black rage swirled within my heart. I swore that one day I would shoot him down. That night, in the pitch darkness of my room, I envisioned his aircraft spewing flames and falling from the sky.

America, Japan, none of that mattered to me. My enemies were each and every fighter pilot. I wanted to become a pilot who was second to none. That was my dream, my deepest desire. I know I've already said this, but I was not afraid of death at all. If I exhausted every effort in combat and then was shot down, that'd be sheer joy, far cleaner than dying in an air-raid shelter or from an illness like malaria or dengue fever. And I certainly didn't want to grow old and become decrepit. Wouldn't you agree?

And yet I wasn't able to die in the sky. After the war, I found myself fighting for my life numerous times. I never once feared death. My body is covered in scars from sword cuts and bullets. Perhaps the Grim Reaper forsook me, and I wasn't able to die. I never thought I'd live to such an old age.

This young man here with me was sent by the syndicate brass as a form of training and also, apparently, to act as my bodyguard. I wish they'd just mind their own business. I'm ready to give up my life anytime. But if I did, there'd be another unnecessary conflict. That's why I keep him by my side.

I lost to Miyabe once. But it wasn't a true defeat because he didn't shoot me down. I didn't really lose. Do you think that's just a convenient rationalization? If so, you'd be incorrect. This isn't about logic. He didn't have it in him to kill me.

From that day on, my life became dear to me. I was afraid of dying in vain. That was the only time in my many years that I valued my own life. Until the day that I could shoot down Miyabe's aircraft, I absolutely had to live. I couldn't go off and die with that business left unfinished. My dream was to fight Miyabe and turn his fuselage into Swiss cheese with my guns and swat him down.

I couldn't actually do that, of course. So instead, I wished to outlive Miyabe. I was determined to hear one day that he'd been shot down by unfriendlies, and then I would laugh at him. That would be my moment of victory.

He died. I won.

Does saying that make you hate me? If you do, you've got it all wrong. He died a kamikaze. It's not like I killed him.

The aviators of the Rabaul Air Corps were soon called back to the interior. All of us were being reassigned. I was separated from Miyabe.

This sounds strange, but I thought to myself, *Don't die yet, Miyabe.* He had to die before my eyes. And I had to survive until that day.

I became an instructor at Iwakuni Base. I was to teach the huge influx of student reservists.

Our job as instructors was so boring it made me sick. The reserves were given only one year of flight training. There's no way anyone can become a competent pilot in a year. The students were passionate and very good, but even so, a year's training was totally insufficient. *What's the point of producing such a vast number of useless pilots?* I thought. As it turned out, the military was planning on using them as kamikazes from the very start.

I begged the flight commander repeatedly to send me back to the front, but my pleas fell on deaf ears.

In October of 1944, I brought the greenhorns with me to Wonsan, Korea, where I had to keep on teaching.

It was there that I heard of Shikishima Unit.

I had absolutely no interest in becoming a kamikaze. I had no issue with falling to enemy fire during combat, but I hated the idea of dying in a special attack. I wanted to die as a fighter pilot. I wanted to be cut down by a master whose skills outclassed my own.

In time, in Wonsan too, HQ recruited kamikaze volunteers. Everyone was given an envelope with a slip of paper inside. On the paper were three choices: "I strongly wish to volunteer," "I wish to volunteer," and "I do not volunteer." We were supposed to mark one of the three options.

The commander said, "It's entirely up to each of you. I don't care if you choose not to volunteer. Consider well before you reply."

I marked "I strongly wish to volunteer." If I made any other choice, there was no telling what they might do to me. The military was that sort of place. I didn't mind being shipped off to the front, but I couldn't tolerate having my wings taken away and joining some island's garrison.

—What if I'd been ordered to become a kamikaze?

I'd have crossed that bridge when I came to it. Even if I only started thinking about it then, it wouldn't be too late. But I definitely wouldn't have said, "Oh, all right then," and gone off to my death.

The following January, a special attack unit was abruptly formed within the Wonsan Air Unit.

My name was not listed among those assigned to the first group. There were a dozen or so pilots that were selected, mostly student reserve officers, and they took off for the interior. They were to sortie from a special attack base on Kyushu.

Then a second and a third wave of kamikaze units were formed and sent off to the interior for their missions.

As I saw them off, I thought that if Japan was being reduced to such tactics, then we were done for. In the first place, there was no way deploying such inexperienced pilots would produce any results. It was obvious that they'd be gunned down by enemy interceptors.

Soon thereafter, I myself was transferred to the interior. My new base was Omura in Nagasaki. It wasn't as a kamikaze. Instead I was to be a part of the fighter escort directly guarding them or establishing air supremacy.

The military didn't officially recognize individual kill scores, but I'm sure HQ was well aware that I had shot down a considerable number of enemy aircraft. By that point almost none of the veteran pilots who had served since the outset of the war was still alive. So the fact that I had served at Rabaul made me seem fairly seasoned.

In March, the American fleet arrived in the seas near Okinawa, and Kamoya Base saw near-daily kamikaze sorties. Most of them were reserves or boy pilots from the Prep Program.

I felt sorry for the student reservists. Sure, it was nice to be pampered and granted a commission right upon entering the military. But they were only taught the basics of piloting an aircraft then sent off to become kamikazes. And I think almost all of them failed to actually strike American warships. An aircraft isn't so easy to handle that barely a year of training could make them proficient in the cockpit.

Faced with an onslaught of unfriendly fighters, there was no way they could escape. Getting away while loaded down with heavy bombs was no easy task, even for seasoned pilots.

At that time, the only goal of the Navy—as well as the Army—was to launch as many kamikaze attacks as they could. Older Type 96 fighters and even some seaplanes were deployed on kamikaze missions. I've heard that in the worst cases, training planes were used, too.

I'm not the type of man who readily sympathizes with others, but I felt very sorry for those young pilots. They thought they were doing it for the sake of Japan and for their families. And after so much distress, their deaths weren't rewarded in any way. Their deaths were a total waste. Their deaths had no value at all.

You might think that kamikaze sorties were solemn, stern affairs. But since it was an everyday occurrence, we grew accustomed to it. At first the ground crews would tearfully wave their hats in farewell, but after a while it became part of the daily routine.

Does that sound heartless? But that's how humans are built. If we didn't grow numb to it, we'd suffer nervous breakdowns. I'm sure that at first the commanders who ordered special attacks felt like they were slicing off a part of their own bodies. But after a while they must have drawn up the lists of pilots like it was just paperwork. I can't blame them for that. That's just how people are.

But it's a different matter if you're the one being sent off to die. You only live once.

They were truly upstanding young men. I had assumed that reserve officers coming straight from college would be a soft bunch. But lo and behold, they were all manly.

I'd seen plenty of officers from the Naval Academy who spouted off brave words but were useless in combat. Meanwhile, the reserve officers sucked as pilots but went off to their deaths with dignity. Once

I saw a Naval Academy graduate raising his voice and asking, "I have to go too?" when he was ordered to join a kamikaze mission. How pathetic.

After the war, I met many yakuza, but the student reservists were so much tougher. They hadn't been handpicked or anything. They'd been taken on in droves, and just a short year before they had been college students. So where did that bravery come from? How could plain students become so strong?

Perhaps the concept of dying for the sake of loved ones really makes ordinary men grow that strong...

What do you think?

Yeah, of course you wouldn't know. How could someone wallowing in today's world comprehend their strength?

The fact is, I don't know, either.

Some kamikazes were boys as young as seventeen. Those kids had such sparkly eyes. "I will happily go to my death," they'd boldly declare, but I could tell that in the bottom of their hearts they were wrestling with terror. On the morning of their missions, all of their eyes would be puffy. They'd probably wept into their pillows all night without even realizing it. Yet they tried not to show any weakness. Damn, they were amazing!

And yet—I'll say it again. Their deaths were completely pointless.

The special attacks were devised as a way for the military brass to save face. By the Battle of Okinawa, the Navy didn't have a single fleet capable of taking on the American military. By all rights, they should have thrown up their hands and said they could no longer fight. But they did not see that as an option. Why? Because they still had aircraft. And so they decided to use all those planes in kamikaze operations. That's what special attack personnel died for.

It was the same with the *Yamato*. There was no way they could defeat the U.S. forces that had landed on Okinawa, but they couldn't just stand by idly and watch the island be taken over. When the Imperial Army was fighting a hopeless battle on Okinawa, the Navy couldn't be sitting on its hands. Could they allow the *Yamato* to remain while other ships had been destroyed? If not, they had to deploy her even if defeat was the only possible outcome.

After the war, I opened several gambling dens. It's the amateurs who don't know how to cool it. Once they've squandered a lot of cash, the blood rushes to their heads, and figuring there's no point in holding onto what little they have left, they bet it all.

For the General Staff, ships, airplanes, and troops were like gambling money. When they were winning, they were stingy, missing the chance to win big. Once the situation gradually worsened and they started losing, they got pissed off and bet everything at once, like typical amateurs.

So was the use of the *Yamato* in a suicide mission a total waste? Did all of the kamikazes in the Battle of Okinawa die entirely in vain? Not so.

At Okinawa, many soldiers and civilians fought a desperate battle. In the face of the Americans' overwhelming advantage, they were ready to die to the last man. Well, does one sit idly because going there would be no use? Mustn't a *bushi* aid them even if he knows he won't survive?

What am I saying… Aw, shit. There's something terribly wrong with me today.

Was the *Yamato*'s sea kamikaze mission a total waste? As far as results go, yes. But Admiral Ito, and the crew of more than three thousand, martyred themselves for Okinawa. The *Shinpu* Special Attack Force was the same.

They may have been killed for the sake of the General Staff and Combined Fleet Command, but what they offered up their lives for was their nation, and Okinawa.

Enough. I'm sick of talking about the *Yamato*.

My task was to guard kamikazes and to shoot down any enemy aircraft that tried to attack them. But by that point, we were already vastly outnumbered and there was no hope for victory. The Americans had positioned picket destroyers well forward of the main task force and were able to detect incoming kamikazes via radar. They could even discern the planes' altitude. If our planes were at 3,000 meters, they'd be at 4,000 meters, and if we were at 5,000 meters, they'd come in at 6,000. They would always be waiting to ambush us from above.

Then, from their cushy position, they would attack. The escort fighters, flown by seasoned pilots, could dodge that first strike, but the inexperienced kamikaze pilots were unable to, and many were felled in the initial assault.

It was extremely rare for a kamikaze to reach the Americans' fleet.

Some kamikazes judged that they couldn't possibly reach the carrier fleet and instead hurled themselves at one of the picket destroyers. That was far more worthwhile, they figured, than aiming for an aircraft carrier and simply getting shot down.

The destroyers apparently found this unacceptable. I saw one ship where the crew had painted a large arrow on the deck as if to show us the way to the aircraft carriers. I was appalled at first, but in time, I felt like tipping my hat to them. A military that's capable of doing that sort of thing is the truly indomitable one, in my book.

The kamikazes were finally unable to sink any large warships but did take out a number of smaller vessels, destroyers and transports and such. I think the American crew who manned those destroyers far ahead of the main task force, where the kamikaze could get to them, were very brave.

Guard contingent fighters had to protect the special attack planes. We were told to put ourselves in the line of fire to protect them if necessary. But that was a bridge that I was not willing to cross.

The most we could do was chase off enemy fighters. But no matter how many unfriendlies we fended off, they kept coming at us, each wave taking out one or two more kamikazes.

Sometimes, the entire kamikaze formation was shot down before my eyes. It was a wretched sight. People think that kamikazes went out in a blaze of glory as they crashed into a warship, but mostly they were shot down long before they got that far. During the Battle of the Philippine Sea, the Americans easily shot down our attack planes and mockingly called it the "Great Marianas Turkey Shoot." During the Battle of Okinawa, they must have had an even easier time taking out our kamikazes.

Only a handful got near the enemy's mobile task force. Even if they went down to anti-aircraft fire, merely getting that close must have been satisfying for the pilots.

After the kamikazes were shot down by enemy fire, the guard

contingent was free to engage hostiles, but we usually didn't dare to. Surrounded by numerous enemy aircraft, it was all we could do to save our own hides. Not to mention that these were F6Fs or Sikorskys, both far superior to the Zero. Had we at least been evenly matched in number, we might have been able to put up a fight, but against a horde of them there was no hope of winning.

The moment you got on the tail of an enemy, another one of them would simply latch onto yours. If you kept firing on the aircraft in your sights you might shoot it down, but you'd end up dead, too. Plus, it took more than a few bullets striking home to take down an American fighter, whereas a single hit could demolish a Zero.

The American pilots were far more competent than they had been at Rabaul two years before, which is why fighter pilots on escort duty were frequently shot down as well. On some missions, not a single plane, the escort included, returned to base.

And by that time, our planes' readiness quotient had sharply declined. Factories in the interior had been ravaged by air raids, rendering them incapable of producing sufficient numbers of aircraft. Many planes simply weren't capable of flight, and more than a few faltered after takeoff. In fact, nearly every day we had kamikazes who were forced to return to base due to engine problems. A number of fighters made emergency landings on Kikaijima Island, but the unlucky ones fell into the ocean.

I didn't forget about Miyabe even while I was escorting kamikazes.

At night, I would lie on an embankment by the runway looking up at the stars, and time and again my thoughts would turn to him. I'd wonder if he was gazing up at the same stars at that moment. Then I'd think to myself, *Don't you die yet, Miyabe. When you die, I have to be there to witness it.*

The Battle of Okinawa lasted for about three months.

During the period, I sortied countless times as part of the guard contingent, or flew on ahead of the kamikaze squad as part of the air supremacy team, engaging enemy aircraft lurking in the skies. On a few occasions, I shot down some enemy fighters before returning to base.

The Americans had captured Okinawa completely by the end

of June. Including those launched by the Army, over 2,000 kami-kazes perished.

Since we'd already lost Iwo Jima in March, losing Okinawa meant that America had filled our moat.

For some time before then, the urban areas of Japan had been under near-constant attack from B-29 bombers launching from Saipan. And after Iwo Jima had fallen, the bombers were escorted by P-51 fighters. In the face of attacks carried out by massive formations of bombers and fighters, the air defense units at various bases around Japan were no more than bugs.

I participated in a number of those battles. The P-51 was an incredible fighter. Those monsters were beyond formidable.

The performance gap between the P-51 and the Zero was so vast it was like comparing an adult and a child. The P-51's cruising speed was 600 km/h, while even at top speed a Zero couldn't hit 600 km/h. Cruising speed is the speed at which an aircraft has maximum fuel efficiency. A Zero's cruising speed was just over 300 km/h, while the P-51's top speed was over 700 km/h. Their bulletproofing and armament were far superior to that of the Zero, too. Moreover, these monsters could leisurely fly from Iwo Jima to the mainland, partake in plenty of fighting, then head on back to Iwo Jima. Zeros had flown between Rabaul and Guadalcanal, but this was an even greater distance.

The P-51's high-altitude performance was extraordinary, and it could readily dogfight at 8,000 meters above sea level. Flying at all was the most that Japanese fighters could do at that height. The engines complained loudly if we forced them to work where oxygen was so scarce. And it got so cold up there that dogfighting would be the last thing on our minds. Our cockpits were fitted with oxygen masks, but there was no protection from the cold. It was not a cockpit designed to withstand double-digit subzero temperatures. Which is why we could only throw up our hands when the B-29s were escorted by P-51s. No other fighter existed that could take on a P-51 at 8,000 meters.

We fought with everything that we had, but every time our fighters sortied to intercept incoming enemy aircraft, they were mercilessly shot out of the sky.

The P-51s and Grummans would nonchalantly drift down and

strafe targets on the ground, too. Buildings, trains, automobiles, people. They had no issue with gunning down civilians running about trying to flee. I don't think they considered Japanese to be human beings. I bet those pilots took shots like they were hunting animals.

But when they came down to lower altitudes, we had a chance to strike back. I shot down P-51s just once, in June of 1945. I had gone out to meet incoming aircraft after a report came in, and on my way back after failing to apprehend enemy aircraft, I discovered a flight of four P-51s firing on a train.

I attacked them from above. They immediately noticed me, but surprisingly, only one of the four turned to challenge me. The other three were going to sit back and watch. I suppose that by then, they considered Japanese planes to be unworthy of their consideration.

At that point, most of the pilots in the Japanese military were barely better than novices, and there were hardly any who could take on the high-performance American military aircraft, not to mention the P-51, which was an invincible fighter. I imagine the pilot of the one that turned towards me had told his fellow pilots over the wireless, "He's mine to kill, so stay out of it." And I'm sure the other three looked on with smirks on their faces. Even though we were at low altitude, the P-51 was challenging me to a dogfight.

I wasn't some rookie, however. I had survived Rabaul, "the Airmen's Graveyard." And Zeros were robust fighters at lower altitudes. After dodging a shower of bullets fired by the P-51, I made a hard turn and ended up on his tail. He slid away, trying to escape, but it was too late. I fired my 20-mm cannons and tore off one of his wings.

After witnessing their comrade's demise, the remaining three fell into formation and came after me from above. I ascended, evading their attacks. I ducked two of them and they flew out ahead, but the third pursued me. He revved up his engine and rapidly drew close. Just then, I went into a barrel roll. He followed. Idiot! I made a tight turn, curving back and pulling up behind him. He panicked and tried to escape by going into a dive, as per their usual tactics, so I could predict his every move. I readied a deflection shot, aiming ahead on his dive trajectory, and fired my 20 mms. I watched as my bullets shattered his windshield. He went into a tailspin and crashed.

The two remaining fighters descended, apparently intending to catch me in a pincer attack. I pulled up, aiming my Zero directly towards one of them. He let loose a barrage of bullets like he was throwing so much sand, but I took careful note of his axis line. All of the tracer bullets went high, passing over my head. Afraid that I was trying to ram into him, he hurriedly swerved right. This was suicide. I fired off every bullet I had left in my machine guns. Black smoke spurted from the underside of the P-51 and it fell away towards the mountains.

The last P-51 had fled and was already far away.

That was the only time I shot down P-51s. I'm not trying to brag or anything. They had made the mistake of dogfighting a Zero at low altitude, and their piloting skills had been rudimentary. Things would have turned out differently against better pilots at high altitude.

This is something I learned after the war, but the famous Sadaaki Akamatsu took on a formation of seventy-five P-51s all by himself, shooting down one before heading back to base. He was one hell of a bullshitter, but on that occasion there had been a large number of witnesses. And his aerial combat skills were truly impressive. Some of those guys who went back to the Sino-Japanese War were seriously not to be trifled with.

I never thought that I wasn't a match for a P-51. I felt that I wouldn't lose a one-on-one fight, and even outnumbered, I was sure I could at least escape unscathed. Since they tended to use hit-and-run tactics, so long as I dodged their first strike they really weren't so scary a foe. It was just that shooting one down was no easy task. But I'm sure it was difficult for young pilots to dodge that first strike.

Beginning in the spring of '45, B-29s carpet-bombed major Japanese cities including Tokyo, Osaka, Nagoya, and Fukuoka, reducing them to burnt-out ruins. Reports of these attacks reached us at Kanoya. It was as plain as day that, no matter how hard we struggled, we would never win the war. Most of our munitions plants had been demolished, making it impossible even to continue fighting, it seemed.

Germany surrendered that May. Japan was the only country left against the rest of the world, and we were heading towards the same fate. By that point, our bases in southern Kyushu came under devastating air raids from American planes flying from Okinawa, and most of our remaining aircraft had been transferred to bases in northern Kyushu. I was transferred to Omura as well.

In July, the entire Naval Air Corps was converted into kamikaze formations. All younger pilots were ordered to conduct special attacks. Veteran pilots were ordered to join ground attack units. It amounted to a proclamation that fighter planes no longer had any role to play.

In August, reports came in that a new type of bomb had been dropped on Hiroshima. Rumor had it that the city had vanished in an instant. Soon after, the new type of bomb was dropped on Nagasaki, too. As Omura was very close to Nagasaki, news of the dire situation reached us quickly. But even upon hearing these things I wasn't agitated. I was only concerned with my own battles. Even if I was the last man standing, I would go out to engage American aircraft.

I was given an order to transfer from Omura to Kanoya right before the end of the war, to escort the kamikazes that launched from there.

It was there that I was reunited with the man who haunted me even in my dreams. Yes, Miyabe. It had been about a year and a half since our parting.

But when I saw his face, at first I didn't even recognize him. His demeanor had completely changed. His cheeks were sunken, his jaw was covered in stubble, and only his eyes shone with a strange light. The Miyabe I'd known before had always been very tidy and clean-shaven. His insignia indicated that he was now an ensign.

Shall I tell you how I honestly felt when I saw him again? I was happy. Don't ask me why, though.

Perhaps it was because over the course of the previous year or so I'd witnessed too much death. Many veteran pilots had died in the course of their duties as fighter escorts for the kamikazes. In part I must have been glad that he'd made it.

"Ensign Miyabe," I called out to him.

He merely glared at me and didn't utter a word in response.

"I've improved a whole lot since back then. I won't lose to you so easily this time, sir."

He gave me a suspicious look and nodded vaguely. Still silent, he turned on his heels and walked away.

He doesn't remember me? The rage and humiliation I'd felt a year ago came roaring back.

It was again my heart's deepest desire to witness his death. I remembered that what had kept me alive until that day was my wish to see him perish before my eyes.

The next day, before daybreak, all aircrew were assembled before the command post. An assortment of planes culled from all over Kyushu stood in rows along the runway. All the engines were running.

In the gloom, amidst the growling drone of the engines, I looked at the blackboard and the lists of the pilots selected for either special attack or escort duty. My name, just like the previous day, was listed among the guard contingent.

After the commander gave his salutation, he traded the customary farewell cups of water with the pilots, who then walked off towards the waiting aircraft. I casually glanced over at them and instantly froze. Miyabe was among the group of special attack pilots.

I immediately broke into a run. Catching up to him, I said, "Ensign Miyabe."

He gave a small jolt and turned around.

"Are you really conducting a special attack?" I asked.

I was left speechless when he nodded.

"It puts me at ease to know you'll be backing me up, Kageura."

With this, he gave me a bright smile, slapped me on the shoulder, and headed towards his bomb-hugging Zero.

This was a situation I'd never considered. To think Miyabe of all people would become a kamikaze... I could only look on in a blank daze as he walked away.

A few minutes later, all the aircraft took off.

My eyes were locked onto Miyabe's plane. To my surprise, his Zero was not a newer Model 52, but the old Model 21 that had been used at Pearl Harbor. Where had they found such an old Zero? A 250-kilo bomb was strapped to its belly.

There was only one thought in my mind: *I absolutely need to protect Miyabe.* That and nothing else.

I would defend his plane, no matter what. I wouldn't let a single bullet touch him. I would shoot down every last hostile that attacked him. If I ran out of bullets, I'd hurl myself at them if that's what it took.

But suddenly the fuselage of my plane began shuddering violently, and smoke started pouring out of my engine.

"You damn piece of shit! Get it together!" I yelled, but the engine failed to recover. I soon fell behind and watched on helplessly as Miyabe and the formation disappeared into the distance.

I screamed at the top of my lungs. I screamed, beside myself, *Lose, Japan! Perish, Imperial Navy! The military can go to hell! I hope all professional soldiers die!*

After screaming my head off, I whispered hoarsely, "Miyabe-san, please forgive me."

When I realized what I'd muttered to myself, tears streamed down my face, endlessly.

A few days later, the war was over.

When I heard the Emperor's broadcast, I fell to the ground and wept, loudly. There were others who cried as well, but none wailed at the top of their lungs like I did. But I wasn't weeping over Japan's defeat. I didn't care about Japan. I had known for a while that we were going to lose.

I cried for none other than Miyabe. Had he lived just one week longer, he would have been saved. He could have gone back to that wife of his whom he loved so dearly.

After the war I became a yakuza. I wanted to take revenge against this insane world. I hated being in a world where the ones in power threw their weight around.

I murdered, too. I killed so many people it's a wonder that I'm still alive today.

But I forgot about Miyabe. I didn't think about him again until today.

"That ends my story," Kageura said brusquely.

He had put on dark sunglasses partway through, so I wasn't able to read his expression. The young man standing behind him had kept his lips tightly sealed.

"That time, though," Kageura suddenly muttered, "Miyabe's eyes weren't those of a man who'd decided to die."

He looked up at the ceiling.

I couldn't think of a reply. Maybe Kageura wanted to say that my grandfather had held on to hope to the very end.

The former yakuza folded his arms. Now he seemed to be staring at me, but his sunglasses made it hard to tell.

After a while he said, "You said your grandmother passed away?"

"Yes, six years ago."

"Did she have a happy life?"

"I think so."

Kageura's expression seemed to soften momentarily. But that might have been my imagination.

"Glad to hear that."

"Did you ever meet her?"

"No," he replied immediately. "I had absolutely no interest in his family."

He abruptly got to his feet then practically shouted, "I'm done with my story. Now get out of here!" His tone was intimidating and final.

I stood up and thanked him. The next instant, something totally unexpected happened. Kageura, sunglasses still on, pulled me into a tight hug. I froze, at a loss for how to react. I could feel the warmth of his thin, old frame. Then he released me.

"Pardon me. It's just that I like young men," he said with a grin, and instructed his bodyguard to see me to the door.

Then Kageura left the room.

The young man led me to the entryway. "I was able to listen to a moving story," he said, bowing deeply.

I bowed in return and left the Kageura residence.

Chapter 11
Final Moments

The hot summer was drawing to a close. So was the journey to learn about my grandfather.

As summer turned to autumn, I set about collating the stories about him for Mom. I plugged the voice recorder into my computer and listened over and over again to the tales. I had asked Keiko to let me handle the job of putting everything together. I thought that she might turn me down, but she had no objections.

"You've really put a ton of work into this project from the beginning, Kentaro. So, of course you should be the one to bring it all together."

I had no intention of hastily writing everything up in a slam-dunk manner. It wasn't my intent to romanticize my grandfather, but I hated the idea of putting his story into words before I was able to convey his true form. But as I listened repeatedly to the testimonials on the voice recorder, I began to think that I should let Mom listen to all of the stories.

I received word from Suzuko Emura that her father Genjiro Izaki had passed away in mid-August.

"He looked very peaceful as he went," she told me at the funeral.

I saw his grandson, Seiichi, when I went up to the small table in front of the coffin to light a stick of incense. At first I didn't recognize him. It was hard to believe that he was the same youth whom I'd met in that hospital room. He had cut off his long hair and dyed it from blond to his original black. We didn't speak, but once he realized who I was, he bowed deeply.

Small changes were taking place in me as well. I opened up my law textbooks that had been collecting dust for some time. And I found myself wanting to try one more time to pass the bar exam.

I'd regained the desire I'd once had to become a lawyer and to devote myself to helping others. Since such a naive motivation and dream had begun to make me feel embarrassed, it was a mystery even to me that I now wanted to pursue that goal more than ever.

At the end of August, Keiko invited me out for drinks. One look at her face told me there was something weighing on her mind.

After we had sat down and ordered beer, Keiko said with forced casualness: "Takayama-san formally proposed to me."

"Oh. And how did you reply?"

She didn't answer.

"I really don't want to have to call that man 'brother.'"

"Please don't say that. He's very sorry for what happened that time. He says he took Takeda-san's insults against his company personally and lost his cool."

"But he still insulted our grandfather. Not directly, but he did insult all of the kamikazes."

"And Takayama-san regrets that. After listening to Takeda-san, he realized that he'd had the wrong idea. You might find it hard to believe, but he was crying when he told me that."

That was very difficult for me to even imagine, but I trusted that Keiko wouldn't lie to me. "Do you really think you'll be happy as a couple?"

She seemed a bit peeved by my question. "Yes, I do think I'll be happy. He loves me, and—"

"And he meets your qualifications for a spouse."

"Is that so wrong?"

I shook my head. To women, marriage is about reality. And he really did seem to love her. Sure, he was biased, but that didn't necessarily make him a bad person. If anything, for an elite like him to admit fault and weep in remorse suggested that he was a fairly sincere human being.

And besides, Keiko was committed to her dream of getting a book published. He was someone who could help her pursue that dream.

"There's just one thing that bothers me," I said. "You haven't said anything about the most important factor."

"What?"

"Do you love Takayama-san?"

Instead of answering, Keiko picked up her beer and silently drained her glass. She ran a finger along the rim.

"And what are you going to do about Fujiki-san?"

Her face went pale.

"Fujiki-san saying that he wanted to marry you was probably him taking a leap into the dark. I think it required death-defying courage for him to ask you."

Keiko looked down. Then she said in a barely audible voice, "I think so, too. I've done something awful, haven't I?"

"I think it was a childish form of revenge. But if you agree it was wrong, then I've nothing more to say. But I do want you to properly apologize to Fujiki-san at least."

Keiko nodded.

"Your life's your own, and I won't say anything more about your marriage plans. You should choose what you think is best."

"Okay," she said.

I changed the subject, talking about how I meant to throw myself into my studies like mad to try for the bar again next year. At first she seemed surprised, but then she smiled and said, "Good luck!"

I wasn't anxious about the exam. Looking back, on my first attempt I had been tripped up by ambition. Failure had sparked impatience. And on the last attempt I had just been dumped, so I was in a very bad state of mind. But now, I surprised myself by how calm and settled I was as I tackled my studies. I felt as though I could simply do my best and then leave the rest up to fate. If I failed, then my plan was to look for a job of some kind. Having a job wasn't a bad thing. In fact, I felt as though I should participate in society by earning a living. And if I felt like it, I could try for the bar again in my thirties, like Grandpa had done.

"By the way, why do you think Grandfather Miyabe ended up dying a kamikaze?" Keiko said out of nowhere.

"This is just a guess, but..." I trailed off.

"It's okay, tell me, Kentaro."

"What Kageura said...the stuff about the *Yamato* heading to

Okinawa even though the crew knew she'd be sunk. It was a point-less death, but they couldn't stand by and do nothing while there were other people fighting in Okinawa."

Keiko looked at me with a serious expression.

"Grandfather saw off many kamikaze pilots, a good number of whom had been his own students. Maybe it made him think that he shouldn't live on when they'd all died."

Keiko looked down towards the table, focusing on the glass before her. Then she replied softly, "I don't think that's it."

I waited for her to expand on her response, but she didn't explain. "About Kageura-san, I think I understand his feelings," she said instead. "He admired our grandfather from the bottom of his heart."

Maybe he did, I thought.

"So is the research over now?" she asked.

"Actually, not quite yet. A few days ago, I got a call from the veterans' group for the first time in a while. There's a man who was a Navy communications specialist at Kanoya, and apparently he remembers a few things about our grandfather. But not much, it seems. Like it's just at the edges of his memory."

"So are you not going to go?"

"Well actually, I want to see the place grandfather took off from for the last time. And I figure while I'm there, I'll go see the man. After that, the journey to learn about Grandfather Miyabe will be over."

"When are you going?"

"This weekend."

Keiko thought for a moment then said, in a firm tone, "Can I come too? No, I mean, take me with you."

The old Kanoya Navy Base was currently used by the Self-Defense Force. It was right near the center of the Osumi Peninsula, and Mt. Kaimondake lay to the southwest.

From Kirishima-ga-oka, a nearby hill, we had a sweeping view of the runway. We learned that they were still using the same one. Bunkers built sixty years ago still remained, too.

I felt very sentimental when I realized I was gazing out over the same scenery my grandfather had so many years ago.

There was a museum adjacent to the SDF base with various materials related to the Naval Air Corps on display. I saw a real Zero for the first time, too. It was far smaller than I had imagined. Some of the wills left by pilots were also on display, but I couldn't bring myself to read them.

I felt I had to get out of there as quickly as possible, and left. Keiko stayed behind, reading some of the wills, but soon after came out with red, weepy eyes. I didn't ask what she thought about them, and she didn't volunteer any thoughts. The kamikazes' sorrow and suffering was something of a common understanding between us.

We paid our respects to the Special Attack Force Memorial, and then left Kanoya city.

Former Petty Officer 1st Class Yasuhiko Onishi lived in Kagoshima city, on the opposite side from Kanoya across Kagoshima Bay. It was a three-hour trek via bus and ferry from one city to the other.

Onishi ran a small inn. Or rather, his son ran it while he enjoyed his retired life.

Keiko and I were shown to the inn's drawing room. It was a sunny one that looked south over a small garden.

The most surprising thing we learned about Onishi upon meeting him was that he spoke the standard form of Japanese. When Keiko commented, "You don't speak in the Kagoshima dialect," Onishi laughed and said, "That's because I'm originally from Tokyo."

He spread open a large notebook on the desk. The pages were yellowed and the cover was falling apart. "I wrote down what I remembered of the war after it ended," Onishi explained as he flipped through the notebook. "I'd written down the names of every one of the kamikazes that took off from Kanoya Base."

I was sent to Kanoya in 1944—that's sixty years ago now. I still can't speak in the local dialect very well, but speaking standard Japanese is useful if you're running an inn.

After the war ended, I thought about returning to Tokyo. But it had been ravaged by fires after the many air raids, my family had evacuated to our relatives' place in Chiba, and there wasn't much to return to. My wife and I were seeing each other here at that point, so I decided to stay put. She'd worked in the bomb shelters at Kanoya as part of the women's volunteer corps. We never spoke to each other during the war, though. We only had our first conversation after the war came to a close.

Her family had run this inn. She had two older brothers who both died in the war. So I was adopted into the family and ultimately took over running the place. Yes, we get along fine.

My job at Kanoya was communications.

Comm specialists did a whole bunch of things, communicating with other units as well as with attack forces. But starting in the spring of 1945, a major part of the job was to receive wires from the kamikaze flights. This was very difficult, heartbreaking work.

By that time, confirming the results of a special attack had become a tall order. Even if a kamikaze successfully rammed himself into a ship, if there was no one out there to witness and report back, we had no way of knowing what had happened.

During the Philippines operation, the formations all had monitoring aircraft to report results, but by the Battle of Okinawa the monitors would be shot down if they sortied with the kamikazes, so none were deployed at all.

The promise that Vice Admiral Onishi made when he spoke to Shikishima Unit, that word of their achievements in battle would be delivered to the Emperor, had long been abrogated. The kamikazes died all alone without anyone knowing their last moments. How sorrowful that is.

So, how to confirm the results of kamikaze missions? Make the pilots themselves do it. Their aircraft were outfitted with radiotelegraphs so that they could make a dispatch right at the moment of the attack. Back then, the wireless phones of the Navy were plagued by static and noise, which made them useless. We had to rely on Morse code transmissions. Those dots and dashes.

A kamikaze pilot reporting "a sighting of enemy fighters" would repeatedly transmit a dot. If he was about to crash into an aircraft carrier, he would send a dash. A very long dash meant "I am about to make my final assault." The pilot would hold down the telegraph key until the moment of impact.

When we heard that tone, our spines froze. It meant that at that very moment a pilot was about to lose his life in an attack. And the instant the tone stopped was the moment their life was snuffed out. But we didn't have the luxury to grow sentimental and grieve their deaths. We had to measure the length of time from the start of the long tone to its expiration in order to gauge whether the pilot had successfully struck his intended target or been taken out my anti-aircraft fire. If the tone ended too quickly, we would judge that the pilot had been shot down by AA fire. If the tone went on for a while, we assumed the pilot had made a successful attack. Basically, it was up to us comm guys to listen to the transmissions and confirm the results of the attack.

The transmissions were the final messages the special attack pilots left in this world, and their way of conveying the results of their mission to HQ. From today's perspective, that's quite cruel to say the least, isn't it? There should have been someone else present to confirm their achievements so the pilots could put aside all distractions and focus on striking the enemy ship. Yet they also had to send out a signal until their last breath in the way of a battle report. I can't think of anything more heartless.

All the kamikaze pilots were truly fine young men. Most of them dutifully sent out long dash tones before their attacks. Even moments before their deaths, they were devoted to every aspect of their mission. They had to dodge terrifying ambushes by enemy fighters, wind their way through a barrage of anti-aircraft fire, then right before diving into an enemy warship, remember to send out a telegraph… Hard to even imagine. The transmitter was attached to their thigh, and in order to press the key they had to switch over and use their left hand on the control stick. To have such presence of mind even in such an extreme situation… On top of which, they hadn't acquired the nerve through experience. It was a once-in-a-lifetime situation, and they still managed to pull it off.

I didn't realize all this at the time. Now I can look back and appreciate how strong they were. None of them panicked in the face of death or lost his head.

I listened to many dashes. I would focus my whole attention, become all ears, to register their last signal. I'd hold my breath for as long as the long tone stretched. There's nothing that can compare to the gravity of that span. When the tone ended, a young man had lost his life. I don't know how to express the sadness and fright of those moments. Each time, it felt like a nail had been driven into my heart.

That tone is still engraved in my mind. I don't know what hertz it was, but when I occasionally hear the same "sound" my whole body goes rigid, my heart starts hammering in my chest, and my knees give out. I don't like listening to music. Sometimes there'll be a long note that's similar to that dash. As soon as I hear it, I'm done for.

You wanted to hear about Miyabe-san.

Yes, I remember him. He was an accomplished pilot, having served since Pearl Harbor. Everyone at Kanoya Base took off their hats to him.

To tell the truth, it had been my dream to become an aviator. I took the entrance exam for the Prep Program but unfortunately wasn't accepted. I know that this is an inexcusable insult to those who died in the war, but actually I'm glad that I failed to get in. Had I been accepted, there's no doubt I would have died a kamikaze.

Ensign Miyabe and I met frequently in the communications room.

Since he was a formation leader, he would come to the comm-shack to ask after the transmission status of scouting parties or attack units. Miyabe-san's rank was ensign, but actually he was a "special duty" ensign. He wasn't the type to swagger about like the officers from the Naval Academy and easily engaged rank and file like me in conversation, so I liked him.

Miyabe-san often flew escort for the kamikaze units that launched from Kanoya.

The escort fighters were not kamikazes. Their job was to defend the kamikazes from attacks by enemy fighters until they safely reached the other side's aircraft carriers. I was just a radioman and didn't know anything about airplanes. But I could imagine how difficult it must have been to fend off an overwhelming number of far superior fighter planes.

In fact, on each mission there were always members of the fighter escorts that failed to return. Sometimes none of them came back. While they weren't kamikazes, they, too, were on special attack missions so to speak. By then even recon planes that had the benefit of speed didn't always return.

I asked Ensign Miyabe about that once. "Are the fighter escorts then not in the same boat as the kamikazes, sir?"

"Not at all," he flatly denied. "To be sure, under these circumstances the support aircraft have a really hard time, too. But at least we have a one-in-ten chance to return from the mission. We can fight for our survival, no matter how bleak the outlook. For the kamikazes, it's zero-in-ten."

Jusshi reisei. Death: ten, Life: zero. This was how the *Shinpu* Special Attack Force was described back then. The word "suicidal" is often used to mean "certain death," but that isn't always the outcome. With the special attacks, though, death was indeed the foregone conclusion. As the old saying goes, "Where there's a will, there's a way." Zero-in-ten odds required an even stronger resolve than that.

The most tragic among the kamikazes were the members of the Divine Thunder Unit.

Those were the ones who manned the Ohka rockets. Among the many horrors of special attacks, none were as atrocious as the use of these. The human bomb Ohka would be loaded onto a Type 1 attack plane and sent off to its target. Who could ever conceive of such a preposterous tactic? When the first Divine Thunder Unit was deployed in early March, none of the eighteen Type 1s that sortied returned to base. Of the thirty Zeros that were in the fighter escort that day, ten didn't make it back. Since there was a shortage of supporting fighters, many a commander and general staffer proposed to Vice Admiral Ugaki that he delay implementing the plan, but he brushed aside their concerns. Lieutenant Commander Nonaka, who led the squadron of Type 1s, apparently said before sortieing, "This is the stupidest battle plan ever conceived."

That day, I waited for telegraphs from the Type 1s, yet not a single one came in. Not even the signal for spotting hostile fighters. The lack of any communications from them was bizarre since the Type 1s each had a dedicated wire operator on board. Even in an ambush, it was standard practice to wire "enemy fighters sighted." But not a single telegraph came in from any of the eighteen aircraft.

A silent protest against the mission, I assumed, on the lieutenant commander's part.

Yet, Divine Thunder Units were deployed many more times after that.

I believe this incident occurred in May. Ensign Miyabe had been ordered on his first Divine Thunder escort mission since his arrival at Kanoya. Six Zeros were deployed to back up six Type 1s. One of the Type 1s, tasked with guiding the formation, did not carry an Ohka. Ensign Miyabe looked unusually pale before he sortied that day.

His was the only plane that ever returned. He reported that all of the Type 1s had been shot down.

The ensign's plane was covered in bullet holes. The tail, especially, was riddled with bullet marks. It was incredible that he'd made it back with his aircraft in such a state.

That night, when I left the comm-shack and was heading back to the barracks, I caught sight of someone in a flight uniform sitting alone on an embankment by the runway. It was a bright, moonlight night. The man was Ensign Miyabe.

When he noticed me, he waved. "Come sit with me, Murata," he called out. That was my original family name.

"Thank you, sir," I said, sitting down next to him.

It was then that I noticed that he smelled of alcohol. I looked over to discover a large-sized bottle of sake by his side.

"How about a drink?" he asked, grabbing the bottle and holding it out. "I don't have any cups, so just drink from the bottle."

"Thank you, but I'll pass, sir. It'd be wasted on me."

Ensign Miyabe didn't seem particularly bothered by my refusal. He took another big swig straight from the bottle.

"The Ohkas will never succeed!" he spat. I was stunned by how loudly he'd said this. "It's hard enough for the special attack planes to get close to their warships. There's no way medium bombers weighed down by Ohkas could ever reach them."

"It's hard even for a special attack plane, sir?"

"The Americans spot us on their radar and launch huge numbers of fighters to ambush us. It's not possible to break through with just a handful of escort fighters. Moreover, the special attack planes are loaded with heavy bombs. Their pilots are newcomers with little experience."

"But there are some who make it to the enemy task force." Since I was on the receiving end of their telegraphs, I refused to concede this point.

"Sure, there's the occasional one that's able to break through, but it's barely one out of a few dozen. Over 2,000 kamikazes have sortied in the Battle of Okinawa. How many of those signaled that they were diving into their targets?"

I didn't have an answer. I had personally heard dozens of strike signals, but out of 2,000 kamikazes that was still a dispiritingly small percentage.

"Even if they're lucky and manage to dodge the interceptors' attacks and make it to an aircraft carrier, they're faced with intense anti-aircraft fire. I have witnessed a number of planes take that final plunge, and I can't even begin to describe how fierce their anti-aircraft barrage is. It was impressive enough at the time of the Battle of the Solomon Sea, but the Americans have far greater AA power now. Headquarters has no idea what the actual conditions are like. Or maybe they do and are just feigning ignorance."

Tears were running down his face. "Pulling off a ramming attack from a nose-dive requires skill. The carrier-based bomber pilots who fought at Pearl Harbor might be able to pull it off, but these young kids can't hack it. You have to dive at a very steep angle in order to avoid their anti-aircraft guns. If you go in at a low angle, you'll get pummeled by them. But if your angle is too steep, you'll end up going too fast, which makes your plane drift. You can do your best to counteract this, but at such high speeds the flaps become awfully heavy, and the vertical rudder is much less efficient. It's not easy to change your angle or direction immediately before you slam into the target. In most cases, you just crash into the sea."

Ensign Miyabe sounded as though he were speaking to an aviation student. He was clearly drunk. That was the first time I had seen him in such a state.

He suddenly grabbed the bottle of sake and flung it towards the runway. The bottle glinted in the moonlight as it arced its way through the air, then smashed into the pavement and splintered into pieces.

"Today, I watched as six medium bombers all got shot down. I couldn't do a damn thing," he said.

Then he howled. It made me tremble.

"Among the Ohka pilots was a student of mine from Tsukuba. Before we departed, he looked at me and said, 'It's a real comfort to know you'll be escorting us, sir.' But right before my eyes, the Type 1 that was carrying him went up in flames and fell away. The crew of the bomber saluted me as they fell," Ensign Miyabe said, glaring at me. "I couldn't save a single one of those planes." His voice was anguished. "Not a damn one!"

"I don't think it could have been helped, sir."

"You don't think?!" he shouted. "Do you have any idea how many men died? It's the duty of the guard contingent to protect the special attack planes, even if it means sacrificing yourself. Yet I let all of them die." Ensign Miyabe gripped his knees tightly and dropped his head. His shoulders were trembling.

I didn't know what words to offer him. I could sense that he was blaming himself and getting lost in a black despair.

"My life rests on all of their sacrifices."

"With all due respect, sir, I don't think that's true."

"Yes, it is. I only survived because they died."

Upon hearing this, I realized just how tormented his heart was. He was all too kind for his own good.

Ensign Miyabe then got up and started walking on unsteady feet towards the barracks. I couldn't even call after him.

In the latter half of the Battle of Okinawa, Ensign Miyabe had clearly changed. He let stubble form along his jawline, and his eyes gave off a strange, dazzling light. He had always been tall and slender, but he grew even thinner. His face was haggard, his features altogether transformed. And he had stopped smiling.

It was as if each sortie as a fighter escort for kamikazes chipped away at his life force.

One early afternoon, seeing him standing on the runway, I felt a shiver run down my spine. As I observed his image wavering there in the hot air reflecting off the runway, it was as though he wasn't of this world anymore. He already seemed to have one foot on that distant shore.

Even after Okinawa was captured by the Americans, kamikaze missions were carried out intermittently.

Soon, however, enemy planes taking off from Okinawa began to conduct near-daily raids. Most of the aircraft and personnel from Kanoya and other bases around southern Kyushu were transferred to northern Kyushu. Kanoya was then only used as a launching pad for kamikaze missions. I remained at Kanoya.

I began to realize that Japan was about to lose. August saw new types of bombs dropped on Hiroshima and Nagasaki, and there was a looming sense of despair that Japan itself would perish.

After the call came down in the latter days of the Battle of Okinawa for all planes to kamikaze, HQ began issuing kamikaze orders as normal attacks. In addition to the student reservists and boy pilots, seasoned aviators from the Preparatory Program and even the Naval Academy were commanded one after another to sortie as kamikazes. Anyone who refused would of course be charged with insubordination.

By that time, however, many pilots were forced to turn around after encountering engine trouble. I'd also heard that more than a few crashed into the ocean well before reaching the American fleet. And I witnessed some aircraft that fell into the sea almost immediately after taking off from Kanoya. No matter how diligent the mechanics were, nearly one out of every three aircraft was forced to return due to engine problems. On particularly bad days, nearly all the aircraft had to come back. Japan was rapidly running out of materials, fuel, and everything else.

It was under those dire circumstances that Ensign Miyabe was ordered to sortie as a kamikaze at last.

The morning of his mission, I went to say goodbye to him. Dawn had yet to break.

It was still dark out, which made it hard to tell who was who, but eventually I found him.

I wasn't sure what exactly I should say. I finally managed to force out, "Good luck in battle, sir."

Ensign Miyabe nodded, but it was hard to read his expression in the darkness.

After a while the engines were started and the pilots headed towards their planes. Then something strange happened.

Ensign Miyabe asked a reserve officer to switch planes with him. The ensign's was a newer Zero Model 52, and the reserve's an old Model 21. By that time, Model 21s were very rare, and that particular one had probably been chucked away at some base to be patched up only now and brought to Kanoya. I was seeing one for the first time.

Ensign Miyabe wanted to fly the antique. He said he wanted to fly the same model of aircraft he'd piloted at Rabaul. A Model 21 couldn't hold a candle to a Model 52 in terms of performance. The Model 52 had far greater horsepower and boasted a higher speed. The Model 21 may have been a more agile dogfighter, but that was irrelevant on a kamikaze mission. Even I knew it would be better to have a plane with greater horsepower and more speed.

The reserve officer that Ensign Miyabe had addressed was quite aware of these things as well, so he refused to exchange planes.

"Ensign Miyabe, you should take the Model 52, sir. You are far more skilled than I. A good pilot deserves a good aircraft," the reserve declared.

"Understood," the ensign said, returning to his own aircraft. But moments later he came back and repeated his request.

"My skills are top notch. I'll be just fine in a Model 21," he said loudly enough to be heard over the roar of the engines.

I couldn't believe my own ears upon hearing this. It just didn't seem like something he would ever say. I had never before heard him brag about his own skills like that. No, that was most certainly not the sort of man he was.

Maybe even someone like Ensign Miyabe wanted to strut a little in his final moments, I wondered then. Or maybe he was insisting on piloting the Model 21 out of stubbornness, out of anger towards the Navy for ordering a brilliant pilot like himself to kamikaze. Perhaps he thought, *Fine, I'll go, but I'll take an old Model 21.*

Or maybe what he said was the plain truth: his nostalgia for the good old Model 21 had won out.

The Zero came to be regarded as a symbol of the Imperial Navy. At the start of the war, she was a peerless fighter. But later on, since they hadn't developed aircraft that could succeed her, the Zero continued to fight on the front lines. The famed warhorse that had once soared across the heavens had grown old and useless. In the first two years after its debut, the Model 21 wreaked havoc across the Chinese mainland and the Pacific, weaving the legend of the Zero's invincibility. Perhaps upon seeing it again Ensign Miyabe felt like he had been reunited with an old war buddy.

He and the reserve officer argued back and forth for a while until the younger man folded, and they switched planes. I remember that scene very well. Their conversation was bizarre enough as it was, but what happened afterwards cemented the events of that day in my memory.

They took off before dawn. Ensign Miyabe didn't return.

Onishi fell silent, a terrible look on his face. After a long silence he said, "There's an unpleasant continuation of this story."

"What is it, sir?"

Onishi seemed hesitant.

"Whatever it is, please tell us."

In response to my prodding, he seemed to make up his mind and opened his mouth. "Six Zeros carrying bombs sortied that day. But one of them was forced to make an emergency landing on Kikaijima Island due to engine problems."

I felt something cold race down my spine. "Is... Was it..."

"Yes. It was the Zero that Ensign Miyabe should have flown: the Model 52. The pilot was the man who had switched places with Miyabe-san."

I was rendered speechless.

"Had Ensign Miyabe not asked to change planes, he might have been the one to survive."

"No, no!" Keiko nearly screamed.

"It must have been fate. The goddess of fortune had abandoned him at the last moment."

"That's horrible!" Keiko yelled.

I was dumbfounded.

Had my grandfather been overcome with nostalgia at the sight of an old Model 21 on his final mission and thought to pilot it to his death? Had my grandfather, who had fought at Pearl Harbor and Guadalcanal in the Model 21, wanted to go down with an old war buddy? If there hadn't been a Model 21 there that day, would he have sortied in the Model 52 and survived?

Was the Model 21 a god of death that led him to the afterworld? Can such a terrifying twist of fate really happen?

No, it couldn't be. It wasn't possible. It seemed all too arbitrary.

That instant, I felt a jolt race through me. "Onishi-san, what was the name of that pilot?" I asked breathlessly.

Onishi seemed briefly lost as to what I was talking about. "Do you mean the name of the pilot that made the emergency landing?"

He put on his glasses and flipped through the pages of the notebook.

"Ah, here it is," he said, pointing.

On the page was a list of the special attack pilots who had died in combat, sorted by date, from August of 1945. I peered at the notebook. Next to five names was another, with the annotation: "Crash-landed on Kikaijima."

"Here." Onishi seemed to be having trouble making it out. His reading glasses must have been out of date.

"May I see?"

Onishi nodded and handed over the notebook. I practically snatched it out of his hands. There, in neat script, were the words:

"Ensign Kenichiro Oishi, Age 23, Student Reservist 13th Class, Waseda University"

"Ahh," I groaned.

"What's wrong?" Keiko asked fearfully. She looked down at the notebook. "Ah!" she cried.

I tried to say something to her, but my voice refused to work. My teeth clacked together.

Finally, I eked out, "Kenichiro Oishi...our Grandpa!"

Chapter 12
Shooting Star

Grandpa leaned back into the chair in his study and closed his eyes.

After a while he opened them and said, "I knew I'd have to tell you everything at some point."

I nodded, speechless. Keiko was sitting next to me.

"When I heard that you were doing research on Miyabe-san, I prepared myself, knowing this day would come." He retrieved a pill from his bottle of heart medication and washed it down with a sip of water.

"Matsuno had insisted that there was no need to tell the children, but I still planned on talking to you about it someday. Just in case the opportunity to tell you never arose, I wrote it all down in a letter for you to read. I left it in the care of a junior lawyer some ten years ago. If I suddenly passed away, he was to give it to Kiyoko."

I met Miyabe-san at the Tsukuba Air Unit.

We received training there to become kamikaze pilots. Not that we had been told as much from the outset. At first, we were trained in the basics of flight technique. Miyabe-san was our instructor for those sessions.

After completing the flight-training course, we students were handed a form on which we were to respond whether we would volunteer or not for the kamikaze units. I selected to volunteer, but in fact I did not wish to do so. I doubt anyone actually wanted to. Yet everyone replied that they would. Were we gutless? I don't think that's correct.

Back then, whether on the continent or on the islands dotted around the Pacific, many troops were giving up their lives every day. The newspapers carried rousing proclamations from Imperial General HQ, but also the phrase "shattered jewels." Given all that, I was willing to surrender my life if doing so would protect my homeland and loved ones. Even if that meant dying a kamikaze.

Yet there was also a resistance to dying. We weren't madmen. We weren't suicide-bound lemmings, joining the hoard, racing off a cliff into the ocean below. We wanted our deaths to have some meaning.

Miyabe-san was gentle in both manner and speech. Despite the countless scenes of carnage he had survived, his quiet demeanor set him apart from the other instructors.

What I sensed more than anything from him, however, was his internal conflict about teaching us how to fly. To repeat, we were to be kamikaze pilots. I felt that it pained him to teach us flight techniques. He would praise us when we made progress, but there was always sadness in his smile.

Miyabe-san was a very compassionate man.

Once, during a training session, there was an accident in which one of our classmates died. While we were still mourning the loss, a certain officer hurled abuse at him and us. Miyabe-san stuck out his neck and defended the honor of the fallen reserve officer.

All of us were ready to give up our lives for him after that.

Had Miyabe-san not spoken up then, his destiny as well as mine might have been different. A person's fate can be drastically altered by the most trivial things. I still find myself confounded by the mysteries of fate.

This happened one month later. We were in the middle of a training flight when enemy aircraft suddenly appeared. Miyabe-san, engrossed in instructing us, didn't notice their approach. Even veteran pilots like him occasionally made such errors.

I spotted the American fighters. I had just completed a dive and was returning to a higher altitude. As if in a trance, without thinking whatsoever, I charged in between the incoming aircraft and the instructor's plane. I have no idea what I was thinking. I had totally lost myself to the moment. I could make myself look good by saying I went in there with the intention of sacrificing myself for him, but

I don't really know if that's the truth. But I knew for sure that I wasn't going to let them lay a finger on Instructor Miyabe.

The trainer planes used by us students were not outfitted with machine guns. Even so, I dashed out in front of the enemy aircraft. Their bullets struck my plane, shattering my windshield. I lost consciousness and began falling, but came to when I was nearing the ground and somehow managed to pull up and fly level. I looked skywards to see an enemy plane plummeting down.

I don't remember very well what happened next. After touching down, I passed out cold.

I was hospitalized at a naval hospital. Miyabe-san came to visit me once. He gave me an overcoat. He had apparently taken note of the fact that mine had grown threadbare and tattered. His overcoat was government-issued, too, of course, but he'd had some work done on it. It had a cotton lining, and leather affixed to the collar.

But spring came before I ever got the chance to put my arms through the sleeves of that coat. I was finally discharged from the hospital and sent back to my unit, but by that point, he was no longer there. Neither were any of my classmates. I thought they had all already died.

And I meant to follow after them.

My emotions at the time were very complicated. At first, I found myself unable to accept that I was to die. I thought the situation was incredibly unjust. But little by little, I started to lean towards acceptance. This was definitely not just a case of me getting swept up in the times, nor was it easy for me to resolve to die. It was a state of mind achieved only after enduring extreme pain and mental conflict. It's impossible to explain such feelings in a few words. I think it would still be very difficult to properly convey them even if I took the time to. I thought about it for a long time after the war. I thought about it after I grew old. But I was never able to reproduce the thoughts I had back then.

Back then I felt like I'd arrived at my answer through some deep thinking, but I'm not even sure about that now. It was an age of insanity, so perhaps my thoughts were insane, too.

But I can say this. We did not accept our fate with wild enthusiasm. We did not go off as kamikazes to die with joy in our hearts. At no other time have I ever thought so seriously about nation and family. At no other time did I give more thought to how the futures of my loved ones might unfold after I was gone.

That July, I received my orders. I was to head to Omura Base in Kyushu.

Right after I arrived, I received a very sad letter from my mother. She informed me that my fiancée had passed away. She was my cousin, and we had been close since we were children. As we grew up, our families naturally assumed we would become betrothed, and we became engaged, though only formally. We certainly liked each other, but I don't think it was romantic love. It was just an innocent sort of companionship. We didn't even hold hands. But when I became a student pilot, I decided to break off the engagement because I couldn't be sure whether I would survive the war.

She had received serious burns in the Great Tokyo Air Raid in May and died two weeks later according to my mother's letter. I'd volunteered to conduct a special attack to protect my loved ones, but I'd lost the person I was meant to protect. When my eyes reached the part of the letter that said she'd called out my name right before she died, I couldn't stop myself from weeping.

In August we heard that a new kind of bomb had been dropped on Hiroshima and Nagasaki.

Omura was a stone's throw from Nagasaki, so news of the disaster spread to us very quickly. A reserve officer in my class who had been a physics major at Kyoto University said, "The bomb that fell on Nagasaki might have been an atomic bomb."

"What kind of a bomb is that?" someone asked.

The physics student explained that it made use of nuclear fission and that it was a terrible weapon with a destructive power so massive, traditional gunpowder-based ordnance paled in comparison.

"Was the bomb used on Nagasaki really this atomic bomb?"

"I don't know. But if the rumors about the level of damage there are true, then it's a possibility. The bomb used on Hiroshima might have been one, too."

If that's true, then Japan might perish, I thought. *If, by dying as a kamikaze, I can defend my homeland, then let me like a brave man. I'll be able to go to where my betrothed is...*

Very soon after, I was ordered to sortie on a kamikaze mission. A classmate of mine, Teranishi, was also called up. We had resigned ourselves to our fates, so I think we were, for the most part, untroubled. We told each other, "Let's go together."

We were sent to Kanoya. I met up again with Miyabe-san there.

He had changed into a completely different person since the last time I had seen him. How can I explain it? His face was almost corpse-like. His eyes were bloodshot, and his whole body emanated a killer instinct. I'd never seen him that way before.

I found myself unable to call out to him. But he noticed me.

"Have your injuries healed?" he asked me, his face impassive.

"Yes, thank you very much, sir."

"Glad to hear it."

That was the extent of our conversation.

The day I arrived at Kanoya, I was ordered to sortie in two days' time. My mind was calm. My only regret was that I wouldn't be able to see my mother one last time to say farewell. That night, I wrote a will addressed to her.

The next day, I went for a walk outside the base. I left the settlement and headed towards the mountains.

It was hot out, but it felt good to sweat. After the following day, I wouldn't be able to sweat.

Every sight seemed precious. Everything was beautiful. Even the grass on the side of the road was endlessly attractive. I crouched down to get a closer look and discovered tiny white flowers bursting from the weeds. The flowers were smaller than the tip of my little finger. *So lovely*, I thought in earnest. That was the first time I'd ever laid eyes on that flower, and I thought it was the most beautiful flower on the face of the earth.

There was a small brook. I took off my shoes and stuck my feet into the flowing stream. The cold water felt great.

I left my feet soaking in the water and sprawled out along the bank. When I closed my eyes I noticed the buzzing of cicadas. It was the first time I found their cries beautiful. And I thought that seven summers later, the cicadas' offspring would sing in just the same way. When I wondered what Japan would be like then, I was filled with great sorrow.

The next day before dawn, we gathered before the command post and listened to the words of our commander.

I was stunned to see Miyabe-san among the group of kamikaze pilots. I'd assumed he'd be escorting us. I thought, *So at last the Navy is killing off this man, too.*

After the ritual cups of water, when everyone was to head to their aircraft, Teranishi and I went over to speak to Miyabe-san.

"I could not have asked for more than to die alongside you, Instructing Officer Miyabe," Teranishi said.

Miyabe-san merely nodded silently and placed his hands on our shoulders. There was strength in those hands. The stubble that had previously covered his face had been cleanly shaven off.

"I never returned the overcoat you lent me, sir." I still have no idea what prompted me to say that to him.

"I don't need it in the summertime, anyway," he replied with a chuckle.

I found myself laughing, too.

"Well then, let's go," he said and walked towards the runway.

All the engines were running. Just as I was climbing into the cockpit, Miyabe-san came over and called out to me.

"Ensign Oishi, I have a request."

"Yes, what is it, sir?"

"Will you switch planes with me?"

He wanted to take the Model 21 that I was assigned instead of his Model 52. The Model 52 was far faster than the old 21. I turned him down, saying the better pilot should have the better aircraft.

Miyabe-san left once, but then quickly returned. He repeated his request to switch planes. After arguing back and forth for a while, I finally agreed.

I got down from the Model 21 and climbed into the Model 52.

The wheel chocks were removed. The fighters began to slowly roll forward, and then took off.

Miyabe-san's Zero flew alongside mine. I could see him in the cockpit. Suddenly, I felt tears spring from my eyes. I didn't care that I was going to die, but I wished from the bottom of my heart for him to survive.

Losing a man like him meant Japan was finished. Was there any way my death could avert his?

I wanted to sacrifice myself for his sake. I vowed to stay right at his side until the very end. If any fighters targeted him, I would shield him. I would take on any and all anti-aircraft fire as well.

The formation headed south. The sky to the east was growing faintly lighter. I recalled the old Japanese word *shinonome*, the reddish hue of early dawn. I marveled at the ancients' way with language.

I turned around to look behind me. Kagoshima Bay glittered. Kyushu's mountains further in the distance were painted green, bathed in the morning sunlight. "Beautiful," I whispered.

I was going to my death alongside a truly magnificent man.

I thought about my fiancée. *I'll be with you soon...*

Mother, I'm so sorry! I shouted in my mind. *My life was a happy one. You raised me with such love. If I'm to be born once more, I hope it's as your child again. As a girl, if possible... So I can stay with you all life long.*

Crying out these thoughts in my heart, I severed all worldly attachments. The beauty of my homeland, my feelings for my fiancée, the yearning for my mother, all of it.

Our upcoming ramming attack on an enemy warship then became everything. And I would die for Miyabe-san.

Yet not an hour into the flight my aircraft started acting up. The fuselage occasionally vibrated, and oil started spewing from the engine. The lubricant spattered on the front of the canopy, which rapidly became covered in a black film. I couldn't see anything out the front.

I continued to fly, trying not to break formation, now and then shifting the angle of my aircraft. *So what? No big deal that I can barely see what's in front of me,* I thought.

But the engine's condition only worsened. The power output drastically dropped and I couldn't keep up my airspeed. I opened the throttle flat-out but still found myself falling behind.

The formation leader pulled up next to me and signaled with

his hands, "What's wrong?" I indicated that my engine was acting up. He saw that my windshield was coated in black grease and gestured for me to return to base. I responded, "No way!" But then the fuselage began rattling and shuddering again.

The leader signaled anew for me to go back before pulling away.

I tried everything I could think of, but the engine refused to come back to life. The rest of the formation flew on, leaving me behind.

"Miyabe-san!" I screamed at the top of my lungs.

Weeping, I turned my aircraft around.

The plane was on its last leg. There was no way I could make it back to Kanoya. I searched for Kikaijima Island on the map. It was roughly fifty nautical miles to the west. It was up to fate whether or not the engine would hold up. If it failed before I reached Kikaijima, I would die. If I encountered an enemy fighter along the way, I would die. It was all down to my luck.

In order to lighten the aircraft, I pulled the cord to release the payload. The bomb didn't drop. No matter how many times I yanked the cord, it wouldn't budge. The bomb was rigged so as to not release. *How cruel are they? I can't even attempt an emergency landing like this.* Command really intended for us to go die to the last man.

Twenty minutes later, I spotted Kikaijima. There were no enemy aircraft in the skies above the island.

Just as I saw the island, the engine gave out completely. All I could do was glide. The windshield was coated in black grease, which reduced my forward vision to zero. If I approached the landing at the wrong angle, the bomb strapped to the belly of the aircraft would explode. I couldn't pull up, so there was no way to retry the landing after the first attempt.

I prepared for death. Just then, I heard Miyabe-san's voice.

"You must not give up, Ensign Oishi. Do whatever it takes to survive!"

I could hear his voice perfectly clearly. Even after sixty years, it's still engraved in my memory. It wasn't my imagination.

These things do happen.

Right before I approached the runway, I banked my plane and looked over the whole airfield. I drilled the distance and angle into my mind and then leveled the aircraft. Then I closed my eyes, having decided to rely on my mind's eye to make the landing.

The image of the airfield stood out in bold relief in my mind— so clearly that it was as though I was seeing it with my eyes. I could even vividly sense when the plane was getting closer to the landing strip. I nosed up, bringing the aircraft level, the correct posture for a three-point landing. The aircraft continued to descend. Altitude fifty meters, twenty meters, five meters—the moment I thought "one more meter," the wheels hit the runway. The plane continued to roll for a distance, then came to a stop.

Even looking back now, I think that it was a miracle. I could never pull off such a landing again if I tried. It was as though I'd been possessed, a rare experience.

I was saved. True, once I returned to the interior, I would be sortieing as a kamikaze again.

I was told, however, that the aircraft's engine was totaled and couldn't be fixed easily.

In the evening, the base's communication specialist informed me that all pilots on our special attack mission, apart from me, hadn't returned.

Miyabe-san was dead…

It was there on Kikaijima that I listened to Emperor Hirohito's broadcast.

"So that was your fate, Grandpa," Keiko said softly.

"It wasn't fate," he stated. "Just as I was about to climb down from the plane, I noticed a piece of paper in the cockpit. It was a note, hastily written, by Miyabe-san."

"What?" I blurted out without thinking.

"The note read, 'Ensign Oishi, if luck is with you and you manage to survive this war, I have a request. If my family is homeless and suffering, please help them.' I think he jotted it down when he went back to the Model 52 before insisting that we switch planes. Do you still think it's by chance that I survived?"

Wordlessly, I shook my head. I'd actually expected as much.

It was only after a while that I could bring myself to ask, "But why?"

Grandpa slowly shook his head. "I don't know, either. However," he said, almost glaring at me, "I think when he got into the Model 52, he could tell the engine was faulty. He must have realized that he'd drawn a ticket for survival."

In my heart, I raised a voiceless cry. What a brutal choice the goddess of fate had given Kyuzo Miyabe at the eleventh hour.

He went back once to his Model 52. He'd wavered, there at the end. But then he shook off his doubts and handed the winning lottery ticket to Ensign Oishi...

Next to me, my sister had her head bowed. Her cheeks were wet with tears.

After a long moment of silence, Grandpa quietly continued his tale.

It took me well over three years to find Miyabe-san's wife.

Their house was in Yokohama, but the city had been reduced to ashes in the Great Air Raid in May. None of their neighbors knew where she had gone.

I returned to college. Whenever I had time to spare, I walked all around their old neighborhood, asking after Miyabe-san's wife, but her whereabouts were a total mystery. Two years later, I graduated from college and got a job with National Railway.

By that time, many of those who had lived in Miyabe-san's former neighborhood had returned, but she wasn't among them. I persistently contacted my reserve officer friends from the Navy, thinking that if his wife was in distress, she might try to contact one of his comrades.

Another year passed with no leads.

At the time, everyone had their hands full just trying to get by. I was incredibly fortunate to have been allowed to resume my education. My mother was a primary school teacher in Tokyo, so we never went hungry.

But that doesn't mean our lives were easy. All I had to wear were my mended and patched clothes from my days in the military. I continued to wear the overcoat that Miyabe-san had given me, too.

It was a friend of mine who worked for the Ministry of Welfare that was able at long last to tell me where Miyabe-san's wife and daughter were. Since she was his widow, she had applied for a bereaved family's pension with the Demobilization Bureau of the Ministry of Welfare. The pension system had yet to be completed, but the Demobilization Bureau had been making preparations for its implementation.

The address was in Osaka. I immediately headed there. This was in the winter of 1949.

Back then, it was a ten-hour trek to get to Osaka from Tokyo. Nowadays you could get to America in the same amount of time.

The day was cold. As I searched for the address, I entered a very poor section of town that could easily have been called a slum. There were rows of barracks-like tenements whose residents were indeed destitute. The entire area gave off an offensive smell.

I felt like my chest was being squeezed. It was so depressing to learn that the wife and child that Miyabe-san had wanted to protect so badly had ended up living in such a squalid neighborhood. No, it was more than just depressing. My response crossed over into something akin to rage.

I entered an alleyway and spotted a little girl standing alone. She wore a red woolen scarf and a skirt covered with patches. She had an affable countenance. And looked at me with lovely eyes. As soon as I saw her, I was reminded of Miyabe-san's face.

"Miyabe-san?" I asked.

The girl turned around and dashed away. I followed.

She went inside one of the row houses. Well, if you could even call it a house. The walls were comprised of random old boards stuck together and the ceiling was a sheet of galvanized metal.

I stood in front of the house. A small wooden board served in place of a proper name plate. On it, written in beautiful script, was the name MIYABE.

"Excuse me, please," I called out in greeting.

"Coming!" a voice replied straightaway, and a woman emerged.

She wore work pants and had a towel wrapped around her head. Her attire spoke of poverty, but she was very pretty.

I was temporarily struck dumb, and found myself staring at her.

Strangely, she, too, stood there looking at me in blank amazement.

She looked at me as if she was seeing a ghost or I was some strange, scary phenomenon.

"My name is Kenichiro Oishi. Your husband was very kind to me during the war."

She gave a start, and then bowed deeply. "I'm Miyabe's wife. I am sure that he is much indebted to you."

"No, I'm the one who's indebted to him."

The little girl from before stood beside the woman.

"Please come inside."

I took her up on her offer. Past the entryway there was no foyer; the door opened immediately on a single tiny room. The floor wasn't tatami matting but boards covered with straw mats. There was a vast number of buttons piled high inside the room.

"Sorry for the mess. This is for my side job." She called her daughter and asked her to go out and buy juice. She took a coin purse from within her blouse and handed her some money.

"Juice! Really?" the girl exclaimed.

"No, please don't go to any trouble," I said, flustered. I took out my wallet and handed the girl some money. "Please use this to buy juice and sweets and anything at all you'd like."

"No, that won't do."

"It's fine. I arrived without announcement and came empty-handed. So please let me pay."

After I repeatedly reassured her, she finally relented and said, "Then I'll take up your kind offer."

I told her about how he had been such a kind instructor during my days in flight school, and that we had been together at Kanoya Base.

But I didn't say anything about the day we had gone on that special attack mission. I couldn't tell her that he had died in my place. Instead, I told her that he'd saved my life during an air battle. She listened to everything quietly.

"It's all thanks to Miyabe-san that I'm still here today."

"Oh then, Miyabe... He was of some help to someone," she said poignantly.

"He helped a great many people, not just me."

"So he didn't die in vain."

As soon as she asked that question, tears sprang to my eyes. "Please forgive me," I said, going on my knees and placing both hands on the floor. "I should have died instead of him." Tears spattered the back of my hands.

"Please, raise your face," she said. "Miyabe died for all of us. Not only him, but everyone who died in the war. They died for the rest of us."

I lifted my head. She was smiling.

"How did he die?"

"He went out honorably, like a true soldier."

"That's consoling," she said and smiled again.

She is such a brave woman, I noted.

"But he lied to me," she said, her tone suddenly cold. "He promised me that he'd come back." Her eyes brimmed with tears. She shut them, sending large drops streaming down her cheeks.

My heart ached as if it were in a vise. I was beset with the same regret that I'd felt countless times over the past four years.

Why did he ask me to switch aircrafts with him then? Why didn't I staunchly refuse to give in to his request? Had I done so, she could be living happily with him now…

Just then, the girl returned. She was shocked to see her mother in tears.

"It's nothing," she reassured her daughter. "We were talking about your father, and that made me a little sad."

"Kiyoko's daddy?"

"Yes, that's right."

"Mom, what was daddy like?"

"He was a wonderful man. He was braver and kinder than anyone else," I answered in his wife's stead.

"But he died."

Once again, my chest clenched painfully.

As I got up to leave, I handed Miyabe-san's wife an envelope I had brought.

"It's not much, but please accept."

"What is this now?"

"It's meager recompense for the debt I owe Miyabe-san."

"I can't take it."

I refused to yield, imploring, "You must. If I couldn't somehow pay back the person who saved my life, I would be something less than human."

After we argued back and forth for a while longer, she finally gave in.

That was how I first met Matsuno.

Every few months, I lied to my mother that I had to go on a business trip and went to visit Matsuno in Osaka. With money each time.

Matsuno would refuse, but I always insisted on leaving it with her. I don't remember the amount anymore, but I think it was close to half my salary. I lied to Matsuno about how much I made, saying that college graduates working for the National Railway received handsome salaries.

Thanks to this, my mother had a very hard time with the family budget. Just as I had graduated and started working, her health had taken a turn for the worse, and she'd had to quit her job as a schoolteacher.

My mother was under the impression that I'd taken up some bad habits, but she never said anything. She knew I'd been part of a special attack unit and assumed that I was trying to forget by being a spendthrift. Meanwhile, my colleagues at the National Railway thought I was being thrifty. I never went out with them, and I still wore my patched-up military clothes. I caught wind of rumors that I was hoarding loads of cash, but I didn't care what anyone thought of me. Some whispered that I was spending all the money on a woman.

That rumor wasn't wholly inaccurate, as I was, in fact, very attracted to Matsuno.

I always took the night train to Osaka. I would head to her house the next morning, and most days we would head into town—Matsuno, Kiyoko, and I.

We went all over Osaka. Shinsekai, Osaka Castle, Dotonbori, Ten-roku, Sennichi-mae. On each trip to Osaka, I could see the progress of recovery there. People's faces grew brighter and the streets bustled. But the scars of the war were still visible all over the place. There were still the ruins of buildings bombed out during the air raids, and black-market stalls stood in some fire-ravaged areas.

There were many disabled veterans loitering in front of Osaka Station. Men missing eyes, hands, legs, or several limbs sat on the streets garbed in white hospital-issued clothes. This was a common sight in Tokyo, too.

Seeing those men made my chest ache. Having fought for their country and lost a part of their bodies, they were being forced to live out painful lives, while the streets around them focused on recovery as though to forget the war. The contrast scared me.

Every time Matsuno passed by the war wounded, she gave Kiyoko some money and had her place it in the donation box.

We would eat lunch at a cheap restaurant. I would talk about my days as a reserve pilot and about how kind Instructor Miyabe had been. Matsuno sometimes looked happy and sometimes sad when she heard stories about her husband.

She rarely spoke of him, but she did discuss their marriage just once. She told me that it had been an arranged marriage. In 1941, after serving in China, Miyabe-san had been stationed temporarily with the air unit in Yokohama. Matsuno's father had worked in the mess hall there and had taken a liking to Miyabe-san, eventually asking him to marry his only daughter. He had probably known at first glance that Miyabe-san would be a perfect match for her. For that alone, I think her father must have been quite a character. He died in 1945, during the air raids on Yokohama. She said that she and Miyabe-san never spoke a word before the wedding.

No matter where we went, everyone mistook us for a married couple and their child. Kiyoko had grown attached to me, and I often walked about with her on my shoulders. After spending a day like that together, I would take the night train back to Tokyo.

This routine continued, once every few months.

On one occasion after several of my visits, Matsuno appeared wearing a skirt. I had only seen her in work pants up to that point, so it was a welcome surprise.

"A friend of mine sold me some material cheaply, so I was able to tailor this," she explained a bit bashfully.

"It looks great on you. You're…"

I wanted to say "very pretty," but the words stuck in my throat.

That day Kiyoko was absent. Apparently, she had gone off to play with some friends from school.

We walked along Shinsaibashi. This was our first meeting where it was just the two of us. My heart pounded in my chest. At the same time, I was beset by guilt.

That evening, while we dined at a restaurant inside Takashimaya Department Store, she asked earnestly, "Oishi-san, why exactly are you so kind to me?"

"Because Miyabe-san saved my life."

"Isn't that just what men do on battlefields?"

"No, I mean he actually risked his life to protect mine."

"When and where?" she practically demanded. "I asked you this before, but you wouldn't tell me."

I was lost for words.

"Please, tell me the truth."

I made up my mind. "All right, I will."

I shared with her what had happened that fateful day when Miyabe-san and I had gone out on a kamikaze mission. All of it.

Partway through the tale, Matsuno lowered her head. Even after I had finished speaking, she kept her face down and didn't say a word.

"Ever since the war ended, I've thought about what Miyabe-san did. Back then, in the midst of a hopeless situation, he found a single spider's thread dangling before him that might be his salvation. If he caught hold of that thread he might be saved—but others would die. And in the end he refused to take that thread for himself."

Matsuno was still facing downwards and silent. At long last she whispered, "I wonder why he chose you."

"I don't know. Or rather—there's only one thing I can think of."

I told her what had happened when I was still a flight student, about the day I'd come to Miyabe-san's rescue and suffered grave injuries, and how he had come to visit me in the hospital—and given me his overcoat.

"I retailored that overcoat," Matsuno said in a small voice.

I recalled how it had a cotton lining and leather on the collar.

"I see. Then Miyabe-san gave me something he truly treasured."

Matsuno looked up. "So Miyabe meeting you on the day he went out as a kamikaze was fate."

She looked at me fixedly. When I saw those eyes brimming with sorrow, I felt my heart seize up with regret. *Why, oh why did I allow him to trade planes with me that day?*

"Please forgive me," I said.

Matsuno looked down, not responding.

"The only reason I am alive today is because of Miyabe-san. So please allow me to do what I can until I feel I have satisfied that debt. He entrusted you and Kiyoko to my care. That's why I was allowed to live. If I'm not able to fulfill my obligation to him, then my life has no meaning."

Matsuno didn't reply, but neither did she reject my plea. In any case, I had no intention of halting my support, no matter how she felt.

My trips to Osaka continued.

After two years, she moved from Osaka to nearby Toyonaka. The new apartment was small, but there were actually two rooms including the kitchen. Matsuno found a job with a transportation company in Toyonaka. The company was affiliated with the National Railway, and I'd used my connections for her.

I'd told her just one lie.

It was true that I supported Matsuno and Kiyoko because I wanted to carry out Miyabe-san's last request, but that wasn't all. I wanted to see her. Likewise, the reason for my visits to Osaka was not entirely genuine. Had I merely wanted to support them financially, I could have just sent them the money. The only reason I took the night train all the way to Osaka was to see Matsuno.

I wonder if she knew. Well, maybe she didn't. After all, I did my best to keep her unaware of my feelings.

Normally, there would have to be some sort of emotional factor for my actions. But Matsuno wasn't the type to say, "Just send me the money."

In this manner, our strange relationship continued for five years.

During that time, my mother passed away, and Kiyoko started middle school. She had grown into an intelligent, lovely girl. I turned thirty. Matsuno was thirty-three.

Then came that day in August 1954.

On the anniversary of Miyabe-san's death, the two of us went to visit his grave. Two years prior, Matsuno had purchased a plot in a public cemetery in the northern part of Osaka and erected a small tombstone for her husband. She did not have the stone engraved with a posthumous name in the Buddhist style. It simply read: GRAVE OF KYUZO MIYABE.

The public cemetery had been carved into a hillside, and the surrounding area was lush and green. There was a temple some distance from the spot, and after visiting the grave, we stopped by there.

It looked empty, and we sat down on the porch of the main hall.

Abruptly Matsuno said, "Oishi-san, thank you for having supported us for so many years."

I was surprised by this sudden remark. *What's she saying?* I thought.

"You have been entirely too generous to us." Matsuno bowed deeply. "I can't allow you to continue to care for us."

"But I still have not repaid my obligation to Miyabe-san."

Matsuno looked me right in the eye. "And when will your obligation be fulfilled?"

I didn't have a reply.

"If you were indebted to him, then you have sufficiently repaid that debt."

"No, not yet," I mumbled.

"Are you going to devote the rest of your life to supporting us like this?"

"And would that be so wrong? Miyabe-san saved my life. No, he died for my sake."

"And what about your own life? What about your happiness?"

"I had a fiancée once. I broke it off as soon as I became a student reservist, but I had intended to be with her were I to return from the war alive."

"What happened to her?"

"She died in an air raid."

Matsuno was silent. We both were for some time, and she was the one to break the silence. "Is your sense of obligation to Miyabe the only reason you've done so much for us?"

I found I couldn't answer her. She looked me directly in the eye. Her gaze was so sharp it felt like she saw right through my heart. Instinctively, I looked away.

"I'm ashamed." I turned my back to her. "I do indeed feel an obligation to Miyabe-san. But that's not the only reason I have been aiding you. I am an uncouth person."

Somewhere a cicada buzzed. I was so embarrassed by my ugliness that I shed tears.

Then I felt a gentle pressure on my shoulder. I turned around to find Matsuno had placed her hand on my shoulder. Large tears spilled from her eyes. "Will you listen to me?" she asked.

I nodded.

"The last time I saw Miyabe, he had just returned to the interior after fighting in the south, and was on leave for a few days in Yokohama. He said to me before he left that he would absolutely come home to me. Even if he had no arms or legs, he would come back."

I nodded.

"Then he said, 'Even if I die, even then, I will come back. Even if I have to be reborn, I will come back to you.'" Matsuno fixed me with a stare. I had never seen such a fierce look in her eyes. "The first time I saw you, I knew that Miyabe had been reincarnated and had come home. You were wearing his overcoat—and when I saw you standing before my house, I thought, 'He kept his promise.'"

I embraced her. She clung fast to me. I cried. She was crying softly, too.

"Do you think it's just another man-and-woman thing?" Grandpa asked after he'd finished telling his tale.

I shook my head. I found I couldn't speak.

"And so Matsuno and I got married. Nine years had passed since the end of the war. After that, we never spoke of Miyabe-san again. But neither of us forgot him, not even for a moment. And Matsuno was a devoted wife until the day she died."

I closed my eyes, recalling my grandmother's face. She was smiling ever happily in my memories. And yet she had led such a life…

"I will tell only you two this," Grandpa continued quietly. "I don't want to tell Kiyoko. This is the only secret from her that I want to carry to my grave."

I nodded, still unspeaking.

"Matsuno suffered terribly after the war. It was very difficult for a single woman with no one to rely on to raise a young child. Do you understand what I'm saying?"

My heart beat faster in my chest.

"Before we married, she told me everything that she'd had to do to survive in those immediate postwar years. I think she hadn't wanted to lie to me. I listened to everything she said and accepted her without even the slightest reservation."

Grandpa sighed heavily. "Matsuno was deceived and became a kept woman of a certain yakuza boss. She never went into detail, but I think she was forced to yield to him because of the gangster's money and violence. Perhaps, after losing Miyabe-san, she'd given herself over to despair."

Keiko covered her face with her hands.

"Normally, it would have been very difficult for her to free herself from the clutches of such a demon. But something surprising happened—something strange enough to make you wonder if such things actually happen in the world."

Grandpa lowered his voice. "The yakuza boss was attacked by someone and killed at the house where Matsuno was being kept. Two other yakuza who were serving as bodyguards suffered severe injuries as well."

I felt something cold race down my spine.

"Matsuno experienced something bizarre then. She was right there at the scene of the murder and saw this man who was wielding a bloodstained sword. Matsuno said she'd never met him before. He was covered in his victims' blood, and as she cowered, trembling in fear, he tossed her a wallet full of money and said, 'Live.'"

Instantly, the image of a certain man floated up in my mind.

"Matsuno thought that he was Miyabe-san, reborn. She knew

that couldn't possibly be true, but sometimes miracles really do occur. Perhaps his spirit had come through somehow. I think Matsuno was under Miyabe-san's protection. Just as he drew her and me together, he'd worked through that killer."

I thought that I might know who the killer had been. I had no evidence, but I felt certain. That man, too, had spent the years after the war searching for my grandfather's wife… He, too, had been ready to sacrifice himself for Kyuzo Miyabe.

Tears spilled from my eyes.

Grandpa stared hard at me. "Was that a shock to you?"

I shook my head. He simply nodded.

"In her final moments, Matsuno thanked me."

I remembered that, too. They were her last words, delivered in a voice so clear it hardly seemed to be coming from someone breathing her last. Then she closed her eyes.

"Do you remember me weeping then?"

I nodded. Grandpa had wailed out loud. He had clung to grandmother's body, his voice wracked with sobs. He'd cried loud enough to fill the hospital room.

"I wanted to say, 'No, it is I that must thank you.' But there was another reason I cried. I saw Miyabe-san then, standing right beside Matsuno. He was wearing his flight uniform. He'd come for Matsuno… I'm sure you don't believe what I'm saying."

Grandpa had a very faraway look in his eyes.

"It's fine if you don't. I myself feel like I saw a phantom. It must have been an illusion. But at the time, I felt it quite clearly. Then Miyabe-san and Matsuno departed together. Just as Matsuno left, she said to me, 'Thank you.'"

"No!" I cried. "Grandma loved you!"

"Yeah, I know she did!" Keiko interrupted too.

Grandpa didn't reply. Tears streaked down his face. "I'm not long for this world myself. When I was young, I was afraid of death. When I was ordered to become a kamikaze, I was scared. I fought back against that fear desperately. But I'm not scared now. I have led a very happy life. I think that when I die, Matsuno will come for me. And I bet Miyabe-san will come get me with her."

Then he said, "Pardon me, but I would like to be by myself for a bit."

Keiko and I left the room.

Night had fallen by the time we left Grandpa's house.

As soon as we passed outside the front gate, Keiko started to cry hard. It was like a dam breaking open.

I hugged her about the shoulders. She clung to my chest and wept. We hadn't embraced since we were kids. I'd never known she was so petite. The only sound along the dark, quiet residential street was her crying. The pavement was wet, perhaps from a passing afternoon shower.

After a while, Keiko regained her composure. As she started to apologize, I shook my head.

"I can't marry Takayama-san," she said. "I'd been worrying over it for a long time, but today my feelings became crystal clear." Her face was wet with tears, but in the light from the street lamps, it looked almost sunny.

"But you might miss out on your chance to become a writer," I joked.

"So what?" she laughed. And then she quietly added, "Kentaro, I didn't tell you this, but I got a long letter from Fujiki-san."

"Okay."

"He apologized for having said it over the phone. He wrote, 'I hope you find happiness.' And then he went over all these memories, even ones that I'd forgotten about. Fujiki-san had always watched over me."

Keiko started to cry again. I didn't say anything. She wiped at her face, and then laughed.

"If I don't marry the person I love, Grandpa will scold me."

She turned her tear-streaked face to me and smiled.

I nodded and looked up at the night sky. I was pleasantly surprised to see it was clear and starry. Never before had I seen such a lovely dome of stars over Tokyo. Keiko looked up, too.

Just then, a bright light shot through the eastern skies. It drew a short line and vanished just as quickly as it had appeared.

Epilogue

Looking back now, I can tell you I think that it must have been the devil himself that was piloting that Zero.

Otherwise, how could it move about with such agility with a 550-pound bomb strapped to her belly? It was unbelievable. I think there was a devil, not a human, in that cockpit.

The Zero approached the ship at an extremely low altitude. It skimmed just barely above the ocean surface, coming up dead center of the carrier's stern. We fired on her with artillery armed with VT fuzes, but the ocean surface reflected the radar, and the shells exploded before reaching their target. Had the bastard figured out the weak point of the VT fuzes?

But even if the fuzes were useless, we could use machine guns once he got close enough. By then, the *Essex*-class carriers were fitted with an awesome amount of anti-aircraft cannons and machine guns. Twelve 5-inch turrets, seventy-two 40-mm machine guns, and fifty-two 20-mm machine guns, like a hedgehog with all quills braced outward. It should have been impossible to take a bite out of that hedgehog.

Once the Zero had reached 4,000 yards from the ship, the 40-mm guns all fired at once. Thousands of bullets showered a single aircraft. Countless varicolored tracer bullets streaked out from all the many machine guns.

At last, I saw flames burst forth from the Zero. "We got 'im!" I hollered. Black smoke unfurled from the Zero as she abruptly pulled up into a climb. The gunners hastily followed the plane's course, but they couldn't match the Zero's sharp maneuver. It ascended, fuselage on fire, then flipped around so the canopy faced down. Once above the carrier, it began arcing back towards the deck, still upside-down. We were left staring helplessly as this devil descended upon us. I had never seen a dive like that. I mean, how could a burning plane pull off such a move?

The Zero plunged at a ninety-degree angle to the ship. I closed my eyes at the moment of impact.

The Zero struck the dead center of the deck. It caused a terrific bang, but its ordnance didn't explode—a dud. The plane burned in the middle of the deck. Bits of the aircraft had scattered about the area. A few seamen told me afterwards that the wings had blown off just moments before impact.

We were all so badly shook up that we couldn't speak.

On the deck lay the upper half of the pilot, torn off. It wasn't a devil. He was a human just like us. Someone gave a scared yell and fired at the corpse with his handgun.

The flames on the flight deck were soon brought under control. Then the captain arrived.

He stared for a while at the torn body of the pilot then said to the dead man, "Good for you, dodging our superb interceptors and anti-aircraft fire and making it this far."

We were all impressed, too. The Zero had broken through our ferocious anti-aircraft barrage in a brilliant manner.

The captain turned and addressed us in a loud voice. "I believe we ought to pay homage to this man. Tomorrow morning, we will give him a proper sea burial."

A wave of distress rolled through the crew. I, too, was shocked.

I thought such a thing was completely unheard of. Had the pilot's bomb gone off as it was supposed to, we could have lost any number of men.

But the captain only glared at us. The look in his eyes made it clear he would hear no objections.

We collected the scattered remains of the pilot. Then someone pulled a photograph out of the breast pocket of the guy's uniform.

"It's a baby."

Everyone gathered around to get a look. I looked, too. The photo showed a kimono-clad woman holding an infant.

"Dammit, I've got a kid too!" Senior Chief Petty Officer Lou Amberson practically spat out. He carefully replaced the photograph back into the dead man's breast pocket. Then he told the seamen under his command, "Be sure to bury him with it."

The body was wrapped in white cloth and laid to rest in the holding area beneath the bridge. As I was wrapping the body, I closed the pilot's still opened eyes.

I remember how his fearsome face turned gentle.

We tossed the Zero's fragments into the ocean. We were unable to remove the lower half of the corpse that was still in the cockpit, so we sent it overboard with the plane. The bomb that the Zero cradled was defused and thrown overboard as well.

The next morning, all free hands were assembled on deck.

Looking back now, I think the captain's attitude was very admirable. I learned after the war was over that his son had been killed in action at Pearl Harbor.

It made me admire what he'd done all the more.

By dawn, most of us had come to feel some respect for the nameless Japanese pilot. Our own pilots, in particular, seemed awestruck. They said the Zero pilot must have flown just above the waves for hundreds of kilometers in order to avoid detection by our radar. Such a feat required superhuman technique and concentration, as well as immense bravery, they pointed out.

"An ace. The real deal," ruled Lieutenant Carl Levinson, the *Ticonderoga*'s own ace. Many of the pilots nodded. "If there are any samurai left in Japan, I'd say he was one of them."

I agreed. But if this man was a samurai, then we had to behave like knights.

As all the free hands stood at attention on the flight deck, a volley of rifles sounded off. The captain and his officers saluted as the shrouded corpse of the pilot slid down the plank and into the waters below.

The body of the Zero pilot, with chains serving as weight, slowly sank into the depths of the sea.

Naoki Hyakuta, born in 1956 in Osaka, earned renown in the television industry as a variety show scriptwriter before embarking on a meteoric second career as a novelist. In addition to his bestselling works exploring twentieth-century history, Mr. Hyakuta is popular for his excellent footwork in the boxing genre. In 2013, *The Man They Called a Pirate* won the annual Japan Booksellers' Award, an honor he deems "much more significant" than his country's lead prize for popular fiction. *The Eternal Zero* is his first work to appear in English.